In memory of Sir Anthony Dawson KCVO MD FRCP

A remarkable man and dearly loved friend, whose medical expertise coupled with his kind and sympathetic manner is best put into words by the following quotation:

'For some patients, though conscious that their condition is perilous, recover their health simply through their contentment with the goodness of the physician'

Hippocrates

Goodbye Tony, God Bless

FUR COAT, NO KNICKERS

Anna King

LITTLE, BROWN AND COMPANY

A *Little, Brown* Book

First published in Great Britain in 2000
by Little, Brown and Company

Copyright © Anna King 2000

The moral right of the author has been asserted.

*All characters in this publication are fictitious
and any resemblance to real persons, living or dead,
is purely coincidental.*

A CIP catalogue record for this book
is available from the British Library.

HARDBACK ISBN 0 316 85174 4

Typeset in Palatino by
Palimpsest Book Production Limited,
Polmont, Stirlingshire
Printed and bound in Great Britain by
Creative Print and Design (Wales)

Little, Brown and Company (UK)
Brettenham House
Lancaster Place
London WC2E 7EN

CHAPTER ONE

'This the lot to go, Miss Donnelly?'

Jimmy Potter, the sixteen-year-old office boy at Laughton & Son in the City of London, nodded down at the bulky wad of letters held firmly between his short, stubby fingers, his eyes quickly flicking back up for another look at the attractive, dark-haired girl, seated behind the tidy walnut desk.

Up until six weeks ago, that space had been occupied by Maude Fisher, a competent woman who had been with the firm since leaving school many, many years ago, and had run the adjoining typing pool, carrying out her duties as personal secretary to Mr Harry Laughton with alarming efficiency.

And when, with much reluctance, she had finally retired, due to ill-health, she had appointed Grace Donnelly, one of the typists from the pool, as her successor. It was an appointment that pleased most of the staff, as Grace Donnelly was a popular young woman. And as Mr Laughton had so far shown no sign of dissatisfaction with his new secretary, it looked as though Grace's new-found position was secure.

Silently watchful, Jimmy gazed in wonder as the long, tapered fingers flew expertly over the raised flat buttons of a Remington typewriter, while thinking that Grace was a lot easier to look at than that old trout Miss Fisher had been.

Without stopping at her task, Grace Donnelly said cheerfully, 'Just this one, Jimmy. Won't be a minute – there! All done.' A large sheet of white, headed paper was pulled triumphantly from the black roller. 'Hang on a minute, will you, Jimmy? I'll just get Mr Laughton to sign this, then I'll be right with you.'

Left alone in the small office, Jimmy leant his backside on the corner of the desk, a soft whistle playing on his lips. Turning his head slightly, he glanced through the glass partition that separated this office from the boss's, and visibly jumped as his eyes met the gimlet gaze of Mr Harry Laughton. As if stung, Jimmy moved away from the desk and began studiously sorting through the pile of letters he had dropped on the desk, eager to appear busy and diligent. True to her word, Grace was back within minutes.

'Here you are, Jimmy, last one. Hope I didn't hold you up.' Grace handed over a long white envelope, a grateful smile on her lips.

Jimmy looked at the pretty face only inches from his own and swallowed nervously. He would have to run like the clappers to get this lot in the last post, but he didn't care, not where Grace was concerned. Gathering up the letters and parcels ready for the post, Jimmy tugged his flat, checked cap further down over his unruly mop of sandy hair, his lanky body teeming with pubescent emotions at being so near to the love of his young life.

Covering up her typewriter, Grace took down a dove-grey swagger coat from a hook behind the door, shrugged her arms into the sleeves, then, carelessly setting a pert, black hat over her dark, wavy hair and picking up her black clutch bag and gas-mask case, said cheerfully, 'I'll walk down with you, Jimmy. If that's all right with you?' Nudging the grinning youth's arm she added playfully, 'Unless of course, you've got a girlfriend waiting for you outside.'

Jimmy's grin faltered, while, much to his chagrin, a hot flush rose over his neck and freckled face as he protested fervently, 'Oh, no Miss Donnelly. No! I ain't got no girl-friend, honest!'

Grace smiled warmly. She liked young Jimmy; he was a nice lad. She was also aware the office junior had a crush on her. And a crush at Jimmy's age could be a very painful affair. Mentally chastising herself for teasing the still-blushing boy, she deftly tucked her arm through his and, to the flustered youth's delight, marched him through the adjoining office and the amused eyes of the girls in the typing pool.

Grace still couldn't believe her good fortune at being elevated to such a coveted position, and was anxious not to appear too superior to the girls she had worked with only a short time ago.

'Night all. Have a nice weekend,' Grace called out as she passed the small row of desks and the five women who were in the process of packing up for the day.

'And you, Grace.'

'Yeah, see you on Monday, Gracie.'

'Ta-ra, Grace.'

One of the younger typists, who had only recently joined the firm, looked pointedly at the lanky youth by Grace's side and giggled, 'Better not let your fiancé see you with Jimmy, Grace. He might get jealous, eh, June.' She winked at her companion while at the same time delivering her a sly dig in the ribs.

Grace immediately felt the youth at her side squirm and try to move away, and tightened her grip on his arm. And when she fixed a steely glance on the two giggling females, the women began to shift uncomfortably on their chairs.

Lifting her chin high, Grace said tersely, 'You may be

right, Gert. After all, Jimmy's a nice-looking young man. As a matter of fact, I've noticed you ogling him on more than one occasion, when you should have been getting on with your work.'

As the indignant typist spluttered to find a suitable rejoinder Grace added icily, 'And it's Miss Donnelly to you, Gert – understand?'

The pert little miss called Gert crumbled under the gaze of the boss's secretary, while her friend June suddenly became very busy with the contents of her open handbag.

Beside Grace, Jimmy felt his slight frame swell with pride at being so soundly defended, and with a new-found confidence he escorted Grace from the typing pool, through the maze of corridors that led to other offices in the large building, then down the stairs that led out to the main door.

As she skilfully negotiated the sandbagged entrance of the dirty-grey office building, Grace gently disengaged herself from the still-grinning youth, saying brightly, 'Well, I'm off home, Jimmy. Have a nice weekend, and I'll see you on Monday. Bye.' And giving a cheery wave, Grace set off in the direction of St Paul's, leaving a forlorn Jimmy standing alone on the busy pavement.

Jimmy had hoped Grace might wait for him while he dropped the mail in the post, and then walk with him to the bus stop. Giving vent to a great sigh of disappointment, the gangly youth cast one last, longing look at the retreating figure. He knew Grace was engaged and therefore out of his reach, but it didn't stop him hoping. Maybe if he got a move on, he might be able to get to the postbox and catch up with Grace at the bus stop. But once again his dreams were shattered as he watched the object of his desire run into the arms of a tall, stockily built man waiting at the end of the street.

His face a picture of dejection, Jimmy Potter indulged in yet another body-shaking sigh. Then, with the resilience of the young, his thoughts turned to the new girl on the sweet counter at Woolworth's. He had planned to stop off there to buy some chocolates for his mum's birthday. Maybe . . . !

Out of the corner of his eye, he saw the postman closing the door of the red pillar box on the corner of Leadenhall Street, the elderly man's hands already drawing in the string of the large, bulky grey canvas sack. With a yelp of anxiety, Jimmy bounded forward, all thoughts of women forgotten, as he raced frantically towards the startled postman, the day's mail clutched in his sweaty hands.

After five minutes of listening to a lecture on the importance of getting the mail to the postbox on time, a relieved Jimmy watched his burden being thrust reluctantly into the canvas sack, before setting off in the direction of Cheapside to buy his mother a birthday present, and maybe, if he was lucky, get himself fixed up with a date for the weekend.

'Stanley! Oh, what a lovely surprise. I didn't expect you to meet me.' Grinning with delight, Grace stood on tiptoe to kiss the long, smooth cheek of her fiancé, before standing back to admire his smart navy pin-stripe suit, white shirt and dark blue tie. 'My, don't you look smart. You didn't dress up in your good suit just to meet me, did you, Stan?'

Stanley Slater's sombre brown eyes gazed down at the lovely face, a tender smile on his full lips.

'I had a job interview, didn't I?' he said wryly, running his fingers through his thick, dark blond hair. 'Me an' a dozen other blokes, and I was the only one who'd bothered to smarten meself up. I suppose it was a bit daft, seeing as I was going after a labouring job. Not that it made any difference. I never even got to see the gaffer, 'cos they took someone on about five minutes after I got there. Still, never mind, eh?' As they walked on, Stanley gave a short, depreciating laugh, while at the same time loosening the knot of the blue tie and unbuttoning his starched shirt. 'Phew, that's better. I can't stand being suited an' booted, which is just as well seeing as how I've only got the one. Gawd knows how the blokes up here stand it.' He nodded at the City gents passing by, in their three-piece suits and bowler hats and briefcases swinging at their sides.

'Anyways, like I was saying,' he tugged again at the knotted tie. 'About the interview. You should've seen the lot of us, Grace. All pretending we weren't that bothered. Well, the younger ones, I mean. The older blokes, the ones with families to support, they . . .' Stanley's head shook with something akin to despair. 'Gawd! It was awful, Grace. The poor bastards looked so . . . so desperate, it . . . Oh hell!'

The pain in Stanley's voice cut through Grace's body like a knife, but she knew better than to offer trite condolences. Instead she took hold of his hand and nestled her face against his shoulder.

Embarrassed at having let his feelings get the better of him, Stanley stopped in his stride, shook off his despondent mood and cried loudly, 'Here, 'ere. No displays of affection in public, if you don't mind, you loose piece. People will start to get the wrong idea.' Adopting a leering tone, he lowered his voice and said, 'What'll two bob get me, darlin'?'

Laughing aloud, Grace shoved the broad chest hard, crying, 'A black eye, that's what it'll get you. Mind you, not travelling in that particular circle, I don't know what the going-rate is.' Grabbing his arm once more she added in mock sternness, 'And you'd better not know either, if you know what's good for you.'

They were nearing the bus stop when suddenly her feet seemed to leave the pavement as Stanley, his strong hand clutching her arm, shouted, 'Come on, Grace. There's the bus. Look lively, girl.'

Before Grace had time to catch her breath she found

herself being pulled forcefully along the pavement, her high-heeled shoes hardly touching the ground as the man by her side propelled her along at breakneck speed.

'Stan – Stanley. Hang on . . . Oh blast!' Her long legs flying, Grace grimly held on to her hat, her face breaking out into a sweat, while her gas-mask case thumped painfully against her side. She'd leave it at home in future, blooming thing. After all, it wasn't as if they were at war, was it! She only carried it because her mother insisted.

Bloody hell! Oh, she'd give Stan what-for later. Making her run like this, especially when she was all dressed up in her good working clothes, and the nearly new shoes she had only just broken in.

By her side Stanley was yelling, 'Hang on, mate. Wait for us!' to a grinning bus conductor who seemed to be relishing the sight of the panting couple chasing his bus. He appeared to think about it for a few long seconds, then, still grinning, he reached up and rang the bell, bringing the red bus to a grinding halt.

'Cheers' mate.' Stanley bounded on to the platform with ease, then turned to where Grace was struggling along behind him. 'Come on, love, get a move on.'

Glaring at him, Grace clambered on to the bus, her face red with exertion, her hat askew, her trembling hands clutching at her bag as if for support. Temporarily winded and unable to answer, she made her way down the bus before collapsing on to a seat by the window.

Dropping down beside her, Stanley held out a sixpenny piece to the conductor. 'Two to the Wick, please, mate.'

Punching out two tickets, the conductor leant across to Grace, asking with mock concern, 'You all right, miss? Bet you never knew you could run that fast, did you?' before letting out a deep, rumbling chuckle.

Despite herself, Grace started to laugh. 'No, you're right there, I didn't.'

Her breath slowly returning to normal, Grace was about to say something to Stanley when he leant forward on the seat, saying quickly, 'There's Bert . . . Oy, Bert. How are you, me old son?'

A young man of Stanley's age looked round from the front of the bus, his tired face lighting up as he espied his friend.

'Wotch'yer, Stan. How's things?' he said eagerly as he made his way down the rocking bus to where his friend sat. With no spare seats to be had, the man leant his lean frame against the rail, planting his feet astride to steady himself.

As Stanley began to tell his friend about the disastrous job interview, Grace took the opportunity to rest her eyes. Making herself as comfortable as possible, she rested her head against the window, feeling the curled edges of the sticky paper that criss-crossed the pane of glass, placed there to stop the glass scattering in the event of a bombing raid. This exercise, like the issuing of gas masks, was looked upon as a waste of time by many people, while those more aware of world affairs were becoming increasingly concerned by the audacity of the German High Command. But in a world still recovering from the horrors of the Great War, its leaders remained impassive as the former housepainter, the comical-looking man named Adolf Hitler, broke promise after promise and continued to increase Germany's territory. At first it was just a piece of land here and there, as if Hitler was testing the water. Then, emboldened by the passivity of the outside world, his armies had overrun Austria, and still Britain and the rest of Europe did nothing, despite the continuous warnings of the former Chancellor of the Exchequer, Winston Churchill, that Hitler would continue to plunder the weaker nations if left unchecked. The general feeling was that if the great statesman was still in office things would be very different indeed. Instead Britain had Neville

Chamberlain to speak for them, and the Prime Minister not only believed Hitler's constant reassurances, but also gave in to him.

Only last week, Mr Chamberlain had returned from a meeting that handed over a democratic Czechoslovakia to Germany, declaring triumphantly that he had won 'Peace with Honour'. And while there were many who despised the Prime Minister's blatant appeasement of the German tyrant, there was also a great deal of relief that Britain wouldn't, after all, be dragged into another war.

Casting a quick glance at Stanley to make sure he was occupied, Grace gratefully closed her eyes again as the bus left behind the dome of St Paul's and entered Cheapside, heading towards Liverpool Street, and from there its final destination – the East End.

She felt so tired suddenly. It had been a long, demanding week, but she couldn't say as much to Stanley. For to mention she was tired after a week's work would be to invite the caustic comment that she was lucky to be in such a fortunate position. And as he said the words, Stanley's face would take on that injured, hard-done-by look she had come to know, and dread, so well over the past year.

As the thought crossed her mind, Grace immediately felt ashamed. Knowing Stan as she did, she knew how deeply he felt the pain and humiliation of being out of work. And knowing he was just one of the million and a half men that were currently unemployed didn't help his wounded pride one bit.

As the rocking motion of the bus lulled Grace into a restful doze, her mind wandered languidly over the past twelve months, back to the day Stanley had asked her to marry him.

He had been employed at that time at Stonbridge & Sons, a small, family building firm, a job he had held since leaving school eight years previously. At twenty-two, Stanley had imagined he had a job for life. Then came the slump, and suddenly orders were being cancelled, and those in the process of completion had gone bust. Arthur Stonbridge, the last surviving son of the company had held on grimly to his business, but finally, and not without a good fight, he had been forced to close down the once-thriving company his grandfather had so proudly started many years before and, in the process, his hard-working workforce had been thrown on to the scrapheap.

Stanley had been optimistic at first. He was a first-rate builder and confident he would easily get taken on in another building firm. But the recession had cut deep and, instead of taking up his trade again, Stanley had been forced to forage for an odd day's work here and there. But for the last couple of months, even that meagre work had dried up. Not that he should have been working anyway – not as he was claiming dole money. Oh, she knew they all did it, but if caught, the law would come down hard on the offenders.

The only time during the past year that Stanley's spirits had been raised had been last March. It was just after Hitler had taken control of Austria, and the Home Secretary, Sir Samuel Hoare, had broadcast an appeal for at least a million men and women to enrol in a Civil Defence Service. Fewer than half that number had responded to the call.

Stanley Slater had been one of the first volunteers. He had jumped at the chance to be doing something, anything, rather than roaming aimlessly around the streets in search of non-existent work, and for a while he had regained a little of his self-respect. But gradually, as the prospect of war faded, so did Stanley's enthusiasm, and within a few months he had chucked it in, declaring the whole exercise to be a waste of time.

As the double-decker bus trundled through Cambridge Heath and down into Well Street, Grace absent-mindedly twisted the small ruby ring Stanley had so lovingly placed on her finger last year, and wondered how long it would be before a gold band accompanied it. At twenty-two, she longed to be married and have children, but Stanley had made it plain there would be no wedding until he found another job. Grace had pleaded in vain for him to let her support them both for the time being. The last time she had brought up the subject, Stanley had walked off in a rage. There was just no way he would countenance being supported by a woman – not even if that woman was his wife.

As the bus came to a sudden, jerking stop, Grace's eyes flew open, then, seeing they had arrived at her stop, she gathered up her belongings and nudged Stanley in the ribs, saying lightly, 'It's our stop, Stanley.'

Still deep in conversation with his friend, Stanley glanced up at Grace, looked out of the taped window, then frowned in annoyance.

'Oh, yeah, so it is.' Reluctantly getting to his feet, he looked at the earnest young man facing him and said, 'Sorry, Bert. This is where I get off.'

Bert Harris, his face filled with disappointment, answered a shade too brightly. 'Yeah, all right, Stan. It was nice seeing you again. Look after yourself, mate.'

As Stanley stood up to let Grace pass, his friend clutched at his arm and in a lowered voice muttered, 'Let me know if you change your mind, Stan. 'Cos to be honest, I don't know what else there's left for the likes of us, only I ain't too keen on going on me own – know what I mean, mate?'

Fully awake now, Grace caught the man's faint words, her head coming up and round to face Stanley, and when she saw the look of guilt in the brown eyes, her stomach gave a nervous lurch of fear.

Never having had the ability to assume a poker face, Stanley looked away from Grace's questioning gaze and said in a voice that came out a shade too loudly, 'Yeah, course I'll keep in touch, mate. Keep your chin up, eh?'

Once on the pavement, Stanley stared after the bus, then down at his feet, before glancing furtively at Grace, and the look in her blue eyes caused him to step back a pace. Quickly regaining some of his assurance, Stanley hitched back his shoulders and blustered, 'That was Bert Harris. He worked with me at Stonbridge's, and got the push the same time as me. Only it was worse for him – the silly sod got married young, an' now he's got a wife and two kids to keep, poor bugger. At least I've only got meself to worry about, thank Gawd . . .'

The thoughtless, casual words were like a blow to Grace's heart, but she kept her feelings in check. There was something far more important troubling her at this moment than Stanley's insensitivity.

'Never mind all that,' she said, noting the irritability in her voice and not caring how she sounded. 'I heard what your friend said as we got off the bus. You're thinking about joining up again, aren't you?' Grace stared hard at her fiancé, her gaze unflinching, and when Stan's face began to colour and his eyes refused to meet hers, Grace moaned, 'Oh, Stan! You promised you'd wait a bit longer. You promised!' And when Stanley bit down on his lower lip and shook his head, Grace suddenly felt as if all the strength had drained from her body, and she wondered why she continued to struggle against the inevitable.

Without waiting for an answer, Grace walked off, her troubled thoughts tumbling around her tired mind.

The idea of joining the Services wasn't a new one, and Grace could understand how a man like Stanley would be tempted into uniform, if only for the security of a regular wage and the return of self-respect. Yet he had promised not to do anything without talking it over with her first. Signing up had always been the final option, a step to be taken when all other avenues had been crossed. Obviously, if the unthinkable happened and war was declared, then

Stanley would have no choice. But to join up just to get off the dole was, to Grace's mind, preposterous.

'Hang on a minute, Grace. Look . . . look, will you wait a minute . . . ?' Stanley was by her side, holding her arm, his eyes pleading with her to understand. 'I ain't gone behind your back, love. Honest I ain't! I wouldn't do that to you, Grace, an' you should know me better than to think that . . . But talking to Bert an' hearing him go on about joining up . . . Well, it got me thinking again, 'cos, like he said, there's nothing for the likes of us as far as jobs are concerned. So . . .' He let go of Grace's arm and shrugged dejectedly. 'Can't we at least talk about it, love? I mean . . . well, it don't do no harm to talk, does it?'

Such was the pathos in his eyes and voice that Grace felt her eyes sting with unshed tears and felt an unexpected urge to stamp her feet like a petulant child. Her mind was telling her she was overtired and to wait until she was in a better frame of mind before continuing this conversation. Instead she slapped at the strong hand holding her arm, snapping angrily, 'Let go of me, Stan. I don't want to talk about this right now, all right! To be honest, I don't want to talk to you at all. So if you don't mind, I'll get off home on my own, OK?

Yet it wasn't the controlled fury in Grace's voice that brought Stanley's head jerking back on his neck, but what he perceived as the arrogance of her words, and suddenly his own anger rose to meet Grace's.

Thrusting his face towards hers, he growled, 'Now look here, Gracie. It's all very well for you to lay down the law, but it's me that's out of work. What d'yer know about it anyway! It's all right for you with your posh job and regular wage, an' there's me with me arse practically hanging out of me trousers an'. . . .' For a moment Stanley thought Grace was about to strike him, and quickly stepped back a pace, while at the same time hurriedly changing tact. Adopting a more conciliatory tone, Stanley now chided gently, 'Oh, now, Gracie, I didn't mean that. You know how me mouth flaps when I'm in a temper . . . Oh, come here, you silly cow . . .' he murmured with an air of resignation as he went to put an arm around her rigid shoulders.

But Grace was having none of it, refusing to be placated like a small child who has been unfairly scolded then cuddled by a repentant mother.

'Don't you silly cow me, Stanley Slater!' she cried loudly, not caring who heard her. 'And don't you try and shut me up . . .' she warned as Stanley made another awkward, fumbling move towards her.

Mortified at being shown up in public, Stanley's face flushed a dull brick red, while his eyes flickered up and down the street in embarrassment as curious passers-by stared in amusement at the young couple at odds on the pavement.

'Look, you're making a fool of yourself, Grace,' Stanley hissed between clenched teeth.

'Making a fool of you, more like,' Grace hissed back at him, knowing full well Stanley's hatred of any form of emotion in public. 'Well, it doesn't bother me one bit, and if you don't like it, you can lump it.' With that she stormed off down the road, leaving a very angry and humiliated Stanley staring after her.

A shabbily dressed man passed by, his grimy thumb gesturing after the retreating figure.

'Women, eh, mate! Can't live with 'em, can't live without 'em. But I'd like to bleeding well try, given half the chance.' With a loud cackle of laughter the man moved on.

After a few minutes, Stanley, his face crestfallen, his shoulders hunched and his hands thrust deep into the linings of his only good pair of trousers, ambled slowly in the direction Grace had taken.

CHAPTER TWO

As Grace turned the corner into Lester Road she stopped for a minute to compose herself. The last thing she needed was for one of her neighbours to see her so upset, for if anyone showed her any form of kindness or concern right now, she'd burst into tears. Not that she knew any of her neighbours that well. In fact, apart from the usual pleasantries when meeting, the Donnelly family remained apart from the other residents in the street. The reason for this went back years to the time of Grace's grandfather, Patrick Donnelly.

Taking a large white handkerchief from her bag, Grace sniffed loudly, her eyes travelling the length of the road to where her home stood proudly at the top of the street, and as always the sight of the three-storey red-bricked house filled her with security. It also served to remind her that the man who had rebuilt the magnificent Georgian house was no longer with her.

'Oh, Grandad,' she whispered softly, 'I don't half miss you.' And as always when remembering the larger-than-life Irishman, who had once been at the centre of her world, Grace saw him laughing at her, playing with her, and often, when her parents were busy, comforting her when she was upset. Like now.

Dabbing at her eyes, Grace looked down the street to see if she was being observed, but apart from a group of children playing marbles in the middle of the road, the street was deserted. And as her eyes lifted her glance settled on the end house: her home, the house known locally as 'Paddy's Castle'.

Tired, angry and tearful, and stalling for time before going home, Grace forced herself to push down the unpleasant row she'd just had with Stanley and let her mind wander back in time to relive and draw comfort from the legend surrounding her late grandfather. Hoping that by doing so, she would shake off the foul mood that was presently gripping her.

The story was well known locally, although, as with many tales, the tale of the Irishman's achievements had received its fair share of embellishment down the years.

It was back in 1874 that the twenty-year-old Patrick Donnelly had arrived on a boat from Ireland. He was just one of many fleeing from a poverty-racked country in the hope of a better life in England. But Patrick had had an advantage over his fellow countrymen, for in his pockets Patrick had held the princely sum of fifty-five pounds, a fortune in those hard-pressed times, and a much-cherished pack of playing cards; cards that he had had in his possession from the age of six, when he had entertained friends and family with parlour tricks, amazing all on-lookers with a dexterity and skill never before seen in one so young. And in the summer evenings when his mother was busy else-where, his out-of-work father, Sean Donnelly, had secretly taught his only son a variety of card games, always with one eye out for his wife, a devout Catholic, who would have severely disapproved of her little boy being taught to gamble.

When Patrick was twelve, his father contracted tuberculosis and died. His mother, who had nursed her husband throughout the terrifying disease, and already worn out with numerous miscarriages, followed him to a pauper's grave barely a week later, leaving a stunned and bereaved Patrick to fend for himself. Neighbours tried to help the orphaned boy, but with barely enough money to keep themselves alive, Patrick had eventually found himself on the streets. Always a resourceful boy, he had managed to live off his wits. And if sometimes he had been forced into petty thieving, he had assuaged his conscious by telling himself it was necessary to survive.

He was fifteen when he won his first few coppers playing cards, and from that day he had been on the constant lookout for bigger and better games.

But big games meant big stakes, and inside knowledge of where such games could be found. For the next five years, Patrick frequented every pub and back-alley club in search of bigger games, putting by a shilling here and there, often starving himself to fund his dream – a stake in a big-time card school – and eventually his efforts paid off. A well-known runner for Dublin's card schools had set Patrick up at a weekly game, charging the eager youth five shillings for his troubles, and with a dire warning to look out for himself. For as the man had explained, such gaming schools weren't known for fair play, and cocky, inexperienced young fellows who thought themselves to be clever, could wind up in a back alley with their pockets empty and a knife in their back. But Patrick had waited too many years for such an opportunity to be easily frightened out of the chance to win some big money, and had ignored the warning.

One night, only days after his twentieth birthday, Patrick, his heart thumping, his pulse racing, and with eight pounds in his pocket, walked jauntily down a flight of steps into a basement of a public house off O'Connell Street. After revealing his name and the name of the man who had sent him, Patrick was admitted into a small, smoky room that stank of whisky, cigars and body odour. A game was already in progress, and as Patrick waited nervously for it to conclude, he noted with some anxiety that the men were playing Twenty-Ones, a game Patrick wasn't overly fond of, being more to do with luck than skill.

Yet when he finally sat down at the green-baized table and felt the cards in his hands as he was dealt a hand of poker, he became more confident. Under the overhead glare of two bracket gas lamps, Patrick's first game began with much amused banter from his elder companions, who were clearly looking forward to having some fun with the fresh-faced youngster, before clearing his pockets. And even when Patrick won the first game, the men remained confident, loudly congratulating him, while winking slyly at each other, as if to say, give the lad his bit of glory before we clean him out.

Patrick lost the next two games, and then he started to win again. One hand after another went his way, while the pile of coins mounted at his elbow.

The other men were no longer smiling, and when after four hours a weary Patrick tried to leave with his winnings, the thick-set man who had admitted him barred his way with such menace that Patrick, with sinking heart, realised for the first time he was in serious trouble. Recalling the runner's words, Patrick continued to play, losing a few hands in order to placate his gambling companions, whose grim faces left the brash young man in no doubt that they weren't going to let him walk away with their money. Fear had gripped Patrick's tired mind and body, but he hadn't battled through a life on the streets without learning some valuable rules of survival.

As dawn broke, Patrick had risen and, ignoring the veiled

threats from his companions, had transferred his winnings to the chamois pouch he had brought his stake in. Realising that there would likely be somebody waiting outside in the street ready to accost him on his way home, Patrick nevertheless made a great show of bravado as he slid the pile of coins into the chamois pouch and placed it with studied deliberation into the inside pocket of his jacket. Not a word was spoken as he left the airless room; none was needed, for the men's brutal expressions and shifty glances spoke volumes.

Once outside Patrick swiftly ran down the adjoining alley he had spied earlier, hiding himself from the view of any passing stranger who might have challenged him. A few minutes later he was heading for the main road, all of his senses alert for danger. Even so, when the two shadowy shapes leapt out on him he was taken off-guard, and although he was fit and strong, he was no match for his assailants. Thick hobnail boots, similar to the ones he was wearing, thudded into his body, forcing him to his knees. Then his head seemed to split open as another vicious blow caught him on the side of the neck. Stunned and bruised, Patrick fell to the ground in agony as the two men ran off. His head pounding and every bone in his body bruised, he had the desire to remain where he was, but a nagging voice in his thumping head urged him upwards. He had maybe ten minutes, fifteen at the most before the men returned.

Dragging himself forward, Patrick staggered to the end of the alley and from there to his lodging room twenty minutes' walk from O'Connell Street. When at last he reached the comparative safety of his room, he swiftly bolted the flimsy door and listened for any sound before sinking gingerly on to the tattered sheets. Then he did an amazing thing: he smiled, then gave a soft chuckle, stopped from laughing out loud only by his swollen, battered face. Then he had carefully pulled off his heavy boots, his torn lips spreading into a grimace of triumph as he turned first one thick heel then the other, revealing a false bottom in both. The cavities were large enough to hold most of his winnings, the rest Patrick had hidden in a concealed pocket sewn inside the wide collar of his jacket. As he had hoped, his assailants had been intent only on the chamois pouch, which he had taken such trouble in displaying.

His carefully laid plans had been the biggest gamble of his life – and it had paid off handsomely. As he packed his meagre possessions into a battered suitcase, Patrick visualised the men's faces when they had emptied the chamois pouch of its pile of halfpennies and farthings and smiled savagely. It was no more than they, and men like them, deserved. It would have been different if Patrick had cheated them but he had won fair and square.

Stopping only long enough to count his winnings, Patrick had left Dublin without a backward glance. This too had been a part of his grand plan, for the men whose money he now held weren't the type to allow any man to humiliate them on such a grand scale, let alone a fresh-faced youth still wet behind the ears. Such men had reputations to uphold, reputations that could be maintained only by setting a bloody example of anyone brave – or stupid – enough to imagine they could take them on and walk away unscathed. And Patrick would be easy to find – the runner who had introduced him to the game knew where he lived.

Three days later Patrick had arrived in England, and like many before him, he had headed for the East End of London, where for the next two years he had continued to live the same lifestyle, until the night he had entered into a card game with three drunken toffs slumming it in an East End pub in Bethnal Green.

Patrick had taken their money with insolent impunity, and when in desperation one of the men had offered his house as collateral against Patrick's entire winnings, the

Irishman hadn't hesitated. At the end of the game, Patrick had come away with a signed pledge for a manor house on the outskirts of Hackney, his heart and mind filled to bursting at his enormous achievement. But this time it was Patrick who had been the victim of duplicity. For on arrival to take possession of the deeds, Patrick had been shown by the sneering debtor not a grand manor house, as he had been led to believe, but a shambling wreck of a building that had been left to rot for many years.

Yet even as Patrick had stared in dismay at his newly acquired property, something inside him had seen the beauty of the once grandiose house, and had resolved there and then to restore the Georgian manor to its former glory. He had never forgotten the look on the original owner's face as he had grabbed the man's hand and thanked him profusely before hurrying inside the ramshackle building to inspect his new home.

That night he had bedded down on bare, rotten floor-boards, with damp pervading the walls and a strong wind blowing through the smashed window-frames; his only company were the rats and mice that scurried into dark corners at his every move. But Patrick hadn't cared. He had a home again. A real home that nobody could ever take away from him, and that cold, windy night, as he had lain awake among the littered rubbish on the creaking floor, he had made a vow to turn the crumbling heap of bricks into a house that would be the envy of all, but more importantly, to build a home that would be a testament to himself long after he had gone.

It had taken five long, lonely years, but with the money he had won in Dublin, together with the winnings from his weekly visits to the gaming clubs in and around the East End, he had slowly restored the manor house to its original state. There were times, of course, when he had come up against someone equally dextrous with the cards and had lost, sometimes heavily, but he had always managed to recoup his winnings at a later date.

In 1881, Patrick married Edith Bishop, a teacher from the local primary school. They had two sons, Samuel and Daniel, and when Patrick died two years after his wife, in 1930, the house passed to his eldest son, Samuel – who by that time had married and had three young daughters, all living in the large family home – with the proviso that, in the event of Samuel's death, the house then be passed on to the surviving son Daniel, and/or any subsequent heirs.

At the time of Patrick's death, the council had already begun to build the new row of terraces in Lester Road, the land having previously been open fields. But number one – with its stone-pillared porch and double-fronted windows on all three storeys, and additional attic space at the back of the house, where two servants had lodged back when the house was owned by the gentry and was now occupied by Daniel Donnelly – continued to dominate the street.

A sudden loud scream brought Grace rudely back to the present. Startled, she glanced up, then relaxed as she saw the source of the piercing yell. One of the small boys playing in the street had been knocked on his back by an equally small companion. A few fists were heatedly exchanged before the small figures resumed their game of marbles. It was a familiar scene, and not one that Grace felt obliged to meddle in.

A sharp wind had sprung up in the rapidly cooling evening and Grace found herself suddenly shivering. She pulled her coat collar up around her ears and gave a small sigh, then she took a cautious look behind her to see if Stanley had followed her from the bus stop. Seeing no sign of his broad figure, she shook her head before slowly crossing the narrow, cobbled road and coming to a stop outside the corner shop. Plunging her hands into her coat pockets, Grace made a great play of staring into the grimy window, while waiting for Stanley to make an appearance; she did not imagine for a moment that her fiancé would have gone home without trying to make amends. That wasn't Stanley's way. He might well shout and rave when he believed himself to be slighted, but not once since Grace had known him had Stanley ever been able to leave her with bad feelings between them. Grace could, quite easily, but not Stanley. And knowing that, she would rather face him out in the street than put him through the ordeal of apologising in front of her inquisitive family.

Keeping her eyes fixed steadily on the grimy shop window, Grace's nose wrinkled in amiable disapproval at the usual haphazard display. Old Benji, as the shopkeeper was affectionately called, had always catered for all purposes and tastes, and this was reflected in the jumbled assortment of merchandise on show – ranging from a wide variety of foodstuffs and household items, such as brooms, buckets and mops, to a motley selection of second-hand clothes. It was well known that at Benji's you could buy anything from a packet of fags to a three-piece suit. And if by some chance Benji didn't have what you wanted that particular day, he would have it waiting the next. An added bonus of shopping at the corner shop was that you could buy goods on tick. This thriving custom was yet another example of how the Donnellys were set apart from their neighbours, for they had never been known to avail themselves of this well-used method of shopping.

Not that the Donnelly family were snobs, far from it. In fact they got on very well with the neighbours. But there was no popping in and out of the Donnellys' house for cups of tea and a chat, as was the custom of the majority of the neighbours. But nobody had ever queried this reticence on their part. It was simply something that had never been done or even thought of. And it wasn't just the grandeur of the red-bricked house that deterred the neighbours from becoming overfamiliar, but rather the quiet dignity of Sam and Hetty Donnelly – both teachers, both educated far beyond the rest of the street, as were their daughters – that served as a constant reminder that the people in the end house were, as the women of the street termed it, posh.

Outside the dingy-looking shop stood a few old wooden crates filled with battered fruit and vegetables. On one of the crates containing some speckled apples sat a ginger tomcat busily cleaning himself with gusto. Grace looked from the cat to the fruit and shuddered. She wouldn't be eating any apples bought from Benji's for quite a while. And when the ginger cat yawned and jumped lazily on to an adjoining crate of cabbages to stretch out for a sleep, Grace mentally reminded herself to tell her nan not to buy any fruit or veg from the corner shop in future.

Glancing up she caught sight of her reflection in the grimy window and imagined her nan's reaction to the cleaning habits of Benji's cat. As if the woman herself was standing beside her, Grace could hear the strident voice of Aggie Harper saying, 'What the eye don't see, the heart don't grieve over. Now eat your dinner and belt up.'

The sound of two women approaching the shop caused Grace to move away slightly from her position, but as she made to walk on she caught sight of a man's reflection in the unwashed window and felt her heart lift. Well! He'd certainly taken his time. Turning to face him, Grace saw the guilty, contrite expression on Stanley's troubled face and immediately softened towards him.

She was about to cross the road to meet him halfway when a sharp burst of pain hit her in the ankle, causing her to cry out in alarm. Hearing Grace's startled yelp of pain, Stan bounded forward, his face filled with concern.

'You all right, Gracie? What happened . . . You hurt, love?'

Bending down to rub her smarting ankle, Grace looked to where three scruffy children were standing wide-eyed, their faces stretched with guilt. Then a boy of about eight with untidy black hair sidled forward warily.

'Coo, sorry, Grace. Did me marble hurt yer? I didn't mean to hit yer, Gracie, honest I didn't!'

Still rubbing her ankle Grace bent down and picked up the blood-red marble. She was quick to notice the look of anxiety that crossed the three dirty faces, as the boys hopped from one mud-streaked leg to another in agitation.

Grace smiled, then held out her hand. 'Don't worry, Billy, I'll live. Here you are . . . And be more careful with it in future,' she shouted after the grinning, running figures as they raced back down the narrow cobbled road.

Stanley stood to one side, unsure whether he should offer any further assistance or be on the safe side and wait for Grace to make the first move in making up their quarrel. And when she glanced up at him and said ruefully, 'I wouldn't say no to a strong arm to lean on. That blasted marble really caught me a wallop,' Stanley eagerly moved closer, knowing that for the moment, at least, their argument was forgotten.

They had barely gone a few steps when Stan, patting at his breast pocket, exclaimed, 'Hang on a minute, Grace. I'm just popping into Benji's for me fags. Won't be long, all right?' Propping Grace up against the wall, Stan gave a reassuring smile and a wink before disappearing into the murky depths of the corner shop.

Left on her own, Grace gingerly tested her ankle by putting her weight on the still-throbbing joint. She was surprised to find she could put her foot to the ground without too much discomfort. Still . . . it wouldn't hurt to play on it for a bit. Not for any sympathy her slight injury might elicit, but more to have something trivial to focus on for a while, a sort of barrier behind which they could both hide, and, in so doing, give them both a chance to get their earlier argument into perspective.

The bell over the shop tinkled as Stanley emerged, then stood to one side to hold the door open as another customer entered the shop.

Breaking the seal on the cigarettes, Stanley flipped out a Woodbine and lit it before saying, 'Here, put your arm round me shoulders and lean on me. Unless you'd rather I carried you to your front door.' The words were spoken lightly, but Grace heard the peace offering in Stanley's voice and smiled tiredly.

'It's all right, Stan. I'm as much to blame as you. I know it's something we have to talk about seriously, but can we leave it until later? I'm really not up to dealing with it right now.'

Eagerly taking the proffered olive branch, Stan nodded. 'Yeah, course we can, love. After all, there's no rush, is there?'

Leaning her weight against Stanley's side, Grace hobbled gamely up the street, grateful that at this time of the evening the neighbours were indoors having their evening meal, sparing her any unwanted solicitations that might arise at her injured state.

As they neared the end house, Stanley experienced the same feeling he always did when approaching Grace's home. It was a mixture of envy and awe that he, Stanley Slater, whose own home had been a run-down hovel in Stepney, could have ever ended up courting a girl from such salubrious origins. Not that the family was wealthy. Old man Donnelly had lived on the edge all of his life, One minute rolling in money, the next without a penny to his name. It was said that in later years, after the old man's once nimble fingers had begun to stiffen with age, the fiery Irishman would bet on two flies crawling up a pub wall in order to win a few bob. But the one thing he had never gambled with was his home. And that in itself said a lot about the man as, being of the character he was, it must have been a grave temptation in his later years, for the house as it stood must have been worth two thousand pounds, or more.

As Grace fumbled in her bag, Stanley's eyes continued to roam the house, and as usual, the grandness of Grace's home merely served to remind him of his own inadequacy. For he would never own such a home. He might well marry into it, but it would never be his, not even if he ended his days within its walls. Yet if he did marry Grace, what would he have to offer in its place? A cheap, one-bedroomed flat in a back street, similar to the place he now lived!

'Are you stopping for tea, Stan?' Grace had her key in the lock, her good foot resting on the red-ochre doorstep.

Jerking out of his reverie, Stanley grinned warmly. 'Yeah, ta, love. I was hoping you'd ask. Mind you, it'll mean giving old Ma Grimes's sardines on toast a miss, but I'm sure she'll serve 'em up for me breakfast. She's not one for wasting food is my landlady.'

Pushing open the heavy door, Grace smiled over her shoulder at Stan, before stepping into the hallway. And Stanley, with a last appraising look at the exterior of the house and mentally comparing it with the grotty two-bedroomed house in nearby Bethnal Green where he rented a room, shrugged his shoulders and followed Grace into the spacious hallway.

CHAPTER THREE

Taking off her coat and hat, Grace hung them on the hall stand, calling out, 'Anyone home?'

Almost immediately a loud, strident voice answered, 'Nah, we've all gone up West for a night out on the town.'

Grace grinned broadly and, gesturing for Stanley to follow, poked her head around the door of the sitting room, crying warmly, 'Well, you might have waited for me. I could do with a night on the town.' Walking into the large, spacious room, Grace leant down and kissed the wrinkled cheek of the small, plump woman sitting in a beige and yellow armchair. 'Hello, Nan. Nobody else home yet?'

Aggie Harper, a brisk, bustling woman in her early sixties, shook her head impatiently.

'What d'yer think! The girls should've been home half an hour ago, an' your mum and dad must be working late again, I mean to say . . .' Twisting around in her seat to look up at Stan she added, 'Oh, hello, lad. I didn't see you standing there . . . Well, come in if you're stopping.' Leaning slightly towards him Aggie peered up, saying, 'You are stopping for your tea, ain't you, lad?'

Standing awkwardly in the middle of the room, Stanley

was momentarily disconcerted by the penetrating gaze in the still-bright blue eyes, and mumbled awkwardly, 'Yeah, thanks . . . If it's all right with you of course, Mrs Harper.'

'Course it's all right, you daft bugger . . .' Then, without seeming to pause for breath, Aggie continued her former train of thought. 'Like I was saying, what's the point of having a job where you can finish at four o'clock in the afternoon if you're gonna stay behind to do extra work? Don't make sense to me. But then, what do I know, eh . . . ?' She smiled over at her granddaughter, now sitting snugly on the brown three-seater settee, and added wistfully, 'All the brains in the family went to me daughter and grandchildren. Still, God gave me a good pair of hands an'—'

Leaning forward, Grace interrupted the familiar banter by saying, 'Yes, and we've all felt the back of them from time to time, haven't we, Nan?'

Aggie's face fell in comical lines of disbelief as she appealed to the young, silent man by Grace's side on the settee. 'Did you ever hear anything like it, Stanley, me own flesh an' blood cheeking me like that?'

Never knowing quite how to take Aggie Harper, Stanley found himself smiling inanely as he answered, 'Um, yeah, well, you know Gracie.'

Aggie moved restlessly in the chair, the smile seeping from her face as she stared at the man by her Gracie's side, wondering, not for the first time, what her granddaughter saw in him. He could be a right miserable git at times. Gawd blimey! It wasn't as if he was a stranger in the house. To look at him sitting perched there on the edge of the settee, like he had a poker up his backside, you'd think he was trying to sell something from a suitcase. Only those cheeky buggers would make themselves more at home than Stanley ever did. She only hoped the lad had a bit more life in him when he was alone with Grace, else her granddaughter was in for a long and boring life.

Clucking her tongue impatiently, Aggie turned, her head coming round to face the wall clock as she cried, 'Look at the time. That shepherd's pie'll be done to a crisp if they don't get a move on.'

At her nan's words, Grace's face fell.

'Nan,' she spoke hesitantly, a note of irritation creeping into her voice. 'Nan, it's Friday. You know Dad won't eat meat on a Friday.' Sam Donnelly, although long since a lapsed Catholic, still refused to eat meat on a Friday, a custom he had never managed to shake off.

And Aggie knew that perfectly well.

'Now, don't go getting your knickers in a twist, me girl.' Aggie wagged a stubby finger under Grace's nose. 'I've done your dad and Danny a nice fish pie, though Danny'll likely turn his nose up at it when he sees what the rest of us are having . . . An' speaking of your uncle, I don't know where the bloody hell he is either . . . Oh, they must've heard me . . .' The sound of the front door opening and voices out in the hallway brought the irate woman half out of her chair. 'About bloody time too!' she called out as she attempted to push herself up out of the armchair.

'Do you want a hand getting up, Nan?' Grace asked, as Aggie seemed to be having trouble getting her large frame out of the snug confines of the chair.

'What!' A pair of blazing blue eyes swivelled to glare at Grace. 'I ain't in me dotage yet, me girl. The day I can't get outta me chair without help is the day I'll be pushing up the daisies.' With much huffing and puffing Aggie hauled her heavy bulk upright just as Sam Donnelly popped his head around the door.

'Hello, love . . . Hello, Stanley,' he called out cheerfully.

'An' what am I then . . . The bleeding cat's mother?' Aggie bridled indignantly.

With all the graceful charm of his Irish forebears, Sam beamed down on his mother-in-law.

'And a beautiful cat's mother, you'd make, Aggie.'

Samuel Donnelly was a tall man with a lean build, red hair liberally sprinkled with grey and twinkling blue eyes. Behind him in the doorway his wife Hetty appeared.

'Is he tormenting you again, Mum?'

Hetty Donnelly was a small woman, who, like her mother, had put on a lot of weight since her young days and was, as her husband often referred to her, well padded. Her chin-length, soft brown curly hair had as yet no evidence of grey, though her husband often teased her about the benefits of the dye bottle. Now her laughing blue eyes were darting from one to another of her family, her gaze settling on her eldest daughter, who had inherited her looks, although, as yet, thankfully, not her build.

'And where have you lot been till this time of the evening?' Aggie bridled while at the same time trying to squeeze her ample frame past her son-in-law, who was blocking her exit. 'I don't know why I bother, I really don't. I . . . Oh . . . Oh, now don't start that lark . . . Look, look . . . put me down, you daft bugger . . .' Aggie squealed nervously as her feet left the floor.

'Ah, to be sure, you're a darling woman, so you are. And if I wasn't a happily married man, you'd have to lock your door at night, so you would.' Sam roared loudly as he held tight to his mother-in-law's ample waistline.

Pretending to be cross, Hetty slapped at her husband's arm crying, 'Put her down, you fool. You'll put your back out one of these days if you're not careful.'

Grace looked on with delight as the familiar scene was played out, while Stanley, as always, merely smiled dutifully. He liked the Donnellys, even old Aggie, though he could cheerfully throttle her at times, but as much as they'd always tried to make him feel welcome, they weren't his family.

Stanley's family, such as it was, consisted of an elder

sister, who had married and moved away ten years ago and never been heard of since, and a variety of distant uncles, aunts and cousins who he wouldn't recognise now if he fell over them in the street. His father had run off when Stanley was eight, while his mother had drank herself into an early grave. He had lived in digs since his sixteenth birthday and was quite happy with his living arrangements, despite his jokes to the contrary. Old Ma Grimes, as he referred to his landlady, led her own life and let him get on with his – and Stanley was happy with the arrangement.

Meeting the Donnellys had, at first, been overwhelming, and even now, after all the time he had known them, he still couldn't manage to be completely at ease with them. The trouble was that Grace thought her family was wonderful and expected everyone to feel the same way about them.

'You all right, Stan? You look a bit down in the dumps. Anything I can do to help?'

Stanley's head jerked up guiltily. Getting clumsily to his feet, he looked at the concerned face of Sam Donnelly and immediately felt ashamed of his thoughts.

The women had left the room, giggling, leaving Stanley and Sam alone.

'No, no, nothing's wrong . . . Well! The usual, you know. Being out of work gets you—'

The sound of the front door banging and the high voices of Grace's sisters giggling in the hallway stopped Stanley's words mid-sentence, which only served to make the young man feel even more ill at ease.

Violet and Polly Donnelly, their faces flushed with girlish glee, burst into the room.

'Hello, Dad, sorry we're late. Old Mrs Spencer wanted us to stay late and finish some stocktaking. I bet Nan's fit to bursting a blood vessel.'

Violet Donnelly, a vivacious nineteen-year-old blonde,

seemed to bounce into the room. She dropped into the arm-chair recently occupied by her grandmother, and sprawled her shapely body carelessly across the upholstery. For a brief moment, Stanley caught a glimpse of pink, frilly satin, then the tantalising vision disappeared. As he raised his head, Stan caught a look of mockery in Violet's large blue eyes as she crossed her legs deliberately.

'Oh, hello, Stan, you here again?' Before Stanley could make a reply, Violet had switched her attention back to her father. 'Two of the girls called in sick today, so Polly and me had to cover for them, as well as manage our own counters. We've hardly had a minute to ourselves all day, have we, Poll?' The question was asked of the sleepy-eyed girl resting her head wearily against her father's broad shoulder.

'Um, oh, yeah, I mean, yes, it has been pretty busy. I'm absolutely whacked.' Both girls worked at Mason's, a big department store in Mare Street, only a short bus ride from home. Pushing a lock of ginger, wavy hair from her forehead, Polly gazed up at her father and smiled tiredly. 'Do you think Nan would mind if I didn't have any dinner? I just want to crawl into my bed and sleep all weekend.'

Hugging his youngest daughter tightly, Sam rested his chin on top of her head, murmuring, 'Best not, love. Any-way, we're all off out tonight to the club. You never know, you might meet some handsome young man who'll whisk you off to some exotic country.'

Polly giggled. 'Fat chance around here, Dad. Anyway, where's Mum?'

Sam glanced over his shoulder, answering, 'In the kitchen with your nan, which is where we should be . . . Oh, oh, here she comes. We'd better get moving.'

There came the sound of heavy footsteps thundering down the hallway, accompanied by a harsh, 'Well, are you lot coming in to eat, or have I been wasting me time all day cooking for the lot of you?'

As they all scrambled for the door, the front door opened and banged yet again, emitting a younger, fatter version of Sam, with none of his brother's self-assurance.

'Sorry I'm late, Sam. Blooming train was delayed, wasn't it.' Danny Donnelly came breathlessly down the passage-way, his chubby face flushed, while further down the hall, Aggie shouted for them all to get a move on if they wanted feeding.

And Stanley thought giddily, *It's like a bleeding train station*. Then Aggie bawled again, 'That you, Dan? Well, get yourself in here with the rest of 'em, or else I swear I ain't gonna cook another meal in this house ever again.'

Hastily scrambling for the door, the party of adults looked sheepishly at each other. With a lot of smiling and raised eyebrows and conspiratorial looks, the Donnelly family con-gregated in the spacious kitchen built at the back of the house, each one taking their designated place at the large table in the centre of the room.

Stanley was relieved to note that Aggie had remembered to set an extra chair at the table for him. Sometimes she forgot, and although it took only a matter of minutes to correct the oversight, to Stanley, still in awe of the rumbus-tious Donnelly family, those few minutes, standing alone, excluded from the rest of them, seemed like hours.

The evening meal was as always – with everyone trying to talk at once, while old Aggie bustled around dishing out the hot plates of food, stubbornly refusing any help, before collapsing triumphant into her own chair.

At the head of the table, Sam looked down at his fish pie and boiled potatoes, then glanced enviously at the plates of heaped steaming shepherd's pie surrounding him. Even Danny, the traitor, had long since turned his back on the childhood custom. With a rueful shake of his head, Sam began his meal. It was silly really, this custom of his not to eat meat on Fridays. He hadn't put his head round the door of the church since Polly's Holy Communion, ten years ago. Yet strangely enough, it was Hetty who helped out at the local church as often as she could, much to the disgust of Aggie, who had a profound distrust of all things popish. Still, there was something inside him that clung to some of his childhood upbringing: old habits were hard to break. Mind you, he mused silently, it would be easier all round if Aggie cooked the same meal for everyone on Fridays. Cantankerous old devil, he thought affectionately.

The woman in question was now looking down the length of the table, demanding, 'Well? Are either of you gonna tell me why it's taken you both two and a half hours to get home? I mean to say, I don't mind what time you roll in, just as long as you tell me.'

Sam looked to his wife, and Hetty, laying down her fork, answered quietly, 'I told you this morning, Mum. There was a meeting after school about the evacuation procedures. I know a lot of people think there won't be another war, please God, but the school board insists the proceedings are maintained. Because if the worst comes to the worst, there'll be precious little time to get organised once it starts.'

Aggie's head appeared to bounce on her shoulders. She hated all this talk of war. It brought back too many painful memories. Her late husband, had been a victim of mustard-gas poisoning, and though he had recovered enough to be shipped home, he had never been the same man, and had died years before his time. Hetty had been only six when her father had died, and when she married Sam, her first thought was to have her mother live with them. Goodness knows the house had been big enough. But the old fellow and his wife had still been alive then, and though Aggie had got on well enough with Sam's mother and enjoyed a laugh with old Paddy, she couldn't have imagined living in the same house with them. She had been quite

happy staying in her old home in familiar surroundings,
although she had often come to stay for weekends and
short stays.

Then when Paddy had died, and there were all the
arrangements to see to and everyone was so upset, Aggie
had come to help out and look after the girls – who were
all still at school at the time – giving their bereaved parents
some time to themselves – for Hetty had come to love the old
Irishman as a father. Strangely enough Aggie hadn't minded
her daughter's strong affection for her father-in-law, for from
the very beginning, old Paddy had treated Hetty as if she
were his own. And somehow the weeks had turned into
months, and the months into years, and now she felt as if
she'd never lived anywhere else.

Though she would never admit it, Aggie was secretly very
proud to live in such a grand house as this one, and when
meeting up with old friends, she would drag them back for
a cup of tea and a chat, her large frame almost bursting
with proud anticipation when she beheld the amazed looks
on her former neighbours' faces as she casually introduced
them to her new home, saying airily, 'Posh? What, this old
place? Well, I can't say as if I've really noticed. I mean, it's
me home, ain't it . . .'

Now she glanced surreptitiously down the table at her
son-in-law, the man who had taken her in and treated her
like his own mother, and thanked God that, at forty-three,
Sam was surely too old to join up. Then again, you could
never be too sure. Look at the last one. Gawd almighty! At
the end, they were practically sending the blind and infirm
over the water, so desperate were they for cannon fodder.

No! No, it was too terrible to contemplate. Besides, the
man had already done his bit in the last war, fighting
alongside his father, and Sam only a bit of a lad at the
time.

Lifting a forkful of meat to her open mouth, Aggie openly

appraised her family and shuddered inwardly at the prospect of losing any of them. The last war had been bad enough – 'The war to end all wars' it had been called. But if this one started, with all the new weapons and aeroplanes to drop the bombs, nobody would be safe. The government knew it too, which was why they were frantically arranging for the children of London to be evacuated. Because that's where that mad bastard Hitler would go for first – the heart of London and the docks.

It wasn't fair, she cried silently. She'd already lived through one war, and she'd been fit and healthy then. Now she was old – old and afraid. Not for herself, but for her loved ones. She glanced up again, as if to reassure herself they were still all right.

They were all chatting noisily, talking over each other, yet still managing to make themselves heard. Then Danny, his cherubic face beaming, shouted merrily above the din, and at his words the hairs on the back of Aggie's neck stood on end.

'. . . I tell you it's true. I heard it from some army captain on the train home.'

Danny was talking to Stanley, who was seated next to him, waving his fork in the air as he spoke. 'The government's gonna bring in conscription within the next few weeks. And that's not the half of it . . .' Seeing that he now had everyone's attention, Danny laid down his fork and assumed a more serious air. 'This army bloke said they're gonna call up every man between the ages of eighteen and fifty-two, so they must be expecting the worst otherwise they wouldn't bother, would they?' Feeling embarrassed at suddenly finding himself the centre of attention, Danny cleared his throat, took another bite of shepherd's pie, then, looking to Stanley for support, said quickly, 'What do you think about it, Stan? I mean, you thinking of joining up, or you gonna wait til you get called up? I mean to say, it'd get you off the dole, wouldn't it? And . . . well – anyway, it's just what I heard . . .' His voice trailed off miserably as he caught his niece's angry glare.

But Grace's displeasure with him was nothing compared to what happened next.

Throwing down her knife and fork with a resounding clatter, Aggie got to her feet, her eyes blazing with fury.

'You stupid little sod! Is that all you can think about? Half the bloody world might be on the verge of being wiped out, and you think it's a good idea 'cos it'll get Stanley off the dole.'

'Mum! Mum, now calm down, Danny didn't mean—' Hetty was swiftly silenced.

'Don't you tell me to calm down, Hetty. I'll say me piece, an' nobody's gonna stop me,' Aggie stormed, while the rest of the family shifted uneasily on their chairs.

Her heavy chest heaving, she jabbed her finger at a now-cowering Danny and shouted, 'Where's your bloody sense, lad? I'd've thought you'd have more sense at your age. What are you now, thirty-four, thirty-five? And still wanting to play cowboys and indians! You was damned lucky to get out of the last one. Another couple of years an' you'd have been called up like your brother. Well, I'll tell you this much, lad. I've lived through a war, and it was bloody terrifying. And there you sit, the pair of you, all excited 'cos you might get the chance to dress up an' play at soldiers. Well, you just might get that chance, Dan, and you too, Stanley . . .' She had turned to Stan, her fear making her unheedful of the hurt her words were inflicting. Stanley's head jerked back painfully as he suddenly found himself the target of Aggie's wrath.

Beside Hetty, Polly burst into tears, her distress momentarily distracting her family from the unpleasant scene taking place. But Aggie was too far into her stride to take any notice of what was happening around her. As Stanley squirmed in his seat, she leant towards him, her eyes turned cold, her lips glistening with spittle.

'Oh, yeah, a war's just what you're waiting for, ain't it, lad? Like Danny just said, it'd get you off the dole, wouldn't it? And it'd only cost thousands of men, women and children their lives. But that don't matter, does it? Oh, no . . . Just as long as you feel like a man again, an' at least we wouldn't have to hear you always going on about how hard done by you are, like you was the only bloke in the world who's outta work—'

'That's enough, Aggie.' Sam had risen from the table, his lean face set hard. 'You know full well that's not what Dan or Stanley meant. Now sit down, woman, and be quiet, else by God I swear I'll throw you out of the room by force if that's what it takes to quieten your tongue.' Turning to Stanley, who sat quietly trembling beside an equally shaken Dan, he said kindly, 'Don't take any notice, Stan. You know how Aggie's mouth runs away with her.' He then shot a fierce glance of reproach at his mother-in-law. But Aggie, her outburst abated, sat slumped in her chair, her eyes downcast as if she had realised the havoc wreaked by her rash words.

Sam stared at the grey, bent head in anger. Lord, but sometimes Aggie went too far. He knew how fearful she was at the prospect of another war, but, God in heaven, weren't they all! There was no excuse for going for Danny and Stan like that. The poor sods were no match for Aggie, and she knew it. She'd never have gone for him like that. No, by God, she wouldn't. As much as he loved her, and treated her like his own mother, he would never have stood for the tongue-lashing she had just handed out. But that was why she had vented her spleen on Danny and Stan. She'd known neither man had the spunk to stand up to her, but she hadn't heard the last of this. No, by God, she hadn't!

Pushing back his chair, Sam reached out and slapped Stanley on the shoulder, saying heartily, 'Look, let's go and have a pint at the Nag's Head before we go to the club, eh?' Looking past Stanley's flushed face, Sam appealed to his brother. 'What do you say, Danny? A quick pint to wash down our dinner. What about it, eh?' He didn't have to repeat the offer. Before the words had left his mouth, Dan was already heading for the door, grateful for the escape route offered, while Stanley, his face scarlet, rose slowly to his feet.

'No, thanks, Sam,' he answered through clenched teeth. 'I think I'll get off home, if you don't mind.' Stepping back he tugged nervously at his tie, stuck out his neck, then, dropping his gaze to where Grace was sitting quietly at the table, added stiffly, 'I'm leaving, Grace, you gonna see me out or what?'

Without looking up Grace nodded, but before she had the chance to get to her feet, Sam placed himself in front of Stan, determined to smooth over the sticky situation.

'Here, just a minute, lad, hold your horses. There's no need to drag Gracie out. Me and Dan will walk along of you, and if we happen to pass the pub on the way and be pulled inside against our will, well, we'll just have to go quietly, eh, Danny?' He shot a questioning look at his brother, who quickly voiced his agreement.

Stan, no match for Sam's forceful personality, shrugged helplessly, his eyes pleading with Grace to help him out, but Grace, knowing if Stan got her on her own there would be another row, refused to meet his gaze. And when she heard the front door bang shut, she was surprised to find herself sighing with relief.

Striding along briskly, Sam kept up a cheerful stream of chatter to help both men forget about the unpleasant scene they had just been a party to. But while Dan, always an easy-going man, responded happily, Stan continued to keep up a stony façade.

Well aware of his future son-in-law's grim mood, Sam again silently cursed Aggie for her loose tongue. The woman never stopped to think before opening her mouth. Casting a quick look at the man walking sullenly a few paces in front of him and Danny, Sam blew out his cheeks in exasperation. Lord, but this was going to be hard work.

On his right, Dan was now chatting away merrily, all rancour forgotten, and Sam was more than happy to let his brother take over the conversation. While he listened to Dan's ramblings, he pondered at the kind of man his daughter intended to marry.

Oh, Stanley was a nice enough young man, but there was a weak streak in him that all his bravado couldn't hide. Still, there was no crime in being weak. Look at Dan. His brother was thirty-five and still stuck in the same clerking job he'd held since leaving school, and still living at home, seemingly perfectly happy with his lot in life. Not that Sam minded, nor Hetty and the girls. After all, the house was still his brother's home, and if Dan would rather live with them than go out into the world alone, well then, he would always be welcome.

But as for Stan! Well, a father always wanted a strong man for his daughters. The problem with Stanley was he wouldn't recognise his abilities – or lack of them. Stanley would always imagine himself to be capable of more than he really was, and would forever blame life's circumstances for holding him back rather than admit he didn't have what it took to make something of himself. And while it was true there was a severe shortage of work, it was no good moping around feeling sorry for yourself. You had to get out and do something to change things, not wait for someone or something to change it for you. But, there you are. His Grace loved the man, and love could often work miracles, although he, Sam, had never known it strong enough to change a person's inbred character.

As the three men came into view of the pub on the corner, Sam blew out a sigh of relief. Ignoring Stanley's protestations of not wanting a drink, he took the young man's arm and steered him into the Nag's Head, thinking as he did so that not only did he strongly want a drink, but he also bloody well deserved one.

CHAPTER FOUR

'Well! That was perfectly horrible. Honestly, Nan, I wish you'd think before jumping in with both feet. Poor Uncle Danny and Stanley were absolutely mortified. You know how sensitive they are and—'

'Sensitive are they?' Aggie swivelled on her chair, her manner calmer now as she looked at the angry faces glaring at her, yet still determined to stand her ground. 'Well, all I can say is if either of 'em are thinking of taking up arms, they'd better bloody well toughen up.'

'That's not fair, Nan.' Grace spoke hotly, her voice unusually harsh when speaking to her grandmother. 'Stan's no coward, and neither is Uncle Danny. You had no right to humiliate them like that, especially Stan. He wasn't the one who brought the subject up, in fact I don't remember him saying a word. It was Uncle Danny who was doing all the talking, and he was just trying to make conversation. You know what Uncle Danny's like. He doesn't mean any harm and—'

'Here, here, that's enough, Grace.' Hetty was busy clearing the table, her normally placid face troubled. 'I think we've had enough unpleasantness for one night. Your nan was wrong to speak out as she did, and I'm sure when she's calmed down she'll apologise to Stan and Danny . . . Won't you, Mum?' Her eyes met and held her mother's, and there was no mistaking the warning in them.

But Aggie wasn't a woman to be easily intimidated, even when she knew herself to be in the wrong. Bridling visibly, she returned her daughter's stare and blustered loudly, 'Now look here, me girl. The day when I can't speak me own mind without having to worry about offending is the day I move out. Now, I'm telling you straight . . . And you can all stop looking at me like I was something the cat had just dragged in . . .'

When her daughter and the girls rose from the table as one, Aggie felt her body deflate, and for one heart-stopping moment she thought she was going to burst into tears. The very notion of such a happening brought her shoulders up straight, but she couldn't quell the uneasy turbulence of her stomach. Taking a loud slurp of her tea, she looked over to where the women were busying themselves by the sink, each one concentrating on their own task, and it was the way they all had their backs to her that made something inside Aggie cry out. *Aw, don't. Don't shut me out. Can't you see I'm scared half outta me wits worrying about losing any of you. Don't you know you all mean the world to me. Please – somebody say something . . .*

As if in answer to her silent plea, Polly came to her side, saying quietly, 'Do you want another cuppa, Nan? There's still plenty in the pot.' Aggie looked up gratefully, her gnarled hand gripping at her granddaughter's long fingers. Thank God for Polly. Polly the quiet one – Polly the peacemaker. Polly, the plainest of the girls, with hair that was more orange than red and a face that ran riot with freckles, and the possessor of the sweetest nature you could wish to find.

'Yeah, thanks, love, ta.'

Giving a loud sniff, Aggie took a crumpled handkerchief from her apron pocket, and on the pretext of blowing her nose, took a quick glance over to where the women of her family were finishing the last of the dishes. Hetty and Grace were talking quietly, Polly was pouring out the tea, and Vi, as usual, was busy doing nothing, her shapely figure slouched against the pine dresser in the corner of the kitchen, her pretty face filled with undisguised boredom. Aggie's eyes narrowed. That one needed watching. The other two had never been any trouble, especially young Polly, but Vi had had an eye for the men since the day she started school, and they in their turn nearly fell over themselves to get to her. There was always some poor fellow hanging around Vi, but while she was more than happy to let her many admirers spend their money on her, she was always on the look-out for someone better. It was just as well Sam wasn't the type of man to stand for any nonsense, else the girl would have gone off the rails years ago.

As it was, Sam had strict curfews for all his girls, insisting they were home at a reasonable time. This law wasn't relevant to Polly, who never went outside the door after work unless accompanied by her family, and Grace, at twenty-two and engaged, was still happy to abide by her father's rules. Vi, though, was itching to kick over the traces, but she wasn't brave enough to defy her father, despite her cocky attitude at times.

Suddenly finding herself under her nan's eagle eyes, Vi shifted abruptly. Detaching herself from the dresser, she said shortly, 'Well, I'm off to the club. Anyone else coming?'

Hetty turned in surprise. 'Yes, in a while, when we've had a wash and a tidy up.'

Vi yawned rudely. 'Blooming hell, Mum. It's only the Legion, not a nightclub up West. I'm going as I am.'

Folding up a damp tea cloth, Hetty said grimly, 'That's up to you, Vi, but you'll still wait for the rest of us. Now if you've nothing better to do, go into the sitting room until we're all ready to go.'

With deliberate slowness, Vi dragged her body across the floor. When she reached the door she stopped, looked over at Grace and said slyly, 'Actually, I don't know if I fancy going, after all. I mean, it's not going to be a barrel of laughs at the club, is it? Not the mood your Stan was in when he left here. It was all right for you, you were sitting next to him, so you couldn't see the state he was in.' She gave a short, spiteful laugh. 'I was sitting opposite him when Nan started. I didn't know whether he was going to burst into tears or slide under the table in a dead faint. Maybe Nan had a point after all. Because between you and me, Gracie, your Stan—'

Grace was already heading angrily towards her sister when Aggie, with surprising agility for her bulk, sprang to her feet and grabbed the startled Violet roughly by the arm, pushing her from the room.

'You shut your mouth, you spiteful little cow. Just because I've opened me big gob and upset everyone don't mean to say you can do the same. I ain't proud of meself for what I said. It came out all wrong, but even so, I never meant it to be nasty. It was, I admit that now, but it wasn't intended. But you ain't got no excuse. You just like being bitchy, and one of these days you'll get a hand across that gob of yours if you're not careful.'

Violet, struggling to free herself from the iron grip, scowled down at the furious woman, her lovely face contorted with rage at being shown up.

'Mum, Mum, for heaven's sake, let her go, you're hurting her.' Hetty hurried towards the struggling women, her face close to tears.

With a muttered oath, Aggie released her grip, and when the front door banged noisily after Vi she turned slowly and sank down in the nearest chair.

For a long while the kitchen was silent as each of the remaining women tried to think of something to say that would banish the ill feeling that pervaded the normally noisy, happy kitchen.

Then Grace, with a loud cry, exclaimed, 'Oh, for heaven's sake! Let's get out of here and get to the club before anything else happens.'

And when, ten minutes later, the group of women left the house, they were all talking again, their high voices masking the tension that still lay between them. But by the time they reached the Legion clubhouse, they were holding arms and laughing, and it was this sight of his womenfolk that greeted Sam as he glanced up from the bar towards the door.

Gesturing wildly, Sam motioned the women over to where an empty table still remained in a corner of the large, square room. Pushing and nudging good naturedly through the crowd, Aggie led the way, thankfully dropping on to one of the four rickety chairs at the cigarette-scarred table. Plopping her best handbag in the middle of the table, she gave a great sigh of relief. This was more like it! The atmosphere in the club, as always, was one of jollity and lively camaraderie. Surrounded by familiar faces, loud laughter and foot-tapping music supplied by the resident three-piece band, Aggie felt the tension seep out of her body like water down a drain. Looking about her, she acknowledged greetings from couples sitting at adjoining tables, her fat face wreathed in smiles as she happily exchanged pleasantries while waiting for Hetty and the girls to get themselves comfortable.

When the women were finally settled in their places, their coats hanging on the backs of the chairs, their handbags resting in a heap under the table, Grace looked around for a sign of Stanley, but the room was so packed and smoky it was hard to see further than a few feet.

When Sam and Danny approached the table with the

drinks, a double port for Aggie, a gin and tonic for Hetty and Grace, and a lemonade for Polly, Grace touched her father's arm, asking loudly, 'Where's Stan, Dad? Isn't he with you?'

Bending down to hear Grace's words, Sam's head jerked up, his eyes circling the room.

'He was here a minute ago, love. He met up with some chap he knows. The last I saw of him, he was over near the band with Vi and this friend of his . . . Oh, there you are . . . See? Over there. Look, right in front of you . . .' Sam was gesturing with the hand holding his pint, causing Grace to lean back to avoid getting splashed with the dangerously tilting Guinness. Following her father's arm, Grace saw Vi's distinctive blond hair nestled between a small group of men and got to her feet.

'Keep my chair for me, Polly.' She bent her head towards her sister, who was watching the activity around her with great enjoyment. 'I'm just going to tell Stan we're here. Won't be a tick.'

As she passed, Hetty reached out and grabbed Grace's arm, saying, 'If you see Vi, tell her I want a word with her.'

Grace nodded and moved on. Squeezing through the merry throng, she reached Stanley's side, and her first thought was one of relief, followed quickly by one of dismay. Stanley was drunk. And Stanley, when in his cups, could be a bit too much at times. Still, she told herself as she ducked a glowing cigarette end held precariously at face level by a passing guest, any change of mood had to be better than the one he was in earlier. With him was Vi, her vivacious face sparkling, her evident good humour obviously engendered by a tall, dark-haired man who was in the middle of telling a witty story to a captivated Stanley. The trio looked so comfortable with each other that for a brief moment Grace felt as if she was intruding; then she slid her arm through Stanley's, saying cheerfully, 'Hello there. I wasn't sure if you'd be here or not.'

Stanley turned, a welcoming smile splayed about his lips.

'Wotch'yer, Gracie, love, how's me favourite girl, then?'

With a bellyful of beer, Stan was positively oozing conviviality. Gathering Grace closer to his side, he waved his free hand to acknowledge his drinking partner.

'This is Nobby, love. We used to go to the same school. Ain't seen each other for years, then, wallop, outta the blue, he shows up in here. Funny old world, ain't it?'

Grace smiled wryly. She couldn't see anything that strange about bumping into an old friend. It happened all the time, especially in places such as these. But Stanley seemed to be delighted at the chance meeting, and that was the main thing.

In the general crush, Grace hadn't had time to look properly at the good-looking, smiling man. Now, as she held out her hand to greet him, her smile faltered as she took in the blue airforce uniform he was wearing. Casting a quick look into Stanley's face, Grace suddenly knew the reason behind his profusive delight at meeting this particular old friend. Swallowing the nagging feeling of misgiving, she took the outstretched hand and gripped it warmly.

'I'm very pleased to meet you, Mr . . . ?'

Stanley roared. 'What did I tell you, Nobby? Has my girl got class, or what?'

The uniformed man flicked an answering smile at Stan, but his eyes remained fixed on Grace.

'And I'm very pleased to meet you, Grace. Stanley here's been telling me all about you. And the name's Nobby . . . Nobby Clark.'

Momentarily disconcerted by the warmth in the stranger's greeting, Grace moved closer to Stanley's side, and when the dark-haired man grinned lazily and turned to the hovering Violet, Grace immediately chided herself for being silly.

As if to compensate for her foolishness, Grace turned to her sister, already busy making herself familiar with Stanley's new-found friend, and said archly, 'By the way, Vi, Mum wants you. You'd better go and see her before she comes looking for you.'

The gaiety slipped from Violet's face at Grace's words, but her loss of composure was swiftly restored as she slipped her arm casually through the arm of the man at her side and, wrinkling up her pert nose, said playfully, 'I suppose I'd better do what my big sister tells me. But, hang on . . . Why don't you come and meet the family? After all, any friend of Stan's is a friend of ours . . . Eh, Gracie?' The look she shot her sister was filled with childish mockery, but before Grace had the chance to answer, Stan, delighted at the opportunity to hang on to his friend for the remainder of the evening, joined in, crying expansively, 'Yeah, that's a good idea. How about it, Nobby? Fancy meeting me relations . . . Well . . .' He dug Nobby slyly in the ribs and winked. 'Sort of me relations. Me and Gracie'll be tying the old knot soon enough – won't we, love?'

Knowing herself to be defeated, Grace led the way back to the table, and while introductions were made all round, she slid back on to her chair and took a long sip at her drink. During the course of the evening more chairs were added around the table, and within a very short time the Donnelly family was hosting its own private party. Sam in particular was thankful to have someone so entertaining join them. Usually the conversation among the men fell heavily on him, so it was a rare treat for him to have someone equally proficient in making the conversation sparkle.

And Nobby Clark could certainly hold an audience. With a seemingly effortless ease, he entertained them all, regaling the group of avid listeners with stories of his life growing up in the East End, and newer anecdotes stored up from his two years in the RAF. And such was his personality that when he revealed he was only on a forty-eight-hour pass, the entire Donnelly family groaned with disappointment, as if a dearly loved friend was soon to be snatched away from them.

When the bell for last orders sounded, the band struck up an old favourite, and while Sam, Danny and Stan rushed to get in a last drink, the women, led by Aggie, joined in a loud rendition of 'Show Me The Way To Go Home' with such gusto that Grace thought her throat was going to burst.

Then it was time to go, and Aggie, her face flushed, her steely grey hair plastered to the sides of her face, tried to rise, only to fall back in a heap. She cried out in a voice smothered with drunken laughter, 'Well, ain't one of you buggers gonna help me to me feet?'

Nobby Clark sprang forward, his grey eyes twinkling mischievously as he hauled the quivering women to her feet, saying, 'Ups-a-daisy, me old darlin'.'

Aggie grabbed at him with both hands, gabbling shrilly, 'Ah, if only I was ten years younger, lad. I'd show you what was what. I never could resist a man in uniform . . . could I, Hetty, love?' The bleary question was thrown over her shoulder as Hetty came to assist the staggering woman, her eyebrows raised in loving exasperation. Considering the way her mother had gone on earlier, she would have thought a man in uniform was the last figure Aggie would have taken a shine to.

'If you say so, Mum. If you say so,' she answered, smiling broadly.

Once out in the cold night air, the group banded together for warmth. With Aggie, Hetty and Sam leading the way, and Danny and Polly close behind, Grace found herself a part of a foursome, as Vi, fearful of losing sight of the handsome man in uniform, clung possessively to Nobby's arm, while Grace tried to keep the inebriated Stanley, who was now having difficulty walking, on his feet.

Seeing Grace's dilemma, Nobby gently disentangled himself from Vi's grip and took the weight of Stanley's heavy body against his own, leaving a disgruntled Violet to trail along behind on her own.

On arrival in Lester Road, Nobby refused all entreaties to come in for a nightcap, insisting he had to get back to his base. Seeing her chance, Violet dropped back from the small group, taking off a high-heeled shoe and making a great show of inspecting the interior as if searching for some foreign object that was hindering her gait. But Hetty, still not forgetting her daughter's earlier behaviour, was having none of it. Grabbing Violet roughly by the arm, Hetty frog-marched the indignant girl inside the house, calling a last goodbye over her shoulder at the silent, grinning airman. And somehow or other, Grace found herself alone with Stanley's childhood friend on the front porch, and without the comforting presence of her family, she experienced a rising uneasiness at the close proximity of the charismatic man.

Nobby, however, was experiencing no such discomfort. Perfectly at ease, he tipped his peaked cap to the back of his head as he gazed in awe at the outside of the house. After blowing a soft whistle through gleaming white teeth he said slowly, 'Bleeding hell! I thought old Stan was exaggerating when he told me his fiancée lived in a posh house – but he wasn't, was he?'

Finding herself growing more uncomfortable by the minute, and grateful for the light streaming over them from the hallway, Grace gave an embarrassed laugh.

'It's a long story. It was left to us by my grandfather. I mean, we're not rich, or anything like that. We all have to work, just like everyone else.'

Nobby lowered his gaze, his probing grey eyes sweeping

over Grace's pink-tinged face. Languidly lifting his hand, he gently ran a finger down the side of Grace's cheek, murmuring, 'Except for poor old Stan'.

Grace jerked as violently as if an electric current had struck her body. She'd been fiddling with the metal clasp of her handbag, which she now snapped shut firmly, saying in a tremoring voice that betrayed her agitation, 'Yes, well, Stan will find work soon. Something will turn up eventually. It always does for men who are good with their hands, like Stanley is.'

Nobby stepped closer, a slight smile playing about his wide mouth.

'Is he now?'

There was no mistaking the inference behind the words and Grace felt her face begin to burn. A hot retort sprang to her lips, then she saw the guileless, open look on Nobby's face, the forthright friendly expression stripping the words of any offence, and found herself smiling. She knew she should say goodnight and close the door on the captivating man, but she couldn't seem to move. It was only when she heard a sudden burst of loud laughter coming from inside the house that the spell was broken.

Stepping back she said lightly, 'It was nice to meet you, Nobby. I'll tell Stanley you had to leave. He'll be sorry to have missed saying goodbye.'

Pulling his cap down over his eyes, Nobby dug his hands into the long pockets of his trousers, gave Grace a long, appraising glance, then winked.

'Don't worry, Grace. I wasn't gonna jump on you. I just ain't used to being with nice girls these days. The sort I meet up with overseas, they're—' He uttered an infectious laugh. 'Don't take no notice of me, Gracie. I always was a bad 'un. You ask Stan, he'll tell you. Anyway, I'm off. Thank your family for me, won't you. For making me feel so welcome I mean. And tell Stan I'll look him up on me next leave if I can.'

Turning from her, the tall figure ran lightly down the three stone steps to the street. 'See you, Gracie. Stay lucky.'

Then he was gone, disappearing into the night, and when Grace slowly closed the front door, she had to wait a few moments for her heart to return to its normal beat before joining her family.

CHAPTER FIVE

'Cor blimey, what a bleeding night. I ain't had that much fun in a long time. What d'yer say, Hetty . . . It was a good night, wasn't it, girl?'

Flopping back in the armchair near the banked-down fireplace, Aggie's head bounced from one to the another of her family for confirmation of her words, her spirits still running high.

Stifling a yawn, Hetty nodded, her face tired but happy.

'Yes it was, Mum, a very good night. But I think it's time we were all off to bed, I'm—'

'Bed! You can't go to bed yet, Hett,' Aggie protested anxiously. She'd had a rare good night out, doubly appreciated because of what had gone on before, and was reluctant to end the party mood. Flinging her arms out towards her daughter she cried, 'Aw, let's have a bit of supper before we go up, eh, Hett! 'Cos I don't know about the rest of you, but all that drink's given me an appetite. Shame the chippie'll be closed by now, I could just go a nice bit of cod and chips.'

'I could do you some chips, Nan.' Polly, her plain face showing no sign of tiredness now, and, like her grandmother, wanting to keep the festive spirit alive for a little longer, sprang to her feet. 'There's still some of the bread left you baked this morning, Nan. I could do everyone a chip sandwich . . . Will that be all right, Mum?' She looked to her mother for approval, and Hetty, conscious that she was herself a little peckish, nodded.

'Come on then, I'll give you a hand. I don't suppose I'd get any sleep anyway.'

'That's the spirit, girl.' Aggie beamed around the room, her eyes lighting on Sam, who had sat down at the piano at the far corner of the room. 'That's the idea, Sammy. Give us a tune, an' we can carry on where we left off at the club.'

Sam glanced up uncertainly. 'I don't think so, Aggie. It's gone eleven. We must have already woken up the neighbours coming in; I don't want them banging on the door complaining.' A slow grin spread over his face. 'Hetty and me have our reputations to uphold, you know. After all, we are professional people, and as such should show an example. Not roll in roaring drunk on a Friday night and start up an impromptu party. We'll get our name up in the street if we're not careful.'

'Bollocks!' Aggie shot back dismissively. 'They might think better of you . . . Oh, all right then, we'll do without the piano. You play like a cat having its teeth pulled anyway. Now your dad . . . Oh, he could play the piano, could old Paddy. And he knew how to have a laugh. You talk about the neighbours, Sam. But not one of 'em ever complained when your dad kept us all up half the night with his goings-on.'

Sam looked over at his mother-in-law and smiled ruefully.

'No they didn't. They wouldn't have dared.'

From the hallway, the tantalising smell of frying potatoes wafted into the room, and when Hetty and Polly entered with two trays piled high with plates of golden chips and fresh bread heaped with butter, everyone in the room drooled hungrily.

With a doorstep sandwich held between stubby fingers, Aggie took a deep bite, licking the corners of her mouth in approval.

'There's nothing like a plate of chips and bread and butter after a good drink, is there?'

Finishing her sandwich, she reached forward for another from the tray, sighing contentedly. 'I was just saying to Sam about old Paddy, Hett. He knew how to enjoy himself. That young fellow tonight put me in mind of him. It's a shame he couldn't stay on for a bit. Oh, he had a silver tongue all right. The sort of bloke you could listen to all night, an' I'll bet he's broken a few hearts in his time. What I can't get over is him being a friend of Stan's. Isn't that right, lad?'

Stan, his mouth full of food, chewed frantically in order to make a reply, but Aggie was carrying on regardless. 'I mean to say, I'd never have imagined you being pally with someone like Nobby Clark, never in a million years. You're as different to him as chalk an' cheese. Still, never mind, lad, it's not your fault . . . Will you be keeping in touch with him, 'cos I'd like to see him again . . . We all would, especially Vi . . . Eh, Vi . . . ! Now where the bleeding hell has she got to . . . ?'

'She went straight to bed, Nan. She said she was tired.' Grace, sitting on the arm of the chair by Stanley's side, gave her fiancé's hand an affectionate squeeze to compensate for Aggie's unfortunate choice of words. But Stanley, still mellow with drink, seemed unaware that he had been insulted yet again, albeit unintentionally.

'Tired!' Aggie snorted. 'More like her nose put out of joint. Still, it'll do her good to be ignored for once . . . Oh, me Gawd! Look at Sam . . . Here, Sam, Sammy, lad . . .' Her raucous laugh carried across the room to where Sam, an empty brandy glass in his hand, had his head laid on the top of the piano, his eyes jerking open in startled surprise.

Smiling tenderly, Hetty crossed the room and took hold of her husband's arm.

'You shouldn't have had that last brandy.' She clicked her tongue in admonishment. 'Come on, love. Let's get you to bed.'

Sam, his face bearing the simplistic smile of a drunk, looked up at his wife bemused.

'Wha . . . what's that, Hetty. Oh, oh, all right, love, all right.' Struggling to rise from the piano stool, Sam threw a beseeching look at his wife and groaned piteously. 'I can't get up . . . Hetty, me darlin'. Will you give me a hand, darlin'?'

Smiling broadly, Hetty went to her husband's aid. With practised ease she lifted Sam's arm across her shoulder while calling to Aggie, 'Here, give me a hand, will you, Mum.'

Aggie pulled herself from the comfort of her chair and took hold of her son-in-law's other arm and hoisted him to his feet, commenting, 'He never could hold his drink, not like old Paddy . . . Here, you, Danny, give us a hand, you big lump, before he has us over.'

Danny sprang forward from the settee like a dog being called to heel. Always wanting to be of use, he took the weight of his brother, his expression assuming the manner of a man engaged in an important task.

With much pulling and panting, Sam was half-carried from the room. As they passed by the door, Aggie, who was pushing Sam from behind, her round face red with exertion, nodded first at Grace, then down to the man lolling in the armchair beside her.

'He takes after your dad for the drink, Grace. Some men get nasty, others get frisky and others get soppy. And you can't get any soppier than the pair of these, now can you? Mind you, I'd rather have them like this any day, Oh yes. Better to be soppy than argumentative like some.'

Grace nodded wryly. 'I suppose you're right, Nan . . .

Look, you help get dad to bed before he has the lot of you over.'

The sound of banging and laughter could be heard down the passage and up the stairs.

Grace looked at Polly and rolled her eyes.

'Lord, what a night. It's lucky Uncle Danny doesn't drink much, or else we'd have him on our hands as well.' Shaking her head in amused vexation, she looked down at the sleeping Stanley and added, 'Help me get Stan over to the settee, will you, Polly? There's no point in trying to wake him. He can sleep it off here; I'm sure Mum won't mind him staying the night just this once.' Standing either side of the armchair, Polly and Grace, like their mother and nan a few minutes since, pulled the drunken man to his feet and dragged him across to the couch, whereupon Stan opened a bleary eye and tried to sit up.

'Wo . . . won't you come ho . . . home, Bill Bailey, wo . . . won't you come home . . .'

'Oh, Lord, he's singing now,' laughed Polly. 'At least he's trying to. Coo, what a racket.'

Letting the heavy form slump sideways on to the settee, the two women stood looking down at him.

'What now?' asked Polly, her shiny face mirroring beads of sweat from her exertion. 'Shall we get him some coffee, or just leave him there?'

'Oh, just leave him there,' Grace answered airily. 'He'll come round in his own good time.'

Hearing soft footsteps outside the door, Grace glanced up to see Vi standing in the doorway, a pair of high-heeled black pumps dangling from her fingers.

'They all gone to bed yet?' she whispered, then, seeing the figure sprawled on the settee she said, 'Oh, Lord, he's not stopping the night, is he?'

Grace's head came up sharply. 'It's none of your business

if he does or not. And where have you been, anyway? We all thought you'd gone to bed.'

Vi shrugged her shoulders defiantly, but was unable to stop herself from sneaking a quick look up the stairway to make sure the coast was clear.

'I fancied a walk, that's all. Anyway, I'm off to bed. See you in the morning . . . Well, sometime tomorrow anyway. Goodnight.'

'Night, Vi,' Polly answered, stifling a yawn. 'I think I'll go up as well, Grace. Unless you want me to keep you company.'

Grace smiled fondly. 'Get up to bed. You look as if you could fall asleep on your feet. Go on. I'll see you in the morning. Goodnight, love.'

Standing with her hand on the doorknob, Polly smiled tiredly at her sister.

'I never thought we'd end up having such a good night. I didn't even want to go out, but I'm glad I did. That friend of Stanley's was a good laugh, wasn't he, Grace? Did you see Vi trying to hang on to him . . . Oh!' Dropping her voice a shade lower, Polly breathed, 'Do you think Vi went after him! Oh . . . she wouldn't have, surely . . .'

Grace's mouth turned upwards in a grimace of annoyance. 'I wouldn't put it past her. But if that is where she went, then it couldn't have done her much good, or else she'd have looked a lot happier than she did when she came in.'

'No, you're right. Goodnight, Grace.'

'Yes, goodnight, love.'

For the next five minutes, Grace wandered around the room, picking up and stacking the dirty plates on a tray ready to be taken into the kitchen. She was bending down to retrieve a dropped piece of bread from the carpet when two strong arms snaked around her waist, causing her to cry out in surprise.

'I thought they'd never go.' Stanley, his face still flushed from the night's drinking, bent down and nuzzled at the soft flesh of Grace's neck, making appreciative noises at the enjoyable task.

Twisting round in the tight grasp, Grace exclaimed sharply, 'Stan, you idiot. You nearly frightened me half to death, creeping up on me like that.' Placing her hands on his broad chest, Grace tilted her head back to get a better look at him. 'Was that all an act? All that singing and larking about—'

Her words were cut off abruptly as Stan kissed her roughly, his hands moving up and down her back. Melting into his body, Grace gave herself up to the passionate embrace without any further protest, until a harsh, familiar voice jerked her back to reality.

'And we'll have none of that malarkey, thank you very much. At least not while I'm around.'

The startled couple sprang apart guiltily, both assuming the air of small children caught out in some minor misdemeanour.

Patting her hair awkwardly, Grace stammered, 'Hello, Nan, we were just . . .'

Aggie gave a short laugh.

'I know what you were doing, girl. I've still got a good pair of eyes in me head. Now you . . .' She dug a short thick finger at Stan's chest. 'You can get yourself off home, seeing as how you've made such a miraculous recovery. And there was me about to fetch you a pillow and blanket for the night. But I'm sure you'd rather be tucked up in your own bed, eh, lad?'

Stan's face suddenly looked sickly white.

'Yeah, you're right. In fact I think I'll be off now.' Glancing feverishly around the room, he caught sight of his hat lying near the armchair and quickly snatched it up. He slammed it down on his head while saying thickly, 'I'll come round tomorrow, Grace . . . About elevenish . . . All right . . . ?'

Looking positively green now, Stan lurched from the room with Grace hurrying behind him.

'Stan, Stanley, are you all right—' But the front door banged in her face, and when she went to follow, she felt her arm gripped tightly.

'Leave him alone, Grace. A fellow doesn't like to be seen throwing up by his girlfriend, so make the most of it. 'Cos once you're married, he won't be so particular, you take my word for it.'

When Grace did as she was told, Aggie hesitated for a moment, then, her face clearing, she burst out hurriedly, 'Look, love, about earlier. I didn't mean to hurt Stan's feelings, or Danny's for that matter. It wasn't them I was mad at, more like the world in general. But I took me bad temper out on them, poor buggers, and I'll apologise properly to Stan, and your uncle Danny, tomorrow. Now I can't say fairer than that, can I, love?' Peering anxiously into Grace's face, she added humbly, 'You don't hold it against me, do you, love?'

The look of uncertainty on the normally implacable countenance brought forth a rush of affection from Grace. Throwing her arms around the broad shoulders, she murmured lovingly, 'Don't be daft, Nan. I could never stay angry with you for long.'

Patting the slim back, Aggie returned the hug, then stepped back to look closely into Grace's face.

'Well, I wouldn't have blamed you if you had, love. And I don't blame Stan for wanting to join up either. I'd probably want to do the same if I was in his shoes. Especially after meeting up with that Nobby Clark tonight, and hearing him talk about what it's like overseas. He made it sound like it was one big laugh. I could see Stan hanging on to every word, poor sod! Still . . .' She squeezed Grace's arm gently. 'Even if Stan does go and enlist, it don't mean to say he'll see any fighting, does it? Not if there's no war to fight.'

Grace blinked rapidly. 'Well, let's hope it doesn't come to that,' she murmured softly, too tired to worry about it any more tonight.

After locking up and turning out the lights downstairs, the two women climbed the stairs. They paused midway at the sound of soft laughter coming from the main bedroom, then there was silence, and with a knowing look, the women tiptoed up the remainder of the stairs.

Two weeks later, Stanley and Bert Harris, Stan's former workmate, met up again for a drink. The following day both men, using each other for moral support, enlisted in the army.

CHAPTER SIX

Events were hotting up over the Channel. Germany had instigated further 'incidents' on the Polish border in a flagrant attempt to justify yet another invasion. Hurried negotiations with Russia were carried out in secret, but it was too late. The shock announcement in August that Russia and Germany had signed a pact of non-aggression fuelled the mounting realisation that war now was inevitable.

By the end of August the gigantic task of evacuating three million of Britain's children to safer zones in the country was complete, leaving their teachers, who had accompanied them, to return to London to await further developments, secure in the knowledge that their young charges were now out of harm's way.

Sam and Hetty Donnelly, like many of their profession, had spent four hectic days travelling on stuffy, overcrowded trains filled with excited and tearful children, the majority of whom, blissfully unaware of the eminent danger at home, had treated the whole procedure as a great adventure.

Now Britain's children were safely billeted in various parts of the countryside, the nation sat back waiting to learn its fate.

The summer of 1939 had seen glorious weather, and as September dawned it looked as if the warm climate was set to hold throughout the autumn.

Barely three days into the new month, the Donnelly family, like the rest of Britain, were waiting to hear the outcome of the Prime Minister's speech.

'Mum, Mum! Will you stop that for a minute, please. We're all waiting for you in the living room, it's a quarter to eleven.'

Hetty stood in the kitchen doorway, her troubled eyes watching Aggie as the elderly woman darted back and forth from the hot stove to the table, laden with vegetables. Dropping another potato into a bowl of water, Aggie looked up sharply.

'I know what the time is, Hetty, and I'm doing what I always do at this time on a Sunday morning, I'm getting the dinner ready. 'Cos whatever Chamberlain has to say, we'll still be wanting our dinner at one o'clock.'

Hetty, her manner brisk now, took the knife from Aggie's hand and laid it down between a pile of carrots and runner beans.

'Yes, I know we'll still be wanting our dinner, Mum,' she said patiently. 'But it won't matter if it's a little late today, now will it?'

Bristling restlessly, Aggie wiped her hand down the front of her apron saying, 'Oh, all right. I'll come an' listen to the broadcast, though why we're bothering I don't know. It's bleeding obvious what he's gonna say, ain't it?'

They were in the hall when they heard the knock on the front door. Both women looked at each other in surprise.

'Now I wonder who that can be!' said Hetty. 'Stan's already here, and we're not expecting anyone else. Oh, look, you go and join the rest of them, I'll see who it is.'

Hurrying towards the door, she opened it to find four

of her neighbours standing awkwardly on the porch, their expressions anxious.

'Oh, hello, Mrs Butcher, and you too, Mrs Castle,' Hetty said, her voice showing her surprise. Behind the two women stood Bert Castle and Reg Watson from number seven. Bewildered by the arrival of her neighbours, Hetty asked, 'Is there something I can do for you?'

The small group shuffled uncomfortably before Rene Castle, a small chirpy woman wearing a floral pinafore and a green turban, under which peeped steel curlers, stepped forward and said hesitantly, 'Look, Mrs Donnelly, I know we've got a cheek. But the thing is, our wirelesses 'ave gorn on the blink, an' we was wondering if we could listen to yours.'

Gathering courage from Hetty's kind expression, Jeannie Butcher, a brash blonde who lived at number four, joined in her friend's request. 'We don't 'ave to come in, like. I mean, yer don't want us all trooping through yer nice 'ouse. But if yer could turn the wireless up an' open the window, we could all hear from out here, like.'

Hetty's eyes swiftly scanned the anxious faces of her neighbours, neighbours she had barely spoken to over the years except when meeting in the street or at the corner shop. And though their conversations had always been brief, they had also been cordial. Now they were asking a favour of her, and judging by the looks on their faces, it wasn't something they had undertaken lightly. Quickly making up her mind, she said stoutly, 'Don't be silly. Come in, come in, all of you. There's plenty of room in our sitting room.'

'Oh, no, Mrs Donnelly, we don't want to put you to any trouble,' Rene Castle protested, her foot already over the doorstep.

'Nonsense,' declared Hetty firmly. Opening the door wide, she gestured the small group into her home.

Murmuring their thanks, the neighbours slowly filed past

Hetty, down the wide hallway. And Hetty was amused to note that although her neighbours were genuinely anxious to hear Chamberlain's speech, they weren't going to let an opportunity to see what the Donnelly home looked like from inside pass by unnoticed.

And look they did. They were only in the hallway for a matter of seconds, but it was long enough for the neighbours to take in the long, wide staircase leading up to the first-floor landing, off which could be seen four stout wooden doors with brass handles; these obviously led to the bedrooms. The landing then branched off in both directions, with whatever rooms they contained not visible from the downstairs hallway. Then there was another smaller, narrower staircase on the right side of the landing, leading up to the attic rooms. Both staircases were carpeted, as was the landing and hallway, in a faded blue-and-gold carpet.

'Coo, it's like a palace,' breathed Jeannie Butcher, unable to disguise her admiration of the surroundings.

Hetty gave a short, pleasant laugh. 'Hardly a palace, Mrs Butcher. The carpets have been here since my father-in-law first moved in, and they'll be here for another good few years yet. The same can be said for most of the furniture, but thank you for the compliment, it's very nice of you to say so.'

Rene Castle, her eyes seeming to be everywhere, asked, 'How many rooms are there, if yer don't mind me asking?'

Conscious of the time, but not wishing to appear brusque, Hetty answered, 'Eleven in all. That's the parlour to your right.' She indicated one of the closed doors. 'And the room next to it is the downstairs toilet, the bathroom has another one – well, you need two with all of us!' Her voice trailed off lamely as she realised her gaff. Here she was wittering on about having two toilets in the house, when, as far as she knew, every other residence in the street had only one toilet, and that was out in the backyard.

Speaking more quickly now, she walked as she talked,

adding, 'We use this side of the house more.' She tapped the first door on the left as they passed, saying, 'This room is the one we call the library, nothing as grand as that, of course, but it's somewhere to sit and read in peace when the fancy takes us. The kitchen is my favourite room. It was originally two rooms, but my late mother-in-law wanted a big kitchen, so it was knocked into one large room at the back of the house. There are four bedrooms on the first floor, and, as I've already said, the bathroom, though you can't see that from the hallway. My brother-in-law has the attic rooms to himself, and this is the main room where all the family congregates.'

She stopped outside the sitting room, slightly out of breath after the lightning, impromptu tour. Pushing the door wide, she announced gaily, 'We've got some company. Some of our neighbours don't have access to a wireless, so I've asked them in to join us to hear what Chamberlain has to say.'

Sam immediately jumped to his feet, a beaming smile of welcome on his broad face.

'Come in, come in, all of you,' he said cheerfully. 'There's plenty of room. Now then, let's get some seating arrangements sorted.' Turning to the two other men in the room, he said jovially, 'Danny, you and Stan get the settee and armchairs in from the parlour, while me and the girls move the furniture around in here to make room.'

As he spoke, Sam was already moving his favourite armchair to one side, his amused eyes catching the look that passed between his female neighbours, which clearly said, *Two three-piece suites – swanky beggers*. Aggie and Vi, who were sitting either end of the sofa, exchanged a look of annoyance at the arrival of the unexpected guests, causing Grace, who was perched on the arm of the sofa to nudge her nan's arm, while at the same time sending a warning glance at Vi. Then she turned to the visitors and smiled a welcome.

'Hello. I'm glad you could join us. The more the merrier, eh, Dad?' She grinned at Sam as she went to help him move the armchair Stan had just vacated.

Standing awkwardly in the centre of the room, the group presented an uncomfortable atmosphere. Then Stanley and Danny reappeared with the settee, and suddenly everyone was busy rearranging the furniture, relieved to have something to do.

'There we are, that didn't take long, did it?' Sam gestured towards the settee the men had brought in from the parlour. 'Would you like to sit here, Mrs Butcher, and you too, Mrs Castle. Make yourselves at home.'

Both women took up the offer gratefully, immediately feeling more at ease now they were sitting down. The two men who accompanied them stood bunched together until the spare armchairs were brought in, whereupon they too sat down, much relieved they were no longer so conspicuous. Then, on the wireless, Big Ben struck eleven. Everyone in the room tensed, then relaxed as the smooth voice of the announcer informed the listening public that the Prime Minister's speech would be delayed for fifteen minutes.

'Maybe there's been some fresh developments.' Sam, his gaze taking in his family and neighbours, nodded hopefully.

Aggie snorted. 'I wouldn't bank on it, lad. That blasted Hitler ain't gonna give in that easily. He's itching for a fight, that one, not that he'll get his own hands dirty. Oh, no! He'll just sit back somewhere safe and give his orders, just like the last lot did.' Suddenly unbending, she nodded towards the man sitting nearest and said gruffly, 'You was in the last lot, weren't you, Mr Watson?'

Reg Watson jumped nervously at finding himself singled out, then, his confidence returning, he stuck out his chin proudly and answered, 'Yeah, I was, Mrs Harper. The First Regiment along with me mates from me old street. Copped a bellyful of shrapnel an' all. Though I was luckier than me mates. All killed they was, I was the only one in me street to get back alive.' Aware he had become the centre of attention, the man shifted his buttocks on the soft cushions, twisted his flat cap nervously, then, his face setting into grim lines, he added stoutly, 'I never thought I'd live to see another war. Not after the last lot. You'd 'ave thought they'd 'ave learnt their lesson, wouldn't you? But nah! There'll always be some clever bugger who thinks he can be cock of the walk . . . Begging your pardon, missus.' He inclined his head at Hetty.

'Gracious, don't apologise, Mr Watson. If anyone has the right to voice an opinion, you have.' Twisting round on her chair, Hetty looked over at Grace and said cheerfully, 'Seeing as we've another fifteen minutes to wait, we might as well make some tea and sandwiches. Give me a hand, would you, Grace?'

As Hetty left the room she turned to Reg Watson and, inclining her head at Sam, said, 'My husband and late father and father-in-law also fought in the last war and—'

Reg Watson looked at Sam in surprise. 'You was in the last lot, sir? Why, you don't look old enough.'

Sam shuffled uncomfortably, uttering a short self-deprecating laugh. 'Huh, I certainly feel it some days. And I was only eighteen when I joined up, and back home again at twenty with trench foot. I was lucky though, I didn't lose any of my toes, unlike some.' Turning in his chair, Sam brought the other man into the conversation by asking, 'I suppose you were too young for the last lot, Mr Butcher?'

Tom Butcher, a pleasant-looking man in his early thirties smiled grimly. 'Yeah, I was, thank Gawd. But I don't think I'm gonna be as lucky this time. Still . . . it'll get me off the dole, so I suppose some good might come of it.'

Grace felt herself stiffen and glanced apprehensively at

her grandmother, but Aggie was keeping her counsel this time. Even she had come to realise and accept the inevitable by now.

Tom Butcher then looked over at the quiet man sitting opposite him, looking slightly out of place in his army uniform, and asked cheerfully, 'So what's it like in the army, mate? Recommend it, would yer?'

Stanley sat forward with a jerking movement and, flexing his fingers in the familiar way he had when excited or agitated, answered, 'Yeah, it's not bad. There's plenty to do, an', like you just said, it's better than being on the dole. Though what'll be like if there's a war is something else. Still, we'll just have to wait an' see, eh?'

When Hetty and Grace reappeared carrying a tray of tea and hastily prepared sandwiches and the remains of last evening's currant cake, the atmosphere lightened considerably.

Feeling more at ease, Rene Castle, accepting a cup of tea but refusing anything to eat, patted a small bulge in the pocket of her pinafore and asked hesitantly, 'D'yer mind if I 'ave a fag, Mrs Donnelly? Only me nerves are all of a twitter.'

'Yes, oh, yes, of course, Mrs Castle. You go right ahead – and anyone else who wants to smoke,' Hetty answered, whereupon the men, including Stanley, gratefully took out their cigarettes and lit up. Stanley had the only ashtray available, and Hetty, looking round for a receptacle to serve as an additional ashtray and finding none close at hand, handed a saucer to her neighbour, at which the horrified woman protested, 'Oh, no, that's one of yer good bits of crockery. I can't flick me ash in that . . .'

'Shush everyone, it's starting.' Sam spoke sharply as the BBC announced the Prime Minister was about to speak. Silence enveloped the room as all trained their attention on the wireless. Outside in the street not a sound could be

heard. All of Britain was listening to their leader's words –
and all were stiff with fearful anticipation.

Then Chamberlain spoke, his familiar voice sounding so
weary and dispirited that before he had uttered his first
sentence, those listening were filled with foreboding. Their
fears were soon founded.

*'I am speaking to you from the Cabinet Room at 10 Downing
Street. This morning the British Ambassador in Berlin handed the
German Government a final note, stating that unless we heard
from them by eleven o'clock that they were prepared at once to
withdraw their troops from Poland, a state of war would exist
between us. I have to tell you that no such undertaking has
been received and that consequently this country is at war with
Germany . . .'*

A startled cry of pure terror from Polly cut the air, and for a
few moments the people in the room were distracted as they
tried to calm the terrified girl. Her face set firm, Aggie pulled
the quivering body of her youngest granddaughter on to her
lap and held her fast, while straining to hear the rest of the
Prime Minister's speech above Polly's heartrending sobs.

*'. . . bitter blow it is to me that all my long struggle to win
peace has failed. Yet I cannot believe that there is anything more
or anything different that I could have done . . .'*

A harsh laugh of derision came from Reg Watson's dry
lips.

'Well, he's got that right, ain't he? He done everything but
crawl on his 'ands and knees ter Hitler, for all the good it's
done 'im . . . Huh!'

The bitterness in the elderly man's voice struck a chord
among those present, for it was true that Chamberlain had
lost the respect of many people by his compromising and
mealy-mouthed attitude towards the German leader, who
seemed hell-bent on conquering the entire Western world
with his newly formed Nazi Party. Yet even in their scorn
of Chamberlain, the British people had hoped fervently his

tactics would work. Well, they hadn't. So much for the soft approach!

Sam, his eyes filled with empathy for the older man's rage, lifted his hand for silence so that they could hear the rest of the Prime Minister's speech.

'Now may God bless you all. May He defend the right. It is an evil thing that we shall be fighting against. Brute force, bad faith, injustice and oppression, and persecution, and against them I am certain that the right shall prevail.'

All those present in the room had fallen silent, yet in that brief space of time the initial onslaught of fear was slowly being replaced with defiance, and when the broadcast ended and Hetty murmured absently, 'Well, we'd best drink our tea before it gets cold,' Aggie roared, 'Stuff the bloody tea, girl, and get out the brandy!'

Her words caused the sobbing girl in her arms to cry louder and, gently, Aggie pulled the shaking form closer to her stout body, murmuring words of comfort.

Apart from Polly, the adults seemed to have taken the news in their stride, for deep down they had known war was imminent. Hadn't they been preparing for such an event for the past year?

The atmosphere was beginning to appear almost convivial as everyone gratefully accepted the offered brandy. And when Rene, another cigarette hanging from the corner of her mouth, said gruffly, 'Well, war or no bleeding war, me old man'll still be expecting 'is dinner on the table when 'e finishes 'is night shift . . .', they all felt themselves relaxing at the normality of the stoic woman's attitude.

It had been barely fifteen minutes since the Prime Minister had finished relaying his doomladen message when the unearthly sinister air-raid siren began to wail and everyone jumped for their lives.

'Oh, me Gawd. The buggers are gonna bomb us!' Rene Castle shrieked wildly. 'I've gotta find me gas mask. Gawd knows where it is now . . . Thank Gawd me kids are safe . . .'

There was pandemonium in the room. Poor Polly continued to scream with terror, expecting a bomb to drop on their heads at any moment.

'Settle down, settle down.' Sam shouted to be heard over the mêlée. 'All of you, get yourselves down to the basement. We'll be safe enough there, I reckon. Come on, everyone, get a move on.' His tone was that of a teacher restoring order among unruly children, and it worked. With startling efficiency the small party scrambled down into the basement of No.1 Lester Road, and waited for the bombs to fall. And when the all-clear sounded without a bomb in sight, the occupants of the basement scrambled shamefaced from their temporary shelter, embarrassed now at the fuss they had made earlier.

On Aggie's insistence, the neighbours stayed to finish their impromptu lunch, aided by a further measure of brandy. A goodly drop was added to the weeping Polly's cup of tea, and within minutes the exhausted girl was curled up in the corner of the settee, mercifully dead to the world for a couple of hours.

Once the neighbours had left, effusive in their thanks for the hospitality they had received, Aggie returned to the kitchen, carrying on where she'd left off as if nothing had happened. As did Hetty, who disappeared upstairs to finish her weekly dusting and polishing of the bedrooms, giving Sam and Danny the opportunity to slip down the pub for their Sunday lunchtime drink.

Everything appeared to be so normal that Grace, left to tidy up after the unexpected visitors, looked over to where Stanley was sitting silently by the fireplace and said in wonder, 'It's like nothing's happened, isn't it, Stan? I mean . . . well, I don't know what I expected to happen after the news, but I didn't expect everything to carry on as usual . . .'
Her voice broke suddenly, and tears began to fill her eyes.

'Oh, Stanley, I'm frightened. You'll be gone this afternoon, and . . . and I might ne – never see you again . . .'

Stanley, his face filled with concern, held his arms out to her. 'Now, don't start that, Gracie, please. You know I can't bear to see you upset. Come here. Come on, come and give me a cuddle. It'll probably have to last me a long time, so let's make the most of it – before your nan comes back and catches us. Or before Polly wakes up and starts howling again.' He attempted a smile as he nodded over at the sleeping girl on the settee, but Grace was beyond being humoured.

Crying quietly, Grace crept on to Stan's lap, and when his arms fastened around her waist, she turned and buried her face deep in the harsh fabric of the khaki uniform and let the tears flow freely.

And when, some time later, Aggie put her head around the door and saw the couple entwined in the armchair, she quietly withdrew without disturbing them.

'Now, are you sure you don't want us to come and see you off, Stan? It would be no trouble, son. We can all pile on to a bus and come with you to the station.'

Stanley shook his head, smiling. 'Thanks, Sam, but like I told you earlier, me mate's kid ain't well, so his wife can't see him off, and I said we'd go together. I can't let him down, can I? But thanks, anyway.'

That Stanley was putting his friend before Grace was evident to all those present, except Stan. But nobody was going to risk causing an upset by commenting on Stanley's tactless behaviour; not today.

As the family stood bunched together on the front porch, Stanley said his goodbyes, kissing the women, and shaking Sam's and Danny's hands fervently as they all wished him luck. Then Bert Harris appeared at the top of the street – looking a lot more cheerful than the last time Grace had seen him on the bus – and with one final wave and a bearhug for

Grace, Stan, his kit-bag slung over his shoulder, ran down the street to join his friend. And with much pushing and backslapping the two men walked off.

Grace stood watching until the figures disappeared from view, her vision blurred from crying, then she slowly went indoors, shutting the door softly behind her.

Later that night, when the house was quiet, Hetty laid in Sam's arms, her head resting on his broad chest. Keeping her voice low, she murmured in the darkness, 'You know, love, I've often wished over the years I could have given you a son. Not that either of us would change our girls, I know that, but I felt at times that I'd let you down by not producing a son and heir, so to speak.'

'You've never said anything about it before,' Sam answered, his surprise evident in his hushed tone.

Hetty snuggled closer. 'No, I know I haven't. And I haven't dwelt on it either. It's just that this morning, when we heard the news, my first thought was "Thank God we never had any sons", and when I saw Stan and his friend, all togged out in their uniforms, looking for all the world as if they were off on some flipping adventure, well, I couldn't help but think how we would have been feeling if it had been our son going off to war – and I was ashamed at the relief I felt, knowing we'd been spared that horror.'

When Sam didn't answer, but simply stroked her hair lovingly, Hetty felt her eyes begin to close and within minutes had drifted off into a restful, contented sleep.

Beside her, Sam remained awake, his mind resurrecting his own youth and the horror of the trenches. Before he slept he lent his own prayer to Hetty's, thanking God for His foresight in giving him daughters.

CHAPTER SEVEN

After the initial outbreak of panic, Britain settled down to the reality of war – a war that soon became complacently known as the Phoney War, for no bombs dropped from the skies as anticipated, and no German soldiers attempted to invade British shores.

Air-raid shelters once again became playgrounds for scores of children – who were brought back home from the country – to play their games of hide and seek, and cops and robbers, while their parents went about their normal routine, their gas masks once again discarded.

But even if people were able to disregard the concept of war in daylight hours, at night the bitter reality was driven home as weary pedestrians and motorists struggled to get home in the blackout. Kerbs, lamp-posts and mudguards on buses were coated with white paint in an effort to help guide people to their destination, but the exercise was futile. People soon realised they were more in danger of being mown down on the streets than obliterated by falling bombs, as once-familiar and well-walked streets became a nightmare filled with hidden headlamps of cars and buses.

But if the British people didn't have the Germans to worry about, the winter of 1939–40 became the worst in living memory. First came the snow, and then the frost, then torrential rain leading to more frost. To venture out was hazardous, and the less mobile slipped and slithered before falling like ninepins on the ice-sheeted pavements and roads. The elderly, in particular, went down in their thousands, their broken bodies filling nearly every hospital and outpatient department in London and the outskirts. Gas, electricity and water were cut off, the powers-that-be answering complaints with the ever-popular excuse, 'Don't you know there's a war on, missus?'

Apart from the inconveniences, of which there were many, life for the majority carried on much the same as usual. The steady stream of children arriving back from the country meant that Sam and Hetty's services were once again in demand. Schools all over the country reopened their doors, much to the disappointment of the children, who had imagined their childhood days would be spent running the streets without worrying about the stuffy boredom of the classroom.

One of the good things to come about during the first year of the war was the gradual thawing of the famous British reserve. Strangers actually began to talk to each other, bonded together by rationing and hardship.

Overseas, Hitler's army continued to march, yet still Chamberlain's government refused to commit themselves to all-out war. The ambiguous attitude of the government not to bomb the German munitions factories – in the hope that they would reciprocate – only served to boost Hitler's confidence that he could conquer Western Europe unhindered. While Britain watched from the sidelines, the German army and airforce first attacked Norway and Denmark, then marched into Holland, Belgium and Luxembourg. But none of these coups could prepare the British people for the unbelievable – France, that bastion of allies, fell to the enemy. And with the fall of France came the turning of the tide in the war.

Britain now had a new Prime Minister – and Winston Churchill soon showed the British public he was a man not open to compromise like his predecessor. Instead of Chamberlain's placating words of comfort, Churchill roared defiance in the face of the enemy, his powerful rhetoric instilling new morale into the listening public.

Meanwhile, the German army had successfully driven across France, pushing the British army further and further back until they were trapped on the beaches of Dunkirk on the northern coast. What followed would go down in the annals of history as one of the greatest acts of heroism ever witnessed, as ordinary men in their hundreds risked their own lives – protected only by small and often flimsy boats – in a daring rescue to pluck their stranded soldiers from the beaches of Dunkirk.

And while England rejoiced in the triumph, it soon because obvious that the time of watching and uncertainty was finally over. The tiny island stood alone, brave and defiant, knowing that the battle had just begun.

'I think I'll go over the park for a couple of hours. Fancy coming with me for a walk, Grace? It's too nice to be sitting about at home doing nothing on such a lovely day.'

Polly looked hopefully at her eldest sister, who was re-reading one of Stanley's letters for the umpteenth time. Raising her head, Grace smiled and folded the letter back into the brown envelope.

'Yes, all right, why not. Hang on a minute and I'll see if the others fancy a stroll.'

Springing to her feet, Grace made for the door, only to be stopped by Polly exclaiming dolefully, 'It's no good asking them, Grace. Mum and Dad are going to the pictures, and after that they're going to some committee meeting; I don't know if Nan's going with them. And Vi's out with her latest fellow, whoever he is.' This statement was accompanied by a rolling of her eyes, eliciting a loud laugh from Grace.

'Looks like it's just you and me, then, Poll.'

'Looks like you and me for what?' Hetty had come into the hallway, pulling on a plain, pull-on felt hat to go with her WVS uniform. The two girls looked at the smart, if a trifle rotund, figure dressed in a green tweed suit interwoven with grey and a dark red jumper.

'Oh, just going for a walk over Vicky Park, Mum,' Grace answered cheerfully, as she pulled on a large floppy straw hat. Polly, too, was trying to look over Grace's shoulder in the long hall mirror, while fixing a hat pin through a beige straw hat.

Talking to her mother's reflection Grace exclaimed, 'Goodness, Mum. You're not going to go out in that lot, are you? You'll be baking by the time you get to the top of the road. Why don't you leave the jumper off. Surely no one would mind on a day like this.'

Pushing her youngest daughter aside Hetty said, 'Let's have a look, Polly, dear. I can never get this hat to sit right.' Then, turning to Grace, she added, 'As a matter of fact the ladies of the committee would very much mind if I turned up half-dressed – even in a heatwave. So I shall just have to grin and bear it. There! That should do it. I'll just see if your nan wants to come with us before I call your father in from the garden. He's probably fallen asleep out there, like he always does after his dinner.' Leaning nearer her daughters, Hetty winked and said drily, 'It's a sign of old age, that is.'

Moving aside to let the girls have the mirror back, Hetty leant her hand on the banister and called up the stairs, 'Mum! Mum, we'll be off in a minute, if you want to come with us. If not, the girls are going over the park, if you'd prefer to go with them.' Peering up the long flight of stairs,

Hetty was about to call again when Aggie's voice floated down impatiently, 'All right, all right, there's no need to shout. I ain't deaf.'

Puffing slightly, the large frame of Aggie appeared at the top of the stairs. Pausing for a moment she looked down at the three women waiting in the hallway, and for a brief second her heart swelled with pride. The trio made a striking picture, with Hetty in her smart WVS uniform, and her two granddaughters in their thin, brightly coloured cotton frocks. Aggie had made them herself. A blue sprigged pattern for her Grace, and a yellow-and-white check design for Polly. Thinking of her dressmaking efforts, Aggie was reminded of her other granddaughter. Descending the stairs slowly she demanded, 'And where's the other young madam. Off gallivanting, I suppose.'

Hetty made a face at her daughters before turning to her mother, saying, 'Now, don't start, Mum. Vi's only doing what most girls her age do. There's nothing wrong with enjoying yourself, now is there?'

Reaching the bottom of the landing, Aggie snorted, 'Enjoying yourself is one thing, off out every night with Gawd knows who is something else . . . Anyway . . . !' Looking from one impatient face to the other, she cried, 'So, I've got a choice have I? Well, ain't I the lucky one. Still, if it's all the same to you lot, I think I'll stay at home with me feet up an' listen to the wireless.' Her eyes twinkling, she nudged Grace, adding, 'I wouldn't want to cramp your style over the park. Not with all them uniforms wandering about looking for a bit of company.'

'Nan!' both girls cried at once, their faces laughingly indignant.

Just then Sam wandered in from the garden, his amiable face glowing red from lying out in the sun.

'You ready, Hett? We'll miss the start of the film if we don't get a move on.'

'Well, I'm ready. I was just waiting for you,' Hetty replied as she adjusted the strap on her leather shoulder bag. 'Now are you sure you don't want to come with us, Mum? It's a Cary Grant film. You like him, don't you?'

Aggie shook her head and snorted, 'Cary Grant, huh! What sort of a name is that. He should've stuck with his own name. I mean, what was wrong with Archibald Leach? I ain't got no time for people what's ashamed of where they come from. And anyway, I don't fancy going out!'

Sam and Hetty exchanged a look of exasperation. Sometimes it seemed as though Aggie moaned simply for the sake of it. Though to be fair to the elderly woman, she had taken Danny's call-up into the army very badly and was constantly worrying about his safety, as were they all. But it didn't do to fret over such things, especially when there was nothing you could do about it.

'All right, Mum, suit yourself. Now you know I'm going to a meeting after the pictures, so I'll be home about seven . . .'

'And I'll be home about six, so make sure my tea's on the table, woman.' Sam landed a light blow on Aggie's rump with the flat of his hand. 'Now, if you'll excuse us, we're off. Don't want to keep Archibald waiting, do we?'

'Silly bugger.' Aggie's comment followed her family into the street.

Coming out at the top of the road, Sam spotted a number six bus and, grabbing Hetty's hand, dashed after it.

'See you later, girls. Have a nice afternoon!' Hetty called out, then saved her breath for running.

Grace and Polly strolled on unhurriedly, giggling like a couple of schoolgirls at the many wolf-whistles they attracted along the way from eager servicemen looking for a bit of diversion on their short leave.

When they arrived at the park, the girls picked out a cool spot underneath a sprawling oak tree, and stretched their long legs out on the dry grass, sighing with contentment.

Throwing her head back so that her face was turned towards the sun, Grace murmured, 'With a bit of luck, we can get a bit of colour on our legs. Save having to smother them in cold tea – not that there's ever any cold tea left, not with Nan. She's a proper teapot if ever there was one.'

'Mmmm, yes, I know. Still, maybe the war will be over soon, then we won't have to worry about rationing any more.' Turning over on to her stomach, Polly looked up at Grace and laughed. 'Mind you, Vi would be upset, wouldn't she? She's never had so much fun. It's a good job Mum and Dad don't know half of what she gets up to, or they'd have a fit. And as for Nan . . . !'

'Yes, well, good luck to her. As long as she's careful, and Vi's not as scatterbrained as she makes out. She knows what she's doing.'

Polly plucked a blade of grass and chewed on it thoughtfully.

'Grace! Do you think, I mean would you come with me to a dance one night?' As Grace stared at her sister with obvious surprise, Polly flushed, a look of embarrassment spreading across her freckled face. 'Vi said she'd take me one night, but I wouldn't feel comfortable going with her, not the way the men all flock around her. I'd be out of my depth. I'd much rather go out with you.'

Grace gave a loud, throaty laugh. 'Well, thanks a bunch, Poll. That's a back-handed compliment if ever I heard one. Are you sure you'd want to be seen out with me and my warts-and-hook nose?'

Polly giggled and flapped her hand at the indignant face.

'Oh, you know what I mean, Gracie. I know you wouldn't go off with some fellow and leave me on my own.'

Pulling a face, Grace leant back against the tree and smiled.

'I know what you meant, silly.' Staring thoughtfully across

the park she murmured, 'I suppose I could do with a night out myself. Apart from Friday night at the club, I haven't been out anywhere since Stan left.' Appearing to make up her mind, Grace nodded and grinned. 'All right, Poll, you're on, and there's no time like the present. How about tonight? I heard Vi saying she was going to the Palais, maybe we could all go together.' As the idea took hold, Grace felt a trickle of excitement in her stomach at the thought of getting dressed up and going out. As she'd just said to Polly, she'd hardly gone outside the front door – apart from to work, of course – since Stan had gone overseas. Grace had hoped Stan's latest letter would contain news of his leave, but he hadn't even mentioned it, even though he must have been due some by now.

Her thoughts turned to her sister Violet, who was constantly out in the evenings, leaving the house all done up to the nines. Well, Grace pondered silently, I wouldn't look too bad myself if I made the effort! Let's see how Vi likes a bit of competition.

Giving herself a mental shake, Grace looked at her youngest sister, a tender smile on her face. The September sun had brought out Polly's freckles, and the orange hair that Polly hated with a passion was braided into a thick plait and pinned to the back of her head. And to Grace's eyes, Polly looked lovely. Already mentally picking out the dress she would wear that evening, Grace grinned at her sister.

'You can borrow my black dress, if you like, Poll. You know, the plain one; you've always said you liked it. It'll look good on you. Though I don't know what Vi'll say when she finds out that two gorgeous young women are going to be keeping her company – Ooh, blast! Where did that come from? It made me jump.' Grace had sat up quickly, her fingers curling around the small rubber ball that had landed in her lap. Spying a small boy standing a few feet away she smiled gently. 'Here you are, love. Come on, I won't bite,' she said gaily as the child hesitated. He was about three or four with a mop of fair curly hair and enormous blue eyes. Eyes that were regarding the two girls warily.

As Grace made to move towards the boy, a loud raucous voice cut through the air.

'Freddie, Freddie, what yer doing, yer little bleeder?'

Looking up, Grace and Polly saw a pretty woman striding towards them, her face heavily made-up and wearing a tight, white dress, gathered at the waist with a wide red belt, and red high-heeled shoes. With every step the heels sank into the turf, causing the woman to lurch slightly as she walked.

'Is 'e bovering yer, girls? The little sod's always running off. I need eyes in the back of me bleeding 'ead with 'im.' As she spoke she gently cuffed the curly head with the back of her hand. The blow was light and without malice. 'Got yer with 'is ball, did 'e? Sorry about that. Give it 'ere, I'll take care of it. In fact I think I'll chuck it in the lake where it won't do no more damage.'

Immediately the child let out a wail. 'No, Mum, don't. I'll be careful wiv it, honest. Don't chuck it in the lake, please, Mum . . . !'

Grinning broadly, the woman scooped up the child into her arms and held out brightly painted red fingernails to Grace for the ball.

'Ta, love. Sorry ter 'ave disturbed yer.'

'Oh, that's all right, think nothing of it.' Grace smiled back.

Polly stared after the mother and child, her mouth slightly open.

'Did you see those nails? And those shoes, phew. I'd love a pair like that, not that I'd have the nerve to wear them. Even if I did, I'd probably break my neck trying to walk in them. They must have had four-inch heels.'

Grace had lain back down on the grass, her eyes closed against the glare of the sun.

'You had a good look. Did you notice what underwear she was wearing as well?'

Polly's head drooped in mock shame.

'All right, point taken. There's no need to be sarcastic . . . Oh, Grace, Grace, sit up – quickly.' A note of excited urgency had crept into Polly's voice.

Startled and a little annoyed at being disturbed once again, Grace raised herself up on to one elbow, the other hand shading her eyes.

'What?'

For an answer, Polly flicked her eyes over Grace's shoulder, murmuring nervously, 'There's a couple of soldiers heading our way. What shall we do, Grace?'

Swinging her long legs round and up under her buttocks, Grace sat back on her heels and said scathingly, 'Well, unless they try and abduct us at gunpoint, I'm staying right where I am.' Squinting against the sun's glare, Grace saw the approaching soldiers, and with a mischievous glance at her sister murmured, 'I don't fancy your one, Poll!'

Blushing painfully, Polly stared down at the grass with studied concentration as the uniformed men drew nearer. And when they both dropped down in front of them saying cheerfully, 'Wotch'yer, girls. Fancy some company?' Polly reached for her hat and began playing with the wide brim.

Grace eyed the soldiers warily then laughed.

'Not really, but I suppose we can't stop you from sitting here. It is a public park, after all.'

The men exchanged hopeful glances. It looked as though they had just struck lucky.

Grinning broadly, the two men sprawled down on the grass and appraised the young women openly. They were both in their mid-twenties, their army uniforms giving them more confidence than either of them had ever possessed in civvy street.

But before they could launch into their newly acquired patter for chatting up the girls, the tranquillity of the afternoon was broken by the all-too-familiar sound of the air-raid siren, its tummy-tightening wail filling the air. There had been many such alerts, especially during the past few months as the RAF had battled the *Luftwaffe* in the skies above London, but despite the fighting in the air, no bombs had fallen in the East End.

'Oh, bother!' Grace, not unduly concerned, looked to her sister, careful to keep her voice steady. Poor Polly always got herself into a panic when the sirens went off. Yet as Grace got to her feet she saw with some surprise that Polly was valiantly trying to hide her anxiety, afraid of looking a fool in front of the two grinning soldiers.

'Don't worry, girls. We'll look after yer, won't we, Lou?'

Grace was now on her feet, smoothing the front of her dress, while keeping a watchful eye on her sister, who was now busying herself putting on her straw hat and the shoes she had kicked off earlier.

'Are you ready, Poll?' Grace asked nonchalantly, her words instantly stirring the two young soldiers, who saw with dismay their prospective companions for the much-prized Saturday-night leave slipping away.

''Ere, hang on, girls. No need ter rush off, there's nothing ter be frightened about. Look! No one else's taking a blind bit of notice.'

And it was true. Apart from a few picnickers who had also risen to their feet, most of the people lazing in the sun seemed to be in no hurry to move. There had been so many false alarms of late, and those that were genuine had resulted in only a few short bursts of fire, that few people bothered to take cover as the authorities insisted.

'Sorry, boys, no offence, but we're meeting someone,

aren't we, Poll?' Grace looked directly at Polly, who looked back blankly, her mind still clearly occupied by the siren.

But then the ack-ack guns started up further off in the park and people began to sit up and take notice.

Stirring uneasily, Grace said sharply, 'Come on, Poll, let's get—'

Her words were cut violently short as the sky overhead darkened as if night had suddenly fallen, then came the deadly drone of aircraft. But this was no lone *Luftwaffe* pilot out to do as much damage as possible before heading back across the Channel before running out of fuel.

Suddenly, there they were. Silhouetted starkly against the warm, blue September sky, the German aeroplanes, their drone becoming a terrifying roar, flew menacingly overhead, the awesome sight temporarily paralysing those below.

Their faces blanched, the girls clutched at each other for support, both looking around wildly, undecided what to do next.

All about them, men, women and children were looking dazed, stunned by the enormity of what was happening.

Then the bombs started to fall!

'Oh shit!' Grace, her eyes wide with fear and disbelief, looked over the road to where fire and smoke were pouring. The sunny day had turned into a nightmare from hell. Chaos erupted as women frantically rounded up their terrified children, while from all sides of the park they could hear the increasingly urgent whistles and shouts of the ARP wardens and the ever-closer noise of bombs falling.

The soldiers, finding themselves the only authority available other than the wardens – who already had their hands full – whirled quickly into action, their fear quickly squashed by their military training.

'Head fer the shelters, girls. Go on, leg it.' Then they raced off across the park in an attempt to maintain some kind of order among the panicking public.

Clutching at Polly's arm, Grace shouted, 'Quick, Poll, we'll have to get to the nearest shelter. We haven't time to get home . . . Poll. POLL! POLLY, move, for Christ's sake . . . MOVE!'

But Polly was transfixed, her white face stricken, her eyes wide and unmoving. Driven by fear, Grace raised her hand and delivered a hard slap to her sister's face. Polly fell back, then, her eyes stretching, she began to scream hysterically.

Grabbing her sister's hand, Grace yelled, 'Come on, Poll, run . . . run . . . !'

Polly needed no second prompting. Their long, healthy legs flying, the two girls tore across the grass, stopping only to help up those who had fallen.

Following the crowd of fleeing people, Grace and Polly raced across to the nearby shelter, where grim-faced air-raid wardens were desperately trying to maintain some kind of discipline among the terrified mob. The elderly men, who for some had been a figure of ridicule during the past year, now came into their own. With great calm and dignity they organised the crowd into the underground shelters, while managing to sustain a steady line of quips to calm the terrified children.

Scrambling for a space on the cold concrete floor, Grace and Polly sat hunched together against the rough surface of the wall, holding on to each other for dear life in the cramped space available. And still people were pouring in, until it seemed as if the very walls would be rent apart. Mercifully the stampede ceased, and with a crisp 'Get yer 'eads down!' the air-raid warden closed the shelter door.

Outside, the engines of the bombers could be heard terrifyingly close-by, as the air outside was literally torn asunder by their deadly cargo, which whistled and crashed to the ground in a deafening rushing noise.

Inside the shelter children were crying and screaming in terror as their mothers tried valiantly to comfort them. With each exploding bomb, everyone crouched instinctively.

'Grace, what about Mum and Dad and the others? Grace, what are we going to do . . . ?'

The shelter rocked as a bomb landed perilously close, setting the terrified children off again.

Grabbing Polly, Grace shouted, 'There's nothing we can do. They're probably in another shelter somewhere, just like us . . .'

A small hand touched Grace's. Startled, Grace peered through the dimly lit space and saw the tear-stained dirty face of the child she had seen earlier in the park.

'Ooh, come here, poppet. Come and sit with us. There, there, you're all right now, I've got you,' Grace crooned softly as the small body nestled against her own. Stroking his head, she mouthed to Polly, 'He must have gotten separated from his mum, poor little mite.' Another loud crash reverberated outside and the plump little body seemed to burrow further into Grace, desperately trying to escape the nightmare. Voices called out in the dimly lit shelter, some prayed while others remained frighteningly silent, as if fearful of drawing the attention of the overhead bombers.

Packed to capacity with terrified people, the noise, both inside and out, was overwhelming.

Then, in a brief lull in the bombing, one wag shouted, 'Fer Gawd's sake, don't nobody fart.'

Despite herself, Grace found herself laughing. Then the shelter shook once more, and, bowing her head, she hugged the child fiercely to her breast with one arm, and held her youngest sister tight with the other.

Beside her, Polly whimpered, 'What about Mum and

Dad and Vi and Nan, Gracie . . . I'm scared, Gracie, I'm so scared . . .'

And Grace, her eyes tightly closed in silent prayer, could offer no more comfort.

CHAPTER EIGHT

'Come on, Vi, be a sport. I'll be off tomorrow, fighting fer King and Country, an' all that old cobblers, so this might be me last chance fer . . . you know what . . .'

Scrunched up in the corner of a battered settee, Violet Donnelly pushed off the roving hands of her soldier companion and hastily rearranged her dress, saying coolly, 'Leave off, Brian, you're not getting me with that old chestnut. And if that's all you're after, then there's plenty of girls willing to do their bit for the war effort, but I'm not one of them.'

Violet reached for her handbag, from which she produced an enamel compact. Flicking it open she scrutinised her features in the tiny vanity mirror, patting and stroking the blond tresses that reached halfway down her back. Satisfied she looked her best, she snapped shut the compact and, turning to the man she had spent the afternoon with, said loftily, 'Well, I'd better be off. My parents like us all to be home for tea. We're a very close family. And besides, I want to get changed for the dance tonight.' Spreading her lips into a wide smile she giggled. 'It's a shame you've got to get back to your base, otherwise you could have taken me to the dance. Still, I'm sure I'll find someone to see me home safely afterwards.'

Brian looked at Vi coldly then lit a cigarette, blowing the smoke deliberately in the pretty face. He had spent his entire month's pay in two days on this woman, and now she was chucking him aside like an oily rag. Tonight she would find another mug to take his place – women like her always did. All at once he felt sorry for the next man who crossed Vi's path. Well, whoever the poor sod was, he was welcome to the teasing little bitch!

Sensing her charms were no longer appreciated, Vi shrugged and rose languidly to her feet. She strolled casually over to the far side of the room, her hips wriggling as she walked, and gazed unseeingly out of the window. Despite her outward appearance, Vi was trembling inside, furious at the attitude her latest conquest was adopting. Bloody men! she thought viciously. They're all the same, expecting you to fall all over them the minute they spent any money on you, and then turning nasty when you wouldn't jump into bed with them.

Biting her bottom lip, Vi continued to stare out of the open window. The flat was on the top floor of the five-storey block and gave a clear view over Hackney Downs. What would Brian say now, she thought, if she was to tell him she was a virgin? Laugh probably. Her vision misted suddenly. It wasn't fair. Just because she liked to have a laugh and flirt a bit, everyone thought she was a tramp. Even her own nan thought so. Oh, the old girl hadn't actually said so, but it was what she thought. Well, sod them. Sod all of them! She didn't care. But the truth was – she did, and it hurt. It hurt terribly, yet she couldn't change the way she was made. And anyway, why should she?

Lifting her chin defiantly, Vi was about to collect her handbag and leave when she heard the first sounds of aircraft approaching. For a brief moment she imagined it to be some of theirs and was reminded of the dogfights so recently witnessed in the skies. Oh, those days had been marvellous. She had climbed to the roofs of many blocks of flats like this to cheer on the Spitfire and Hurricane pilots as they battled the German *Luftwaffe*, shouting herself hoarse at the thrilling sight. She smiled at the memory. Then her smile froze, changing immediately to a look of horror as the ominous dark formation of German bombers appeared overhead.

At first, too shocked to move, she stood rooted to the spot. Then, whirling round, she screamed wildly, 'They're here, they're here!'

Racing across the room Violet grabbed her handbag from the coffee table and headed for the door, heedless of the soldier in whose company she had spent the past two days, and who was now looking at her as if she'd gone mad. Then he too heard the steady drone of aeroplanes and with only a brief look out of the window he hurled himself after the fleeing figure.

All through the flats, doors were opening and banging shut, neighbours calling out anxiously to each other, asking after loved ones who weren't at home, hoping one of the neighbours might know of their whereabouts. But in essence it was every man for himself. Pushing people out of her way in her haste to get to the shelters in the courtyard, Violet didn't stop to run down the stairs, instead she vaulted each flight in a single bound, her legs reverberating with each impact, until she reached the ground floor.

Clambering over the stacked sandbags at the flats' entrance, Vi stumbled and fell, grazing her knees. Instantly she was pulled roughly to her feet and given a hard shove in the small of her back.

'Quick, Vi, get yerself in the shelter.' Brian was at her side yelling into her shocked, frightened face. 'Hurry up, yer silly cow, run fer it. I'm gonna go back an' make sure everyone's out.'

Violet, her face stretched in disbelief, clawed wildly at his arm screaming, 'Don't be such a bloody fool, Brian. It's every man for himself . . . Brian! Brian, come back, you'll be killed—'

But the khaki-clad figure took no notice, and Violet wasn't going to wait around for his return.

Violet raced off behind the fleeing crowd, reaching the shelter just as the first bombs began their deadly mission. She was the last one into the shelter, but before the warden closed the heavy corrugated door, she looked on in horror as a hail of stick-like missiles dropped directly on to the block of flats she had just left – and Brian had just ran back into. Then the whole building collapsed like a pack of cards, spewing out great clouds of smoke and rubble.

Screaming hysterically, Vi called out, 'Brian, Brian . . . Oh, my God, Brian!'

The heavy hand of the warden pushed her inside the shelter and banged the door shut, saying tersely, 'It's no good, love. He's copped it. Now, be a good girl and sit down quietly, we might be 'ere for a long time.'

Numbed with shock, Violet, for the first time in many years, did as she was told without a murmur.

The cinema was packed with customers eager for some light-hearted entertainment to cheer them up after a hard week's work. What with rationing and daily warmongering in the papers, the British people were in dire need of a pick-me-up. And what better way to forget all your troubles than the cinema, where for half a crown you could get a few hours of escapism.

Seated in the front row of the two and six stalls, Hetty settled herself more comfortably in the plush seat.

'Have you got the chocolates, Sam? I'm that hungry I could eat the whole box.'

Beside her, Sam grinned. 'Well, it wouldn't be the first

time, would it? You'd better watch out, or you'll end up as fat as your mum.'

In the midst of taking off her hat, Hetty spun round, her eyes twinkling.

'Are you saying I'm getting fat, Sam Donnelly, because if you are then—'

Behind them a man cut in waspishly, 'D'yer mind, missus. I've come ter see the film, not listen ter you nattering.'

Looking over her shoulder Hetty replied tartly, 'Well, sorry, I'm sure.' And with a sharp dig in Sam's ribs, she placed the opened box of chocolates in her lap, and settled back to enjoy the film.

When the sirens sounded halfway through the main film, the film-goers let out a communal groan of irritation. Some began heading for the exit, while others, determined not to miss their weekend treat, remained in their seats.

'We'd better go, love, just in case.' Sam, already on his feet, was still watching the big screen.

With a sigh of impatience Hetty said, 'It's probably just another false alarm. Let's stay and see the end of the film, Sam.'

When her husband raised his eyebrows in mild disapproval Hetty groaned.

'I know what will happen. We'll just get outside and the all-clear will go, then we'll have to pay to get back in again.'

Gently taking hold of his wife's arm, Sam said gently, 'Not if we keep our tickets. Now come on, you know—'

Sam's words were cut off as a gigantic thud exploded somewhere nearby, but it was when the entire screen fell out on to the first row that pandemonium broke out.

Her face white, Hetty quickly got to her feet.

'Don't say I told you so, Sam Donnelly, or I'll bash you one . . . Oh, Sam . . . the girls. Sam, our girls!'

A sudden deafening roar drowned out her words as

the cinema took a direct hit, obliterating everything. And everyone in it.

Aggie sat on a lumpy mattress in the basement, her face streaked with tears, her thick fingers pulling and wrenching at each other in her agitation. With her were some of her neighbours and their children, the noise of the latter nearly drowning out the crumping sound of the falling bombs nearby.

Sam had turned the basement into a shelter at the outbreak of war. He had deemed the basement, built well below ground level, to be safer than the customary Anderson shelters, and had extended the use of it to his neighbours if the need ever arose.

Well, the need had arisen, and at the first sighting of the enemy aircraft, Jeannie Butcher and Rene Castle, together with their combined seven children, had hammered on Aggie's door pleading to be allowed in. Reg Watson, now an ARP warden, had seen them all safely settled in the basement before dashing off to attend to his duties.

Leaving their children, who seemed to be thoroughly enjoying the excitement, except for Rene's eldest daughter, Linda, who looked scared to death, Rene and Jeannie came and sat either side of the trembling, distraught Aggie.

'Come on, Aggie, old girl,' Rene cajoled earnestly. 'They'll be all right, won't they, Jeannie?' She looked to her friend for support.

'Course they will,' Jeannie responded heartily. 'Probably all tucked up in a shelter somewhere, worrying about you, ain't that right, Rene?'

The onus of conversation back on her shoulders, Rene shrugged, not knowing what else she could say. Flicking her eyes over her children, her glance rested on Linda, a surge of relief sweeping her body. If her sixteen-year-old daughter hadn't come home an hour after her nine-o'clock curfew last night, then Rene wouldn't have forbidden her to leave the house for two days, and she would now be out there in the thick if it somewhere. And judging by the frightened face of her Linda, she too had come to the same conclusion.

The smaller children were running around the basement, screaming and shouting as they played at being soldiers, pretending to be shot, then jumping up again, and Rene, grateful of the diversion, let out a bellow of rage, 'Keep the bleeding noise down, yer little buggers, or I'll land yer all a good clout round the head.'

'That goes for you lot an' all,' Jeannie warned her three boys.

Aggie, sandwiched between the two women, continued to tremble, her mind forming the same words over and over again: *Please God, let my family be all right . . . Please God! Let them be safe somewhere.*

CHAPTER NINE

When the all-clear siren sounded – after what seemed to be an eternity – Grace and Polly emerged, dirty and dishevelled, from the shelter. After the darkness of the jam-packed subterranean shelter, their eyes squinted against the glare of the early-evening sun. Their legs were cramped from crouching in a sitting position for such a long period, and many of their companions stumbled, as they too scrambled from the leaden tomb. The young boy was still holding tight to Grace's neck, as if his very life depended on it, his plump face streaked with dirt-channelled tears.

Grace looked around warily, half expecting to confront a scene of total annihilation, and was relieved to see only a few smouldering craters amidst the parkland and an equally small number of fires scattered, seemingly haphazardly, above the chimneys of the rows of terraced houses on the opposite side of the park.

'Blooming hell! I expected the whole park to be gone, the amount of noise that was going on . . . Are you all right, Poll?'

Polly, her eyes wide, her face startling white against the grime that layered her freckled skin, remained silent. Only her fingers seemed to have any life, as they fiercely gripped the arm that held the child so protectively.

Grace winced as Polly's nails dug into her exposed flesh, but no sound escaped her lips. Instead she hoisted the child on to her hip, making soothing noises to placate the bewildered young boy, while every instinct in the body urged her to run towards home. The desire to be with the rest of her family was tearing at every fibre of her being, but outwardly she remained calm, knowing that if she were to show the slightest sign of fear, her sister, as well as the child, would collapse into hysteria. It was only her stoic demeanour that was holding them together.

All around people were making their way home, or looking for friends and family from whom they had been separated during the frightening and unexpected attack from the skies. It still seemed unreal, like a bad dream, one from which you could urge yourself to awake. But this was no dream, and Grace was terrified – not for herself now, but for what she might find when she and Polly arrived home.

Suddenly the small body jerked in Grace's arms, one grubby finger pointing to a spot nearby, his face lit up with excited relief as he sobbed, 'Shoe, Mummy's shoe. C'mon, lady, let's go and get my mummy's shoe. She'll be looking for it.'

Grace's eyes followed the pointed finger, her body slumping with relief at the thought of relinquishing her burden. Then her heart skipped a beat. There, lying on its side only a few yards away on the gravel path, among the newly formed debris thrown up from the park, lay a solitary red shoe.

And it was this pathetic object that finally brought home the true tragedy of the day.

Turning away swiftly, Grace looked around for some form of authority, needing desperately for someone to tell her what to do with the child. Two ARP wardens were busy dispersing the crowd with good-humoured banter, despite their own desperate need to return to their own homes and families.

'C'mon, you lot. Ain't yer got no homes ter go to?'

Someone in the crowd called back, 'I bleeding well hope so, mate. It was there when I left it a couple of hours ago.'

The warden grinned tiredly. 'Just get yerselves off ter yer own shelters in case the buggers come back. Come along, people. Look lively.'

The man's words had a startling effect on the silent Polly. Her eyes nearly popping out of her head, she dug her nails deeper into Grace's arm, crying hysterically. 'Did you hear that, Grace? He said they might come back. We'll be killed . . . We'll all be killed!'

Feeling like screaming herself, but unable to indulge in the luxury of relieving her pent-up emotions, Grace thrust her sister away impatiently, her fear bringing a harsh, jarring note into her voice.

'Pull yourself together, Polly, for heaven's sake! The poor little sod's frightened enough without you screeching in his ear.'

Polly reared back, her face stricken, her head drooping in shame, while her feet shuffled anxiously on the rubble-strewn ground.

Shifting the weight of the child once more, Grace turned his face into her shoulder, at the same time jerking her head at Polly.

'Look! Over there, Poll. It's his mum's shoe. Well . . . I assume it must be. Shoes like that aren't exactly common, are they?' She had dropped her voice to a whisper. 'Goodness knows where the poor woman's got to. She wasn't in the shelter – at least, not the one we were in . . . Oh, there, there! Don't cry, sweetheart, don't cry. It'll be all right . . .'

Still stung by Grace's harsh words, Polly had momentarily put aside her own fear, and when her gaze travelled over the ground and came to rest on the discarded shoe, her eyes filled with tears.

'Ooh, Grace. Oh, the poor woman. She must have—'

'Sshh, keep your voice down, he'll hear you . . . Oh, for goodness' sake, there must be someone around who can help. Oh! Excuse me. Could you help us, please?'

Grace had grabbed at a passing warden. Quickly explaining the presence of the child and the ominous significance of the shoe, Grace waited hopefully for the uniformed man to advise her while the child continued to thrash around in her grasp, calling out piteously, 'Mummy! Mummy's shoe, Mummy's shoe. Me go and get Mummy's shoe and find my mummy.'

''Ere, give him ter me, love. I'll take him ter the church hall over the road. The Red Cross 'ave set up a temporary infirmary there. Maybe his mum'll be there. An' if she ain't . . . Well, I'm sure they'll take care of him, poor little sod.'

Now that she was about to be relieved of her burden, Grace found herself torn between her urgency to get home and being loath to relinquish the small body that clung so trustingly to her neck. Then the situation was taken out of her hands. With great tenderness, the elderly warden took the child with practised ease, his kindly weathered face bent close to the quivering tear-streaked face of the young boy.

'C'mon, me brave little soldier. You come with old Charlie, an' we'll see if we can find yer mum, eh?'

At the mention of his mother, the little boy's grimy face lit up in delight. Quickly transferring his allegiance to the kindly stranger, he looked at Grace, crying gleefully, 'Bye, bye, lady. I'm gonna find me mum.' Then, shyly, he leant forward and placed a wet, sticky kiss on Grace's cheek.

The touching gesture was almost the undoing of Grace, but she gamely swallowed hard, gave the boy a final hug, then waved him goodbye. Then the warden was gone, carrying the child in the direction of the nearby church.

'Come on, Grace. I want to get home and make sure everyone's all right.' Polly was tugging at Grace's arm, and this time Grace needed no more urging.

The short journey home was like travelling through a foreign country. Familiar streets, streets they had passed through only a few hours earlier, now appeared alien. Windows had been blown out of houses and flats, the pavements and roads littered with shattered glass, bearing testament to the disaster that had befallen the tough East Enders. Isolated pockets of smoke hung in the air, but, as far as Grace could tell, there were no major fires to be seen. The streets were teeming with people examining the damage to their homes, all stunned and angry, but nowhere was there any sign of panic. And this realisation alone brought a light quickness to Grace's step.

'Well, if this is the best Hitler can do, then we've nothing much to worry about, eh, Poll?' Grace turned to her sister as they picked their way over a small pile of rubble in the road. 'I was expecting it to be much worse than this . . . Oh, look, Poll, it's Vi . . . Here, Vi. Vi, over here!' Grace waved furiously as her sister came into view. 'Blooming hell, Vi, you look terrible. Mind you, I don't suppose we look much better.' Grace gave a shaky laugh, and was amazed that she could even smile, let alone laugh. Maybe she was gathering courage from the apparent calm of the people milling around the street.

Linking her free arm through Vi's, Grace kept up a steady stream of nervous chatter to mask the eerie silence of her sisters, who where walking either side of her in an apparent daze.

'We were over the park when it started. Lucky there were shelters nearby. Coo, it was horrible down there, like being buried alive . . . Well . . .' She emitted a self-conscious cough. 'That was an unfortunate choice of words in the circumstances, but you know what I mean. Anyway . . .'

Leaning into Violet's side, she asked shakily, 'Where were you when it started, Vi?'

Violet jerked away sharply, then shrugged.

'With a friend,' she answered dully, pushing a lock of dirty blond hair behind her ear. 'He ran back into the flats to see if he could help anyone still in there and a bomb dropped on them. He's dead of course, and that's a shame. He wasn't a bad sort of bloke. Still . . .' She lifted her shoulders listlessly. 'I don't suppose I'd have seen him after today anyway. His leave was up. I only went round to say goodbye.' A short gurgly sound came from her throat. 'And it was definitely goodbye, as it turned out. There won't be any love letters arriving from him, will there? And there was me hoping we could keep in touch.'

Shocked at Vi's story, and her seemingly heartless attitude, Grace could find no answering platitudes, nor could she summon up any false sympathy for Vi's friend, whom she had never met. And never would now by the sound of it. Oh, Lord! What was she thinking? Violet had witnessed the death of a friend in the most horrible circumstances imaginable. It didn't seem possible, yet Vi had spoken of it as if describing an accident involving a pet dog. Grace stared into her sister's face, still beautiful in spite of the grime and dirt from the polluted air, and thought quickly, *She's in shock. We're all in shock. How could we be otherwise on such a day as this. Oh! Let's get home. Let's get back to normality.*

They entered the street by the corner-shop end, and had hardly stepped foot in the road when a shrill scream of delight split the air. Aggie was storming towards them, her fat face wreathed in undisguised relief. Hurrying behind her came the neighbours, their expressions bearing testimony to the welcome sight they made.

'There yer are, Aggie. What did I tell yer?' Rene Castle yelled triumphantly. 'I said they'd be all right, didn't I . . . Well, didn't I?'

Aggie made no answer. She was too busy gathering her granddaughters to her heaving bosom.

'Oh, me angels, me angels. I've been half outta me mind with worry. Where've yer been? Oh, what does that matter, you're here now, that's the main thing . . . Here! Where you sliding off to, madam?'

When Aggie had descended on them, Violet had instinctively moved to one side, thinking her grandmother would be concerned only with Grace's and Polly's welfare. It had been a long time since Vi had been held in her nan's arms, and even in such an emotional moment as this, she felt unsure of her welcome. But if her body was refusing Aggie's comforting arms, her mind had different ideas. Vi felt hot tears spring to her eyes and dashed them away self-consciously, but not before Aggie had spotted them. Aggie recognised the struggle raging within Violet, and her throat swelled with raw emotion; for what she was witnessing was a reflection of her own blasted stubbornness and pride. Gently freeing Grace and Polly from her embrace, Aggie looked hard into the tear-filled, defiant face and cried loudly, 'C'mere, yer silly cow!'

At the strident voice Vi deflated like a balloon, and when she found herself enveloped in the familiar fleshy, sweaty arms of her grandmother, she broke down completely.

'Oh, Nan, it was horrible, horrible. I was so . . . so scared.'

'There, there. Now come on. We was all scared, love. Nothing to be ashamed of in admitting that. I nearly shit a brick meself when I saw all them planes flying overhead, an' when the bombs started ter drop, I nearly dropped one meself . . . Still! We're all safe now, that's the main thing. And as soon as yer mum and dad get home, we'll have a real celebration.'

All the girls' heads came up in unison.

'Wh – what do you mean, Nan?' Grace was the first to

find her voice. 'I thought they were indoors.' Yet even as she spoke, Grace knew that if her parents had been home, they would have been the first ones flying down the street to meet them. Her stomach listed sharply. 'Where are they, Nan? Have they been home yet?'

Ushering her granddaughters ahead of her like a mother hen, Aggie made reassuring noises.

'Now don't start me off again, for Gawd's sake. They'll be home soon. We'd've heard if anything had happened to them. They're well known around these parts. They're most likely helping out somewhere, 'cos you know yer mum and dad. They wouldn't be able to walk by if someone needed help. An' there's likely many a poor bugger needing a helping hand today. Now c'mon an' let's get indoors. We'll probably meet them on the way, you'll see. They'll be coming round the corner any minute now, with yer dad yelling his head off for a cuppa and as mad as hell into the bargain. You wait an' see . . .'

An hour later there was still no sign of Sam or Hetty, and the tension was becoming unbearable for those waiting for them to return.

Pacing up and down the spacious kitchen Grace pleaded for the umpteenth time, 'Look, Nan, let me go and look for them. I won't go far, I promise. Just to the top of Well Street and back. It won't take me ten minutes and—'

'NO!' Aggie shouted, the fear inside her growing by the second. If she hadn't the girls to think of she'd be out there herself looking for her daughter and son-in-law. But she did have the girls to consider, and not for anything was she going to let them out of her sight again today.

A sudden loud knocking at the front door brought them all to their feet in a huddle in the middle of the room.

'I'll get it,' Grace shouted as she ran down the passage-way.

Reg Watson, dressed in his ARP uniform stood on the doorstep, his lined face etched with tiredness.

'Hello, Gracie, love. Can I come in a minute?'

Standing to one side Grace gabbled, 'Yes . . . Yes, of course you can, Mr Watson.'

'Who is it? Oh, it's you, Reg. Come in, come in.' Aggie ushered the man into the hall, but not before casting a quick look over his shoulder into the street, praying for some sign of Hetty and Sam. Her spirits fell as the familiar loved ones failed to materialise.

Leading the way back to the kitchen, Aggie placed a steaming mug of tea in front of the weary man.

'Here, get that down yer, Reg. It's as weak as piss water, an' there's no sugar, but it's better than nothing.'

Reg Watson gratefully took a gulp of the hot liquid.

'Thanks, Aggie, ta, I needed that.'

'Would yer like a drop of something in it, Reg?' Aggie asked solicitously.

Reg shook his head regretfully.

'No, thanks, Aggie, I'm still on duty. As a matter of fact, that's the reason I'm 'ere.' He took another long slurp of his tea. 'I've just come ter make sure you've registered your cellar as a shelter. I did tell Sam he had ter register it last year, but I don't know if he did or not. D'yer know anything about it, Aggie?' He shot a questioning look at the elderly woman.

With more important things on her mind, Aggie bristled impatiently, wondering why the man was bothering her with such a trivial thing.

'I don't bleeding know, Reg. You'll 'ave ter speak ter Sam when he gets in. Anyway, what's so bleeding important about registering our cellar?' A thought suddenly struck her. Aggressive now, she glared at the warden. ''Ere, you lot ain't gonna make us share wiv the whole bleeding street, are yer? I don't mind a few of the neighbours in an emergency, but I ain't opening it up as a public shelter.'

Reg uttered a dry laugh. 'Nah, nothing like that, Aggie. It's just that the authorities like ter know about basements and cellars in case of a direct hit . . . Oh, Gawd! I'm sorry, Aggie . . .' Reg's head jerked back nervously as Polly let out a wail. 'I didn't mean ter put the frightners on yer, love.' He addressed the tearful Polly, who seemed ready to drop to the floor in fright.

Clicking her tongue Aggie turned to Vi, saying, 'Take Poll into the other room, Vi, will yer? Get her ter lie down on the sofa for a while, she's had a shock.'

Violet had changed into her siren suit, as had her sisters, in case of another raid, unlike her nan who was still wearing the dirty floral dress she'd had on all day. More composed now, and feeling flushed with a camaraderie towards her younger sister, Vi said kindly, 'All right, Nan. Come on, Poll. Let's get you lying down. You'll feel better after a sleep.'

Still in a daze, Polly let herself be led from the room.

The door had hardly closed behind the two young women before Reg said quietly, 'I think it'd be better if yer all got yourselves down the basement, Aggie. And you'd better take enough food and drink ter see yer through the night, an' all.'

Aggie spun round to face him, her expression grim as she demanded roughly, 'Yer think they'll come back tonight?'

Placing his now-empty mug on the table, Reg nodded.

'I'd lay money on it, Aggie. The docks 'ave taken the worst of it so far. Words coming through the whole of docklands is burning. And not only the docks, but the houses down there an' all, which means that the blackout'll be no bloody good tonight. The whole city will be lit up once it gets dark, an' Hitler's not gonna miss a chance like that, is he?' Pushing himself back from the table, Reg asked. 'By the way, where is Sam? I thought he'd be here with you.'

Aggie and Grace exchanged a look of concern, but it was Grace who answered.

'That's the problem, Mr Watson. We don't know where they are, and we're worried sick. They—'

The wail of the siren cut into her words.

'Oh, no, not again!' Grace cried.

Reg moved hurriedly towards the door, slamming on his steel hat.

'Get yourselves down the basement, the lot of you, and I'll see what I can find out about yer mum and dad.'

Grace had followed Reg to the front door, and as he turned the handle, he paused, 'By the way, d'yer know where they were going when they left here?'

Grace answered quickly. 'Yes. They were going to the pictures. I'm not sure which one. I think it was the Plaza . . . Wh – what? What's the matter, Mr Watson? Why are you looking at me like that?'

The warden had already averted his red-rimmed eyes but not before Grace had glimpsed the look of horror in them. Grace felt something jump within her, like a live being. It travelled from her stomach to her chest and into her throat, and for a few seconds she stopped breathing.

Watching the dawning horror flooding Grace's face, Reg felt his legs go weak. He had just come from the Plaza. The whole place was gutted, with no sign of any survivors; but the firemen were still trying to get through. But not now. Not with another raid starting. Oh, dear God Almighty! Not Sam and Hetty. Because if they'd been in the cinema when the bomb dropped then they must be dead. No one could have survived that blast. Not from the devastation he'd witnessed at the Plaza.

Grace was clutching his arm in desperation.

'What is it, Mr Watson? You know something, I can tell by your face. Tell me, Mr Watson, please . . . Tell me . . .'

The stricken warden could only stare wordlessly into the

terrified blue eyes of the young woman standing before him. Never in his life had he felt so inadequate, so useless. Nearby he could hear the crumping noises as the bombs began to fall nearby and, gently, he disengaged himself from Grace's frantic grasp.

Shaking his head he muttered helplessly, 'I'm sorry, Gracie, I'm sorry. You'd better get them all down below before it gets too bad. Go on, love. See to your sisters and your nan. They're gonna need yer now. Bye, love . . .'

Grace stood frozen in the doorway. It was a nightmare. That's what it was, a nightmare. This couldn't be happening; it just couldn't.

The sound of the falling bombs was growing closer, and as Aggie, Polly and Vi ran out into the hall, Grace took control, grateful for something to do to distract her from the unspeakable thoughts that were torturing her mind.

'Come on, you lot, don't hang around. Get down the stairs. I'll grab some food and a bottle of milk, in case . . .'

Ignoring the cries of panic, Grace marshalled them all down the basement steps, avoiding eye contact with anyone. Only Aggie, her pale eyes suddenly painfully aware, continued to stare at Grace, but Grace skilfully avoided her grandmother's silent, pleading look.

There was nothing definite after all. Her mum and dad might have left the cinema early. They might even have changed their minds about going. They did that sometimes.

The second air raid was now in earnest, although down here in the basement the noise was muted. Settling herself comfortably on the mattress beside Polly and Vi, Grace hugged her knees. Without being aware of it, she began to hum a well-known popular tune.

Only once did she raise her head. And when she caught Aggie's knowing, anguished stare, Grace stopped humming, dropped her head to her knees and forced her mind to go blank.

CHAPTER TEN

There was no time to grieve, not with Goering's *Luftwaffe* bombing London day and night without respite. During the infrequent lulls, the people of the East End managed to bury their dead, but not so the Donnelly family. In their tragic case, there were no bodies to lay to rest, no special place where the bereaved family could visit their dead loved ones to gain comfort and solace.

The cinema where Hetty and Sam had perished had simply been left, the emergency resources already stretched to the limit in a bid to combat the inferno that was sweeping through the East End and beyond. Though, as Reg Watson confided to Rene and Bert Castle in a rare moment of quietness, it was probably for the best, because from his experience, and remember, he had told them, he'd already been through one war so he knew what he was talking about, those people in the cinema had more than likely been blown to bits on impact. And if there was one thing worse than removing bodies from bombed buildings, it was trying to piece bits and bobs of them back together for a decent funeral. No! It was much better this way, even though it made it hard for the Donnelly family to accept their loved ones were really gone, which was what funerals were really for, weren't they? To say your goodbyes properly and give yourself time to mourn. Still, there was nothing anyone could do to change things now, and after all, the girls still had their gran, and she them. And if anything else was needed, they had their neighbours to turn to.

'You sure, Gracie, love? Only I've gotta queue up for me own rations, I might as well get yours while I'm there, save both of us standing around for hours.'

Rene Castle was sitting at the kitchen table, her usually chirpy face solemn as she regarded the young, pale-faced woman standing by the sink. Like the rest of the street she still couldn't believe Sam and Hetty were gone. If the tragedy had happened before the war then no one would have felt it as hard. But they'd all grown close since the start, and Rene, like many others, wished they'd made the effort to be more friendly in the past. Then again, if the war hadn't started, Sam and Hetty would still be alive, and she herself wouldn't be sitting here now preparing to go off and stand in line for hours for a measly piece of liver, or a couple of chops if she was lucky. That was if there wasn't another blasted raid before she'd had the chance to get her meagre provisions.

Raising her head she glanced anxiously at the slim figure and sighed heavily. Poor Grace. It looked like the responsibility for looking after the family had fallen on her young shoulders for the time being, and that had puzzled everyone, for old Aggie had always appeared so strong, so resilient. Now she was a mere shadow of her former self. She'd hardly been seen out of doors since that terrible day, preferring to stay in her room with the curtains closed, even during a raid. Whereas young Polly wouldn't move from the basement, terrified to set foot outside in case the bombers appeared. And as for that flighty piece Vi! Rene tutted in disgust. Talk about gadding about with her parents hardly cold. Out every night she was, all tarted up to the nines and heading up West, and staying up there an' all. Mind you, a lot of people had taken to staying up the West End during the night raids. It was a lot safer than round the East End at the moment. But still! Vi should be giving her sister some support instead of letting Grace take all the burden. It wasn't right! But there you were, life was rarely fair, and she had her own troubles to keep her occupied.

As if reading her mind, Grace asked quietly, 'Have you thought any more about sending the children away, Rene? It must be terrifying for them having to put up with all that's going on.'

Rene gave a loud exclamation of derision.

'Huh! They're having a whale of a time, the lot of 'em. Every morning they're outta the shelter and straight on to the bomb sites, little gits.' Gathering up her shopping basket, she added laughingly, 'You should've seen what my Billy brought home yesterday. A bit of shrapnel as big as a bleeding bomb. I nearly had a heart attack when he threw it on the table. Proud as punch he was an' all. It's the biggest bit found so far, so he tells me an' his dad. So of course he's cock of the walk now among his mates. Anyway, I wouldn't 'ave the heart to send 'em away again. They hated it the first time, cried the whole while they was there, poor little sods, though I'm the one who has nightmares about anything happening to them. But as Tom says, if a bomb's got your name on it—' Rene broke off, appalled at her lack of tact, but Grace smiled sadly.

'It's all right, Rene. You don't have to watch every word you say.' Busying herself at the sink, Grace added, 'Actually, Rene, you could get my shopping, if you don't mind. I don't like leaving Nan and Polly if I can help it. It's bad enough during the week while I'm at work, but I like to stay with them at weekends if I can.'

Grateful to be of help, Rene answered quickly, 'Course I will, love. 'Ere, give us your ration books an' I'll see what I can pick up.'

With the ration books carefully stowed inside the large shopping bag, Rene made to take her leave. 'Oh, by the way. Any news of your young man coming home on leave, love?'

Grace shook her head. 'No . . . Well, not that I've heard. Stan did try to get some compassionate leave, but they weren't family . . . Mum and Dad, I mean. It would have been different if we were married, but as it is . . .' She spread her hands and smiled weakly. 'But Uncle Danny's coming home on sick leave. You remember I told you he'd been injured. Nothing serious, thank goodness, just a flesh wound, so he says in his letters, but he's been given a month's pass. Then he's got to report to the army doctor to see if he's fit to go back at the end of the month.'

Rene nodded. 'Well, that's something, ain't it, love? And it'll be nice fer you to have a man about the house again, even if it is only fer a little while.'

As she left the house Rene thought: Not that Danny will be much help, if she was any judge of character. Oh, he was a good man, and kind, there was no doubt of that, but what Grace and the family needed now was a strong man, someone who would take charge and give Grace a bit of breathing space. More important, someone who could take over and give the girl a chance to grieve properly. 'Cos at the moment she was propping everyone else up, an' it wasn't fair, nor natural. It couldn't go on for much longer, 'cos that poor cow she'd just left was building up a store of trouble for herself. She might carry on as normal for days, even weeks, but she couldn't keep it up for ever. There was a dam building inside of her, and sooner or later it would break. Quickening her step, Rene nodded to herself. And the sooner the better, as she saw it. Else young Grace was heading for a nervous breakdown. And what would the rest of them do then, if their life-raft was suddenly swept out from under their feet! Shaking her head sorrowfully, Rene set off for the shops and the battle of the queues.

Grace waited until the front door banged, then slowly carried on with the washing in the sink. What she really wanted to do was to slide to the floor, curl up into a tight ball, and howl and scream and cry, and in so doing let the anguish and pain that had been building ever since that awful day roar and gush from her tortured mind. Maybe that would give her some blessed relief from the dreadful loss she had sustained. But she wasn't allowed! Oh, no! Good old Grace would hold the fort, see to everyone's needs, give them all the time in the world to grieve in peace, while she got on with the rigours of everyday life . . . It wasn't fair. It wasn't bloody well fair. Why should she be denied the luxury of grieving? Why? She felt her throat contract and tears beginning to prick behind her eyelids, but as usual she pushed down her feelings. Almost savagely, she flung a saucepan into the rapidly cooling water and began to scrub the enamel pot until her fingers bled.

'Who was that?' Aggie had come downstairs, shuffling into the kitchen and slumping on to the nearest chair.

Without turning round, Grace answered gruffly, 'Only Rene. She kindly popped in to see if I needed any help, and, unlike I normally do, I didn't refuse. She's getting the shopping for me, so at least that's one worry off my mind, and, as they say, every little helps.'

Aggie looked at the slim back of her eldest granddaughter and, noting the harshness in the normally soft voice, felt a moment's panic. *Gawd help us. Don't let Grace crack now, please. Just let her hang on for just a few more weeks, and then I'll be able to take over the reins. But not right now. I wouldn't be able to cope, not yet.* She needed more time. *And what about*

Gracie? Her mind threw back the sharp reprimand. *What about her, eh, or don't her feelings count?* Aggie's head drooped forward in shame as an overwhelming sense of guilt swept through her tired body and, not for the first time since the tragedy, she wished wholeheartedly she had gone with her Hetty and Sam to the pictures on that fateful day, then she would have been spared the grief and guilt that was with her every waking moment.

Gulping loudly, Aggie said, almost timidly, 'Yeah, well, she's a good sort, is Rene. In fact all the neighbours have been good. It was the same last time round. People you didn't speak to from one month to another suddenly got all chummy. I expect thing's will go back to the way they were after it's all over . . .' When the mug of tea was placed before her, Aggie gratefully wrapped her hands around the steaming brew and said softly, 'I ain't been much help ter you, have I, love . . . Oh, now, don't try an' spare me feelings,' she added quickly as Grace, her face contrite now, made to speak. 'I know what I've been like these past three weeks, an' I ain't proud of meself, but it's partly your fault.'

Grace, her face twisted in bewilderment, said hesitantly, 'My fault? How?'

Aggie reached out and gripped Grace's hand tightly.

'Yeah, that's what I said. If you hadn't been so strong, I would've had to be. It goes like that sometimes. You get a couple of people faced with bad news, or some disaster, an' if you want ter wallow in self-pity, you've gotta get in first before anyone else starts to go to pieces. 'Cos if the other people involved start to fall apart, then the strongest of the bunch will be left ter cope. It's always been that way, and always will be.' As she continued to talk, Aggie felt a new strength beginning to grow inside her. Leaning across the table she grasped Gracie's hands and said sadly, 'And that's what I meant just now. If you'd gone ter pieces when we heard about your mum and dad, then I wouldn't have had any time to dwell on it. I would've had ter take charge an' look after all of you. But you was a bit slow, an' that gave me time to crack up an' shove all the responsibility for looking after us all on ter your shoulders, Gawd forgive me!'

When there was no response from the young woman, Aggie looked up almost fearfully into Gracie's white, strained face, and realised that talk alone wouldn't help her Gracie. She had to do something positive, to let her granddaughter know she was sincere and not just rabbiting on in an effort to get out of taking some of the load from Gracie's shoulders. It was then that the resilience that had got Aggie through life slowly began to creep back.

Swallowing back the last of the now-cold tea, Aggie shifted her weight more comfortably on the chair and said more firmly than she had sounded in a long while, 'There'll be no more sleeping upstairs while the raids are on, I promise. I . . . I suppose some part of me, some cowardly part, was hoping a bomb would drop on me head an' wipe out all the pain. But it looks like God wants me to stick around fer a while, so I ain't gonna push me luck any more. Tonight I'm coming down the basement with you and Poll . . .' At the mention of her youngest granddaughter, Aggie looked around the room and sighed, 'She still down there?'

Grace nodded wearily. 'I'm afraid so, Nan. She's hardly left, apart from visiting the bathroom. I don't want to make a fuss, though, not right now. If she feels safer down there . . . Well, she's not doing any harm, though it's a pity she's lost her job. Although I can't blame her boss for sacking her. I mean, where would we be if we all buried ourselves away from reality! You've got to go on as best you can, otherwise we might as well be dead.'

Aggie's neck snapped back on her shoulders at the obvious slight, and she waited for Grace to apologise, but no apology was forthcoming. She tried to think of something to say or do, anything that would take away the hostility that had crept back into Grace's face and voice.

Just for something to do, Aggie lumbered to her feet, her heavy body shaking as she walked slowly over to the window. She peered through the net curtains, and the sight that met her temporarily blotted out her own problems.

Turning sharply she exclaimed loudly, 'You didn't tell me the houses over the back had been hit. When did that happen? Was anyone killed?'

Grace joined Aggie by the window and, her manner more amenable now, she answered, 'No, thank God! That was the first thing I asked Rene this morning. It must have happened during the raid last night . . . Well, that's stating the obvious, but the people from the three houses that were hit had to move out. Nobody knows where they've gone. The last I saw they were trundling up the road with a barrow filled up with bits and bobs they'd managed to salvage. It was pitiful to watch. Then again, it's happening every day somewhere in the East End.' Grace flicked her eyes towards her grandmother and added, 'I'm surprised you didn't hear anything. Poll and me were kept awake half the night with the racket that was going on outside. It must be nice to be able to sleep through anything—' Grace stopped suddenly. Here her nan was trying to make an effort, and all she could do was keep making sly digs at the poor woman. Beside her, Grace felt the bulky frame stiffen in anger.

Then, in the old familiar voice, Aggie said harshly, 'All right, Grace, you've made your point – loud and clear. You got stuck with the dirty end of the stick!' The proud body seeming to swell with indignation, Aggie continued, 'You can take a rest now, 'cos I'm taking over from now on.' Shuffling over to the kitchen door, Aggie pulled down her black shiny coat and said gruffly over her shoulder. 'Where was Rene heading? I might as well stretch me legs and keep her company.'

Grace remained looking out of the window, her eyes focused on the bombed-out houses opposite, knowing that if she turned to face her nan, she would crumble and apologise, and that wouldn't do either of them any good.

'I think she said she was going down Well Street. I wasn't really listening to be honest; I had other things on my mind.'

Aggie, in the process of buttoning her coat, stopped and stared at the rigid figure of her granddaughter, and could find no resemblance to the once-amenable, kindly Gracie. Once again she felt the guilt rising inside her. Blinking back the tears that threatened, Aggie turned and was about to leave the room when the sound of the front door banging shut brought her to an abrupt halt.

'Morning all.' Vi sauntered into the kitchen and dropped on to a chair. 'God, I'm whacked. I've hardly had a wink of sleep all night. Any tea going, Gracie?' She looked up at her sister hopefully.

'Only what's in the pot. It's probably stewed by now, but it's better than nothing.'

Vi looked warily from her sister to her nan, who was busily fastening the last button of her coat, then back to Grace, suddenly aware of the tension in the room. Not wanting to become embroiled in whatever was going on, she poured herself a cup of tea, took a sip, then grimaced.

'Phew, that's a matter of opinion. It tastes like cat's—'

Her words were cut off as Grace whirled on her, shouting, 'Well, if it's not good enough for you, then get off your backside and make a fresh pot.'

Vi's eyes widened in amazement. She had never heard Grace talk like that before. And where was her nan going? Like Polly, she hadn't left the house since the first night of the air raids. Something was going on, any idiot could see that, and Vi wanted no part of it. Uneasily rising to her feet she made a great pretext of yawning, then, addressing no

one in particular she said, 'I'm off upstairs for a kip while
it's quiet, see you later.'

Neither of the other women made any comment as Vi
sidled from the room. The truth was both women had
enough on their minds without worrying about Vi, who
was a grown woman, after all, and more than capable of
looking after herself. If she wanted to spend all her free
time up the West End enjoying herself, well, let her.

'Well then, I'm off,' Aggie said, her voice loud and strident. Slapping her black felt hat down firmly over her head
and clearing her throat, she made a final go at getting some
kind of response from Grace. 'When did your uncle Danny
say he'd be arriving home?'

Grace, hearing the silent plea for reconciliation in her
nan's voice turned and answered quietly, 'Oh, he said in
his last letter he'd be here in the middle of next week,
providing there are no hold-ups.'

Noting the softer tone in Grace's voice, Aggie's spirits
lifted. Not wanting to push her luck too far, she asked
hesitantly, 'And what about Stan, any news?'

Grace shook her head tiredly.

'No, nothing, well, apart from his letters saying how sorry
he was to hear about . . . about Mum and Dad, and how
he had tried his best to get some leave on compassionate grounds.' Swallowing hard, Grace attempted a watery
smile, eager now to make peace with her nan. 'I'm hoping
he'll get some leave over Christmas . . . Not that we'll
be doing much celebrating this year,' she added, a lump
settling in her throat as she lowered her head to avoid eye
contact with her nan.

Aggie was experiencing similar feelings, and was strongly
tempted to risk another rebuff by taking Grace in her arms.
But she quickly squashed the notion: what Grace needed
now was some time to herself, as did she.

Pulling herself together she said, a bit too loudly, 'Well,

I'm off out now, love. Why don't yer try and get your head down fer a few hours, it'll do you the world of good.'

Huffing and puffing, Aggie made to leave the room when Grace's voice stopped her departure.

'You won't need your hat and coat, Nan. It's quite warm outside.'

'It might be for you youngsters, but us old 'uns feel the cold. Anyway . . .' She fell quiet, her layer of chins wobbling slightly. 'I wouldn't feel right going out without me black hat and coat on.'

Tears sprang to Grace's eyes as she swallowed once again over the painful lump that seemed to be permanently lodged in her throat these days.

'All right, Nan. I understand. I'll . . . I'll see you later.'

Left alone once more, Grace wondered what to do with herself. She should really go down and check on Polly, but like Vi she, too, was tired, desperately tired, both in mind and body. Even though the basement afforded them good shelter, she hadn't been able to sleep for worrying about her nan lying upstairs.

Then there was the horrendous journey to and from work each day. There was no longer such a thing as a regular route to the City. Instead people were shunted from one bus to another, squashed amidst a crowd of like-minded commuters who had also been bombed off their usual route. Often they arrived at their workplace feeling like they'd already done a day's toil. Sometimes they arrived to find their premises bombed and to be ordered by the ARP wardens to return home until further notice. The cockney bus drivers had soon discovered alternative routes, and it wasn't unknown for travellers to be whisked down an unfamiliar side street, while the cheerful driver dodged craters and bomb sites, all the time keeping up a steady line of patter with the conductor designed to keep the passengers happy. And, surprisingly, people in the main were happy.

Thinking of work brought to mind young Jimmy, the office boy. Now seventeen, he was all talk of joining up, despite Gracie's earnest entreaties. She wouldn't be surprised to arrive at work one day to find him already gone. For, like Stanley, and countless others before him, the young lad couldn't wait to take up arms for King and Country.

Her eyes felt so heavy, and there was an alarming churning in her stomach and chest, as if something inside her was about to explode. Maybe if she was to rest her head on the table for five minutes she would feel better. Yes! That's what she'd do. Just rest for five minutes . . . !

Up above, Vi had slowly kicked off her shoes and stretched out on the feather quilt covering her bed, her eyes solemn. She hadn't expected to see her nan up and about looking more like her old self. Nor had she expected the awful atmosphere that had greeted her arrival. Well! Whatever that had been about, no doubt the pair of them would patch things up between them. Vi had been banking on finding Grace on her own, hoping her sister might break the news of her impending move to her nan.

Stifling another yawn, Vi looked up at the ceiling and sighed. She had long outgrown the small department store, and had been thinking of changing jobs before all hell had been let loose. With Polly losing her job, Vi felt easier about giving in her notice, which she couldn't have done if she still had to look after Polly. Now that problem was solved she still had to face her nan. Not that she intended to tell the whole truth. She uttered a short laugh of derision at her own expense. God! She could just imagine everyone's reaction if she announced she was thinking of becoming a hostess up West. Her nan would class that the same as going on the streets.

Suddenly angry with herself, Vi swung her legs over the

side of the bed and lit a cigarette, yet another change in her altered world. Directing a cloud of smoke across the room, she thought back to three nights ago. An Airforce officer had taken her to a posh nightclub, and Vi had been interested to see the hostesses at work. And when the officer had laughingly commented, 'You should have a go at that, Vi. You'd make a packet with your looks,' she had laughed at the suggestion, but the idea had stuck. She had gone back the following night and had been welcomed with open arms by the manager of the club, and by the time she had left, she had been offered a job to start whenever she wanted.

Plumping up her pillows, Violet turned over in her mind all the details the manager had explained to her with a view to becoming a hostess in his club.

There wasn't a salary as such. In fact she had to pay the club two pounds a week for the privilege of being employed in such a top-class establishment. It was all done above board, with the management presenting their hostesses with a bill for the said amount supposedly representing coffee and sandwiches consumed on the premises. The hostess could then charge each man she danced with at least a pound a time. She would also expect the man to keep her company for the rest of the evening, while spending freely the whole time she was with him at his designated table. A hostess who is offered a drink always asks for champagne. When she is offered a cigarette she announces she smokes only a special brand that can be bought from the cigarette girl at the club. Of course, the particular brand in question costs six shillings for a box of twenty-five. The cigarette girl also carries a wide variety of flowers, chocolates and dolls. And, of course, if the gentlemen at the table wants to impress his companion, then he is only too eager to buy whatever it is his new-found friend desires. A typical velvet doll for sale is worth about sixteen shillings. The customer pays three guineas and the hostess sells it back to the cigarette girl for a pound. This practice, so the manager had informed Violet, was the most popular among his hostesses. They all love the cute velvet dolls, and so they should, the smartly dressed manager had laughed, seeing as how the same doll is bought for them three or four times a week.

A sound from the street brought Violet out of her reverie. Stubbing out her cigarette, she debated whether to go downstairs then decided against it. And in that moment she decided against taking the job at the club for the present, even though she could earn up to twelve pounds a week, a small fortune compared to what she was earning now.

Not that anyone from around here would ever know the exact nature of her new profession, but still. It didn't feel right just now. Not with her mum and dad dead for less than a month. Memories of Sam and Hetty swam in front of her eyes, eyes that immediately filled with tears.

Laying her head back on the feather pillow, she tried to sleep, but images of her parents kept intruding on her thoughts. With a muffled moan she turned over, burying her face in the soft pillow.

Like her grandmother and sisters, every time Vi imagined herself over the tragedy, something set her off again. Oh God! How long was the hurt going to last? Would it ever go away? Would it ever lessen . . . ?

CHAPTER ELEVEN

The arrival of Danny in the middle of October was a much-welcomed distraction in the bereaved Donnelly household – for a while.

Grace, like the rest of the family, had secretly hoped that the time spent in the army would have toughened up the mild-mannered man, but within hours of his arrival, it had been painfully obvious that Danny Donnelly was still the same shy, timid, dithering man he had always been, and so the much-needed strength the women had been hoping for was again denied them. Instead they found themselves comforting Danny, and he, as was his character, allowed himself to be cosseted. To be fair, he was devastated by the loss of his brother and sister-in-law, and no one would have denied his right to mourn, but now, over a week into his fortnight leave, Grace and Aggie were having to look after him as if he were a ten-year-old boy instead of a grown man – and a uniformed man to boot. It was as Aggie commented to Grace late one night after Danny had gone to bed, 'Gawd knows how he gets by in the army, 'cos them buggers ain't known for soft-soaping anyone. He can't even make up his mind if he wants a cuppa or not without one of us telling him.'

Grace had replied, 'He's probably completely different away from home, Nan. Like you said, the army wouldn't put up with any wishy-washy behaviour. Uncle Danny just needs someone to lean on right now, that's all.'

'Yeah, well, we could all do with someone to lean on, love. Only some of us have got to lean on ourselves,' Aggie had snorted back tersely.

Danny's injury, a flesh wound to the thigh, had healed completely and with only six days left of his leave remaining, the shy, rotund man sat at the kitchen table he had eaten at all of his life and looked apprehensively at his niece. He had cleared his throat three times before Grace, who was staring dismally into a stew comprising mainly vegetables and lamb bones, finally realised her uncle was trying to catch her attention and asked guiltily, 'Oh, sorry, Uncle Danny. Did you want something?'

Now that he had her attention, Danny jumped nervously on the wooden chair before stuttering, 'No, Gracie, love . . . Well, that is . . .' Agitatedly he rubbed the back of his neck, making it redder than usual before continuing awkwardly, 'I was wondering if you'd think it wrong of me if I went out for a drink, only I . . .'

Grace put down the ladle she had been stirring the broth with and smiled tenderly.

'Oh, don't be daft, Uncle Danny. Of course I won't think wrong of you. In fact I'm surprised you haven't gone out sooner. After all, you won't get much chance once you go back, will you?'

Getting to his feet, Danny paced the floor worriedly.

'I know, love, but it doesn't seem right me going out for a good time when Sam and Hetty—'

Swiftly Grace interrupted. She couldn't face another torrent of tears and self-recrimination. 'Now, stop that, Uncle Danny,' she said fervently, seizing his large, flabby hands. 'You know Dad wouldn't have wanted you to go on mourning, nor would Mum for that matter.'

Danny still blamed himself for not being here when the bombing had started, a guilt compounded by his lateness in getting home. He had had no control over either incident, but grief is never rational.

Gently bundling him from the kitchen, Grace walked him to the door, her voice soothing. 'You go and have a drink . . . And, Uncle Danny . . . Have one for Dad. He'd have liked that.'

Danny swallowed, a film of tears forming over his eyes, and for one horrible moment Grace thought he was going to break down again. Then he squared his shoulders and in a voice gruff with emotion said, 'All right, Gracie, I'll do that. I'll have one for your mum too.'

Grace laughed shakily. 'Well don't have a drink on too many people, or you won't be able to walk back from the pub.'

Passing by the door to the basement, Danny nodded towards it, saying, 'You'll have to do something about young Poll, Gracie. It's not right her spending all her time down there. I'm worried about her, love. I mean I know she has to grieve, but it's not natural her barricading herself in the basement from morning till night. Have you thought of getting the doctor in to see her?'

The question, although mildly put, brought Grace's hackles up. Of course it wasn't natural the way Polly was behaving, but then things hadn't been exactly normal lately. As for getting the doctor in . . . Good God! Every doctor in London was run ragged with Blitz victims, and here was Danny suggesting she get one to pay a home-visit in order to coax a frightened and bereaved young woman from the safety of her own basement.

Urging herself to remain calm, Grace pasted a smile on her lips, saying firmly, 'I'll see to Polly, Uncle Danny. She'll be fine, don't you worry. It's early days yet and I don't want to put any pressure on her; it might make things worse. She's safe where she is, and me and Vi and Nan are down there every night with her, so she's not completely on her own.'

After another five minutes of dithering, Danny finally left the house, much to Grace's relief. Waving him off, she retraced her steps to the kitchen and turned down the heat under the stew. Then, remembering her sister, went down to the basement with a cup of tea and biscuits, intending to keep Polly company for a while.

As Danny turned the corner at the top of the street he collided with a a khaki figure.

'Oh, sorry, I wasn't looking where I was – bloody hell! Stanley. Where did you spring from?'

Eagerly grabbing the soldier's hand, Danny pumped it furiously, his face wreathed in smiles.

Stanley dropped his kit-bag on to the ground, his body breathing a sigh of relief at the unexpected welcome. In the split second of recognising Danny, he had pondered what to say in the face of what had happened. Assuming a solemn air, Stanley looked into the pudgy face and muttered slowly, 'I was sorry to hear about Sam and Hetty, Danny. I got home as soon as I could. I wish it could've been sooner, but you know what the red tape is like in the army.'

Danny's face fell. Shaking his head sadly, he murmured, 'I know, I know, Stan. There's no need to apologise. I never got home until last week, and that was only because I was wounded . . . Oh, nothing serious,' he added swiftly as he saw Stanley scan his body for apparent injury. 'Just a flesh wound in my leg. It's healed now, but I've still got another six days before I'm due back. I was just off down the pub for a drink . . .' Again his voice faltered. His face etched in confused guilt, he added, 'I asked Gracie if she minded, and she said—'

Stanley's hand came out to clasp Danny's shoulder reassuringly.

'Give over, Danny. You don't have to explain yourself to me. It ain't none of me business what you do, but Sam would've been the first one to tell you not to dwell on it too long.'

Danny looked into the broad face eagerly. 'That's what Gracie said . . . I don't suppose you fancy coming with me for a quick one, do you, Stan? I don't like drinking on my own . . . Oh, no, of course you don't,' he said awkwardly. 'You want to get off and see Grace, don't you . . . Maybe later?' he added hopefully.

'Yeah, of course, mate. I'll have to see what Grace says, so I ain't promising, but I'll see what I can do, all right?' Jerking his head back, he asked hesitantly, 'How they bearing up . . . ?'

Danny's head shook sorrowfully.

'Same as you'd expect, I suppose. Aggie seems much the same, though from what the neighbours say she was in a state when it happened. She's not in at the moment. I heard her go out earlier on with one of the neighbours. They've probably gone to see what food they can buy or scrounge. I've hardly seen Vi, she's always in and out of the house. Nothing's changed there, eh?' He attempted a watery smile. 'Polly's the one who's taken it the hardest . . . But, here, I'm keeping you from Grace. I'm sure she'll give you all the news better than I can. She's been great, has Gracie. I don't know what the family would have done without her – nor me, come to that. But, look, you get off. And if you can persuade Grace . . . well, I'll be in the Hare and Hounds. See you later, Stan.'

Danny stopped, then gripped Stanley's hand tight, and when Stanley saw the emotion starting to build in the portly face he disengaged his hand firmly but kindly and, swinging his kit-bag back up over his shoulder, said, 'Yeah, see you later, Danny.'

Marching off down the road, Stanley blew out his cheeks

in profound relief. That was one out of the way. Now he had to face the rest of the family and he was dreading it. Since joining the army Stanley had seen a lot of death and was surprised at how quickly he had become immune to it. But this was different. He had been genuinely fond of Sam and Hetty, even though he had felt overwhelmed by them at times. When Grace had written to say they had been killed, he had been gobsmacked, then he had tried every trick in the book to get some leave, without success – until now, and then it was only a forty-eight-hour pass. Still, he told himself, it's better than nothing.

Striding down the familiar street, Stanley stopped outside number one, Paddy's Castle, and found himself relieved to find it still intact, even though he knew he'd have known if any misfortune had befallen it from his meeting with Danny.

Dropping the kit-bag once more, Stanley stepped back and let his eyes roam over the house he had dreamt of for the past year. Then, with the start of the Blitz, the nightmares had started, where he returned to find a mass of smouldering rubble, and no Grace. *Here! Here! Snap outta it, mate*, he chided himself sternly. *The house is still standing, and Grace is waiting for you inside.*

But Sam and Hetty aren't. And things will never be the same again, a little voice in his head reminded him.

Bracing himself for the emotional reunion that faced him, Stanley puffed out his chest, took a deep breath and knocked loudly on the stout wooden door.

Grace was just coming up the basement steps when the knocking started. Tutting with annoyance, she debated whether or not to ignore it, then felt ashamed at her reaction. It was probably one of the neighbours knocking to ask if she needed anything.

Placing the tray that contained the remains of her and Polly's afternoon tea on the hall table, she brushed back a stray wisp of hair from her forehead and opened the door, her jaw dropping in disbelief when she saw who was standing on the doorstep.

'STANLEY!' She screamed in delight, before being swept up into strong arms and carried down the hallway. Crying and laughing she clung on to the uniformed body wildly, not believing what was happening.

But before she could get her breath, another loud cry filled the hall, and there, standing behind them looking like a lost waif, stood Polly, her eyes and mouth wide as she beheld the entwined couple. Her mouth opened and closed futilely, then the tears began to course down her sunken cheeks. Grace saw her sister shuffle towards them and felt her throat tighten at the sight she must present to Stanley. Quashing the thought that she would have liked a few minutes of privacy with Stanley, she beckoned her sister, and when Stanley's arms enveloped both women, the three of them broke down unashamedly, letting their grief wash over them like a healing balm.

The public bar in the Hare and Hounds was almost empty at this time of the evening, and Danny, feeling a little self-conscious, was about to finish off his beer and leave when he became aware of someone standing at his table. Looking up he saw Beryl Lovesett, the resident barmaid, and immediately made to rise.

'Oh, hello, Beryl. Sorry, were you waiting on my glass?' Danny floundered hopelessly.

'Gawd help us, Danny. I ain't after your glass. I was just coming over to say hello an' to ask how you were keeping. Can I join yer?'

Almost falling off his chair, Danny leapt to his feet, spluttering, 'What! Oh, yes, of course you can, Beryl. Please, sit down.' When the woman was seated Danny sat back down, then, his eyes darting to the bar, asked nervously, 'Is it all right? I mean, you won't get into trouble, will you?'

Beryl laughed gaily. 'Course I won't, yer silly devil. It's me break, an' I'll 'ave a port an' lemon if you're asking.'

Again Danny stumbled to his feet, his hands going instantly to his pocket for his wallet.

'Yes, of course. Just a minute, I'll be right back. Um . . . Right then, a port and lemon coming up.'

Watching the bumbling man make his way to the bar, his face as red as a beetroot, Beryl made herself more comfortable. Taking a cigarette from a small packet of Capstans, she inserted it between blood-red lips, her brown eyes narrowing as the smoke filtered up to her attractive face.

Beryl Lovesett was thirty-three, with blond hair straight from a bottle, a full figure, which she used to her advantage, and was, at the moment, looking for a way out of her present life. She had been working as a barmaid for over five years, always hoping that some day she would latch on to someone with a bit of money to his name. So far she had been unsuccessful in her quest. There had been no shortage of men in her life – one in particular she'd rather forget – but none had come up to her expectations. Now it looked as if her luck might be about to change. Her painted lips smiled cruelly as she recalled Danny's obvious excitement and eagerness. Poor, pathetic bastard. He had been coming into the bar for years making sheep's eyes at her, but she'd never given him any encouragement, looking on the plump, bashful man as a joke.

But things had changed. Now that his brother was dead, the house in Lester Road belonged to Danny Donnelly, and though she had never seen the house, she'd heard about it, and a house such as the one described must mean there was a fair bit of money that went with it. That was one consolation about working in a pub. There was never any shortage of local gossip. Of course there were still Danny's nieces and the old girl living there, but if things went according to plan, she'd soon turf them out. This was the best chance of owning a decent house she'd ever have, and she wasn't going to let the opportunity of obtaining a cushy billet pass her by.

As Danny approached the table with the drinks, Beryl pasted a warm, welcoming smile on her lips. This should be a walkover. The man was obviously desperate for a woman. The only snag was he would be going back to base soon, so she would have to work fast.

The drinks were deposited on the table with shaky hands and Beryl had to lower her eyes to hide her contempt for the pathetic man trying so hard to make a good impression. Oh, this was going to be easy. Like taking sweets from a baby. Danny Donnelly was the answer to all her prayers. And the beauty of it was she wouldn't even have a husband to worry about, because once that ring was on her finger, and Danny was back overseas and sending her half his paycheck, she'd live the life of Reilly. No more standing on her feet for twelve hours a day for a poxy wage, not if she could pull this off.

Smiling sweetly, Beryl played up to the inexperienced man, and Danny, his enthusiasm painfully evident, was soon completely bowled over by the good-looking blonde. Carefully hiding her excitement at the ease with which her newly formed plans were going, a triumphant Beryl sent Danny off for more drinks. Her scheme would never have been possible in ordinary circumstances, but these days couples were meeting and marrying within days with the aid of special licences. Oh, she'd thought it all through carefully. The only thing missing up until now had been the man himself; and now she had found him. Now all she had to do was carry it through.

It should be easy enough. After all, there was a war on, wasn't there? And people and circumstances changed during wartime.

At closing time, slightly drunk and delighted at his good fortune, Danny walked Beryl home. And when, after he had delivered her safely to the door of her flat, she asked him to stay a while, pleading nervousness of the nightly raids, Danny was only too happy to oblige. No woman had ever treated him as Beryl was doing, and after the trauma of losing Sam and Hetty, Danny was ripe for the attentions of a woman like Beryl Lovesett.

Babbling nervously, his arms and hands jerking in pleasurable agitation, Danny unwittingly stepped into the expertly laid trap, thinking happily that his luck was finally turning for the better.

CHAPTER TWELVE

Stanley's short leave flew by, the majority of it spent with both Grace and Polly, much to the young couple's annoyance. They'd had no time on their own, but Grace, seeing the change in Polly brought about by Stanley's presence, couldn't stay annoyed for long. Now it was the last evening, and Grace was determined to have Stanley to herself for the short time they had left. With Aggie's help, the couple managed to creep out of the house without Polly in tow, then, like two naughty school-children, they ran to the pub holding hands, their journey interrupted by frequent stops down dark alleyways for a kiss and cuddle, the exercise leaving them both edgy and frustrated.

On arrival at the pub they were surprised to find Danny propping up the bar, his face more alive they they'd ever seen it as he engaged in deep conversation with the brassy blonde behind the counter.

'Strewth! The sly old devil.' Stanley grinned in amazement. 'Looks like Danny's got his foot well in there. I'd never have thought he had it in him. No wonder he's been looking so pleased with himself. Mind you, he's jumped in at the deep end with our Beryl. She's been round the track more times than a greyhound. Still! He doesn't seem to be complaining, does he?'

Grace watched the scene at the bar, her face set in lines of disapproval. She'd be the last one to deprive her uncle of some happiness, but not with an old brass like Beryl Lovesett. Grace didn't know the woman, except by reputation, and none of it good, though the men would disagree on that score.

'Oh, Gawd! Look at your face.' Stanley was laughing down at her obvious disapproval. 'Don't be such a misery, Gracie. Danny ain't doing no harm, an' you said you wanted him to have a good time before he went back.'

Grace tossed her head impatiently. 'Don't be so silly, Stan,' she said sharply. 'Uncle Danny wouldn't know how to cope with a woman like that.'

Stanley, his face still wearing a boyish grin, answered gleefully, 'Well, he don't look as if he's doing too badly from where I'm standing.'

And he was right. Grace had never seen her uncle act in the manner he was adopting now. It was obvious to all watching that something was going on between the barmaid and the eager customer, and suddenly she felt uncomfortable.

'Let's go somewhere else, Stan.' She pulled on Stanley's arm. 'I don't want to be forced into a conversation with a woman like that.'

But Stanley had no intention of leaving. Shaking off her hand he said, 'Now who's being silly? You don't even know her. She's quite nice as a matter a fact, and a good laugh. Perhaps she's just what Danny needs right now. Where's the harm in it?'

Stanley was staring hard at her now, his face set in lines of disapproval at what he considered her narrow attitude. Grace saw the condemnation in her fiancé's eyes and looked away. Maybe he was right. After all, her uncle would be leaving in a couple of days. And, as Stanley said, where was the harm in it!

Allowing herself to be led over to the bar, she went to stand by Danny, her manner awkward.

'Hello, Uncle Danny,' she said in a stilted voice.

'Wotcher, Danny, how's it going?' Stanley, no sign of embarrassment on his face, winked suggestively at the startled Danny.

'Oh, um, hello, you two. I didn't know you were coming here tonight.' Danny, his new-found confidence slipping away, shuffled his feet and looked to the watching barmaid for support.

Beryl, quick to notice the disapproval on the young woman's face, felt her backbone stiffen in anticipation of trouble. She knew Grace by sight, though the young woman hadn't been in the pub for well over a year now. And it was apparent that the snooty piece didn't think much of her uncle's choice in women friends. Well, she was in for a few more surprises, wasn't she! Beryl's hard eyes raked Grace from top to bottom, taking in the royal blue swagger coat and the light blue two-piece costume beneath it. The girl was a looker all right, Beryl conceded reluctantly, and she knew how to dress. Both the coat and costume were a couple of years old, but of good quality and showed off the girl's glossy nut-brown hair and blue eyes perfectly. And it was the eyes that held Beryl's attention, for they were fixed on her in open dislike. Taken off-guard by the open hostility, Beryl swallowed hard, then turned her attention to the men. Nodding to Danny she uttered a shrill laugh, so false and grating it set Grace's teeth on edge.

'D'yer want another one in there, love?' she asked familiarly, while at the same time stroking the back of Danny's hand. The gesture wasn't lost on Grace, who visibly bridled at the blatant display of intimacy. Beryl saw Grace's look of discomfort and renewed her efforts. Turning to the good-looking man by Grace's side, she batted her eyelashes, stuck out her chest and said cloyingly, 'It's Stan Slater, ain't it? You ain't been in here much lately, but I never forget a face, 'specially a good-looking one.' Again she let out a braying laugh, this time with both men joining in.

Grace could only stand and stare in amazement. What was the matter with men? They only had to have some woman make a fuss of them and they lapped it up like puppies at their bowls. Out of the corner of her eye, Grace saw the look of triumph on the painted face and smiled grimly. So, all this was for her benefit, was it? All right then, let the old trout have it her way for the evening. By this time next week, both men would be gone. She'd be a fool to spend Stanley's last night in conflict with a woman she would probably never see again unless she came back to the pub, and that wasn't likely once Stanley had gone back to the army.

Slipping her arm through Stanley's, Grace, smiling archly, said, 'Yes, he is quite handsome, isn't he? I'll have to keep an eye on him. Some women will go after anything in trousers, you know the type.'

Both men fidgeted with embarrassment, yet to Grace's astonishment her normally docile uncle turned on her, saying sharply, 'You're not being very pleasant, Grace. Beryl is a friend of mine, and I'll thank you to be civil.'

Deeply shocked that her beloved uncle could turn on her, Grace lowered her head in confusion. Oh, God! Why had they come here tonight of all nights? All she'd wanted to do was spend some time with Stanley, and now it had all gone wrong. She looked to Stanley for reassurance, but found his gaze, too, was filled with accusation. She would have fled from the pub had not Stanley taken her arm and led her to a corner, depositing her none too gently on to a rickety chair.

Bending down he hissed, 'What's up with you? The poor old sod finally gets himself a girlfriend and all you can do is take cheap shots at her. Well, it ain't on, Gracie. Not all women went to posh schools and were brought up in good homes, you know. And they weren't all lucky enough to get a job in a fancy office working with toffs and toffee-nosed bitches in tailored suits. Now I'm going back to the bar to get us some drinks. Then I'm gonna invite Danny to join us, and his lady friend when she gets a break. So try and be nice to her, for Danny's sake, all right?' With that he stormed off, his back held rigid the way it always was when he was annoyed.

Grace slumped back on the chair, her eyes filling with tears. Not because Stanley had told her off, that had never worried her overly, but because it didn't take much to set her off these days. And Stanley knew that. So why had he taken that woman's side against her? Her hands clenched into fists in her lap. She'd a good mind to leave and let the pair of them fawn over the made-up tart to their heart's content. But Stanley would only come after her and start another row. No! As much as it went against the grain, she would just have to grin and bear it for the evening, for everyone's sake.

So when a hesitant Danny appeared at the table, she smiled up at him warmly, saying apologetically, 'Sorry, Uncle Danny, I didn't mean to be rude to your friend. Will she be joining us for a drink later? I'd like to apologise properly.'

At her words, Danny's face lit up with relief. Dropping down on the chair opposite, he gabbled happily, 'Oh, that's all right, love. We've all been out of sorts lately. Not surprising with all that's happened, is it? Let's forget about it, eh?'

Deeply ashamed, Grace patted Danny's arm. 'Thanks, Uncle Danny. You're a good man.' *Much too good for the likes of that one*, her inner voice added, refusing to be silenced.

When Beryl joined them later, Grace struggled to be amenable, but it was hard going, and when the woman had to return behind the bar, Grace only just stopped herself from letting out a huge sigh of relief.

At least she wouldn't have to go through that ordeal again. Now she could concentrate on spending the rest of the night with Stanley.

Leaving Danny behind, the young couple left the pub, each one contemplating the hours left to them and praying there wouldn't be an air raid tonight. No sooner had the thought crossed their minds than the now-familiar wail of the siren cut the air.

'Oh, damn and blast!' Grace cried in despair as the searchlights lit up the sky. Suddenly remembering her uncle she cried, 'Uncle Danny. We'll have to go back for him.'

As she turned, Stanley gripped her arm.

'Don't be daft. He'll go down the cellar with the rest of them. C'mon, let's get moving . . .

'Cheer up, girl. It might just be a light raid,' Stan said jovially as they hurried along. 'Come on, Gracie, race you home. First one into the basement's a—' A bomb fell nearby, drowning out his words. Grabbing hands they raced towards home, to be met at the door by an anxious Polly, for once not safely ensconced down below stairs.

'What are you doing out here, you silly cow?' Grace shoved her youngest sister back inside the house roughly. 'You stay downstairs when its safe and stand out on the doorstep in a raid. What's the matter with you? You trying to get yourself killed?'

''Ere, leave the poor little mare alone. You've been in a right old mood tonight.' Stanley, his lips pressed into lines of anger, wrapped his arms around the shivering Polly. Over the top of the ginger head he mouthed to Grace, 'I'm beginning to wish I hadn't bothered coming home . . . Oh, Gawd! You ain't gonna start crying again, are you? Bleeding hell! Can't I say anything without you bawling?'

Aghast at the cruel words, Grace could only watch as Stanley led Polly down the basement stairs, for all the world as if *she* were his fiancée!

'Oh, good, you're home.' Aggie came bustling along the corridor, a flask under each arm and a tray of sandwiches piled high on a large platter. 'Vi's already downstairs with some squaddie. They were just about to go out when the siren went off. Let's hope it's only a short raid. I don't fancy spending the night with a strange bloke – not at my age, though Stan'll probably be grateful to have another soldier to keep him company . . . Gawd! Here the buggers come again. Here, help me with this lot, Gracie, there's a good girl . . .'

Angry and frustrated at the way the evening had turned out, Grace followed her grandmother down the steep steps to the large room below. Resting the tray on the top step, she pulled the door firmly shut, took a deep breath to regain her composure, then carried on down the stairs.

The basement had been made comfortable at the start of the war, with bits and pieces added at different intervals. Two double mattresses, intended for the rag-and-bone man, lay propped up against the far wall ready to be made up into beds should the need arise, and the spare three-piece suite from the dining room was now arranged in the centre of the room for added comfort.

Placing the tray on the coffee table, Grace looked to where Vi was sitting on the arm of the armchair, a uniformed man sprawled in the chair itself. But the man with Vi was no squaddie, as Aggie had said, not according to the stripes on his arm.

Grace uttered a silent disparaging laugh. She should have known Vi wouldn't lower herself by entertaining an ordinary man from the ranks.

As if conscious of her thoughts, the man leant forward, saying, 'Sorry about imposing on you like this, miss. I did offer to go to the public shelter, but your grandmother kindly offered to let me share the amenities here.'

Startled, Grace handed the officer a mug of tea.

'Oh, that's quite all right. We often have the neighbours in if it's a heavy raid, so we're used to company.'

Taking the offered mug, the man winked, reached into his pocket and produced a bottle of brandy.

'I don't know about the rest of you, but I prefer my tea a little stronger. Anyone else like some?'

Grace shook her head, but Aggie, her face lighting up at the sight of her favourite tipple, eagerly held out her mug.

'Cheers, mate, you're a gentleman.' Taking a long pull at the fortified drink, Aggie smacked her lips in appreciation. 'Ah, that's better. A couple more of these an' I won't be worrying about no bleeding bombs . . . Oh, thank you kindly, I don't mind if I do,' she added affably as another good measure was poured into her mug.

'Did you see Uncle Danny on your travels, only he's not come in yet?' Vi, her long legs dangling provocatively over the side of the chair, addressed Grace.

Still smarting from the episode in the pub, and Stanley's subsequent behaviour, Grace answered curtly, 'Yes, we saw him in the pub, but he stayed on after we left. The siren went off when we were halfway home. I was going to go back for him, but Stan said he'd probably go down the cellar with the rest of the pub regulars. I hope he's all right, he . . .'

But Vi was no longer listening, her attention consumed by the smartly dressed man lounging in the large armchair.

Embarrassed at being ignored, Grace dithered a moment before settling herself in the other armchair, the settee already being occupied by Stanley and Polly. Looking at the entwined couple, Grace felt a lump form in her throat, then she shook her head crossly. Come on, girl, get a grip on yourself, she admonished herself sternly, ashamed for feeling so weak and weepy.

Getting up again, she crossed over to the officer and, holding out her mug, said with forced gaiety, 'I think I will have a drop, thank you. I might as well, after all there's nothing much else to do, is there? Cheers!'

Because of the clement weather, the *Luftwaffe* seized the opportunity to mount a large-scale raid that evening, which meant that everyone had to bed down for the night. Polly and Grace shared one mattress, while Vi, protesting beneath her breath at being separated from her officer friend, was forced to bed down beside her nan. The two men, meanwhile, had to make do with the settee and armchairs pushed together. Altogether the sleeping arrangements were comparative luxury compared to the conditions of the ordinary public shelters, and everyone tucked up warmly in the basement was aware of their good fortune.

Grace had slept soundly, due in part to the generous helping of brandy she had imbibed. So when she felt someone pulling at her arm she didn't awaken instantly as she usually did, but groaned and turned back over on her side. But the feel of hands on her body became more insistent, until she was finally dragged from her peaceful slumber.

Groggy with sleep, she half sat up on the mattress mumbling, 'Wh . . . what . . . What is it? What's the matter?'

She felt a finger press lightly on her lips, warning her to keep quiet.

'Sshh, it's me, Stan. Keep your voice down. We don't wanna wake anyone up.'

Inching her way to a sitting position, Grace looked at the gloomy outline crouching on the floor, her eyes screwing up in bewilderment.

'Stan!' she whispered. 'What's going on? What do you want at this time of the night?'

In answer she felt a warm hand on her leg, then she smelt brandy-laden breath on her cheek and shrank back in disgust, with Stan moving closer until their bodies were touching.

'C'mon, love. Let's go over to the sofa, we'll be more comfortable there.' His lips were nibbling at her ear, the stink of alcohol making Grace gag. 'Hurry up, Gracie, we ain't got much time left. I'm gonna have to leave as soon as the all-clear goes, and we ain't had a minute to ourselves since I got here.'

Disgusted and angry, Grace shoved the heavy body away, hissing angrily, 'Are you mad? Do you honestly expect me to . . . to . . . with all of my family in the same room? Not to mention a complete stranger who could wake up at any minute. Get away from me, Stan. Go on, clear off. You're drunk. You stink of it.'

When the heavy body paid no heed and began to press down harder on her, Grace kicked out wildly, her legs thrashing around furiously as fear began to grow inside her at this man who had suddenly turned into a stranger. Suddenly, one of her kicks found its mark, and with a muffled groan Stanley fell back holding his stomach.

'What'd you do that for?' he cried piteously. 'I only wanted a bit of a kiss and cuddle.'

Scrambling on to her knees, Grace faced him in the darkness, her whole body trembling with rage.

'I know what you wanted, Stan, and I can't believe you could act like this. What's gotten into you, you . . .'

A low mumble came from the mattress and Grace quickly bent down to her sister, who was attempting to sit up.

'Grace! Gracie! Is that you, Gracie? What's the matter? Is anything wrong?'

'No, no, nothing's wrong, Poll,' Grace whispered reassuringly. 'You go back to sleep, love. That's it. Go back to sleep.' Tucking the blanket up around Polly's neck, Grace moved closer to her sister as if for protection. But Stanley had already slunk away back to the sofa. Yet even when she heard his drunken snores she continued to sit bolt upright, afraid to close her eyes in case he came back.

'Don't worry, miss. I'll keep an eye on him. He won't bother you again, you have my word on it.'

Grace jumped at the sound of the strong, timbered voice that came out of the darkness, forgetting for a moment about the man who had been forced to stay the night with them. Deeply ashamed that her ordeal had been witnessed by a stranger, Grace mumbled, 'Thank you,' before burying herself under the blankets with Polly. But it was a long time before she managed to get back to sleep.

'Come on, you lot, rise and shine. The all-clear went half an hour ago, you lazy buggers.'

Bustling around the room, Aggie laid down a tray filled with mugs of tea and hot, buttered toast, the heady aroma bringing the occupants of the basement awake.

Leaning up on her elbow, Grace sniffed the air then nudged the sleeping girl by her side.

'Wake up, Poll, it's all over for another night, and Nan's made breakfast. Come on, lazy bones, get up.'

Mumbling and groaning, Polly sat up, her nose, like Grace's, sniffing the delicious smell of breakfast, which overrode the heavy stench of brandy and cigarette smoke from the previous evening.

'Ooh, Nan. Toast with butter. Where did you get that from?' Clambering over Grace, Polly, looking more animated than anyone had seen her in a long while, scrambled to the coffee table, her eyes widening further at the sight of the four eggs perched resplendently in china egg cups. 'Coo, eggs! Can I have one, Nan?'

Aggie, her face wreathed in pleasurable smiles, tapped at the grasping hand with a teaspoon, saying quickly, 'Hang

on, girl. We'll have to share 'em. Half each, so don't be so
bleeding greedy. And as for where I got them, well you can
thank Vi's friend for your breakfast.' Jerking her head over
to where the officer was sitting, an amused smile on his
face, Aggie explained, 'He gave 'em to me last night when
he called for Vi, but I thought I'd save 'em for breakfast.
An' that's real butter on the toast, so get stuck in before it
gets cold.'

Polly, her mouth watering in anticipation of the treat in
store, looked over at the figure in the armchair and said
shyly, 'Thank you. I haven't had an egg for ages. Where
did you get them? Are you in the black market?'

A loud concerted gasp of dismay greeted this tactless
remark, but the soldier grinned good naturedly.

'Nothing so glamorous, I'm afraid, Polly. I got them from
the store at the barracks. I'm only sorry I couldn't get any
more, seeing how much they're appreciated.'

Shoving Polly aside, Aggie poured out the tea, saying happily, 'Here, I'll share one egg with you, an' Grace can share
with Vi. That'll leave one each for Stan and—' She broke off,
embarrassed at not remembering the man's name.

'Chris,' the man laughed. 'My name's Chris, and you can
have my share. I can get plenty more where that came from.'
His face changing suddenly, he looked over to where the
still figure of Stan lay on the sofa and added grimly, 'I don't
suppose Stanley will deprive you ladies of an egg either, so
you might as well have one each.'

Polly looked to Grace for confirmation, her face lighting
up when Grace nodded in agreement.

'Chris is right, Poll. Stan can get his breakfast when he
gets back to the barracks. Go on, take one.'

The four women sat cross-legged around the table, and
within minutes the tray was cleared.

Wiping her mouth, Grace rose to her feet, saying regretfully, 'I suppose I'd better get ready for work, though after

that heavy raid, it's going to be murder getting to the City this morning.'

'You work in the City?' The question was tinged with surprised admiration, causing Grace to blush.

'Yes, I'm a secretary at an office block off Leadenhall Street. We deal in stationery. It's not a very big firm, but I like it.' She laughed self-consciously. 'I just hope it's still standing when I get there. There's always a worry that I'll arrive to find a pile of rubble where my building used to be. Anyway, I'd best be off.' Holding out her hand, she said, 'It was nice meeting you, Chris, and thanks again for the breakfast.' She smiled, indicating the remains of the breakfast tray.

'My pleasure, Grace. It was nice to see it appreciated.'

Violet, who had been watching the scene with bored indifference, now joined Grace on her feet.

'Speaking of work, I suppose I'd better get a move on myself, though I don't have to leave as early, seeing as how I only work up the road.'

Once out of the basement Grace said to Vi, 'He's nice, Vi. How long have you been seeing him?'

Walking ahead of Grace up the stairs, Vi shrugged. 'I only met him Friday night, but I won't be keeping in touch. He's all right, but not exactly a barrel of laughs. Besides, who wants to get serious these days? It's hardly worth the effort. They're here one minute and gone the next. Unless of course you manage to get a ring on your finger.'

Grace made a face behind Vi's back, then, remembering Stanley still sleeping down below, exclaimed. 'Oh, my Lord, Stanley. I forgot all about him. He's supposed to be back at camp by nine o'clock. I'd better go and wake him up or we'll have the military police after him.'

She was halfway down the stairs when she recalled the unpleasant scene from the early hours and felt her stomach tighten in distaste. It would be easy to blame Stanley's outrageous behaviour on the drink he'd consumed, but she'd seen him drunk many times, and never once had he turned nasty. So why had he last night? Shuddering at the memory, she hesitated. She really didn't want to face him, but she had no choice.

The sound of voices in the hall brought her head up, a look of relief coming to her face as Stanley, looking the worst for wear, emerged from the basement followed by the rest of the group.

Seeing Grace standing on the stairs, Stanley gave her a watery smile.

'Morning, darlin'. Gawd! Me head's splitting. You ain't got any aspirin, have you? It feels like there's a couple of German tanks moving about inside me head.'

The open, guileless smile on Stanley's face showed he had no recollection of last night. Either that or he had suddenly developed an excellent talent for acting.

Immensely relieved she wouldn't have to face a confrontation, Grace answered lightly, 'There's some in the kitchen. Ask Nan, she'll get them for you, I have to get ready for work.'

Stanley's smile faltered, his forehead creasing in befuddlement at the unmistakable frostiness in Grace's voice. Then he remembered Danny and his new lady friend and realised why Grace was in a mood. Glumly he made for the kitchen where Aggie was busy washing up the breakfast plates. What a bleeding leave this had turned out to be. And he'd been looking forward to it so much as well. Not having to face the family's grief over Sam and Hetty's deaths, of course, that had been awful, but he had hoped he and Grace would have had some time to themselves, maybe even . . . !

'What's up with you?' Aggie demanded brusquely. 'You've got a face on you like a smacked arse.' Falling on to a chair, Stanley replied dolefully, 'I think I had a few too many last night. What with the beer at the pub and the drink Vi's friend was handing round. I wasn't gonna take any, not with him being an officer, but he's all right, ain't he? Not like some of 'em; look at you like you was something they found on the bottom of their boots, some of 'em do. Nah, Chris is all right in my book . . . 'Ere, got any aspirin, Aggie? Grace said there was some in here.'

Throwing Stanley an exasperated glance, Aggie took a small bottle from a cupboard under the sink and handed them to him, remarking archly, 'Chris now, is it? I shouldn't get too matey, if I was you, Stan. He might have been friendly enough last night, but he couldn't've been otherwise in the circumstances, could he? But I doubt if he'll be asking for your regiment so he can keep in touch. A bit out of your class, lad.'

Stanley's face flushed at the reprimand. Of course he wasn't going to make any assumptions about Lieutenant Green, he wasn't that daft – though to hear Aggie talk you'd think he was a complete idiot. Swallowing two of the white tablets down with a drop of milk, he grimaced at the bitter taste they left in his mouth. Yet it wasn't only the tablets that caused his discomfort. He had imagined a hero's welcome, but it hadn't turned out like that at all. Apart from the initial greeting, Grace hadn't exactly been all over him. To be fair, she hadn't had much chance, what with Polly following them everywhere, then the raid had put a damper on a cosy evening alone. But she could have spent some time with him during the night when everyone was sleeping. He frowned, his memory hazy at the events of the night. He could just remember trying to wake her up, but nothing after that. But seeing as he had woken up on his own, it was obvious she hadn't broken her neck to be with him. Then there was Vi, sneering at him with that superior look of hers, and Aggie quickly reverting to treating him like a schoolboy instead of a grown man fighting for his

King and Country. In fact the only people who had looked on him with any respect were Polly and Danny, and to be brutally honest, he couldn't take much pride from those two. Poor Polly had been desperate for a man to lean on, anyone would have sufficed, and Danny . . . Well, it didn't take much to impress Danny.

His face clearing, Stan thought back to the previous night and smiled slowly. Maybe there was more to Danny than met the eye. The sight of the normally bumbling, painfully shy man falling all over Beryl Lovesett had been an eye-opener and no mistake. Thinking of the man in question, he was about to ask Aggie if Danny had been back home yet, then changed his mind. He didn't want to take the chance of Aggie asking any awkward questions. If Danny decided to introduce Beryl to the family he wouldn't be around to see the commotion that would surely follow.

All of a sudden Stanley had the desire to be back among his mates. Rising to his feet, he cleared his throat loudly and said, 'Well, I'd better be off, Aggie. Thanks for putting me up, I appreciate it. See you.'

Putting the plates and mugs away, but carefully leaving the egg shells on a spare plate to be noticed if Rene or Jeannie popped in, as they usually did in the morning, Aggie swung round to face the ill-at-ease man, then blew out her cheeks in exasperation. Like Danny, the army hadn't changed Stanley. He was still the same inept, defensive little git he'd always been. You'd think he was saying goodbye to a stranger instead of a woman he'd known for years, and the grandmother of the woman he intended to marry. A pang of guilt attacked her conscience. All right, so she wasn't the easiest person to get along with, but if Stanley intended to marry into the family he was going to have to get used to her ways, instead of expecting her to fall on his neck in gratitude for the slightest little thing he did. To be fair to the lad, he had managed to prise Polly out of the basement, although whether his good work would be undone the minute he left remained to be seen.

Aggie took a few steps towards Stan then stopped as she saw the sudden alarm that crossed his face. She had been about to give him a kiss goodbye, but he could whistle for that now. Once again the old thought reared its head in her mind. What on earth did Grace see in him?

The same thought was going round Grace's confused, tired brain as she changed into a clean blouse and skirt for work. The leave she'd been waiting for for so long hadn't turned out as she'd hoped. And as painful as it was, she had to face the truth. All the time spent apart from Stanley hadn't strengthened her love for him, and after last night something inside her had died and could never be brought back to life. The worst of it was she couldn't say anything, not with Stanley returning to the front line. It would be cruelty of the worst kind to tell him now she didn't love him any more.

Sinking down on her single bed, she dropped her face in her hands in despair. Maybe she was feeling this way because she still hadn't got over the shock of her parents' deaths. No sooner had the idea crossed her mind than she dismissed it angrily. Of course she hadn't got over her mum and dad dying, maybe she never would, not completely. But one thing she did know for sure, and that was their deaths had nothing to do with her altered feelings for Stanley. If anything, the tragedy should have brought them closer, but instead of the strength she had so desperately needed from him, Stanley had let her down once again. It wasn't his fault, he just didn't have it in him to be the man she needed. And as she ran down the stairs to say goodbye, she knew he never had, she just hadn't seen it before. But even though she had no intention of telling him the wedding was off, neither would she be a hypocrite. There would be no loving kisses and passionate embraces of goodbye.

Grace was spared the embarrassment of any awkward farewell scenes by Violet's friend offering her a lift to the underground. Gratefully seizing the opportunity to avoid a possible prolonged farewell, Grace gave the stunned Stanley a quick hug, said she would write as soon as possible, and hurried out to the waiting car. The last she saw of her fiancé he was standing on the doorstep, his kit-bag at his feet, looking for all the world as if he'd just received the biggest shock of his life. Beside him stood Polly, clinging to his arm, her face tearful as she said her goodbyes. As the car turned the corner, Grace caught one last glimpse of them and thought they looked for all the world like a couple.

The journey to Bethnal Green took longer than usual due to the night's heavy raid, and when Grace alighted from the car she thanked the officer warmly before hurrying down the stationary escalators to her platform, where dozens of people were busy tidying up their belongings after a night spent on the cold, draughty platforms. As always, Grace was amazed at the cheerfulness of these people, some of whom had spent the entire night on the filthy tracks, there being no more room on the crowded platforms and escalators.

When the train pulled into the station, Grace clambered aboard, eager to get away from the depressing sight of so many people with their few pathetic belongings, a large number of whom no longer had a home to return to and would have to find temporary accommodation in an over-crowded church hall or empty classroom.

Spotting an empty seat at the far end of the carriage, Grace hurried towards it, just beating a well-dressed man to the punch. Plopping down triumphantly, she rested her head against the rail and closed her eyes, feeling a curious sense of well-being, almost as if she had just had a miraculous escape.

CHAPTER THIRTEEN

The entire family was, to put it in Aggie's words, gobsmacked. Here was Danny, that mild-mannered, ineffectual
man, who as far as his family knew had never had a girlfriend in his life, here he was, standing facing them telling
them he had got married, the inane grin plastered over his
sweating face making him look like a simpleton. And the
loose piece he'd married hanging on his arm and gazing
up at him like he was Douglas Fairbanks, instead of a near-
middle-aged man with a receding hairline and a pot belly.

'Look, I know it's a shock to you all.' Danny was staring
at the group of women, who in turn were gazing back at
him as if witnessing an apparition. 'But it was all a bit
quick. Sort of a whirlwind romance, wasn't it, Beryl?' He
asked cloyingly of the woman at his side. All eyes turned
to the flash-looking blonde wearing a cheap grey two-piece
and a straggly piece of fur around her neck.

Beryl felt the penetrating gazes of the women in her
new husband's family and stiffened her spine. Bloody lot
of toffee-nosed cows, looking at her like she was something
the cat had just dragged in. Even the old biddy, who looked
just like any other East End housewife, was glaring at her

like she was rubbish. Well! She'd show them. They could do and say what they wanted, it was no skin off her nose. She had a ring on her finger now, and if they didn't like it then they could bloody well lump it.

The atmosphere in the kitchen was stifling, and even Polly was wishing for the siren to go just to relieve the tension. But the worst was yet to come.

Gathering courage from the striking woman who was looking at him in open admiration, Danny cleared his throat, stuck out his ample chins and said firmly, 'I can see it's been a great shock to you all, and I'm sorry about that, but there it is. I'm married now, and I hope you'll make Beryl feel welcome while I'm away. After all, she is one of the family now.'

Danny's words finally loosened Aggie's tongue. Shambling forward on the chair, she screeched, 'What d'yer mean, make her feel welcome? You telling me you're leaving her here with us while you go swanning off back overseas? Oh, no. No, you don't, Danny, me lad. All right, so you've got married, that's up to you, Gawd help you . . .' She shot a withering look at the stony-faced blonde. 'But she ain't living with us and that's an end to it.' Shaking her massive body, Aggie glared at the flushed man.

It would be fair to say that the women had thought there'd been enough shocks for one morning, in fact for a lifetime, but they were in for a further surprise. For Danny, seeming to grow in stature, for the first time in his life raised his voice – and the effect was startling.

'And I'm telling you, Aggie, that Beryl is my wife and she'll be living in my home. Yes, you can look, all of you. But this is my home. I don't like to bring this up, because I know how painful it is for all of us, but the fact is that with Sam gone the house passes to me. We've already talked it over . . .' Here he stopped for breath and patted Beryl's arm for moral support. 'And we've agreed that Beryl will take over my rooms while

I'm away, so she won't actually be living with you, although she will have the run of the house. I'm sure it'll all work out fine and you'll be the best of friends in no time,' he finished hopefully, his eyes flickering at the emptiness of his words, his short burst of bravado rapidly fading under Aggie's furious gaze. Suddenly anxious to get away from the accusing eyes that seemed to be boring into him from all directions, he said over-brightly, 'Come on, darling, I'll show you where you'll be living from now on.'

With a triumphant look at the stupefied women, Beryl took her husband's arm and swept from the room, her head held high.

The silence in the kitchen lasted until the incongruous couple had left the room, then Aggie, looking fit to burst, exclaimed, 'Bloody hell's bells! Tell me I'm dreaming someone. Somebody tell me I'm having a bleeding nightmare, 'cos I don't believe what I just heard.'

Slowly sinking down on a chair, Grace shook her head.

'It's no nightmare, Nan, I only wish it was. I knew Uncle Danny was seeing her, but . . .'

'You knew?' Aggie thrust her face forward, her eyes wild. 'You knew your uncle was seeing that trollop and you didn't say anything? Well . . . !' She threw out her arms, then, bringing her fist down on the table with a thump that made them all jump, she shouted, 'Why the bleeding hell didn't you tell me? You know the poor sod ain't got the brains he was born with, not where women like that are concerned. Fur coat an' no knickers, that's her sort, out for a cushy billet provided by some poor git who keeps his brains in his trousers – which accounts for most men . . . And did yer see that mangy bit of fur hanging round her neck? Huh! There'll be some poor cats going about with their arses hanging out tonight. Oh, my Gawd! What are we gonna do? 'Cos I'll tell you this much, I won't be able to stick it under the same roof with a woman like that. One of us'll have to go 'cos . . .'

'Don't talk daft, Nan. You're going to have to lump it like the rest of us; we don't have any choice.' Violet, a cigarette between red-painted lips, stared hard at her grandmother. 'Like Uncle Danny's so forcefully pointed out, this is his house now, and we're just the boarders. Oh, I know he'd never throw us on to the streets, but he's not going to be here, is he? And there's always the possibility that he might not come back. So . . .' Raising her eyes to the ceiling, she said bitingly, 'Unless we all want to find new homes, I suggest we keep that in mind when dealing with the new Mrs Donnelly, because she doesn't strike me as the sort who would put up with being treated like dirt in her own home.' With this parting shot, Violet left the room in a cloud of perfume, her heels clicking on the kitchen lino before being muffled by the hall carpet.

All the aggression seemed to seep from Aggie's large frame as with anxious eyes she appealed to her remaining granddaughters: 'He wouldn't let that tart chuck us out, would he? I mean, I know your uncle's a bit soft, but he wouldn't stand for that, not Danny. He'd never choose a loose bit of fluff over his own flesh an' blood . . . No. No! I don't believe it.' But there was a sudden lack of certainty in her voice, which Grace and Polly were quick to notice. Yet there was nothing they could do to comfort the elderly woman.

The sound of footsteps overhead brought their eyes upwards, and each wondered what was going on upstairs.

'Well, what do you think, darling?' Danny, his face split into a wide beam of pleasure, watched as his wife inspected his rooms.

First Beryl had looked at the bedroom, with its comfortable wide bed covered in a silk padded quilt, its double wardrobe and chest of drawers, all standing on a faded but good-quality patterned carpet. Walking slowly into the adjoining room she saw two green armchairs – a bit the worse for wear but, like the rest of the furniture, of good quality – stood either side of a long, highly polished coffee table, on which rested a small, tidy stack of magazines. Over in the corner was a walnut bookcase, filled with hardback books of all descriptions. Not much of a reader herself, except for trashy magazines, Beryl passed the bookshelf disinterestedly, stopping by a gramophone resting against the wall, and the small stack of records piled neatly in the corner on a small sideboard.

She kicked off her shoes and, making herself comfortable in one of the armchairs, she lit a cigarette. Narrowing her eyes up through the smoke, she thought quickly. It was a lot better than she'd hoped for, but if those cows downstairs thought she was going to stay cooped up here once Danny had gone back overseas, then they had another think coming. Raising her gaze she looked at her husband, who was anxiously awaiting her approval. Poor bastard! He looked as though he'd just shown her around Buckingham Palace, though compared to the flat she'd been living in, this was a palace. And it was all hers. But Christ! She had earned it. Not for having to share Danny's bed – that was no hardship to a woman like her; five minutes and it was all over. No! That had been the easy part. It had proved more difficult getting Danny to agree to a quick wedding. He had gone on and on about it not being proper getting married in a register office, and how he wanted to wait until his next leave so they could get married in a church – and a Catholic church to boot. For a mild man, Danny could be remarkably stubborn when he wanted to be. She had had her work cut out there, but eventually she'd had her way. Though she'd had to do all the necessary running about to obtain a special licence. All Danny had had to do was turn up. But it had all been worth it. She was now set up for life.

She spread her generous lips into an inviting smile and beckoned her new husband over, and like a boisterous puppy he bounded gratefully to her side.

As she held the plump body in her arms, Beryl gazed over Danny's shoulders in amusement. Let him have this last night thinking he was a real man. It wasn't worth making a fuss at this late date. He'd already shown he had some guts by facing up to that old harridan downstairs; she didn't want to take the chance he might direct some of that strength at her if she showed her true colours now.

Drawing him down further into her voluptuous bosom, she smiled inwardly. She'd done it. She had a smashing house and Danny's pay to look forward to. Life was going to be a lot easier from hereonin. And if something happened to her new husband . . . Well, wouldn't that be too bad. And it could easily happen. After all, there was a war on!

CHAPTER FOURTEEN

During the run-up to the second Christmas at war, the Blitz on London and the East End lessened, although Manchester and Liverpool suffered considerably from heavy raids. The people of the beleaguered East End began to hope they would be able to enjoy a Christmas without the dreaded air-raid siren spoiling the festivities. And in this their hopes were granted. Christmas Eve saw the beginning of an unofficial truce in the *Luftwaffe*'s aerial-bombing campaign, and on Christmas Day families sat down in peace to enjoy their dinner of meat or poultry, which they had managed to buy or find from dubious sources, accompanied by vegetables many had grown themselves, and followed by a rare treat of a Christmas pudding made with precious eggs and fruit hoarded for the occasion. Those less fortunate had to make do with puddings made with dried egg and grated carrots, parsnip or mashed potatoes. Yet even these were consumed gratefully in the peaceful lull, a lull that lasted through Boxing Day – and was savagely shattered on 27 December when another major attack on London brought an end to the Christmas peace and left around 600 people dead or injured in its ferocious wake. There followed a quiet weekend, giving the people of the East End a brief respite to catch their breaths before the next onslaught. But it was the City that became the next victim in Hitler's passionate desire to bring London to its knees. On Sunday evening between six pm and nine thirty pm, the *Luftwaffe* dropped 127 tons of HE and more than 10,000 incendiary bombs, starting a series of massive fires which threatened to turn the City into one huge conflagration. But while the German bombers could destroy buildings, they couldn't destroy or dampen London's fierce spirit for survival.

When Grace arrived at the tube station on the Monday morning, she found the station closed. Undaunted, she, along with dozens of others in the same boat, set off on the long walk to the City, all cheerful, all determined to get to work come what may.

'What a bleeding performance, eh?' The young cockney woman who had accompanied Grace on the hazardous journey grinned cheerfully. 'I only hope me firm's still in one piece. I heard the whole of the City got a right pasting last night. Bastard Germans!'

As they picked their way carefully over piles of rubble that lay in nearly every street, the two women chatted amiably until they came into sight of St Paul's.

'Well, at least the buggers didn't get the cathedral, thank Gawd. Anyway, this is were I turn off. Nice meeting you, Grace. Hope your building's still there – and mine.' The woman crossed her fingers and gave Grace another reassuring grin before they went their separate ways.

Readjusting her gas-mask case over the padded shoulder of her blue swagger coat, Grace carried on walking down Cheapside, her anger growing as she picked her way carefully through streets lined with fire hoses and past smouldering buildings still emitting choking black clouds of smoke. Mingled with her rage at the wanton destruction wrought by the enemy bombers was pride and admiration for her fellow countrymen. It was truly heartening to see and hear their good humour flourishing in such devastating circumstances. Some banks remained closed due to fires still unchecked nearby, but their staff were waiting patiently outside to begin work as soon as the doors reopened. Groups of firefighters, their filthy faces lined with exhaustion from their heroic efforts to combat the infernoes, were wearily rolling up the mountain of hoses to be replaced on their fire engines ready for the next onslaught. Grace's heart went out to them all. One fireman, resting his aching body against a crumbling wall, looked up as Grace passed and emitted a soft whistle. Beneath his steel helmet was a face streaked with soot and grime, and eyes almost dead from lack of sleep, but still the valiant man managed to ask, 'Wotcher, darlin', fancy coming out for a drink tonight?'

A surge of emotion tightened Grace's throat. Going over to where he lay, she smiled broadly.

'Can I bring my husband and six kids with me? They'd enjoy a night out.'

The man grinned back. 'If you're paying, yer can bring your whole bleeding family. But let's make it another time, eh, love? I'm gonna rest me eyes for a bit; I was working late last night . . .' Even before he finished the sentence the man's eyes fluttered and closed, his head falling to one side as he slipped into an exhausted sleep.

Grace walked on, her fingers crossed that her building has escaped the previous night's blitz.

Finding the narrow road to her office block impassable, Grace took yet another detour trying to avoid the spray from a hose lying unattended amid the debris. Then her heart seemed to come up into her mouth as she looked aghast at the huge, empty space where her offices had once stood. All that remained was a smoking, smouldering pile of bricks and mortar.

'Oh, no!' A low moan emitted from her lips. Then her

attention was caught by the sound of her name being shouted frantically. Raising her head she saw Jimmy Potter, the office junior, running towards her, his face lit up with excitement.

'Cor blimey, what a palaver. I couldn't believe me eyes when I got here. It's like those newsreels you see at the pictures, ain't it? I mean, I've seen plenty of bombed houses and shops since it all started, but never nothing as bad as this. Looks like Hitler meant to wipe out the whole city, don't it?'

Bemused, Grace could only continue to shake her head in a daze.

'Old man Laughton's here, an' the other guv'nors from the rest of the building . . . Huh! I mean what used to be the building. There's a couple of girls from the typing pool here an' all. C'mon, Grace, come over with the rest of us and find out what's gonna happen – I mean about our jobs. Looks like we're outta work, Grace. It don't bother me much, 'cos I'm gonna join up. Me mum's been trying to stop me, but I reckon she'll be all right about it now I've lost me job. At least I'll still be able to pay her some housekeeping if I join up an'—'

'Be quiet, Jimmy!' Grace spoke brusquely as she pushed past the abashed young man.

Jimmy, a look of embarrassment replacing his excitement, hurried after the slim figure, anxious to redeem himself in Grace's eyes.

Walking hurriedly alongside, he said in a calmer voice, 'Could you come an' have a word with Gert and June, please, Miss Donnelly. They're in a bit of a state. Not crying or making a fuss or anything like that, just sort of like shocked. They don't know whether to stay here or go back home, an' Mr Laughton's busy with the other guv'nors and the police.'

Grace had never taken to either Gert or June, the two younger typists: they were much too sure of themselves for Grace's liking. But when she saw them sitting atop a pile of rubble, their normally pert faces now looking dazed and lost, Grace immediately tried to comfort them.

'Oh, Miss Donnelly,' Gert said as she got unsteadily to her feet. 'Isn't it awful? Poor Mr Laughton's lost his business; he looked dreadful when he arrived and saw the damage. I felt so sorry for him.'

Her friend June now joined in, saying, 'What shall we do, Miss Donnelly? It doesn't look like there's much point in hanging around here, does it? I mean we're not going to get much work done today, are we . . . ?' She ended on a nervous laugh.

Grace patted her shoulder absently. 'Just stay where you are, both of you, and I'll see if I can find out anything. Though, like you said, there doesn't seem to be much point in staying.'

Leaving the girls with Jimmy, Grace made her way to where Harry Laughton was standing with two men she knew from the other offices, and, waiting until he caught sight of her and moved away from his colleagues, she said sympathetically, 'I'm so sorry, Mr Laughton. I don't know what to say really. Is there anything I can do for you?'

Harry Laughton shook his head tiredly and smiled ruefully.

'Thanks, Grace, but there's nothing to be done today. I'll stay here and see when I can get relocated, but there won't be much happening today. Maybe not for weeks. There are a lot of us in the same boat. You get yourself off home and I'll get in touch as soon as I have some news for you . . . Oh, and could you tell the others as well?' he added, nodding towards where his depleted staff sat waiting for instructions.

Anxious to help in any way she could, Grace said quickly, 'Of course I will. And, please, if there's anything I can do to help, let me know, won't you?'

But Harry Laughton had already turned back to his fellow businessmen, each one trying to develop contingency plans that had been made early on in the war for just such an occasion.

Seeing there was nothing to do here, Grace made her way back to where Jimmy and the two typists were eagerly awaiting news.

'I'm sorry. There's nothing much I can tell you, except to go home and wait until Mr Laughton gets in touch with us.' Grace hesitated, wondering if she should tell them what she knew. When war had first been declared, Harry Laughton had confided in Grace that if Germany bombed the City, he, like many other small businessess, wouldn't be able to afford to set up again in London, and would probably have to transfer the offices to the bigger, safer cities. When Grace had asked if he had any particular place in mind, Harry Laughton had told her he had a brother in business in Hampshire, and if the worse happened, he would probably transfer his business there. Grace didn't know if that plan was still on the cards, but she did know that neither she nor any of the others would be able to take up their old jobs if Mr Laughton moved so far away.

Gert and June looked to each other for support, then, as if of one accord, they shrugged.

'Well, thanks for trying, Miss Donnelly,' said Gert, 'but I think we'll stick around for a while until Mr Laughton has time to talk to us himself – no offence!'

'None taken,' Grace replied as she turned to leave.

Then she remembered Jimmy.

'Will you walk with me a bit, Jimmy? That's if you've nothing better to do.'

The gangly youth bounded to her side, relieved she was no longer cross with him.

Tucking her arm through his, more to help clamber over

the mountains of rubble that littered the pavements than any form of affection, Grace said, 'Sorry I was so short with you earlier, Jimmy, but it was a hell of a shock to find the entire street gutted. I know we've been half expecting it since the war started, but you never think it will really happen. Between you and me, I don't think Mr Laughton will start up again in London, it's too risky. But don't take that information as gospel. It's just something Mr Laughton said to me when the war started. As for now . . . I'm as much in the dark as you. Anyway . . .' She gave his arm a squeeze. 'What were you saying about joining up? You're too young yet, Jimmy, so don't go rushing to get yourself killed.'

Pushing back the brim of his cloth cap, Jimmy, his face unusually serious, looked at Grace, and said earnestly, 'I could just as easily get killed here, Grace. Half of me street was bombed two nights ago, an' there was seven people copped it. I didn't know them all that well – you know what it's like, say good morning, or bloody weather, that kind of thing, but them going like that . . . It shook me up, Grace. Made me realise how any of us could go just like that. It made me mum stop an' think an' all. She still ain't keen for me to join up, but she ain't as dead set against it like she was before the Blitz started. Me dad says I ought to go. He was in the last one, and he says if a bullet or bomb's got your name on it, then there's no point trying to dodge it.' A slow, almost frightened smile came to his lips. 'I'll tell you a secret, Grace. All me talk of joining up and fighting the Hun, well, I mean all that, but every time that siren goes it scares the sh – I mean, it really frightens me. But I'm still gonna enlist. I'll be eighteen next month, and I ain't gonna waste time trying to get another job as an office boy, not when I could be doing a man's job,' he finished lamely and Grace's heart went out to him. In that moment she knew she would probably never see him again and impulsively bent over and kissed his cheek.

'Bye, Jimmy. I hope I'll see you again, but if not . . . Well! Good luck.'

The youth's eyes reddened suddenly and he coughed to hide his emotion, saying, 'This bloody smoke's everywhere. I'm gonna see if I can get a cuppa off of the Red Cross. They've been handing it out all morning. I've already had one, but I don't suppose they'll know if I go back for another.'

Suddenly awkward, Jimmy shuffled his feet, the toe of his shoe kicking up pebbles of dirt. Quick to notice the young lad was nearly on the point of tears, Grace, who was also starting to feel emotional, said briskly, 'I don't suppose they'll notice. Anyway, I'm off home. Goodbye, Jimmy. And like I said before, good luck.'

She left him staring after her, the way he had done many times before. But this time Jimmy knew it might be the last time he would ever see Grace. Giving his eyes a surreptitious wipe with the back of his hand, he went back to join the two girls, still waiting hopefully for news of their jobs.

And Grace, looking after his gangly figure through misted eyes, whispered huskily, 'Goodbye, Jimmy. May God watch over you and see you safely home.'

Walking quickly away, Grace waited until she was well out of sight of her former work colleagues before sinking down on a lump of rubble, her face held despairingly in her hands. With her defences down, the now-familiar rush of anxiety and deep fear came surging through her. She had experienced these same feelings repeatedly since the night of her parents' deaths. They would start in the middle of her stomach and work their way slowly up to her chest and throat. Once there she would feel a weakness overtake her, and in her mind she could see clearly a dark, welcoming tunnel waiting for her, beckoning her towards the blackness that would afford her the release from all the anguish and grief that remained locked up tight inside her, and which, up until now, she had managed to fight off. But now, with the devastation she had just witnessed, and the certain knowledge that she would never again make the journey to her place of work in the City, and see the same familiar faces surrounding her, her defences began to crumble.

Maybe she would have succumbed to the inviting blackness, where she would no longer have to try and fill every moment of her days, leaving her too drained to dwell on the fact that her beloved parents were dead, and the knowledge that they still lay buried amidst a pile of rubble, left to rot alongside strangers, instead of the serenity and dignity of a proper burial place. Maybe if a passing policeman hadn't stopped by her side, dropping to his knees in concern at her obvious distress, she would have slipped silently towards the dark tunnel of her mind, but as soon as she heard his deep, cockney voice ask anxiously, 'You all right, love? I mean ter say, d'yer need any help in getting back home?' her head snapped back on her shoulders, and, taking the constable's arm for support, she once again push down those feelings.

Looking up into the warm concern of the middle-aged man, Grace attempted to smile, saying, 'Thank you, but I'm quite all right now, honestly.'

Feeling the constable's eyes still on her retreating back, Grace climbed carefully over the mountain of bricks and broken shards of glass, holding a handkerchief over her mouth and nose to avoid breathing in the smoke and dust that filled the air around her, and began the long, arduous journey home.

CHAPTER FIFTEEN

Upon entering the house on her return, Grace hung her coat and hat on the hall stand and took a quick look at her reflection in the long mirror on the wall, then groaned. God, what a mess she looked. Her hair and clothes stank of smoke and her face looked like it hadn't seen a drop of water for weeks. She had a sudden longing for a hot bath – a proper bath with loads of bath crystals and piping-hot water up to her neck. Instead all she could look forward to was a measly five inches of water, the amount now allocated per person, or two if you were really patriotic, and a sprinkling of the last remaining crystals she had hidden away in her chest of drawers. Hidden because of Vi and Beryl, who had already depleted Grace's hoard of bathing luxuries. It wasn't that she was mean, but those two took liberties. Grace hadn't been surprised when Vi got pally with her new sister-in-law, for Beryl was cut from the same cloth. Not that Vi was as common as Beryl, nor had she acquired a reputation, as yet. But working in a nightclub up West wasn't, to Grace's way of thinking, the most respectable of jobs. Still, it was Vi's choice, and seeing as she herself was now out of work, she hadn't any right to criticise her sister, not when Violet was the only one bringing money into the house.

Nevertheless, Grace worried about her sister. Since starting her new job she had become even more outrageous in her behaviour. Sometimes she didn't come home for days at a time, and when she did she offered no explanation for her absence. And Aggie, that once fierce matriarch, had long since stopped trying to curb her spirited granddaughter's nefarious activities. Then there was Beryl, her despised sister-in-law, who now stuck to Vi like glue, hoping no doubt that some of Vi's glamour and popularity with the men would rub off on her. Not that Vi seemed to mind; both women liked a good time, it was something they had in common – and common was the right term for Beryl. If Vi didn't watch out, she would find her name linked to Beryl's, in more ways than by marriage.

Tucking a lock of dirty hair behind her ear, Grace walked slowly down the hallway towards the kitchen, then stopped in startled amazement as the sound of laughter came roaring from the sitting room. It wasn't the usual polite laughter or false gaiety that had replaced the natural enthusiasm the house used to ring with; this laughter was genuine, and loud. The kind of laughter only her nan could make. Then Grace's eyebrows arched even higher, for along with the raucous sound of Aggie was the pealing laughter of Polly – Polly who had barely smiled since the death of her parents.

Her face creased into lines of puzzlement, Grace hurried towards the sound. As she flung open the door she heard a man's voice crying loudly, 'I tell you it's true. As true as I'm sitting here. If you're in the army you get three sheets of toilet paper each time you go. One up, one down, and one to polish . . . Honest!'

'Get outta it, you daft bugger . . . Oh! Gracie. What you doing back home?' Aggie, tears of merriment running down her fat face, turned to where Grace was standing, stunned, in the doorway. The sound of her grandmother's voice brought Grace back to earth. Moving into the room, she walked over and kissed Aggie's cheek.

'We've been bombed out, Nan. I'm surprised you didn't already know. There must have been something on the wireless this morning after I left.'

Still wiping her streaming eyes, Aggie said, 'Yeah, it did say the City had copped a bellyful, but it ain't all gone, has it?' The elderly woman gazed in anticipation at Grace.

'No, most of it's still standing, but my office got a direct hit. There's nothing left but a pile of rubble. It's like a mad-house up there . . .' Shifting around to where the dark-haired man, fully dressed in the smart dark blue airforce uniform, sat idly in the armchair, Grace, aware of her pounding heart, said almost shyly, 'Hello, Nobby. When did you get here?'

Nobby Clark, his handsome face suntanned, leant forward, his hands resting on his knees, and grinned.

'Just after you left. Which is a shame. I could've saved you a journey. After that raid last night, I'm surprised anything's standing. It's lucky the weather was so bad, otherwise the bastards would've done more damage. As it was, it was a deliberate attempt to set the whole of the City on fire. And they nearly succeeded. A few of us went up after them, but all we could do was scatter them a bit.'

'You were up there?' Polly was staring at the uniformed man, her face filled with awe.

Grace, watching her youngest sister intently, noted how different Polly was when there was a man around the house. First with Stanley and Danny, and now Nobby Clark. It seemed only the men had the power to buoy up Polly's spirits and quell her terror of the chaos in which they now lived. Out of Sam's three daughters, it was Polly who had been a proper daddy's girl, so it was understandable that she, more than her sisters, had come to rely on a male figure to lean on.

Glancing back at Nobby, Grace admitted that out of the three men who had visited them since the tragedy of their parents' deaths, only Nobby came close to possessing her father's strength of character. You could almost feel the power of the man, the comforting presence he engendered just by being here. Yet as her rapidly pounding heart reminded her, it wasn't just comfort Nobby Clark represented. *Oh, don't be so daft*, she chided herself. He's a good-looking bloke. Even in civvies he would turn heads, but add to that the glamour of the RAF uniform, and he must have the women falling all over themselves to get at him.

'I was very sorry to hear about Sam and Hetty, Grace.' Nobby was addressing Grace now, his face sombre. 'I didn't know or I wouldn't have intruded on you all. I know I met them only for a few hours, but I took to them straight away. They were nice people. It must've been very difficult for you all.'

As always, at the mention of her parents, Grace's throat tightened, a rush of emotion threatening to overwhelm her. Polly too began to weep silently and Aggie cleared her throat furiously to hide her feelings.

'I'm sorry. I shouldn't've come. Look, I'll be on me way an'—'

'No . . . Oh, no, don't go, lad.' Aggie was the first to protest.

Then Grace added her voice: 'Nan's right, Nobby, don't go, please. You're the first person who's made us laugh and forget it all since it happened.' Which was an insult to Stanley and Danny, but Grace was finding it increasingly difficult to care about Stanley's feelings, and her silent betrayal of the man she had once loved was deeply disturbing to her.

'Well . . . If you're sure I'm not putting you out.'

'Don't be silly . . .'

'. . . Of course you're not putting us out . . .'

'. . . Oh, don't go, Nobby, please.'

All three women seemed to speak at the same time, causing them all to laugh with relief.

Nobby looked at the women facing him, and the hopeful, anxious faces told their own story. It was only his second time meeting them, but he felt, as he had that first night, as if he'd known the Donnelly family all of his life.

Slapping her knees triumphantly, Aggie bawled happily, 'Right then, that's settled.' Heaving herself from the armchair, she looked down at the young man. 'You're staying for dinner, and supper an' all if you've got time. I've managed to get a couple of pieces of liver and a few bits of streaky bacon. It ain't much, but mixed up with some onions and mashed potatoes, it'll go down a treat.'

Happily bustling from the room Aggie strode down to the kitchen, her step lighter than it had been in ages. She took a small parcel wrapped in brown paper from the larder and unwrapped the precious liver and bacon, her nose wrinkling suspiciously. Rene had brought it by early this morning, tapping her nose and winking, 'Ask me no questions, an' I'll tell you no lies. That'll be a bob, please, Aggie.'

Aggie had paid up gratefully, thinking it would save her legs queuing for her weekly rations from the butcher in Well Street. Now she wasn't so sure. The bacon was mostly fat, and the liver appeared to be a funny colour. Come to think of it, she hadn't seen the ginger tom outside Benji's for a while! Chuckling at her own joke, Aggie looked through the open door down the hallway, from where she could hear clearly Nobby's deep voice. Then she heard Polly laughing, the clear, tinkling laugh Aggie had almost forgotten, coupled with the softer laughter of Grace. Oh, wouldn't it be lovely if he could stay a few days! Nobby Clark was better than all the tonics and tranquillizers handed out by harassed doctors in these trying times. If only her Gracie had picked someone like Nobby instead of Stanley Slater . . . !

Aggie gazed into space, her expression thoughtful. Things weren't right between Grace and Stanley. She hadn't noticed it when Stanley had first arrived home. They'd all been overjoyed at seeing him turn up unexpectedly on the doorstep, herself included. But once the euphoria had subsided there had been a marked difference in the way Grace had acted towards her fiancé. And the morning he'd left it had seemed as if Gracie couldn't wait to get away from him. When she'd asked her granddaughter if there was anything wrong, Grace had laughed it off, claiming everything was fine. But Aggie sensed something different. Any further doubt had been dispelled the minute Grace had walked in the sitting room and seen their visitor. The way Grace's face had lit up on seeing Nobby told its own story. A worried frown crossed over the fat face. If what she suspected was true, then there was bound to be trouble. Nobby Clark wasn't the kind of man to take no for an answer, and if he was after Grace he wasn't going to be put off by an absent fiancé.

As Aggie placed the liver and bacon into a pan of sizzling fat, her face took on a determined expression. Well! If that's the way things were shaping up, she certainly wasn't going to put her oar in. She had never thought Stanley good enough for her Gracie, but Nobby Clark . . . Now there was a man worthy of any woman, and he couldn't find better than her Gracie. Humming under her breath, Aggie turned her concentration to the dinner.

Once again Grace found herself standing outside the house with Nobby Clark, but this time there was no reassuring light from the hallway to protect her. Even as she said softly, 'Thanks for a lovely evening, Nobby. You've really cheered us all up,' the words seemed to echo those she'd spoken to him over a year ago.

That evening, too, had seen the family strained, and it had been Nobby who had brought them all back together with his unflagging humour and charismatic charm. As on that occasion, tonight Nobby had taken them to the pub for a few hours, and for Aggie, who hadn't been out for a drink since the start of the Blitz, it had been a much-needed outing. Even Polly had left the security of the basement to venture out on the streets, such was the overpowering personality of the man by their side. Now, at eleven o'clock, both Aggie and Polly had settled down for the night in the basement, with Grace saying she'd wait up for Vi and Beryl. Not that anyone was concerned about Beryl's whereabouts, but Grace liked to know Vi was home safe, that is when she deigned to come home at all – though to be fair to her sister, Vi did normally phone if she intended staying out all night. Plus tonight it gave Grace the perfect excuse to spend some extra time alone with Nobby. Sitting side by side on the top step, Grace wrapped up in her grey winter coat, and Nobby looking like an advertisement for the RAF in his thick navy coat and peaked cap, they looked the perfect couple. With only the stars for illumination in the blackout, Grace could feel Nobby's presence enveloping her like a shroud, wrapping her up in a cocoon of security. It was a wonderful feeling, and one she was wishing would go on for ever.

'There! I told you there wouldn't be any raid tonight. The weather's too bad for flying.'

Nobby smiled into the darkness, his breath coming out in puffs of cold air in front of Grace's face. They could barely see each other, but they felt the heat from their bodies mingling. The intimacy generated from such close proximity was causing Grace some uneasiness, but she made no move to leave Nobby's side.

The young couple had been chatting amicably for nearly half an hour, when Nobby, the tone of his voice changing, said somberly, 'You know, one of the worse sayings in the world – to me that is – is "I know how you feel", when usually the person saying it hasn't got a clue. But I *do* know how you're feeling, Gracie. That's the reason I've come home. I didn't say anything to the others, but my mum and dad were killed in much the same way as yours were. They were in the shelter in the garden when it took a direct hit. There were six of them in it when the bomb dropped – Mum and Dad and four of our neighbours. Some of our other neighbours told me that when the fire brigade and the wardens turned up they said there was no hope of anyone being left alive and so no point in trying to get them out. A couple of the neighbours tried to shift the rubble off the shelter, then another raid started and they had to leave it. When they came back out the same spot had been bombed again. There was absolutely nothing left of the garden, or the house, and half the street had copped it as well.'

Her heart full, Grace leant closer.

'Oh, Nobby, I'm so sorry. I had no idea. Why didn't you say something?'

In the darkness Nobby shrugged, his body now slumped in dejection, the grief he had hidden so well all day now welling up inside him.

'What'd be the point? You all had enough on your plate without me telling you me own problems.'

The feelings Grace had been fighting all evening now came dangerously close to bubbling to the surface. Touching his arm gently she murmured, 'Nobby!'

He turned and gazed down at the shadowy face so close to his then moved his head closer, and Grace's heart seemed to stop beating. Ignoring the warning voices in her head she lifted her face to his and when his lips came down on hers the world and everything around them disappeared. There was no war, no problems, no one to care about, no Stanley, no guilt. Nothing existed except the presence of this man whose lips and arms were conjuring up feelings she had never experienced before.

The magic of the moment was rudely shattered by the sound of high-pitched giggling and the clicking of high heels unsteadily approaching them.

'That you, Grace?' Violet's voice pierced the night, high with drunken gaiety.

Startled and suddenly flustered, Grace tried to pull away from Nobby's embrace but he held her firm. Clearing her throat she stuttered wildly, 'Yes, it's me. Look, Vi . . . Look who's come to visit us.' Grace could hear her voice rising and cursed herself for acting like a schoolgirl caught out in some playground misdemeanour.

Vi tottered closer, her eyes squinting into the gloom, trying to make out the shadowy figure with her sister.

'That you, Stan? I thought you'd gone back overseas. You can't have got another leave already . . . Ooh . . . !'

'Hello, Vi. Grace has been telling me about your new job. Bet it's a change from serving behind a counter in Mason's.'

Staggering up the steps, Vi plopped down on the cold stone step beside the uniformed figure.

'Well, well, look who it is. Nobby Clark. The Brylcreem boy himself. If you've come looking for your friend Stanley, you're too late. The dashing hero's already departed to fight the dreaded Hun . . . Unless it was someone else you came to see!'

Grace stirred anxiously. Violet sober was a handful. Violet drunk was impossible.

Angry at Violet, and more so at herself, Grace said angrily, 'Get yourself in the house, Vi. You're drunk . . . And where's Beryl? I thought I heard the two of you staggering up the road, unless she's passed out in the gutter. It wouldn't be the first time.'

Vi rolled her eyes mockingly. 'Ooh! Aren't we the miss prim and proper.' Clutching at the heavy overcoat of the silent man, Vi giggled. 'She's talking about our new sister-in-law, Nobby. A bit on the rough side, is Beryl, but she knows how to have a good time.' She waved her arm drunkenly, gesturing into the darkness. 'She was behind me a minute ago.' Then she lowered her voice dramatically, whispering, 'She's with a friend, a very nice soldier, but don't tell Grace, she wouldn't approve. Our Gracie hasn't got any vices, Nobby. I keep telling her, we could all be blown to bits any minute, but she won't take any notice. Good old Gracie. Always the model of respectability, always the golden girl, everyone's favourite . . .' Vi's voice trailed off, suddenly weary.

The change in her sister's tone wasn't lost on Grace. Disengaging herself from Nobby's grasp, she got to her feet. Holding out her hand she said, softer now, 'Come on, Vi. I'll help you in. You can—'

Vi's arm shot out, brushing away the helping hand roughly.

'I don't need any help, thank you.' Getting unsteadily to her feet, Vi peered down at the shrouded figure of the well-built man and said sneeringly, 'Well, you won't be able to turn your nose up at me and Beryl any more, Grace. Because from where I'm standing, you aren't any better than either of us.'

Mortified, Grace watched her sister stagger into the house, then leant against the stone pillar, her head drooping on to her chin. Vi was right. These past few months Grace had constantly remonstrated with Vi for her gadding about, and here was she, an engaged woman, falling into the arms of the first man to come along.

She heard Nobby scramble to his feet and instinctively shrank back from his touch. But Nobby wasn't a man to be put off lightly.

Laughing softly he took her arms. 'Don't take any notice of her, Grace. There's no comparison between the pair of you. She knows that as well as you do. She's just trying to justify herself. Though why she thinks she has to, I don't know. She's a grown woman who can do as she wants, and if she feels guilty about how she behaves, well, that's her problem, not yours.'

Grace moved uneasily. 'You'd better go, Nobby. I'm sorry if I've given you the wrong impression, but . . .'

The grip on her arms tightened. Then Nobby, no trace of amusement in his voice, growled, 'I didn't get the wrong impression, Grace. The first time I saw you with Stan I knew he wasn't right for you. And now you know it as well, so don't come that old cobblers with me.' When Grace's head dropped further down her chin, Nobby relented and relaxed his grip. Gently, he lifted Grace's chin with his finger, and whispered tenderly, 'You and me, we're right for each other, Grace. I've fallen for you, and I think you feel the same way. I'll go now, but I ain't giving up.'

When there was no reaction, Nobby's eyes narrowed and he stepped back. Pulling his peaked hat down over his eyes, he turned up the collar of his heavy overcoat, and said tersely, 'I've got four days' leave and I promised Aggie I'd call in tomorrow, an' I ain't gonna disappoint her. Whether you're in or not is up to you. Goodnight, Gracie.'

Then, like that night over a year ago, he gave a cheery wave and vanished into the night.

CHAPTER SIXTEEN

'Nan, I'm off out now. Do you want me to pick up anything?'

Grace was in the hallway bundling herself up in her
winter coat, hat and gloves in preparation for braving the
February wind.

Aggie, standing in the doorway of the library, a duster
in one hand and a tin of polish in the other, laughed.

'Yeah. I'll have two pounds of best steak, no fat, a pound
of bacon, two dozen eggs, a couple of pounds of butter and
sugar . . . Oh, and don't forget me tea. You'd best get me a
couple of packets, I don't want to run out . . . !'

Grace grinned happily.

'So, it's the usual, then?'

'Where you gonna try today, love?

'Oh, I thought I might ask around Liverpool Street. There
are plenty of offices there, trouble is, there are lots of women
like me in the same boat. Bombed out of one office and
looking for similar employment.'

Aggie nodded vigorously. 'Well, ain't that what I keep
telling you? You're wasting your time trying to get the same
sort of job you had before. All you're doing is wasting shoe

leather.' Pausing for breath, Aggie looked anxiously at her granddaughter. She hated to see Grace looking so worried, and the last thing she wanted was to add to Grace's problems, but the bald truth was that they needed another wage coming in. They had been living on the small life insurances paid out after Sam and Hetty's deaths, but that was nearly gone. And with Polly still too scared to venture far from home, and that lazy cow upstairs keeping all of Danny's army pay, they were in desperate need of funds. If it wasn't for Vi tipping up a regular amount of housekeeping, Aggie didn't know what they would have done.

A nagging unease rippled through Aggie's large frame, but was quickly squashed. So what if Vi had a job working in a nightclub? It was all perfectly decent and above board. All right, so she had gone off at the girl at first, but, as Vi had explained, she was only checking in the coats of the customers, and some of them were generous with tips, so where was the harm!

Aggie had refused to take any of Vi's money at first, but that stubborn pride had soon vanished. Now she lived in dread of Vi moving out and getting a flat somewhere away from the East End, though her granddaughter had so far shown no sign of wanting to leave – as long as she was left in peace to do as she pleased.

'You're probably right, Nan, but I have to try. If I've no luck today . . . well, then I'll have to think of something else. Maybe I could get set on in a factory. There's plenty of warwork going.' A mischievous smile lit up her face. 'And if I really get desperate, I can always take Benji up on his offer!' The elderly Jew in the corner shop had offered Grace a job weeks ago, an offer Grace had hastily refused, much to Aggie's annoyance.

'And what's wrong with that?' Aggie now demanded indignantly. 'You'd be near home with no bus or train fares to find, no hours spent trying to get to work, not knowing if the place'll still be standing when you get there. Oh, no, me girl . . .' She shook her grey head vigorously. 'I'd take the job meself if it was offered, and so would half the women in the street, but old Benji only offered the job to you 'cos he's always had a soft spot for you.'

Grace's eyebrows rose in surprise. 'Really! I've never noticed. I only go in there once in a blue moon, so I can't see how he can have a soft spot for me. Anyway, I'm off . . . Oh, I nearly forgot the ration books. Won't get much without those, will I?'

Aggie bustled into the kitchen to fetch the books, which Grace took and quickly left the house before her nan could say any more about her prospects of finding work. That is, the work she was used to. On the spur of the moment Grace changed direction and walked towards the end of the street where the small shop was situated on the corner. If anything it looked grimier than ever. If she ever did take a job here, the first thing she'd do would be to get a large bucket of water and soap flakes and give it a good clean. Never mind that the almost nightly bombing created clouds of smoke, dust and fumes, it was no excuse to be dirty. It was different for those people with their water supply cut off, but their street had been lucky so far. The water had only been off for a day at a time.

Shaking her head, Grace set off to wait on the corner of Well Street for the number six bus. While she waited she thought of the letters that lay in her bottom drawer at home, and experienced a moment's panic. What if someone should find them . . . ? Then she relaxed. Who was going to go to the trouble of searching her room? Laughing at herself she plunged her mittened hands further into the deep pockets of her coat, then she looked searchingly up the road for any sign of her bus. But the road was empty.

Grace stamped her feet then began pacing up and down, her thoughts whirling around her head. She had received two letters from Stanley in the past month, and three from Nobby in the space of two weeks. It was fortunate for her she was an early riser, else someone else might have picked up the letters for their Gracie from the mat and seen the strange handwriting.

As yet she hadn't replied to Nobby's letters, for the simple reason she didn't know what to write. With Stanley it was easier. She knew now she didn't love him any more, but that was something she would have to keep to herself until she could see him face to face. Until then the feelings she had for Nobby Clark would have to remain under wraps. But knowing he was stationed in England, and could turn up on her doorstep any moment, caused a ripple of excitement to run through her.

Oh, don't be so daft, she rebuked herself sternly, he's not going to be able to just drop everything and come calling whenever he felt like it. Not with the Blitz still raging and every fighter pilot on standby. There was no chance of another leave until the Blitz was over, and the Lord only knew when that would be.

When the bus turned up Grace had to stand all the way to Liverpool Street.

Four hours later she was on the same bus coming back.

The conductor, remembering her from earlier in the day, quipped, ''Ello, 'ello, you following me, love, and me married with eight kids . . .'

Weary though Grace was, the cockney conductor's cheery attitude raised her spirits immediately.

'Eight kids, eh? You've been doing your warwork then.'

The man grinned. 'I know, I know. It's hard work, but someone's gotta do it.'

Getting off at the bottom of Well Street, Grace stood in line for another hour for her meat rations. Then she had to join the dwindling queue outside the grocer's, but because of the lateness of the day, she came away empty-handed, her heart sinking at having to tell her nan there would be no tea today. Her feet were aching, she was tired, cold and hungry, and all for nothing. Maybe she would have better luck up Mare Street.

She was trying to decide what to do when a bus came along and, without thinking, Grace jumped aboard. At least she would save her aching feet from having to walk to the high street. Grace paid her fare, sat down, and leant back tiredly against the seat, fighting the desire to close her eyes for a moment's rest. It was only a short journey, a matter of three stops, and she didn't want to take the chance of falling asleep.

Maybe it was because she was so tired and it was beginning to get dark that Grace got off at the wrong stop. Whatever the reason, she walked up a side street, and, turning the corner into Mare Street, she found herself standing in front of the ruins that had once housed the Plaza cinema. As if a door had slammed shut in her face, Grace stood motionless, staring down at the heap of rubble. None of the family had come this way since the night Sam and Hetty had died, preferring to keep their loved ones alive in their minds, the way they had last seen them. And now, by either design or simple misfortune, Grace was staring down at the burial ground of her parents.

A swirling mist came down over her eyes as she tried to back away, tried to flee the awful scene, but her legs refused to obey her. A sudden high-pitched scream brought Grace's feet from underneath her, and then she was on her knees, her fingers pulling away the bricks and mortar that were her parents' grave, while the screaming went on and on. Her knees scraped and pouring with blood, as were her hands, she continued to scrabble among the debris, calling out frantically, 'It's all right, Mum. It's all right, Dad. It's me, Gracie. I'll get you out. Just hold on . . . Just hold on . . .' And still the screaming persisted from somewhere. Then hands were pulling at her, trying to stop her getting her parents out from beneath the debris. Only then did she realise that the screaming was coming from her own lips.

Viciously hitting out at the hands that were trying to pull her away, she cried piteously, 'Please, help me, someone help me.'

In the deepening gloom she could see a small crowd had gathered, their faces solemn and embarrassed at the young woman's raw grief. Trying to reassure them, Grace looked up and again cried, 'It's all right, I'm not mad . . . really I'm not . . . But my parents are buried under there. They might still be alive. Please . . .' She held out her bleeding hands in supplication. 'Please, won't anyone help me get them out?' Her eyes flickered from one face to another, and the men and women began to shift awkwardly, lowering their gazes, unable to witness the anguish in the young woman's tear-filled eyes. Then they could only watch helplessly as the woman turned her back on them and continued to claw amidst the ruins of the cinema.

It was then that three women stepped forward and dragged the screaming, fighting Gracie away, shouting, 'It's all right, ducks. Yer'll be fine. Just tell us where yer live an' we'll get yer safely back 'ome. C'mon, love, tell us where yer live, an . . .'

But Grace kept on screaming and lashing out at the restraining arms, until one of the women lifted her hand and brought it down sharply across Grace's face. Stunned, Grace could only look from one face to another in bewilderment. Why wouldn't they help her? Why wouldn't anyone help her? Then her inner voice screamed, *Because they're dead, you stupid bitch. They're dead and buried. They're dead, they're dead. They're never coming back . . . Never, never, ever . . .*

Her body now limp, Grace felt the darkness enfold her, then the rushing dark tunnel came spiralling towards her, and this time she was unable to fight it. Her head lolling back on her shoulders, she let herself slide down towards the darkness, and felt the velvety comfort of the black void softly surround her. With a soft sigh, she gave herself up to the comforting arms and sank into a place where no one could hurt her any more.

The hours turned into days, and the days into weeks as Grace drifted in and out of consciousness, her mind hovering between the real world and that other place, where it was warm and comforting and dark; where there were no worries, no heartache, and, most important of all, no responsibilities.

But Gracie's character was too strong to allow her to slip into total insanity. She was aware of her family sitting by her bedside, crying and coaxing her to come back to them, but she hadn't wanted to come back, to return to the agonies and turmoil of life.

Yet as the dark winter faded, and spring burst into being, bringing with it lighter, warmer days and a welcoming lift of spirits, Grace began her journey back to reality. Finally, she awoke from her long sleep and looked with clear eyes at her surroundings. She was in a room that contained only two beds, the other being empty, and as she struggled to sit up she became aware of the heady smell of freshly picked flowers, which adorned the room.

Blinking rapidly, she forced herself to sit upright, and as she did so, a nurse, her young fresh face beaming with delight, exclaimed, 'At last! We were beginning to think you were never going to wake up. Proper Rip Van Winkle you've been. All right for some, eh!'

Grace looked at the cheerful face with bemusement and tried to speak, but found she couldn't utter a word. Even if she had been capable of speech, she wouldn't have been able to get a word in as the nurse kept up a steady line of patter, until, seeming to run out of breath, she took hold of Grace's hand and, in a softer tone of voice said kindly, 'Oh, I am glad you're back with us.' Patting Grace's unresisting hand she added, 'I'd best go and tell the doctor you're awake, else he'll skin me alive for not letting him know straight away. You rest now, and I'll be back in a tick.'

True to her word, the nurse returned almost immediately with the doctor, who, like the nurse, seemed delighted to see her sitting upright and alert. He checked her pulse, then stuck a cold thermometer under her tongue, just as she was about to speak.

'Well, well, you've given us all a great deal of concern, not least your family – who should be bursting through the door at any minute.' He smiled as he checked his watch, his broad, blunt features stretched into a wide smile.

When the thermometer was removed and Grace was finally able to speak she asked haltingly, 'Are . . . are you a psychiatrist? And . . . and am I in a . . . a mental ward, or a pro . . . proper one?'

The doctor, seeing the sudden fear spring into the lovely eyes, took hold of her hand and, in a gentle but firm voice, answered, 'We don't have mental wards in this hospital, my dear. But yes, I am a psychiatrist. And before you say another word—' he interjected swiftly as he saw alarm flicker over the pale, attractive face, 'listen to me, Grace. You are not mad, and never have been. Just as we all suffer from physical illness at some time in our lives, many of us also suffer an illness of the mind; that doesn't make you mad, not in the sense you're referring to. In your case, your mind desperately needed rest, and anything could have set if off. Unfortunately for you, it was triggered off by a traumatic incident. You could just as easily have been having a good knees-up down your local pub when—'

'I don't normally go in for a good knees-up, as you put it, Doctor. But I just might let my inhibitions have a night off soon. I . . . I think it would do me a power of go

. . . good . . . Oh, dear . . . Oh, dear me, I'm so . . . sorry
. . . I . . . !'

As the nurse moved forward, the doctor silently shooed
her away, mouthing the words, 'Don't let the family in until
I tell you to, understand?' The fresh young face nodded
earnestly.

Even as the nurse was leaving the room, Grace could
hear Aggie's strident voice in the corridor, and instead of
feeling joy at the sound of her nan's voice, she experienced
a moment's panic and clutched at the doctor's hand, 'Please
. . . Please, I don't want to fa . . . face them yet. I'm sorry,
I ca . . . can't explain, but I . . . !'

'It's all right, Grace. I understand.' So saying he rose and
swiftly drew the dark green curtains across the windows
and shut the door firmly before returning to her side. He
pulled the bedside chair closer to the bed, and watched as
the fear faded from his patient's eyes and her taut body
relaxed. He understood only too well her fears at seeing
her family, for he had witnessed the same fear many times,
and understood the reason for it. For no matter how loving
a family – and Grace Donnelly did indeed have a loving
family, of that there was no doubt – human nature being
what is was, after the initial cries of relief and tears that followed the reunion, the family would, without realising it,
begin to assume that person was fully recovered. And before
too long they would begin to relate their own troubles, thus
replacing the burden of responsibility that had helped send
the unfortunate patient over the edge in the first place back
on them.

Gently stroking her hand, the kindly man asked softly, 'Do
you want to talk, Grace? I mean *really* talk, without having to
watch what you say, or worry about offending or upsetting
anyone? To talk about yourself, and what you want and
need, without feeling selfish for putting yourself first for a
change? Or would you rather I left you in peace?'

In answer, Grace gripped the strong hand tightly and, after a few quiet minutes, she began to talk.

She talked right through visiting hours, before falling into an exhausted sleep, and when she awoke, the doctor was still there, sitting by her bedside as though he had never left. And Grace began to talk again. And when the Donnelly family turned up at evening visiting time, they were once again, firmly but kindly, sent away. And still Grace talked, until dusk began to settle over the room and the side-light was lit as the nurses performed the nightly ritual of putting up the blackout shutters, before dispensing the night-time cocoa or hot chocolate, if they were fortunate enough to have some in the supply cabinet. The nightly drinks were normally made up with powdered milk, but for Grace, in this, her first night back in the land of the living, the nurses had scrounged some milk for her hot drink. And, after being helped to the toilet by two nurses, she climbed wearily but happily back into her bed, drank her hot beverage gratefully, clasped the tired doctor's hand warmly, then settled down for her first night's restful sleep since the war had begun.

'There yer go, love. Now, is there anything else I can get fer you, before I go out, or would you rather I stayed with you?'

Aggie, her fat face filled with love and concern, bustled around Grace, who, despite the warmth of the April sun, was bundled up with blankets on the settee, with three large pillows plumped up under her head.

Looking up into the dearly loved face, Grace smiled and said jovially, 'I'm fine, Nan, honest . . . And, Nan . . . now look, don't go taking offence, but I'm not an invalid, you know, and much as I appreciate all the attention and fuss, I feel like a fraud, lying around being waited on hand and foot when what I should be doing is getting off my backside and out into the world again, looking for a job.'

When there was no answer, Grace peered at Aggie's face, and was surprised and heartened to see the concern for her well-being mixed with relief.

'You sure, Gracie, love? Only I ain't gonna push yer into going back ter work, not if yer don't feel up ter it.'

'Oh, Nan, of course I'm up to it. My legs are still a bit wobbly, but if I could find something local . . .'

'Like Benji's . . . ?' Aggie asked almost fearfully. She knew only too well that her Gracie was worth more than working in a corner shop, but it would be a start, sort of get her used to being out and about. And old Benji was forever asking about Grace. The old boy was getting on and badly needed help running the shop, but he wouldn't take on just anybody, and had hinted many a time that he'd be only to happy to take Grace on. In the meantime Aggie had been helping out a few days a week. The money had come in useful, and she felt she was sort of keeping the job open for Grace should she decide to take it, before anyone else got their feet behind the counter – and there were many women in the street who would be only to glad to take on such a cushy job.

Grace, too, was thinking along the same lines. It wasn't the sort of job she was hoping for, but it would help get her back into the swing of things. Then later on, when she had fully recovered her strength and confidence, she would try again for the type of work for which she had been trained. She hitched herself up higher on the pillows and playfully smacked the back of Aggie's hand.

'If Benji still wants to take me on,' she said, 'then you can tell him I'll start on Monday. In the meantime, I'm getting off this settee, and out into the garden to get some sun on my face. I must look as if I've been buried and dug up again.' She laughed merrily.

At the sound of the old Grace laughing, Aggie's body slumped with relief. Then, her face wreathed with smiles, she said gaily, 'Well, I'd best be off then. Someone's got to do some work around here. I'll be back at dinner time; I'm only working the morning today.'

With a last hug, Aggie almost bounded from the room. When the front door slammed, Grace lay for a while before pushing back the suffocating blankets and swinging her legs over on to the carpeted floor. She still felt a bit unsteady on her feet, and she had lost a lot of weight during her illness, but that period in her life was behind her. Now she had to look to the future.

Once out in the garden she flopped into a large wicker chair and took out, for the umpteenth time, the letters from Stanley and Nobby from her pocket. Both men had been informed of her illness, but neither had been able to get any leave to visit her – and for that she was grateful. She was going to take the doctor's advice and concentrate on herself for the time being. She wasn't going to worry about either Nobby or Stanley, for each in their own way caused her anxiety, though both of them genuinely cared for her; she didn't want to be bothered with any form of hassle at the moment.

Deciding against re-reading the letters, she held up her face to the healing rays of the sun and relaxed, letting her mind dwell on the changes that had occurred during her absence. Vi was still working up West, but she had been spending more time at home while Grace had been in hospital, and since she had returned home. That wouldn't last once Grace was up and about again, but it had shown that despite her airs and graces, she still loved her family. Then there was Beryl – no change there. Her sister-in-law had carried on as usual, having a good time on her uncle Danny's money. But the biggest change had been in Polly. That once shy, timid girl had altered greatly, the reason being the company of Linda Castle, Rene's daughter, who had latched on to Polly and coaxed the frightened girl from the basement and out into the world again. They were both now working in the Mare Street branch of Woolworth's, and now the lighter evenings were back, Polly had actually been going out with Linda after work. Only to the social club down at the local church, and she was always home before dark, much to Linda Castle's annoyance, but at least she was going out, and that was the main thing. Before Grace's breakdown, she had imagined her younger sister would spend the duration of the war down in the basement. Grace gave a short laugh. The experience she had been through had been horrendous, but some good had come out of it, and with her nan back to her old belligerent self, it meant Grace had less to worry about, and that in itself would help speed her recovery. Shifting herself to a more comfortable position she closed her eyes and let her body relax, her mind drift aimlessly, and soon, despite her resolution to stay awake, she felt herself floating away into a restful sleep.

Surrounded by the salty smell of pickled herrings, overripe fruit and vegetables that were on the turn, Grace smiled at the last customer of the day, then locked the door, and turned the door sign to closed. As usual, minutes later there was a banging on the door accompanied by a pleading voice asking to be let in, a plea that Grace ignored. She had been working in the shop for only three weeks, but had soon learnt that if she let in one late customer, there would be another and another. In fact she would have been stuck in the shop until midnight if she had carried on being so soft.

When the banging finally ceased, Grace made her way to the back of the small shop, calling up the stairs, 'Benji, I'm off now. Do you need anything before I go?'

When there was no answer, Grace assumed the elderly man had fallen asleep, as he so often did, and was about to leave when she heard the shuffling, slippered footsteps on the stairs and waited by the door.

'Oy vey, Gracie, you should have woken me. I would

sleep my life away given the chance, and at my age that isn't a good thing.' Laughing at her employer's kindly face, Grace answered, 'Come on, Benji, you're not that old.'

Samuel Benjamin looked fondly at his assistant. Since Grace had started work, he had felt a giant weight lifted from his shoulders. At seventy-five, he no longer had the energy he had once possessed. He should have employed someone years ago, but had been afraid of being stuck with somebody who would have taken advantage of him, or helped themselves to his stock – or worse still, been light-fingered with the takings. With Grace he had no such misgivings; he trusted her implicitly.

'Wait a moment, leibchen,' he said softly as he disappeared into the back room. He returned with a small parcel and tapping the side of his nose, he whispered conspiratorially, 'Here's a little something extra for all your hard work, but don't tell anyone where you got them from, else I'll have a mob knocking down my doors.'

Grace peered into the bag and saw a packet of tea and a brown bag containing at least a pound of sugar. She leant down and kissed the withered face gratefully.

'Thanks, Benji. I appreciate it, and so will my nan. She does love her tea, bless her.'

'And why not! She's a good woman is Aggie. If she'd been twenty years younger I would have taken her on full time, but then I wouldn't have had the pleasure of your company.'

Slightly embarrassed, Grace coughed, said her goodbyes once more, and left the old man to lock up after her.

Grace hurried home, a bounce in her step as she anticipated the look on her nan's face when she handed over the small items that were like gold dust these days.

She bounded into the kitchen grinning from ear to ear and cried out, 'Nan! Nan, where are you? I've got a little treat for you. I—'

She stopped suddenly at the sight of her nan sitting at the large table, her face filled with anxiety. Grace's mouth turned dry with fear. Something had happened; something awful!

'Wha . . . what is it, Nan? What's happened?'

Aggie raised a fear-filled face to her granddaughter before saying in a trembling voice, 'I'm sorry, love. I . . . I should've brought it straight down the shop as soon as it arrived. But . . . but, I couldn't . . . I couldn't face you. I'm sorry, love, I'm really sorry . . .' Sniffing into a large handkerchief, Aggie blew her nose loudly before taking a long brown envelope from her apron pocket and reluctantly put it on to the table, averting her eyes as she did so.

For a long, agonising moment, Grace stared down wordlessly at the official-looking letter, her heart beating erratically.

'For Gawd's sake, Gracie, open it,' Aggie barked nervously, already guessing what it contained. It must be news about Stanley. If it had been concerning Danny, then the letter would have been addressed to Beryl.

With shaking hands Grace opened the envelope, her face turning white as she read the contents.

Seeing the blanched look spread over Grace's features, Aggie slumped down further in her chair, her fingers beating out a nervous tattoo on the wooden table. When Grace remained silent, Aggie's already frayed nerves snapped.

'Fer Gawd's sake, Gracie, what is it? What does it say?'

Grace tried to speak but found her vocal cords temporarily blocked. Then, clearing her throat loudly, she whispered hoarsely, 'Stanley's been captured. He's been declared a prisoner of war. He . . .' Her voice broke. 'Oh . . . Oh, Nan, poor Stanley. He'll never survive, he's not strong enough. Oh, Nan, Nan . . .'

Aggie, lumbering from her chair, gathered her granddaughter into her ample arms and found herself uttering

useless words of comfort. And while she was comforting Grace an unbidden thought sprang to her mind. Any
notion of her Grace getting together with Nobby Clark
were now well and truly scuppered. No sooner had the
thought crossed her mind than she felt a deep sense of
shame. Poor Stan. He wasn't a bad bloke, just weak and
immature. And as Grace had just said, a man such as
Stanley would have a hard time coping with the rigours
of a prisoner-of-war camp. Everything she had ever said
or thought about Grace's fiancé came back to haunt Aggie,
and she knew in that awful, gut-wrenching moment, that
if Stanley didn't survive the war, she would never forgive
herself for all the thoughtless, unkind words she had heaped
on the poor lad over the years.

CHAPTER SEVENTEEN

'Are me seams straight, Vi?' Beryl Donnelly twisted her head to check the black pencil line that ran from her heels to the top of her thighs. 'I can't see properly.'

Violet, already dressed for a night up West, put down the magazine she had been reading and glanced up from the bed.

'Yes, they look OK to me. Hurry up, Beryl, we'll never get out at this rate.'

Picking up a beaded evening bag, Beryl shrugged her arms into a fur coat of dubious origins and said, 'All right, keep your hair on. Gotta look me best, don't I? We can't all have film-star looks naturally.'

The grudging remark held no malice, simply fact. Vi, as usual, looked stunning. She was wearing a long midnight-blue dress and her mother's pearl earrings and necklace, an anniversary present bought for Hetty by Sam many years ago.

When the pair entered the dining room Aggie looked up first at her granddaughter, who looked like she'd just stepped off the big screen of a Hollywood movie, and then to the elder woman in a cheap black dress that ended just below her knees, a ton of make-up, huge paste diamond earrings, and the mangy fur coat, and snorted, 'Like I'm always saying, fur coat no knickers, that's you, Beryl Lovesett. It's written all over yer.'

Beryl's face froze. Tightening her blood-red lips she snarled, 'Listen, you old cow, don't push your luck. And it's Beryl Donnelly now, and don't you forget it. You keep forgetting this is my house while Danny's away, so you watch your mouth, or else you might find yourself out on the street.'

Vi stepped in to Aggie's defence.

'Leave off, Beryl. You're not going to throw anyone out. My uncle may be a bit soft, but he would never stand for that, and well you know it.'

With a look of grudging gratitude, Aggie looked up at Vi and said shortly, 'By the way, that Chris chap phoned again this afternoon. He left a number where you could reach him, only you'd better be quick, he's only got a three-day pass.' When Vi shrugged her shoulders and made to leave the room, Aggie bounded forward in her chair, her face and voice showing her exasperation. 'For Gawd's sake, girl, what's the matter with you? A nice fella like that falling over himself to see you, and you ain't even got the common courtesy to answer his calls.'

Violet, her face stony, picked up a black cashmere shawl and carefully placed it around her white shoulders.

'Look, Nan, I don't want to see him, all right? And if he had any sense, he'd have taken the hint by now. Anyway, I can't stand here chatting, or I'll be late for work.'

Aggie peered at her granddaughter through narrowed eyes.

'Bit dressed up for a hat-check girl, ain't yer, Vi? Course, not that I'd know anything about it, seeing as I've never been in a nightclub in me life, and never likely to either.'

Very slowly, Vi picked up her clutch bag and, without looking at her grandmother, said softly, 'I'm a grown woman, Nan, and answerable to no one, not even you. You get your housekeeping every week, don't you? But if you're that worried about my way of life, I can always move out.' Moving languidly towards the door, Vi added over her shoulder, 'I don't know what time I'll be home, so don't wait up.'

Behind her, Beryl directed a smile of pure malice at the elderly woman she loathed, saying sneeringly, 'Yeah, don't wait up, *Nan*, you wouldn't want to lose your beauty sleep, would you?'

But Aggie, shaking with rage, shouted after the retreating couple, 'I don't need it, not at my age, but by God, a couple of months sleep wouldn't do you any harm, you blowzy old tart.'

Any further retort from the furious Beryl was cut short by Vi, who quickly manhandled her sister-in-law from the house.

Alarmed to find she was trembling, Aggie rose stiffly and tottered over to the drinks cabinet, where she poured herself a good measure from the rapidly dwindling brandy bottle. After a couple of swallows, Aggie felt the warm liquid course through her body and she leant her head back on the antimacassar and closed her eyes restfully, glad for a bit of peace and quiet. But her contentment didn't last for long, for as always her thoughts returned to her granddaughters, and the constant worry of what was to become of them.

She had long stopped believing that tale Vi had first spun her about working as a hat-check girl. Aggie didn't know how much those women earned, but it certainly wasn't as much as Vi seemed to. The housekeeping money alone, which Vi gave her each week, was equal to a week's pay. Not that Aggie wasn't grateful, but it didn't stop her worrying, especially now she was hanging around with that old tart Danny had married. Yet even though Aggie wasn't sure what Vi did at that club she worked at, one thing she was sure of, and that was any money Vi earned was earned respectfully. Her middle granddaughter may have an eye for the men, but she was no tart. That much Aggie would bet her life on.

Raising her eyes upwards to where Grace and Polly were playing records in their room, Aggie gave a deep sigh. As much as she fretted about Vi's dubious lifestyle, she sometimes wished her other two granddaughters would get out a bit.

Since Hitler had deemed his plan to bring London and the south-east to its knees by the constant bombardment a failure, he had turned his attentions overseas, thus giving the much-beleaguered Londoners a chance to rebuild their bombed homes. But although London had come through the massive onslaught, the price paid had been terrible. During the Battle of Britain and the subsequent Blitz, 915 RAF aircraft had been lost, compared to 1,733 *Luftwaffe* planes. And though Aggie had little sympathy for the destruction of the German planes, she often thought that the pilots and crew, although the enemy, had still been men and young boys with families, only following orders, the same as their own lads.

The bombs still fell over London, but nothing as horrendous and unrelenting as those terrible days between September 1940 to May 1941.

Now it was October, and England maintained an optimistic spirit in public, while beneath its bravado there lurked a great anxiety, wondering what each new day would bring. Even posters of their formidable leader Churchill, which seemed to beam down from every street corner, failed to bring them any new hope. But every now and then, his broadcasts, delivered in a strong, resolute voice would momentarily lift the spirits of the war-weary populace and instill in it a new inspiration.

With autumn just around the corner, the news broadcast

from the BBC was decidedly gloomy. Tobruk and that tiny island Malta were under siege, added to which were the horror stories coming out about the atrocities committed in far-away countries such as Russia. According to the news reports, it wouldn't be long before the German tanks were at the very gates of Moscow. And still those bastard Americans refused to come to Europe's aid. Oh, some of them had sent their old cast-off guns to the Home Guard, a motley collection of out-of-date sporting guns and dilapidated tommy-guns, last used by Al Capone and his cronies, and for this magnanimous gesture they expected the people of England to fall on their knees with gratitude.

Then there were the rumours about concentration camps being set up in Germany to inter the Jews that Hitler despised so much.

As she shifted in her chair, Aggie tried to put the awful pictures from her mind. God knows they had enough problems of their own in this country without worrying about the fate of people thousands of miles away. Still . . . !

Aggie took another swallow of her brandy, looking regretfully at the small amount left in the bottom of her glass. For a few moments she was tempted to refill it, but decided against it. Who knew when she would he able to get her hands on another bottle? The one on the sideboard had been brought round by Chris, the officer who was still keen on Vi, despite the runaround she was giving him. Vi hadn't been home at the time, and Aggie had been reluctant to accept such a precious gift, but the young man, well, he was young in her eyes, though he must be in his early thirties – well anyway, he had insisted she take the small bottle of brandy. Oh, he was a nice man. As well as the brandy, he had brought with him eggs, bacon, sugar and tea, then apologised for not being able to bring more. Aggie had been profusive in her thanks, but wisely decided not to ask how he had come by such treasures. Likely he had raided the supply quarters at the army barracks, but Aggie wasn't about to ask any awkward questions.

Dancing footsteps overhead, accompanied by soft laughter, attracted Aggie's eyes to the ceiling and brought a smile to her wrinkled face. At least she always knew where Grace and Polly were in the evenings. Grace had virtually taken over the running of the corner shop, and, thanks to young Linda Castle, Polly was back at work. Not only that, but she had started to go out to the social club after work, although she still hadn't plucked up enough nerve to go out at night. Aggie had a great deal to be thankful to Rene's daughter for, but it had to be said, and Rene had said it herself, Linda was a flightly piece, her eyes always firmly fixed on any pair of trousers that passed her way. Then again, she was still very young, and Aggie didn't suppose there was any real harm in the girl. Even so, Aggie was always relieved when the nights drew in, and Polly was safely back home.

Aggie knocked back the last of her brandy, sighed and put the empty glass on the coffee table by her side. Then she smiled warmly as she picked up a framed newspaper clipping and gazed fondly at the grinning face of Nobby Clark. Nobby Clark the hero, a hero whom she regarded as a very dear friend. Pride swelled her body as she read for the hundredth time the account of Nobby's brave actions. He and his crew had been on the way back from a bombing raid over France, when three Messerschmitts had appeared out of nowhere over the Kent countryside. Caught by surprise, the small Mosquito aircraft had taken a direct hit to the wing tail, followed by a savage burst of gunfire on the left side of the plane. Nobby's navigator, Bill Williams, had taken two bullets to his chest. Somehow Nobby had kept the plane flying, although he knew it was only a matter of time before it crashed. But if they were going to go down, he was going to take some of those bastards with him. With expert skill, Nobby managed to evade the heavier aircraft and shoot down one, while badly crippling another, whereupon the remaining Messerschmitt moved in for the kill. Opening up with all guns blazing the German fighter hit the left wing of the smaller plane, and Nobby felt a sickening lurch in his stomach as the plane spiralled out of control and dropped like a stone towards the green countryside below. With only one wing intact and the tailgate on fire, Nobby miraculously managed to keep the plane from plummeting too fast. Without his expert skill both men would have been killed instantly. But the story didn't end there.

The plane caught fire, black, oily smoke pouring from the damaged engine rapidly filling the cockpit. It was only Nobby's immense skill that brought the plane down safely in a jerking, stomach-turning crash-landing.

Knowing he hadn't much time, Nobby had quickly unbuckled his safety harness and jumped from the blazing plane. But instead of running for cover, he raced around to the other side of the plane and dragged the seriously injured navigator from his seat.

They had barely moved a hundred yards when the small aircraft exploded, sending large chunks of metal hurtling through the air.

Three pieces had lodged in Nobby's body, one in his arm, one in his leg and another in the small of his back.

Two farmers, who had watched the fight in the skies, came running to Nobby and Bill's aid, but both men were beyond awareness of their saviours' presence.

Now, some six months later, Bill Williams was still in a military hospital, and would be for some months yet, but Nobby was back in Hackney, honourably discharged from the airforce and decorated with the DFM for his gallant action in saving his navigator's life at the risk of his own.

Aggie ran her fingers lovingly over the grainy picture. If only Stanley hadn't been captured, she was sure Nobby and Grace would have gotten together by now. But while poor Stanley was incarcerated in a POW camp neither of them would even contemplate such an alliance. Even she, Aggie, could understand their feelings. It would be the utmost betrayal to Stanley if Grace started a relationship with another man while he was suffering in such terrible conditions.

But that didn't mean Nobby couldn't come round and visit them as a friend, which he did often. It was one of the few bright moments in Aggie's life when she opened the door to his smiling face. He was now running two stalls, left to him by his late father, and by all accounts he was making a good living. But then who could resist those mischievous eyes and that cheeky grin, certainly not the women who frequented the markets. He had one stall in Roman Road market, which he ran on Tuesdays, Thursdays and Saturdays, and another one in Petticoat Lane on a Sunday morning. The other three days he spent building up his supplies. Aggie didn't know how to describe the nature of Nobby's stalls, for, like old Benji, he seemed to sell everything under the sun.

The sound of running feet down the stairs brought Aggie's mind back to the present. Looking up, she smiled at her granddaughters, gratified to see the happy, flushed smiles on their faces.

'Been having a good dance, 'ave yer? I thought you was gonna bring the ceiling down the way yer was clumping about.'

Grace came over and sat on the arm of Aggie's chair, her eyes immediately going to the photo Aggie held in her hand. As always, Grace's heart gave a painful leap when she saw Nobby's face, but she was always careful not to show her feelings.

'Vi and Beryl gone out already?' she asked quickly before her grandmother could start regaling Nobby's virtues.

Aggie snorted, all thoughts of Nobby temporarily forgotten.

'Yeah, they've gone out, thank goodness. If I had to spend any more time in that woman's company I wouldn't be responsible for me actions.'

Grace and Polly raised their eyebrows at each other over Aggie's grey head. They had no need to ask who their grandmother was talking about.

'God! That woman makes my blood boil,' Aggie stormed. 'For two pins I'd land her one right in the mouth. Whatever possessed Danny to take up with an old trollop like that . . . !'

Stroking the grey hair tenderly, Grace said softly, 'I don't know why you keep on getting at her, Nan. It won't do a blind bit of good. You're not going to drive someone like her out with words; she's too hard-faced for that.'

Shifting round in the armchair that barely contained her girth, Aggie wagged a finger under Grace's nose.

'I can't help it. Just looking at her gets me back up. Aw . . . what's the use.' She gave a heavy sigh and heaved herself up from the sagging chair. 'I'm gonna make some tea, d'yer want some?'

'No thanks, Nan.'

'What about you, love?' she asked Polly, who kept looking at the clock. They didn't go down to the cellar now until ten o'clock or until the siren went, whichever came first, and they had a good couple of hours before thinking about bedding down for the night. Yet Polly was showing no signs of anxiety; in fact she looked bored.

Polly declined her grandmother's offer of tea and when Aggie had left the room, Grace slid down on the sofa beside her sister, her mind racing furiously. What Polly needed to fully restore her confidence was a good night up West in a proper nightclub, instead of the drabness of the church's social club.

'*Oh, who are you trying to kid, Grace Donnelly?* she rebuked herself silently. *The fact is, you're bored and lonely and could do with a good night out, so don't go fooling yourself that it's Polly you're thinking about.*

Even so, she cleared her throat and asked hesitantly, 'Why don't me and you go out, Poll? Vi and Beryl are always having all the fun, so why don't we do the same? After all, it is Saturday night, so we don't have to worry about getting up in the morning. And it's not that late, is it? It's only just gone eight. What do you say, Poll?'

Polly's eyes widened in amazement, and Grace was quick to note the element of fear that had suddenly crept into them and the nervous plucking of the black skirt that covered Polly's knees.

'Oh, I don't know, Grace . . . I mean, I don't mind going out any more, you know that, but at night I . . . I still get a bit frightened. Sorry, Grace, I . . .'

Immediately ashamed for putting her sister into an awkward position, especially after the way she had progressed during the past months, Grace lowered her head in embarrassment. It had taken courage for Polly to leave the safety of the basement to go out and find a job, even with the ebullient Linda by her side. And she had started a social life again, albeit a small one. But both Aggie and Grace always noted the relief in Polly's eyes when she was back home and settled in for the night. Now here she was, trying to push Polly that one step further, instead of leaving her to build up her confidence in her own good time.

Patting Polly's knees, Grace rose, and, forcing a light note into her voice, said, 'It doesn't matter, Poll. It is a bit late to think of going out, after all. Maybe some other time, eh?'

Deep in her own thoughts, Polly nodded, her mind conjuring up images of the nightclubs Vi and Beryl were always raving about. It was a completely different life to her own, and even before Grace had brought up the subject, Polly had often lain awake at night wondering what it would be like to get really dressed up, put on a bit of make-up and wear the few pieces of jewellery she had accumulated on her birthdays over the years. Oh, it would be wonderful, if only she could muster the courage to actually do it. It would be different if they were going out in the company of a man, she wouldn't be so frightened then.

Shrugging her shoulders with regret she whispered to the empty room, 'I will do it; I will . . . But . . . but not just yet. Maybe next weekend . . .'

Out in the kitchen, Grace's thoughts were running along the same lines – Polly was always more relaxed when in the company of men. The germ of an idea that had crept into her head earlier now gathered momentum, and, once again berating herself for being a hypocrite, she slipped out into the hall, took a deep breath, then, with trembling fingers, dialled a well-known number.

It was half an hour later when there was a knock on the door, bringing a note of annoyance from Aggie's lips as she had just settled herself down to listen to the nine o'clock news.

'Who the bleeding hell's that at this time of night?'

She looked hopefully at Polly, who was curled up on the sofa, her mind still dwelling on what Grace had asked earlier, and Aggie sighed gratefully as the young girl unfolded her legs and made for the front door.

Grace, upstairs keeping out of Polly's way, also heard the door, her face falling in disappointment as she heard Polly say listlessly, 'Oh, it's you. You weren't out very long. Did you forget something?'

Beryl's strident voice carried through the house as she pushed past the young girl.

'Yeah, as a matter of fact. Not that it's any business of yours.' Hurrying up the stairs, she met Grace on the hall landing. 'I suppose you want to know all me business an' all?'

Grace shrugged disdainfully. 'Don't flatter yourself, Beryl. I couldn't care less what you do.'

Yet when Beryl emerged seconds later, stuffing a small packet into her handbag, Grace couldn't resist asking slyly, 'Forget your weekend supply, Beryl? I must say it comes to something when a woman's got to buy her own protection. I was under the impression men took care of those details. Not that I'd know, of course, not having had the benefit of your experience.'

Beryl's face twisted into a snarl of rage, but before she could make a suitable rejoinder there was another knock on the door, and both women heard Polly's happy voice crying, 'Oh, Nobby. Oh, how wonderful to see you. Have you come for a visit? Oh, Nan will be pleased.'

Her sister-in-law forgotten, Grace's face broke into a smile of pure happiness, a smile that faltered into a look of astonishment at Beryl's reaction to Nobby's arrival. The painted face had turned white under the heavy make-up, and the open bag she was holding slipped nervously from her fingers, scattering its contents all over the hall carpet.

'Whatever's the matter with you, Beryl? It's only Nobby Clark, a friend of the family. What are you getting so agitated about? You've hardly ever said two words to the man.'

But Beryl was making herself busy collecting up the spilt contents of her handbag, a procedure that took considerably longer than the action required. It was only when she heard Nobby go into the sitting room that she moved. And move she did. With quick bounds, as if the very devil was after her, Beryl was down the stairs and out of the door before Grace could catch her breath.

Grace, her face thoughtful, descended the stairs slowly. It wasn't like Beryl to avoid a good-looking man, yet ever since the day she had been first briefly introduced to Nobby she had made it her business to stay well out of his way.

As she entered the sitting room the smile returned to her face at the sight of Nobby sitting beside Polly on the settee, chatting together like old friends. Conscious of her rapidly beating heart, Grace played her part to perfection.

'Why, Nobby, this is a nice surprise. We didn't expect to see you tonight. Was there something special you wanted, or is this just a flying visit?'

Nobby looked up, his deep grey eyes holding hers for a fraction of a second, before laughing gaily, 'Actually, I wouldn't say no to a cup of tea. And before you say you haven't any to spare, I've brought me own.' Leaning forward, he tapped Aggie's knee, saying playfully, 'There's a good pound there, Aggie, better than that measly two ounces a week you get on your rations.'

Aggie's face split into a huge grin. For if there was one thing she liked more than a drop of brandy, it was a good strong cup of tea. Reaching out a grateful hand, Aggie took the brown paper bag, then asked slyly, ''Ere, yer ain't dabbling in the black market, are yer, son? Not that it bothers me, but Gracie here's got strong moral principles about that sort of thing, ain't yer, love?'

But for once Grace wasn't interested in where Nobby or Vi's unwanted boyfriend Chris got their dubious supplies from. Tonight she had more important things on her mind.

Taking the tea from Aggie, she said quickly, 'I'll make it, Nan. You listen to the news. I won't be long.'

Before she left the room she gave Nobby a conspiratorial look, and he answered her unspoken question with an imperceptible nod of his dark head.

The door had no sooner closed after Grace when Nobby, his face bearing a serious expression, took hold of Polly's hands and said quietly, 'Actually, it's you I wanted to see, Poll. I need a favour, and you're the only one I can ask.'

Polly squirmed on the sofa, her eyes wide in aston-ishment.

'Me!' she squealed. Nobody had ever needed her help before – well, not for anything important. Her face alight with excitement, she asked breathlessly, 'What is it, Nobby? You know I'd do anything to help you if I can.'

Nobby shifted on the comfortable cushions, his eyes momentarily dropping from Polly's eager gaze. Lord! He hated deception of any kind, but as Grace had explained over the phone, something had to be done to free Polly of her fear of going out at night. Casting his mind back to the brief phone call, Nobby frowned as a thought crossed his mind. To his mind, Polly had come along in leaps and bounds since Grace had been in hospital, and certainly bore little resemblance to the cowed, terrified girl she had been during the first terrible months of the Blitz. So, she still didn't like the thought of going out at night, but she would get over that particular fear in her own good time. Why then had Grace asked him to . . . ? A surge of hope swept through his lean body. Could it be . . . could it possibly be that Grace was using Polly as an excuse to be with him? A broad smile crept on to his face, a smile that prompted Polly to say, 'You look happy, Nobby. I thought you came round to ask me a favour of some kind. You don't look to me as if you've got any problems.'

Startled, Nobby immediately assumed what he hoped was a solemn expression, and answered, 'It's like this, Poll. I've asked Grace to come out with me a dozen times or more – just as friends, of course,' he added hastily, knowing how fond Polly was of Stanley, and how deeply worried she was about him being held in a POW camp. If she had any inkling of the strong feelings he had for Grace, then the young girl would have no part in the scheme he and Grace had planned – or should he say the scheme he had in mind. Maybe Grace had been truthful in her desire to help Polly, yet . . .

Clearing his throat, he sat forward until he was sitting on the edge of the sofa, then, dropping his hands between his knees in what he hoped was a gesture of uncertainty, he continued in a soft voice, aware Aggie was sitting only a few feet away, her attention seemingly held by the voice on the wireless. 'The thing is, Poll, she won't agree to a night out with me. She feels she'd be being disloyal going out and having a good time while poor Stan's being held prisoner. And to tell the truth, I don't think she trusts me motives,' he laughed softly. 'But if you were to come with us, sort of pretend a night out was for your benefit, then she wouldn't have any excuse. Would you, Poll? It'd mean a lot to me, and Grace could do with a bit of pampering after what she's gone through. What d'yer say, Poll? Will you help me out?'

Polly's body stiffened slightly, the old fear returning as she contemplated leaving the safety of the house at night. And yet – this was Nobby asking. Nobby, her friend, who had never asked a favour of her in all the time she had known him. How could she refuse those penetrating, kindly eyes? Plus she had promised herself that she would lose her fear of the night, and what better way than to have Nobby by her side? Nothing bad would happen to her or Grace while Nobby was with them, and, oh, wouldn't it be lovely to have a night out up West . . . !

Quickly now, before she changed her mind, Polly jutted out her chin and, in a determined voice, said breathlessly, 'All right, Nobby, you're on.'

Surprised and delighted that Polly had agreed, Nobby nevertheless detected a tiny tremor of fear and uncertainly in Polly's voice, and because he was genuinely fond of the red-haired, freckled young girl, he said with authority and confidence, 'If you're worried about a raid tonight, Poll, then don't be. They won't be over tonight, there's no bombers' moon to guide them. Trust me on this, I know what I'm talking about.'

Polly looked into Nobby's kindly, solemn eyes and immediately relaxed. Trust me, he had said. Of course she trusted him, trusted him with her life, so great was her confidence in this man.

Jumping to her feet, she cried merrily, 'Tell Grace to get a move on, then, Nobby. I'm going upstairs to change into something a bit glamorous.' Grinning, she leant down and added, 'I'll have to pinch something from Vi's wardrobe, or borrow something from Grace, because I certainly don't have anything in my wardrobe suitable for a West End club, and I wouldn't want to embarrass you.'

Gazing up into the flushed, excited face, Nobby felt a lump come to his throat.

'You'd never embarrass me, love. Not if you was dressed in rags.'

Polly's flush deepened, then she almost ran from the room.

Nobby heard her calling to Grace, then the sound of both young women running up the stairs. All at once he felt drained and guilt-ridden. The look of absolute trust in Polly's eyes had momentarily stunned him. Oh, he knew he had a gift with words, especially with women, but never before had he witnessed such unwavering faith in him, and the memory left him feeling humble.

He'd almost forgotten Aggie's presence until she cut into his thoughts, saying artfully, 'Yer should've taken up acting, lad. You'd have given all those film stars a run for their money after that performance.'

Nobby stared guiltily, then grinned.

'Where you listening the whole time?'

'Course I was, it was a lot more interesting than all that

doom an' gloom on the wireless.' Her demeanour suddenly altering, she leant forward and, staring him directly in the eyes, said, 'You're a good bloke, Nobby Clark, an' if things were different, there's nothing I'd like better than to see you and my Gracie make a go of it. And don't pretend you're not interested. I ain't that old that I can't spot a man in love when I see one. And if it's any consolation, Grace feels the same about you. But don't ever tell her I said so, else me life won't be worth living.'

A rush of happiness raced through Nobby's mind and body. So Grace did love him. He hadn't read the signs wrong, she really loved him. But the sudden euphoria vanished as quickly as it had come. Whether she loved him or not, nothing could ever come of it until Stanley was safely home, or . . . !

'Here, Nan, how do I look?' Polly came waltzing into the room wearing a smart black dress that belonged to Grace. Her hair, for once, was hanging loose around her shoulders, and although she would never be termed a beauty, she looked in this minute a very attractive young lady. Close behind her followed Grace, who was wearing a red dress that reached to her mid-calves, a dress her nan had made for her before the war, and she'd never had the chance to wear until now.

'Well, will we do?' Grace asked gaily.

Nobby got to his feet, his eyes shining in admiration.

'I'll have to keep all the other fellows away with a stick. Have you got one I can borrow, Aggie?'

Happier than she'd felt in a long time, Aggie waved her hand at Nobby, laughing, 'Get away with yer, yer daft bugger. And don't keep me girls out too late, or you'll have me ter answer to.'

Nobby bowed at the waist to the grey-haired woman, then, offering an arm to each girl, he escorted them grandly from the room.

CHAPTER EIGHTEEN

When the two young women walked into the Top Hat nightclub, their eyes widened in childish excitement and delight. Up until now, their nights out had consisted of an evening down the local pub or at the social club with their family. But this place . . . well! It was like something you saw in the films. As their feet sank into the deep, plush red carpet, their eyes swept the large, luxurious room. Overhead hung revolving, crystal globe-shaped chandeliers, and on the bandstand three men in tuxedos were belting out a perfect rendition of 'Ain't Misbehaving', while smartly dressed couples danced and jiggled along to the catchy tune on the small dance floor.

Glancing first at Grace, and then at Polly, Nobby grinned in delight at the sparkle in their eyes; their faces seemed to have had years taken off them. Then he looked down at their feet and almost laughed aloud as he saw their feet tapping in time to the music.

A well-groomed man came towards them, his weathered face lighting up at the sight of his customer.

'Well! As I live and breath, if it ain't me old mate, Nobby Clark. Good to see you again, mate. It must be years since we last met up.' His shrewd eyes flickering to Grace and Polly, the man gave a soft chuckle. 'See you ain't changed much, Nobby, only it used to be one at a time. Seems you're getting greedy in your old age.'

The smile slipped slightly from Nobby's face. He didn't want the man getting the wrong idea about Grace and Polly. His voice a shade terse, he said tightly, 'These two young ladies are very good friends of mine, Pete. In fact you could say they're like family.'

Immediately realising his mistake, and anxious to make amends, the man called Pete ushered them like royalty to a front side table near the band. Then, clicking his fingers at a nearby waiter, he ordered a bottle of champagne 'on the house'.

'Thanks, Pete, but there's no need to go overboard,' Nobby responded drily.

The manager's body swelled with importance.

'Leave off, Nobby. It ain't everyday we get a hero visiting the place. Anyway, enjoy your meal, and if you need anything, just give me a call.' Turning to the two girls, he bowed slightly saying, 'Ladies,' before returning to the rest of his clients. And it was with great amusement that Grace and Polly listened to the cockney man greet an obviously affluent couple in a voice that wouldn't go amiss on the nine o'clock news.

Picking up a leather-bound menu, Nobby inclined his head to the still slightly overawed girls and said lightly, 'Well? Are you gonna order something to eat, or just sit there reading?'

Smiling, Grace looked down at the menu, written in finely printed gold italics, her face turning to horror.

'Nobby! You can't afford any of these meals. Bloody hell, it's daylight robbery.'

Thinking of all the women he had known who had tried to squeeze the last penny out of him, Nobby grinned affectionately.

'Don't you worry about the prices, Gracie. This is my treat, remember. I promised you two girls a night to remember, and I'm gonna keep my word.' Assuming an expression of mock sternness, he growled, 'Now order something, or else I'll do it for you.'

Despite Nobby's words, both young women felt uncomfortable, and, as if by telepathy, they both chose the cheapest item on the expensively bound menu, an unselfish action that didn't go unnoticed by Nobby.

Halfway through her roast beef, Polly gave an appreciative sigh and asked, 'Where do these places get all this lovely food, Nobby? We're lucky to get a scragg-end of lamb or mutton, unless someone hears the butcher's got something special in, then there's a mad stampede and you're lucky if you're not trampled underfoot in the rush.'

Tapping his nose conspiratorially, Nobby said, 'Some things are best left unasked, Poll. Although a lot of the food is legally bought, it's just a question of who you know and how much you can afford to pay. Now, eat up and then we'll have a dance.' His eyes twinkling, he added slyly, 'Of course you'll have to toss for who gets the honour first. Even I can't dance with two women at the same time – at least, not any more.'

Grace put down her fork and asked solicitously, 'Do your injuries give you much trouble, Nobby? Only you never talk about them. You've never even told us just how serious they were, except that because of them you could no longer fly.'

Nobby placed the last morsel of his steak into his mouth, wiped his lips on a white napkin and frowned.

'I didn't bring you two out to talk about my war wounds, but seeing as you've asked, no, they don't give me much trouble. It was my back that was the main problem. You can't fly a plane for twelve hours on end with a dodgy back, can you?' He spoke casually, as if talking about a sprained ankle received in combat. What he didn't mention was the months of agonising pain he had endured from his injuries, nor did he mention the addiction he had developed to morphine while in the military hospital. But that was all behind him now. His back still played him up on occasions, as did his leg and arm when the weather was cold, but compared to his friend Bill Williams, who was still receiving treatment for third-degree burns, Nobby counted himself very fortunate indeed.

'They did offer me a desk job, but I ask you,' he spread his arms wide, the smile returning to his lips. 'Can either of you see me sitting behind a desk from nine to five shuffling papers? Nah, I'm better off working the stalls. It's a good living and I enjoy it. I used to work for me dad when I was a nipper, and I'd've been quite happy to make a living out of it, but me mum had other ideas for me. She wanted me to better meself, so as soon as I was old enough, I was sent into the RAF to train as a pilot. Course, we didn't know there was gonna be a war then. If we had, me mum might have had second thoughts about spending all that money to educate me so as I could join. Because they don't take any old riff-raff, you know. Oh, no, you have to have some kind of decent education to show for yourself before they'll even consider taking you on. Mind you, I don't expect they're so fussy now. Can't afford to be, can they?'

They were just finishing their dessert when a loud braying laugh brought the girl's startled eyes up in a horrified gaze.

'Oh, no!' breathed Polly. 'It can't be.'

Cautiously turning their heads, both girls sneaked a look at the dance floor, and sure enough, there was Beryl, wrapped around a portly, middle-aged man, who seemed to be thoroughly enjoying the blonde's lavish attention.

'What's up?' Nobby asked curiously, his gaze following that of the girls.

Polly groaned. 'It's Beryl, our sister-in-law. Lord! I hope she doesn't come over here and embarrass us.'

'I shouldn't worry abut that, Poll,' Grace reassured her sister. 'For some reason, whenever Nobby's around she avoids him like the plague.'

Listening to the conversation, Nobby's eyes narrowed, his face thoughtful. He was sure he knew that woman. On the few occasions they had met, the brassy blonde had, as Grace had pointed out, quickly made herself scarce, and that alone was surprising. From what he had heard of Danny's new wife, she'd have the trousers off a corpse if the coffin lid wasn't nailed down. But where did he know her from?

The dance over, Beryl, her arms still draped around the sweating man's neck, happened to look towards the bandstand. The glittering smile froze on her face. Not at seeing her nieces, but at the handsome man accompanying them. Steering her companion swiftly around, she hurried him back to a table at the far end of the room.

'Whew! Thank goodness for that.' Polly breathed a sigh of relief. 'It's bad enough having to put up with her at home, let alone having her spoil our night out.'

But Grace wasn't listening. Her face solemn, she let her eyes scan the large room. If Beryl was here, then so must Vi. And if Vi was here, then it wasn't in the capacity of a hat-check girl. Both girls had handed in their wraps on the way in, and it certainly hadn't been Vi who had been behind the counter. Oh, who was she trying to kid, Grace thought angrily. She had never bought that story about Vi's new job. Not with the money she brought home. Then there were the new clothes she was always buying. Dresses that would take a year's clothing rations. Suddenly she felt sick, the wonderful evening ruined by a chance encounter. Oh, why had they had to come to this nightclub? There were dozens dotted around the West End, and Nobby had to go and choose this one.

Getting to her feet she said shakily, 'I'm going to the ladies' room, won't be long.'

Bending down to pick up her bag, Polly said brightly, 'Hang on, Grace, I'll come with you,' which was the last thing Grace wanted, but what could she say?

The long, plush-carpeted cloakroom nearly took their breaths away. There was a long line of toilets, facing which were gilt-edged oval mirrors and hand basins with gold-plated taps. The sheer opulence of the place nearly drove the worry of Vi from Grace's mind. But not for long, for when she emerged from one of the cubicles there was Vi, a worried look on her lovely face, a smouldering cigarette clasped tightly between nervous fingers, leaning against one of the basins.

Before Grace could utter a word, Vi began to speak quickly.

'It's not what you think, Grace. All right, so I lied about the hat-check job, but what I'm doing isn't wrong.'

Grace swept past her sister, her cheeks flushed with shame and embarrassment. In spite of Vi's wild ways and constant stream of boyfriends, Grace had never in her wildest thoughts imagined her sister would end up on the game. Beryl, yes! But not Vi. God, if her nan found out, the shock would likely kill her – that is if her nan didn't kill Vi first.

'Oh, hello, Vi. I thought you must be somewhere around, seeing as the ghastly Beryl's here. Have you finished work for the night, or are you on a break?' Polly, her freckled face wearing a beaming smile, laid her bag on the tiled surfaces of the basins and began to wash her hands, talking all the while. 'I bet you're surprised to see me out, aren't you, Vi? I can't hardly believe it myself.' There was a note of pride in her voice. 'But I'm having such a wonderful time, you never know, I might start wanting to come out every night.' Then she gave a short self-deprecating laugh. 'That'll be the day, eh! The first sound of the siren and I'll be scuttling back down the basement, trampling everyone who gets in my way.' Then her chin came up proudly. 'But I'm not afraid tonight, and I'm going to savour every, lovely last minute of it.' Giving her hair a final scrutiny, and still unaware of the silent animosity that was flowing between her sisters, Polly put her brush in her bag, snapped shut the clasp and said brightly, 'Are you two coming back outside, or do you plan to stay in here all night?'

Forcing a light note into her voice, Grace said quickly, 'We'll be out in a minute, Poll. I just wanted to have a word with Vi about Beryl.' The lie slipped easily off Grace's tongue. 'We don't want her ruining our evening, do we, and she might if she gets drunk.'

'Good Lord, no!' Polly replied, horrified at the thought. Glancing back at the still-silent Vi, Polly said seriously, 'Honestly, Vi, I don't know how you put up with her. She's as common as muck, and if you keep hanging around with her people might start to think you're the same. Anyway, I'll see you both in a minute.'

But it was a good five minutes before Grace and Vi had the chance to talk, what with the constant stream of women walking in and out of the cloakroom. Finally they had the place to themselves, and it was Vi who spoke first, her words tumbling over each other in a desperate attempt to tell Grace the truth before they were interrupted again.

As she listened, Grace's stony face began to relax, and when Vi finished Grace's whole body slumped with relief.

'You silly cow!' she exclaimed angrily. 'I can understand you not letting on to Polly and Nan, but you could have told me at least.'

Vi shrugged, a thin smile on her lips.

'What, you! Miss prim and proper? I thought the least you'd have done was tar and feather me.'

A watery smile broke over Grace's face.

'You daft mare. But seriously, Vi, isn't it dangerous? I

mean, don't any of the men cut up rough at the end of the evening when they realise you're not going to . . .'

'Not going to go home to bed with them, you mean.' Vi laughed. 'It's not like that, Grace. All the men who pay for my company know it's only for the evening. I'm a hostess, that's all. Of course you do get the odd one who has a few too many and gets nasty, but the bouncers soon throw them out. As for me keeping company with Beryl . . . Well, she isn't a bad sort really. Plus it's company for me on the journey here and back home. Sometimes, on special occasions, like a private party, the place can be open all night. The doors are locked, of course, to keep out uninvited visitors; if they weren't, we'd have the police closing us down. The club only has licensing hours up until a certain time. That's why I sometimes don't come home until the following morning. It's because I've been working all night. Speaking of which, I have a customer waiting for me, and Polly and Nobby will be wondering where we are.'

'Wait a minute, Vi.' Grace touched her sister's arm lightly. 'There's been something on my mind for months, but I was afraid to ask. It's just that . . . well, I just can't understand why you're so worried about any of us finding out what you were really doing for a living. As you're always telling us, you're a grown woman now and can do as you please. So why all the secrecy? And another thing I've been puzzled about,' she hurried on before they were interrupted again by another woman wanting to use the toilets, 'with all the money you're earning, and the hassle of keeping your work secret, why on earth do you stay at home? Surely it would be easy for you to get a place of your own. You can certainly afford it . . . Not that I want you to leave home,' Grace amended hastily. 'It's just that . . . well, like I said, it doesn't make sense.'

Violet lowered her eyes, then busied herself lighting up a cigarette. Taking a deep lungful of smoke she answered quietly, 'The thought has crossed my mind more than once, believe me, Gracie. I've even looked at flats and bedsits, but none of them felt right. They . . . they weren't home, you see . . . Oh . . . !' Vi puffed at the cigarette impatiently, her eyes avoiding Grace's concerned gaze. 'I know what you all think of me. Always out for a good time. Never thinks of anyone but herself, that's our Vi, and it's true to some extent. But believe it or not, I'm a home body at heart. That's a laugh, isn't it? Me, the gadabout, a home body. But it's true. Besides, while I'm at home, I can still feel Mum and Dad; it's as if they're watching over me somehow. And sometimes at night, when I can't sleep, I go into their room and sit on their bed and talk to them as if they were still there . . . Oh, you must think I'm mad!'

Embarrassed now at baring her soul, Vi ground out the cigarette in a glass ashtray. Then she gasped in surprise as Grace threw her arms around her, saying in a voice trembling with emotion, 'Oh, Vi. Why haven't you ever said anything about how you felt? Don't you realise we all feel the same way. Our home is what Mum and Dad made it, and as long as it's standing, they'll always be close by.'

Her voice sounding strained, Vi gave a short laugh, 'Yes, well, don't go spreading it about. I wouldn't want to lose my image, now would I?'

As they made their way back though the tightly packed tables, Grace tugged on Vi's arm and asked hesitantly, 'Is Beryl a hostess too?'

Vi threw back her head and laughed loudly. Then in a pseudo-grand voice said, 'My dear, even hostesses have standards!'

Stopping only to say hello to Nobby and Polly, Vi swept past and was soon lost to view.

'You were a long time, Grace. Have you and Vi fallen out again?'

Grace looked at Polly fondly. 'No, we haven't fallen out

again, nosy. In fact we had a nice little chat. Cleared up a few things that were bothering me – and that's all I'm telling you, so don't ask any more questions.'

As she lifted her glass of champagne to her lips Grace caught Nobby's gaze, and what she saw reflected there caused her eyes to drop. He knew! Without being told, Nobby knew what Vi did for a living. But then Nobby Clark had been around. He'd probably known all along what Vi was doing – or guessed; but he'd never even mentioned it. Then again, why should he? After all, it was no business of his how Vi earned her money, she thought rebelliously, her inbred loyalty towards her sister surfacing.

When the band started to play a popular tune, Nobby dragged Polly to her feet, and amidst much giggling protest from the delighted girl, Polly let herself be whirled around the floor under the glittering globes.

Feeling a little awkward at being left on her own, Grace watched the dancers, her feet tapping to the lively music. She nearly jumped out of her skin when a deep voice, only inches away from her ear, said, 'Would you like to dance?'

Flustered and feeling completely out of her depth, Grace stuttered, 'Oh, no. No, I'm sorry, but I'm with someone.' She gestured towards the dance floor, while at the same time cursing herself for her gauche behaviour.

Eager to make amends for her stilted refusal, Grace's eyes flickered upwards towards the uniformed man, a spark of recognition registering. Then she remembered.

Feeling all kinds of a fool, she smiled gaily, 'Chris! Oh, it's wonderful to see you again. Nan said you'd phoned a few times and . . .' Too late, Grace realised her gaffe and flushed with embarrassment.

Noting her discomfort, Chris pulled out a spare chair, saying, 'May I?'

'Of course. Lord, where are my manners tonight. I think I've drunk too much champagne and . . .'

Gently placing a strong hand over Grace's slim fingers, Chris said softly, 'It's all right, Grace. You don't have to worry about hurting my feelings. I know Vi's not interested in me, and I know what she's doing here. But you know what, Grace?' He smiled broadly, 'I'm a persistent begger, and besides, what else would I have to do on such a short leave? Anyway, enough about me, how's your fiancé? Stanley, wasn't it?'

Grace felt her face burn at the memory of that night, then she remembered where Stan was and all animosity vanished.

Lowering her eyes she said simply, 'He's in a POW camp, and that's about all I know.'

'Oh, Lord, I am sorry, Grace, I had no idea. Poor begger. It must be dreadful for you waiting for news of some sort. That's the worst part, isn't it? Not knowing.'

Grace was about to reply when a gruff voice said tersely, 'This table's taken, pal, and so is the lady.'

Startled, Grace looked up into Nobby's thunderous face, a nervous Polly hanging on to his hand.

'Nobby! Don't be so rude,' Grace snapped back at the glowering face. 'This is Lieutenant Chris Green, an old friend of mine – well, Vi's actually. He only stopped by the table to say hello.'

At once Nobby's countenance changed, his face taking on a sheepish expression.

'Sorry, mate.' He extended his hand, saying, 'Nobby Clark's me name, I'm a friend of the family, so to speak, and their protector for the evening. Their old nan would hang, draw and quarter me if I let anything happen to one of her girls.'

Returning Nobby's firm handshake, Chris said laughingly, 'I think you may be underestimating the redoubtable Aggie. I'm sure she could think up a worse fate than that.'

Nobby's eyes widened. 'So you've met Aggie, have you? I didn't realise you knew the family that well.'

Chris raised his eyebrows. 'I don't actually. It just happened I'd arrived to take Vi out for the evening when there was a big air raid. We all ended up sleeping down in the basement – and very comfortable it was too. I've never forgotten that night. Even though I was a virtual stranger, the whole family treated me like a special guest. As for Aggie . . .' Chris extended his hands. 'What can I say? Once met, never forgotten, though I've seen her a few times since, when I've gone round hoping to catch Vi in, but . . .' He shrugged then grinned. 'Anyway, I suppose I mustn't intrude on you good people any longer, so I'll say goodnight.'

Instantly Nobby was on his feet.

'Is there somewhere else you've got to be?'

Chris Green fiddled with the brass buttons of his uniform, saying lightly, 'Only my bed and a cup of cocoa.'

Nobby grabbed the man's arm firmly.

'In that case why don't you stay and spend the evening with us? I could do with an extra man around. Like I told the girls, I can only dance with them one at a time.'

Now that Nobby knew the attractive man was interested in Vi, poor devil, and therefore posed no threat to himself, he was all the good-natured host.

Ordering another bottle of champagne, and two packets of De Rizers from the cigarette girl, the four of them settled down to a relaxing evening. Now and then Vi would glide on to the dance floor with her customer for the evening, but if Chris noticed, he didn't make any comment. By the time they left the club it was gone eleven, and it was as they were waiting hopefully for a taxi that Chris, tapping at his breast pocket, exclaimed, 'I must have left my lighter on the table. Won't be a minute.'

Grace and Nobby exchanged glances, wondering if the

lighter was an excuse to go back in to try to have a word with Vi. Polly, on the other hand seemed oblivious to everything around her, and it was no wonder the way she'd been knocking back the champagne and wine as if it was water, when the strongest drink she'd ever had in her life up until now was orange juice. Grace only hoped her nan would be in bed when they got home so she could smuggle Polly upstairs and into bed before Aggie saw the state she was in.

'Sorry about that.' Chris came hurrying towards them. 'It was in my trouser pocket all the time . . . Here, quick, there's a taxi.' Jumping out into the road he waved down the gloomy shape of a black cab, its shrouded lights making it barely visible in the blackout.

They were no sooner sitting down when Polly laid her head on Grace's shoulder and promptly fell asleep.

Grace laughed softly. 'You two will have to help me get her into the house without nan seeing her, that is, if it's not taking you out of your way, Chris?'

Instantly Nobby bridled with indignation.

'It ain't gonna take two of us to carry a little slip of a girl like Poll. I might have been a bit injured, but I'm not a cripple.'

Grace, ignoring Nobby's outburst, leant towards Chris in the darkened taxi and said wryly, 'A bit injured, he says. He only shot down two Messerschmitts after they'd almost wrecked his plane. Landed in a Kent field, got out, then went back for his navigator. A minute later the plane burst into flames and our reluctant hero here caught flying scraps of metal in his leg, arm and back. Not that that would stop him trying to carry Polly, even if he did do himself a worse injury, stubborn old begger.' She tapped Nobby's knee affectionately. 'And we're all very proud of him. He was awarded the DFC, so what do you think of that, Chris?'

Although it was dark in the taxi, Chris could feel the affection flowing between Grace and Nobby. He had to admit he hadn't taken to Grace's fiancé, thinking at the time that a woman like Grace could do much better than a man like Stanley Slater. But things were different now. You didn't dump a man while he was being held in a POW camp. Not a woman like Grace anyway. Shrugging his shoulders, he dropped the idea from his mind. It was no business of his. After all, he hardly knew these people, although it didn't feel that way – he felt as if he'd known them for years.

Nudging Nobby in the ribs, he said with admiration, 'Congratulations, Nobby. I've never met a hero before. Well, not a properly decorated one. Well done. It must have taken some guts to do what you did.'

As always when his heroic actions were mentioned, Nobby became abashed, and swiftly changed the subject.

As the taxi drove slowly through the night, Grace felt her own eyes begin to close. The last thing she remembered hearing was Chris and Nobby discussing America's reluctance to enter the war, both of them scathing in their remarks about the so-called super-power country that was sitting on its backside watching the world fall apart around it.

On 7 December that year, the Japanese bombed the naval base at Pearl Harbor, killing 3,300 service personnel in the process.

America had finally entered the war.

CHAPTER NINETEEN

'Now look, Mrs Collins, I've told you, we don't deal with under-the-counter stuff in here, so it's no good you going on about it. In fact we're running very low on stock just now. Mr Benjamin is waiting for a delivery. We've got some dried eggs and some tins of spam and just enough to cover your tea and sugar ration for the week.' Grace, her face set, stared at the shabby plump woman with distaste. Week after week she was in here demanding all sorts of provisions, refusing to believe that Benji's cellar wasn't well stocked for his favourite customers. It was now May 1943, and provisions were getting harder and harder to come by, but people like Mrs Collins would always believe shopkeepers kept a special stash under the counter or down the cellar.

With a loud sniff, Mrs Collins cast a withering look at the young woman behind the counter and said tartly, 'Don't give me all that old cobblers, Grace Donnelly. The whole street knows about your gentleman friend supplying you and the rest of your family with black market stuff. And him supposed to be a hero an' all – huh!'

Grace's face turned scarlet at the nastiness in the woman's tone. Resisting the urge to lean over the counter and slap the

woman's mottled face, she said between clenched teeth, 'For
your information, Mrs Collins, and you can pass it on to your
cronies, Mr Clark is a legitimate businessman, and any little
treats he kindly gives us is more for my nan's sake than the
rest of us, and—'

'Bollocks! You can tell that tale to the next flying pig yer
see go by, miss,' The outraged woman's chest was heaving
with indignation, so much so that the buttons on her shiny
black coat seemed in danger of popping off. 'I heard yer nan
down the market last week bragging about the joint of beef
you'd all had for your Sunday dinner, and fresh strawberries
and cream for afters. And you stand there bare faced and tell
me Nobby Clark's not running a black market scam with
you an' your family reaping the rewards.'

Her eyes glittering dangerously now, Grace moved from
the back of the counter.

'Get out . . . Go on, get out of this shop before I do something I'll regret, you nasty, evil-minded little woman.'

But the woman, believing herself to be in the right, stood
her ground.

'You can't order me about, yer cheeky little madam. It
ain't your shop, yer just the hired help. I wanna see old
Benji.' Bristling with rage now, the woman bellowed, 'Well,
don't just stand there gawping, go and get the old Jew boy
out here. Can yer 'ear me back there, Benji. Get yerself out
'ere and face me yerself, yer bleeding old Jew boy, I – 'Ere
. . . 'ere, wot you doing yer little bitch. Take yer hands off
of me before I land yer one.'

But Grace, infuriated by the contemptuous manner in
which the woman had addressed her beloved friend was
past caring. With a strength she didn't know she possessed
Grace grabbed the woman by the back of the neck and
tried to push her from the shop. But even with her temper
raging to boiling point, Grace could budge the woman
no further. Sweating now, and beginning to feel foolish,

Grace valiantly gathered all her strength, but the woman was built like a Sherman tank. Determined to throw the woman out, even if she gave herself a heart attack in the process, Grace continued to push and shove, but all to no avail.

Then salvation arrived. The bell over the shop door tinkled, and there, framed in the doorway, stood the formidable figure of Aggie. Not one to waste words, she said sharply, 'Need a hand, love?'

And Grace, the sweat now pouring down her face cried, 'Oh, yes, please, Nan.'

At the sight of Aggie Harper, the irate customer suddenly seemed to lose her confidence. Blustering wildly, she stuttered, 'This ain't no business of yours, Aggie Harper. This is between me an'—'

She got no further. Two strong, brawny hands grabbed the woman at the back of her neck, and with Grace pushing from the rear, Mrs Collins found herself thrown bodily from the shop on to the cobbled pavement, much to the amusement of some passers-by.

Struggling to regain some of her dignity, the humiliated woman stepped back a few steps and yelled at Aggie, 'You've got some nerve, Aggie Harper, acting all righteous, when the whole street knows you're in with Nobby Clark and his black market scams. I'll bet you don't have ter eat dried eggs and spam fer yer breakfast, do yer? Or queue up fer hours outside the butcher's and grocer's.'

As Aggie advanced on the shouting woman, her fists clenched by her sides, Mrs Collins, either through bravery or sheer stupidity, added sneeringly, 'And then there's those two whores coming home every night with a different man. Our own boys were good enough fer them before, weren't they, but now the Yanks are here, our soldiers don't get a look in. But then they don't have the money to throw around like the Yanks, do they? Or have packets of nylons and chocolates to hand out to whoever takes their fancy—'

A heavy fist smashed into the woman's mouth sending her sprawling flat out on the pavement. Then Aggie was standing over her, her face contorted with fury.

'You ever say anything about me family again an' I'll put yer into hospital. D'yer understand, yer vicious bitch, you? Now get outta me sight before yer get me toe up yer arse to help yer on the way!'

The injured woman rose unsteadily to her feet, her mouth pouring with blood.

'I'll 'ave the law on yer, Aggie Harper, you see if I don't . . .'

But Aggie was already walking away, pulling a horrified Grace alongside her.

Back in the shop, Grace had to sit down before her legs gave way. She had seen her nan in a temper many times, but had never realised how violent she could be if provoked.

'You stay there a minute, love, an' I'll slip out back and brew us some tea. By the way, what was that all about? She another one thinks you've got mountains of supplies hidden away?'

Grace nodded ruefully. 'I'm afraid so, Nan. And she's not the only one, but she is the nastiest. Still! I don't suppose she'll be back here in a hurry.' Reaching up she took hold of Aggie's gnarled hand. 'Thanks, Nan. I don't know what I would have done if you hadn't come along.'

Clicking her tongue Aggie retorted, 'You'd 'ave managed somehow, love. I've never known you to give up without a struggle. Anyway, where is Benji? I'd 'ave thought he'd have come out to see what all the rumpus was about. He ain't going deaf, is he?'

Weakly, Grace shook her head.

'No, at least not that badly. He's having his afternoon nap, and once he's asleep nothing wakes him. I worry about

him, especially at night, because he never hears the siren
go off.'

Aggie patted Grace's shoulder.

'Well, let's hope he goes on leading a charmed life then,
eh! Anyway, you sit there and I'll go and brew up.' Aggie
walked away but then stopped in her tracks. ''Ere, he won't
mind me using his tea, will he, love? I know he doesn't mind
when he's down here and I pop in fer a chat and a cuppa, but
seeing as he's upstairs asleep, I don't want him thinking I'm
taking liberties.'

Grace shook her head. 'No, he lets me make as many
cups as I want. Besides, you know how much he enjoys
your company. He wouldn't begrudge you a cup of tea,
whether he's here or not.'

Aggie grinned slyly. 'Better not let Ada Collins hear yer
say that, love. Especially after that smack in the mouth I gave
her defending old Benji.' Chuckling to herself Aggie went
behind the heavy curtain that partitioned the shop from the
living quarters and, as she'd done on numerous occasions,
made herself at home in the kitchen.

And as Gracie listened to her nan humming out in the
small kitchen she reflected wryly that Aggie hadn't picked
up on that odious woman's references to Vi and Beryl. And
even though it went against the grain to admit it, there
had been a ring of truth in the woman's spiteful words.
That crack about Nobby supplying them with black market
goods had hit home. Although whenever Grace tackled him
about it, he always had a plausible explanation as to how he
had come by the treats he was always bringing around the
house. The eggs, butter, fruit and occasional joint of meat
were, he had told her on numerous occasions, bought from
a farmer out in Kent, a man Nobby's father had apparently
fought with in the first war and had remained friends with
until his death. The tea that Aggie loved so much came
from an army warehouse, together with the extra sugar

that always accompanied it. For although Nobby had been in the RAF, he still had many friends serving in the army.

Grace still had her doubts, yet what could she do? Refuse to accept the gifts and risk the wrath of her nan who had become used to eating and drinking as well as she had before the war? Worse still, openly accuse Nobby of theft and lose his friendship, maybe for good? Grace shivered at the thought. Life now was only made bearable by Nobby's visits and the Saturday night excursion up West to a club or to see a play, always with Polly in tow, of course, as chaperon. Not that Grace didn't trust Nobby; it was her own feelings she was wary of. The very thought of spending an evening alone with Nobby always reduced her limbs to jelly, and then guilt would set in, as she remembered Stanley and the barbarous conditions under which he was living.

Uncomfortable with the direction her thoughts were heading, Grace squirmed on the straight-backed chair and thought instead of the other accusation thrown in Aggie's face. It was true Beryl and Vi had become friendly with the visiting Americans, and indeed at first there had been a different one knocking on their door almost every day. But for the past four months, both women had settled down with two American officers. Vi's friend – an amiable, attractive man in his mid-thirties, a colonel no less, named Chuck Downing – was always made welcome by Aggie. Of course, the fact that he always brought Aggie either chocolates or a small bottle of brandy had nothing to do with her affable acceptance of him! But Beryl's gentlemen friend, a top-ranking general by the name of Donald Laine, like all the other men she had tried to sneak into the house, had never got his nose past the door. They had all seen him, standing on the doorstep, a portly man in his late fifties with a kindly face, and wondered how on earth Beryl had managed to snag a general, even one who was getting on a bit, and was certainly nothing to set any woman's pulse racing.

Maybe, as Grace had pointed out, the man was probably lonely and desperate for some female company. To which Aggie had retorted loudly, 'Female company, be blowed. He just wants ter get his leg over, like all the rest of 'em. And we all know how accommodating our Beryl is, don't we?'

When Beryl had complained in loud, colourful language that this was her house and she could bring who she liked into it, Aggie would calmly say that in that case Danny wouldn't mind knowing about her entertaining other men in his absence. This threat always shut Beryl up quickly, but the murderous looks she directed at Aggie on these occasions showed only too clearly what would happen to the old lady if Danny didn't make it back home. Grace shivered. Poor Uncle Danny. He was so trusting and obviously adored his wife, as was proved by the letters that frequently tumbled through the letterbox from overseas.

''Ere yer go, girl. Get that down yer. There's nothing like a nice cuppa to steady the nerves.'

For a moment Grace was tempted to ask Aggie if she had any suspicions about Nobby's activities, then decided against it. Aggie thought the sun shone out of Nobby's backside, and even if she did know something, she would defend his name to the death.

The tinkling of the shop bell led both women's eyes to the door, and as Grace stood up to serve the three women who entered, they ignored her completely, directing their attentions at Aggie.

'Is it true, Aggie? Did yer smack old Ma Collins in the mouth?' A small, sharp-faced woman who lived across the road from them was looking at Aggie with open admiration, as were her companions, who also lived in the street.

Aggie's huge breasts appeared to swell with proud satisfaction, and as she related the incident to the avid listeners, Grace sighed and went out the back.

It was nearly five o'clock, and Grace always brought Benji up a cup of tea if he hadn't come down to the shop by now. As she waited for the kettle to boil she wished it was six o'clock so she could go home. She was tired and still shaken by the violent confrontation that had taken place. If she asked, she knew Benji would let her go early, but she didn't like to take liberties. So she waited for the kettle to boil, her ears picking up on the slight embellishments Aggie was adding to the story.

A shuffling sound behind her made her jump, then she relaxed.

'I was just going to bring you up your tea, Benji.' She smiled at the elderly man dressed as always in a shiny black suit with a dark grey waistcoat.

The elderly man came further into the kitchen and sat down at the small table. He smiled warmly.

'Oy vey! And who could sleep with all that noise going on, tell me that, Gracie.'

Grace laughed. 'You seem to manage to sleep through the warning sirens at night, or are you just too lazy to get out of bed?'

The old man took the mug of tea, his face suddenly solemn. Putting down his tea, he looked up at Gracie and said softly, 'You don't have to defend me, leibchen. I am used to being called much worse than Jew boy.'

A flush rose over Gracie's cheeks. So he had heard after all. Oh, Lord! If she could have got her hands on Ada Collins at that moment, she would have smashed her in the mouth herself for belittling this kindly old man who had never done anyone any harm in his life. Nor had Grace ever heard him complain, despite the horrific tragedies he had suffered.

Benji had arrived in England back in 1928 with his wife Eva and their two sons. After Benji and Eva had established themselves in the shop, their sons, by then in their early twenties and unable to find work, had returned to Germany, where they had found work as labourers. That had been back in 1937. A year later, Benji's beloved Eva had died suddenly from a heart attack, leaving him devastated. His sons had come over to England for the funeral, begging their father to go back with them to Germany, while at the same time Benji tried desperately to keep them in England. The rising power of Adolf Hitler and his army of Nazi thugs was becoming a dangerous threat, particularly to the Jewish population. Already there was talk of concentration camps being built to dispose of this unwanted race. But Benji's sons had laughed off the threat as sheer propaganda. Now they were dead, tortured then gassed in the Holocaust.

The news of his sons' fate had been delivered in a letter by his only surviving relative, a cousin living in Berlin. Benji hadn't heard from him since.

Benji peered into his mug, then lifted watery brown eyes to Grace and asked, 'Would you mind if I went back upstairs, leibchen? I didn't sleep very well last night, and to tell the truth . . .' He winked and nodded in the direction of the shop. 'I'd rather be back upstairs, it will be safer. Shalom, Gracie.'

'Shalom, Benji. I'll see you tomorrow. Goodnight.'

The shambling figure making its way up the stairs didn't turn, but raised its hand in farewell.

Grace waited until Benji had disappeared then her eyes immediately found the clock on the wall, willing the minutes to pass quickly so she could go home and get some peace and quiet.

The noise hit her as soon as she opened the door. Somebody, probably Polly, had brought down the gramophone from Danny's room and the sound of the Glenn Miller Band was blasting throughout the house.

As she hung up her coat, Grace thought wryly, *So much for a bit of peace and quiet.*

In the sitting room, Polly was dancing with Linda Castle, while Aggie, who had arrived home only twenty minutes before, tried to make herself heard over the throbbing music.

'Turn the bloody thing down, can't yer! Yer'll 'ave the neighbours in complaining if yer keep up that racket.'

Polly, her face flushed with exertion cried happily, 'Oh, Nan, don't be such a wet blanket. It's the new records from America. It's called swing music.'

'Swing music, be blowed!' Aggie shouted back. 'I'll bleeding well swing fer you two if yer don't turn down the noise.'

But Polly, laughing gaily, came over to Aggie, gave her a big hug and said gleefully, 'Come on, Nan. Why don't you try it. It's fun – honest.'

Aggie's face nearly turned purple.

'What me, jiggle about like some lunatic, showing me drawers off to all and sundry? No thanks.'

But Polly's high spirits refused to be dampened. Taking hold of Linda's hand she laughed. 'Come on, Linda, let's show Nan and Grace how to do the jitterbug.'

'All right,' Linda answered, her pretty face animated, her long fair hair shining with vitality. She was a friendly, outgoing girl who loved life and made the most of every minute of every day. Grace surmised that Linda must be nineteen by now, making her two years younger than Polly. Yet looking at the pair of them, you'd have thought them the same age. Both girls had their hair caught up in a ponytail, and were wearing full skirts, which ended just below the knees, and white cotton blouses.

Now Linda was holding Polly's hand, crying cheerfully, 'Stand well back, ladies. There's gonna be a lot of arms and legs flying about.'

Grace, her good humour restored by the happy atmosphere, sat on the arm of Aggie's chair and waited while Polly put on 'In the Mood'. Then she watched in amazement as the two young women went into a wild routine of twisting and turning, their bottoms stuck out, sliding through each other's legs, their arms waving wildly as their feet went out in all directions. Grace found herself laughing at the comical antics of the two girls, so much so that the tears began to roll down her face. Aggie, too, was finding it hard to keep a straight face. She glanced up at Grace, then towards the two sweating girls and let out a howl of merriment. But Polly and Linda weren't put off, and when the record ended they both collapsed on to the sofa, their faces beaming with satisfaction.

A frantic banging on the front door brought Aggie's head up sharply.

'There! What did I tell yer. Some Nosy Parker's come ter complain about the noise, I bet. Well, I'll soon see them off with a flea in their ear. Bloody cheek. Begrudging folk a bit of fun in their own homes, when there's precious little of it to be had anywhere else.'

The two sisters grinned at each other. Their nan was an enigma. One minute telling them to keep the noise down in case the neighbours complained, then ready to do battle if they dared to do just that.

Straining to hear the conversation going on at the front door, all three young women jumped back in alarm as Aggie, her large frame moving quickly into the room, shouted excitedly, 'Quick, all of yer, that was Rene. Our boys 'ave just shot down a German plane over the marshes. The pilots parachuted out, so yer know what that means, don't yer?' At the blank looks gazing back at her, she yelled, 'The parachutes, you idiots. So don't just sit there with yer mouths open, come on, otherwise there won't be enough silk left fer a bleeding hankie by the time we get there . . .

And pick up something heavy ter bring with yer, just in case the Germans wanna make a fight of it.'

All three young women looked at each other apprehensively, then Grace lifted her shoulders and said, 'I'm game. Anyway, we can't let Nan go on her own. You never know what might happen to her.'

Polly gasped in fear. 'You mean she might get hurt, Grace?'

Grace laughed. 'No, you silly cow. I was thinking of those poor pilots if Nan gets her hands on either of them.'

So, armed with a frying pan and two heavy saucepans, Grace, Polly and Linda followed the running Aggie down Well Street, round the back turnings, and were soon running up towards the Downs. Unfortunately, about fifty other women had the same idea, and by the time the four women reached the plane it was surrounded. The two German pilots, their hands held high over their heads, looked scared to death, as they stared at the horde of women, all of of whom were armed with pitchforks, spades or glittering kitchen knives.

Pushing and shoving her way to the front of the mob, Aggie demanded of the woman next to her, 'Well? Where are they?'

The woman looked puzzled for a moment. 'Where's what?' she answered, then, realisation dawning, she leant forward and whispered in Aggie's ear, 'We've hidden them til the law and the army's been and gone. 'Cos yer know what them buggers are like. They'll confiscate those parachutes, saying it's spoils of war or some such cobblers. Then they'll give them away to their girlfriends or wives. Nah!' She tapped the side of her nose. 'They won't find 'em, nor the two spare ones we found in the plane.'

Aggie's mouth dropped in amazement. 'Yer ain't been daft enough ter go into a burning plane, 'ave yer? Christ! Nothing's worth taking that risk for.'

The woman smiled proudly. 'It wasn't on fire, well not much anyhow, just the tail end. Me and a few others were in an' outta there in five minutes. Look, over there, see!'

Aggie peered in the direction the woman was pointing and saw the wrecked aircraft.

Just then the local bobby arrived on his bicycle, its wheels wobbling dangerously.

Assuming an authoritative air, he commanded, 'Come on, ladies, the law's here now. I'll deal with this, so you lot can get yourselves off home before one of you gets hurt.'

One of the women laughed scornfully. 'Oh, yeah! I can see them two Jerries shitting themselves at the sight of you and your truncheon.'

Before the red-faced man could make a suitable retort, he was saved from further embarrassment by the arrival of two army trucks. As the bevy of troops disembarked, the women fell back, and the two prisoners, relief flooding their faces, went with the British soldiers silently and without fuss.

A high-ranking officer stepped forward.

'All right, ladies, there's nothing more to see.' Then, winking at the group of women, he said softly, 'We'll be gone in a few minutes, then you can collect the parachutes from wherever you've hidden them and divvy them up between you. Good day, ladies, and many thanks for keeping the prisoners under surveillance until we arrived.' With a nonchalant salute, he strode off, issuing orders left and right, one of which was to deploy two soldiers to stand guard over the enemy plane until reinforcements arrived, and within minutes the trucks were trundling down the road, the lone policeman following as quickly as he dared on his teetering bike.

As soon as the men had disappeared the women huddled together in a wide circle, and suddenly four *pregnant* women were delivered of four healthy parachutes.

To be fair to everyone, the women who had risked going

into the plane got the biggest share of material. Large squares of the voluminous silk were cut with a pair of shearing scissors brought along especially for the occasion. As Aggie and the girls had arrived last they managed to get only a few yards between them, but they were satisfied with their haul. After all, they hadn't done anything for it. Rene had fared little better.

They were halfway down Homerton High Street, past the Hackney Hospital, when the first explosion rent the air, followed moments later by another deafening blast. Thinking a bomb had dropped nearby, all the women fell to the ground, their hands covering their heads. But it wasn't a bomb that had caused the explosions. The plane had suddenly, and without warning, exploded.

Within minutes the army trucks were racing back to the scene, and as the women rose shakily to their feet, Aggie said hoarsely, 'Bleeding hell! If that had gone up half an hour earlier those women would've been killed, and all fer a bit of silk. Makes yer think, don't it?'

Thoughtfully and not a little shaken by the fright they'd had, the women carried on walking until, breaking the silence, Linda said to Rene, 'Me and Polly was thinking of taking a walk round the shops, Mum. I know they'll all be closed by now, but we just wanna do some window shopping.'

Rene turned and looked at her daughter suspiciously.

'As long as yer don't go over the park, or if yer do, you'll stay well away from that POW camp. Now, I'm warning yer, Linda. If I hear you've been over there chatting up those Germans, I'll have the skin off yer back, understand?'

The opening of a POW camp in Victoria Park hadn't gone down too well with the East Enders, many of whom had their menfolk overseas fighting the very people that were now strutting around the compound, calling out to any girl or young woman walking by. It was also well known that a few of the women weren't averse to climbing over the heavy wire gates that housed the prisoners.

Linda returned her mother's gaze steadfastly and said indignantly, 'What d'yer take me for, Mum! I wouldn't go within a mile of the place. Besides, I'm not a little kid any more, an' I can take care of meself, yer know I can.'

Breaking into the conversation between mother and daughter, Aggie looked at her friend and said cheerfully, 'Aw, let 'em go, Rene. Like Linda says, they're not children, and besides, it'll mean we can have the place to ourselves, while we sort out the silk over a nice cuppa tea without having ter listen ter that infernal record player blaring away.'

As they headed home, Aggie said gleefully, 'I'll bet Jeannie will be flaming mad at missing out on this. Trust her to pick today ter go an' visit her sister. Still . . .'

Grace walked on behind her nan and Rene as they carried on their conversation, both of them in high spirits. Stifling a yawn, Grace looked back at the retreating girls, her brow furrowed. She liked young Linda, but still couldn't help wondering if she was the right sort of person Polly should be going out with. No sooner had the thought crossed her mind than she shook her head in amusement. She still thought of Polly as a little girl, but her sister was now twenty-one and could do as she pleased. Besides, it would do Polly good mixing with an outgoing girl like Linda.

CHAPTER TWENTY

At the same time as the German plane had crashed over the marshes, Nobby Clark was holed up in a locked warehouse in one of the many backstreet warrens in Bethnal Green. There were three other men in the warehouse, all dressed in smart three-piece suits and wearing large hats that almost obscured their faces, and as Nobby stared at his companions, he cursed himself for ever getting involved with the Davidson family. It had seemed like easy money at first, now as he was now learning to his cost, nothing in this life was ever easy.

When Nobby had taken over his late father's stalls, he had found his father had plenty of loyal and regular customers. Unfortunately as the war bit deeper into the nation's economy, it had become increasingly difficult to find anything worthwhile to sell. Not a man to be defeated easily, Nobby had racked his brains for a way to replenish his dwindling supplies. First he had looked up some old army friends and, with the aid of a few backhanders, had managed to obtain tins and other perishable foods, discreetly smuggled out of the army barracks and into the back of his old van. This he did once a month. It was so easy it was

almost laughable. He would drive up to the army gates in
the van, where he was instantly recognised by the guard on
duty, and once into the barracks he would open the back
doors and help his friends load up the back of the van. And
if he was lucky, he would get a couple of gallons of petrol
as well – all for considerable remuneration of course.

Then there was the old farmer friend of his father in Kent.
Nobby could remember golden summer days when he and
his family had visited the farm for a day out, and the young
Nobby would run wild all over the farm playing with the
animals and riding the farmer's old bike over the green hilly
fields. The elderly farmer had welcomed Nobby with open
arms the day he had arrived to give the old soldier and his
wife the sad news of his parents' deaths. They had talked
for hours, reminiscing about old times, and when Nobby
had told of his difficulty in getting enough foodstuffs to
stock his stalls, the farmer had immediately offered to help.
It was what Nobby had been hoping for, but he would never
have brought up the subject himself, for he was genuinely
fond of the old couple, and would have hated for them to
think he had only made the visit to line his pockets.

So a deal was struck, and once a fortnight Nobby would
visit the farm and come away with fresh eggs, butter, vegetables and fruit. And if an animal had been slaughtered
that day, he would also receive a goodly portion of the
carcass. All of this cost Nobby money, but whatever he
paid out, he trebled instantly. All of the women who came
to his stall were only too pleased to pay over the odds for
some decent food, although Nobby was careful who he sold
his prohibited supplies to, as the local bobby patrolled the
markets regularly, on the lookout for black market goods.

But since the authorities had started to clamp down on
the farmers selling their produce to civilians, Nobby had
found it difficult to obtain his regular supply of fresh produce. The old farmer still managed to hide away a goodly

assortment of supplies for his old friend's son, but Nobby, knowing the penalties the farmer could face if found out, had reluctantly brought their brief partnership to an end. He still visited the farm and, despite his protests, never came away empty-handed. Like last week, when three punnets of strawberries, a dozen eggs and a joint of beef had been thrust into his hands upon leaving. When he had attempted to pay for the goods he had been sent on his way with a fond laugh and an extracted promise to come and visit again soon. These particular presents had landed up in Aggie's kitchen, and for once he had been able to look Grace straight in the eyes and tell her they had been given to him by an old friend.

Then his army supplies had started to dry up, due to the fact that the two guards who supplied Nobby had been caught red-handed pilfering from the store rooms, and were presently languishing in an army jail awaiting trial.

Just as things were getting desperate for Nobby, he had gone to his local pub one night and had started chatting to the Davidson brothers and their cousin. It had been a pleasant evening with much beer supped, and when they were all sufficiently inebriated the Davidsons had offered him a deal. With much nudging and winking, they had implied they had plenty of contacts, and if Nobby was interested they could keep his stalls stocked from now until the end of the war. Warning bells had gone off in Nobby's head, but, slightly drunk and desperate to maintain his livelihood, he had agreed to join them. However, only by way of buying the stuff, he had added – he wanted no part in the obtaining of it, nor did he want to know where it came from. The men had agreed and shook hands on the deal.

As good as their word, the Davidsons had kept Nobby well supplied, and as the months went on Nobby found he was being offered more goods than he could handle. To rectify the problem he had hired a garage in the grounds of his flats, and prayed a stray bomb wouldn't land on his spoils of war.

However, of late his conscience had started to trouble him, not from buying black market goods but because of the way they were being obtained. The papers had been filled recently with stories of lorries being hijacked, warehouses being turned over, and consignments of goods being brought in by merchant ships mysteriously vanishing while being unloaded. Even then Nobby hadn't worried unduly – not until an elderly man guarding a warehouse in Stepney had been viciously beaten about the head during a robbery and was at present fighting for his life in Hackney Hospital. That had been the end for Nobby. Although he couldn't be sure the Davidsons had been responsible, he had a gut feeling it had been them. Now he wanted out, only it was looking as if it wasn't going to be that easy.

Phil Davidson, the elder of the brothers, was sitting on an upturned crate, a cigarette hanging from his thin lips, his eyes hard and cold.

'So, our war hero's lost his bottle, has he?'

Nobby felt his hands clench into hard fists by his side, although he knew he couldn't take these men on single-handedly. If he even tried, they would kill him, or leave him so severely maimed he would never be whole again. He also knew that to show fear would be fatal.

Keeping his voice firm he said, 'I ain't lost me bottle, Phil, but it don't take much bottle to beat up an old man and leave him near dead.'

Phil Davidson threw his cigarette on the floor and raised his eyebrows ambiguously.

'And what makes yer think that job was down ter us, Nobby? There's plenty of other geezers doing the same thing we are, it could have been any of 'em.'

One of the other men stepped forward, growling impatiently, 'Let's cut out the crap, Phil, an' let him know what's what.'

Peter Davidson, Phil's brother, moved towards Nobby menacingly. When he was only inches from him, he ground out viciously, 'Listen, Clark, you've had it cushy up till now. We've done all the dirty work, and risked getting nicked, and all you've done is sit by and take whatever we gave you, no questions asked. Now you've 'ad enough and yer expect us ter just let yer walk away knowing what yer do about us. What's ter stop yer from shopping us to the coppers?'

Nobby stood his ground, his grey eyes meeting the small shifty eyes of Pete Davidson. His voice harsh, he barked, 'Don't be a fool, man. If I did that, I'd be dropping meself in it as well, wouldn't I? You don't have ter worry about me opening me mouth; the sooner I forget about you lot the better I'll sleep at nights.'

Nobby looked past Pete to Phil, saying, 'You know I won't squeal, Phil. I've got too much to lose. The coppers would hardly say, "Thank you, very much, Mr Clark, you can go home now." I'd be nicked quicker than yer could say "It's a fit up".'

Phil drew another cigarette from a crumpled pack and stuck it into the side of his mouth.

'That's all very well, Nobby, an', like yer say, you'd be nicked the same as the rest of us, but,' an unpleasant smile tugged at the corners of his mouth, 'the only problem is, while you'd get a few years fer buying stolen goods, me and the other two,' he jerked his head behind him, 'well now, we've got more ter lose, ain't we? I reckon we'd be lucky ter get off with twenty years, if not more, while you'd be out walking the streets a free man. Nah! Sorry, mate, that's not good enough. Before we dissolve our partnership, we'd like a bit of insurance, just in case, like. And once that's done, you can piss off. There's dozens of geezers who'd snap our hands off fer the chance to get in on our racket.'

George Davidson, Phil and Pete's younger cousin, shuffled forward impatiently.

'Fer Gawd's sake, Phil, get a move on. I got a heavy date tonight. Just tell him what he's gotta do and we can be on our way.'

Nobby looked warily at George. The Davidson brothers were tough enough, but their cousin wasn't quite right in the head. Not mad exactly, but he'd think nothing of slipping a knife into your back if he felt like it.

The sinking feeling in the pit of Nobby's stomach was becoming acute, though none of the men present would have guessed it. Keeping his voice hard he said gruffly, 'All right, let's stop pissing about and get down to it. What exactly do I have ter do to get rid of the lot of you?'

Phil took a long drag on his cigarette, his eyebrows rising in mock disapproval.

'That ain't very nice, Nobby. But all right, like yer say, let's stop pissing about. There's a lorry arriving next Thursday stocked up to the hilt with booze. Whisky, brandy, vodka, you name it, the lorry's carrying it. We won't spoil your conscience by telling you how we found out. Let's just say we've had the information from a reliable source. And you, Nobby, mate, are gonna be with us when we turn it over. Like I said before, it'll be a kind of insurance, just to make sure yer don't rat on us. Once the job's done, yer can be on your way, and if yer get any ideas in the future about going ter the coppers, the idea of having been involved in a hijacking should stop yer.'

Nobby felt beads of sweat break out on his forehead. He was in a tight hole and could see no way out of his predicament. If he refused, then he was certain he'd be found one night in some dark alley with a knife in his back. And if he agreed, he'd be party to a major crime.

The choice he faced wasn't good. He was no angel and, as Phil had pointed out, he been keen enough to handle the stolen goods and make a good profit out of them, but what they were suggesting went against every fibre of his character. All right, so maybe he was a hypocrite, and a thief into the bargain. But now he wanted out, and the only way he could see to achieve his aim was to go along with the Davidsons on their next job, and pray to God it went smoothly, and, more importantly, the lorry driver, or drivers, didn't get hurt.

He was still mulling the problem over when George sidled nearer, his rank breath flowing over Nobby's face, his lips smiling cruelly as he said, 'I seen yer the other day with a couple of tarts. Nice looking, the dark-haired one. Wouldn't mind of bit of that meself.' Reaching into his trouser pocket he pulled out a flick knife and pressed the spring to reveal a wicked-looking blade. 'It'd be a shame if anything was ter happen ter her. I mean, there's a lot of nasty geezers about, blokes who wouldn't think twice about slicing up a pretty face just fer the fun of it.'

An icy fear crept up Nobby's spine, then with a roar of rage he leapt at the leering man, his face contorted with rage. Ignoring the knife, he grabbed George around the throat and threw him up against the wall snarling, 'You scum! You touch one hair of her head, or any of the family for that matter, and I won't care if they bang me up fer life, or if I end up swinging from the end of a rope, 'cos I'll kill yer. D'yer understand, yer miserable bastard, I'll kill yer.'

Rough hands pulled Nobby off the grinning George and shoved him on to a wooden crate.

'That's enough,' Phil barked harshly at his cousin, who was still grinning inanely. 'You go anywhere near Nobby's girl and I'll see ter yer meself. We may be no angels, but we don't go in fer beating up women.' Turning back to Nobby, who was breathing painfully, Phil said softly, 'So what's it ter be, Nobby? You in or not?'

And Nobby, looking into the cold black eyes, answered bitterly, 'I don't seem to have much choice, do I?'

It had gone eight o'clock, and Aggie and Grace were just finishing the last of the washing-up from their late dinner. As always after this chore was out of the way, Grace and her nan sat down for a mug of tea and a natter.

'Polly looked a bit flushed when she came in, did yer notice, Gracie?'

Shaking her head, Grace replied, 'I can't say that I did, Nan, though she did shoot upstairs a bit sharpish after dinner.' A slow smile crept over Grace's lips. 'Maybe she met some boy over the park, and good luck to her if she has. Some of Linda's personality is beginning to rub off on her, she – Oh! There's the door. It must be Chuck, I'll get it.'

Grace opened the door to the tall, good-looking American, and, ushering him into the sitting room, called up the stairs, 'Vi. Vi, Chuck's here.' When there was no answer, Grace smiled, saying, 'She's probably got the record player on. I'll pop up and tell her you're here.'

Chuck Downing, six feet tall and dressed in his colonel's uniform, was absolutely gorgeous. Never before had Grace been jealous of Vi regarding her men friends, but this one . . . Phew . . . !

'Thank you, ma'am. I'll just sit myself down here and wait, if that's OK with you?'

The softly spoken drawl sent a shiver up Grace's spine. The American had been a regular visitor to the house these past four months, and it seemed as if he was as besotted with Vi as she was with him.

Grace hurried up the stairs, knocked on Vi's door then entered. Vi was in her underwear covered by a nylon wrap-over, sitting at the dressing table applying her make-up.

Looking at her sister through the oval mirror, Vi said, 'Anything wrong?'

Walking over to the single bed, Grace sat down and gazed at Vi's reflection.

'What? Oh, no, nothing's wrong. I just came up to tell you Chuck's here. I did call up, but you couldn't have heard me. Still, seeing as you mention it, there is something I'd like to get off my chest.'

'Oh, yeah.' Vi eyed Grace warily in the mirror.

'Oh! Now don't start getting your back up, Vi. I only wanted to say that I'm sorry I didn't take to him at first. I mean, none of us tried to make him feel welcome, did we? It was only because I thought Chris was such a nice bloke, and better suited to you than some American who might be here today and gone tomorrow. But Chuck obviously makes you happy, and that's all that matters. But don't you worry about when he has to go back overseas? I mean, it's not like our boys – when the war's over, he'll go back to America, and I don't want to see you hurt, Vi.'

Putting down her brush, Vi seemed to be deliberating as to whether to share something with Grace. Then, her face lighting up with excitement, she said happily, 'He's asked me to marry him, Grace. Oh, not now, of course. I'm not about to rush into marriage like poor Uncle Danny did. No! We've made proper plans. Before we even consider a wedding date, I'm going to go over to America and stay at his home for a while, to see how I fit in.' Seeing Grace's face crumple, Vi hurriedly came to sit beside her on the bed. 'Don't look like that, Grace. Nothing's settled yet. The war could go on for years, and who knows what might happen in the meantime.' Attempting to make light of the situation, Vi smiled wanly. 'If I do go, you'll all be able to come over for your holidays.'

Vi peered anxiously into Grace's face, pleading, 'You won't say anything to Nan, will you, Grace? She'd go mad, you know she would. She's still hoping I'll settle down with Chris. I just wish he'd stop phoning and coming to the club. Not that he causes any trouble. He just sits there, nursing a couple of drinks for an hour or so then leaves. And believe it or not, Grace, it upsets me. Chris is a nice bloke, one of the best, and I know he's in love with me. But I don't feel the same way about him. I like him, and I feel sorry for him, but I don't love him.'

When Grace asked quietly, 'Have you told him about Chuck's proposal?' Vi looked away, suddenly embarrassed.

'No, not yet. I mean I will, when everything's settled, but I don't want to make any announcements . . . well, just in case.'

Horrified, Grace stared at the averted face and said sharply, 'I hope you don't mean you're stringing Chris along just in case this thing with Chuck falls through. Oh, Vi, you wouldn't! Chris deserves more consideration than that. It's not fair to keep him hoping there's a chance for him when you know damn well there isn't.'

Vi rose sharply from the bed and strode back to the dressing table, where she began to powder her face furiously.

'You've no right to preach morals to me, Grace. There's poor Stan locked up in a POW camp, God knows where, and you're out almost every night with Nobby. A blind man could see you're in love with him, but you still keep sending letters care of the Red Cross to Stanley, hoping they'll be able to find out where he's being held. So don't accuse me of giving Chris false hope when you're doing the exact same thing.'

Grace's face turned white. Vi's barb had struck home forcefully. In an attempt to justify herself she stuttered, 'You can't compare me with you, Vi. For a start Polly's always with me and Nobby, and it's only once a week. As for Stanley – what else can I do? I don't even know if he's received any of my letters, but how could I write and tell him I don't love him any more with the state he must be in? To do such a thing would be cruelty beyond belief, and I just couldn't do it, Vi.'

Her face suddenly contrite, Vi muttered, 'I know, I know. It was a wicked thing to say. Even I wouldn't be that hard-faced. But I don't envy you when Stanley gets back home, Grace. You don't know what sort of state he'll be in. In fact, you might never be able to tell him the truth, not if he's really in a bad way.'

Grace hung her head. That thought had crossed her mind a dozen times a day. If Stan returned home an invalid she would be stuck with him for the rest of her life.

Leaving Grace's side, Vi picked out a calf-length black dress from her wardrobe and slipped it over her head. Stopping only to have a last look in the mirror, she said, 'By the way, I've cut my nights down at the club to three evenings a week. It was Chuck's idea. He's never been very happy with what I do for a living; which is ironic, seeing as that's how me met in the first place. He wants me to give up the job completely, but I'm not that much of a fool. I like my independence. Anyway, the manager wasn't very pleased.' She gave a soft, tinkling laugh. 'The funny thing was that Beryl asked the manager if she could step into my shoes, so to speak. You should have seen the look he gave her. I mean, I know she's not bad looking for her age, but she looks cheap and tarty, and the Top Hat only employs the best hostesses. That's why she's been so off-handed with me lately. She seems to think it's my fault she didn't get the job. And of course her nose is out of joint because she won't be able to go up West every night like she used to. Still! She's managed to latch on to Donald. He's no oil painting, and he's old enough to be her father, but he's got plenty of money, and that's all Beryl cares about. To be truthful, I'm glad of a break from her company. She was a laugh at first, but she can get on your nerves at times. Not only that, but my conscience has been bothering me lately about Uncle Danny, and what she's getting up to behind his back. I know it's a bit late in the day for me to start moralising, but better late than never.'

As they left the bedroom Vi clutched at Grace's arm, saying awkwardly, 'Thanks for the talk, Grace. I've been busting to tell someone about me and Chuck for ages, and I promise that the next time I see or speak to Chris, I'll tell him the truth, because, as you say, he's worth more than being led on when there's no hope of us getting together.'

After the couple had left the house, Grace spent the remainder of the evening with her nan and Polly, playing cards and listening to the radio until ten thirty, before retiring for the night.

CHAPTER TWENTY-ONE

'Are you sure you're not feeling well enough to come out with us tonight, Polly? We're not going far, just to a club in Stoke Newington near where Nobby lives. We could always come back home if you feel worse.'

Grace was sitting on the edge of Polly's bed, her heart hammering with guilty excitement. Part of her was hoping Polly would make an effort to go out, while another part of her prayed that her sister would remain in bed. She looked down on the forlorn figure, whose eyes were streaming above a bright red nose, brought on by a bout of hayfever.

Sniffing and sneezing, Polly dabbed at her red, puffy eyes and said miserably, 'Don't be daft, Grace. How can I go out looking like this? You'll just have to go without me for a change. Now, if you don't mind, I'd like some sleep.'

Grace left the room quietly and went downstairs to where Nobby, as usual, was regaling Aggie with more humorous stories.

'Honest, Aggie, I saw it myself. Stuck up on a wall it was, a big poster saying: "Flies spread diseases, so keep them buttoned". And I'll tell yer something else, Aggie, it wasn't directed at our boys. It was a blatant dig at the

Yanks. 'Cos they've been putting it around as if it's the last chance they're gonna get.'

Wiping the tears of laughter from her eyes, Aggie replied disdainfully, 'Yeah, well, yer can't blame the Yanks if it's on offer. And there's plenty of women who'd do it for ten woodbines lying down, an—'

'And five standing up,' Nobby completed the familiar saying, whereupon both roared with laughter as if hearing the joke for the first time.

Noticing Grace, Aggie enquired, 'Poll no better, then, love?'

Grace shook her head. 'No, Nan. She's worse if anything.' Turning to Nobby she said hesitantly, 'Maybe we should leave going out for another time, it—'

'What d'yer mean, not go out, just 'cos Polly's a bit off colour?' Aggie said tersely. Turning to Nobby she added roguishly, 'Anyone would think she's afraid ter be on her own with you, lad. Bleeding hell, if I was thirty years younger, yer wouldn't have ter twist my arm to get me out on me own. Go on, yer daft cow, get out and enjoy yerselves.'

Faced with both her nan's annoying insistence and the silent pleading in Nobby's eyes, Grace picked up her cardigan from the arm of the chair, kissed Aggie on the cheek, then, arm in arm with the handsome man by her side, her insides churning with anticipation, she looked forward to the night ahead.

The evening had been wonderful. They had dined on steak and chips and shared two bottles of wine, while enjoying the spectacle of the numerous young couples doing the new dance craze, the jitterbug. The club, a sort of social hall, was filled with GIs, much to the annoyance of the British tommies home on leave, for the women seemed to have eyes only for the fast-talking, gum-chewing Americans.

'Bleeding hell!' Nobby laughed loudly, as he watched a young woman being swung and flung every which way in time to the swing music. 'I've never seen so many pairs of knickers on display in one room in all me life.'

Then, with a twinkle in his irresistible eyes, he said mischievously, 'Come on, Grace, let's have a go, it looks like fun.'

Grace looked at him in mock horror. 'Give over, Nobby, I can't dance like that. I can just about manage a decent waltz. And even if I could, your back would never take the strain of chucking me about like that.'

Grabbing her hand, Nobby pulled Grace to her feet, declaring indignantly, 'We'll see abut that, madam, I ain't in me dotage yet, thank you very much.'

Pulling her on to the packed dance floor, Nobby leant close and whispered, 'I hope you didn't forget ter put yer drawers on tonight, or I'll find meself having ter fight off the entire American and British armies.'

Her face alight with merriment, Grace replied, 'Now you come to mention it, I had a feeling I'd forgotten something when we came out tonight.'

Trying to copy the other couples, who appeared expert at the new dance, Nobby and Grace ended up laughing so much they had to stop their efforts. Besides which it was pretty dangerous to be in the middle of the dance floor with arms and legs swinging in all directions. Nobby had already collected two kicks up his backside, while Grace had just narrowly missed being smacked in the face by an outflung hand. They were about to return to their table when the band changed to a softer tune.

'Now that's more like it,' said a jubilant Nobby, who was determined to have at least one dance with Grace before the evening ended.

Snuggled warmly in Nobby's arms, Grace laid her head on his broad shoulder, while the singer in the band gave a tear-jerking rendition of 'A Nightingale Sang in Berkeley Square'. When the music stopped, they remained as they were, loath to be separated. Then the band continued with the softer music by playing 'Moonlight Serenade'. When they stopped playing, Grace and Nobby stood still, hopeful of another slow dance, but they were disappointed. Without seeming to stop for breath, the small band immediately launched into another swing-dance tune.

Yet even seated back at their table, with Nobby's arms still holding her close, Grace could feel the wonderful intimacy they had shared during those two short songs, and found herself wishing the feeling could go on for ever.

They left the club at eleven, but no sooner had they stepped outside than the high-pitched wail of the siren went off. Almost instantaneously dozens of searchlights lit up the sky. Scores of people, all of them praying it would be a short raid, headed for the nearby shelters, but it was over an hour before the all-clear sounded.

Dishevelled, tired, and above all extremely thirsty, Grace climbed out of the shelter hand in hand with Nobby, to be met by the sickly sweet smell of cordite, burning wood and the air thick with brick dust. The street had been hit hard by the German bombers, and Grace watched with tears in her eyes as hordes of people scrabbled among the ruins of their homes, trying to salvage what was left of their possessions.

Then she felt her arm being pulled roughly.

'Come on, love. There's nothing we can do here. The ambulances and fire engines will be here shortly.'

Puzzled as to why Nobby was trying to rush her along, Grace looked over her shoulder, her legs almost giving way at the gruesome sight of a man lying in the gutter, his head yards away from his body. Oh God! She was going to be sick, or pass out, or both.

Leaning against Nobby's chest she cried piteously, 'Get me away from here, please, Nobby, get me away.'

Within ten minutes they were in Nobby's flat, and the first thing he did was to pour them both a large measure of brandy. He had seen too many dead bodies to be as affected by the sight of the decapitated man as Grace had been. Yet he had never become completely immune to the sight of the dead. When it was children, that was different – then the grief was compounded with hatred and rage against the men who had butchered the helpless innocents. Faceless men, dropping their deadly cargo on to the ground below, not even thinking of the deaths they caused, because it was their job. Just as it had been his job when Churchill had ordered the raids on Berlin in retaliation for the merciless bombing during the Blitz.

Throwing back his brandy he quickly poured himself another, wondering how many children he had killed or maimed as he had rained his bombs down on the city below. But a bomber pilot couldn't think like that. They were given orders and carried them out without question. Even so, every now and then, like this evening, seeing the devastation and the bodies of the unfortunate few who hadn't made it to the shelters on time, brought it all back. So what gave him the right to condemn the German pilots who dropped their bombs indiscriminately? He was no better than they were. He too had blood on his hands, and no matter how many times he argued with himself that they were at war, he still had trouble at times in justifying his actions.

'Could I have another one, please, Nobby? I'm still shaking.'

Nobby jumped at the sound of Grace's voice. He had almost forgotten she was there. As he refilled her glass he said, 'I'd better phone Aggie to let her know we're all right, and to make sure they are too. You'll have to stay here tonight, Grace. There's no telling just how much damage has been done, and I doubt there'll be any kind of transport running after this little lot.'

'All right, Nobby,' Grace said absently, her mind still trying to shake off the horrific sight she had witnessed. 'Can I have a wash? I feel filthy.'

As he dialled Aggie's number, Nobby nodded.

'The bathroom's through there.' He jerked his head in the direction of the small hallway. 'Oh, Aggie . . . Yeah, we're both all right, how about you lot?'

Grace waited, then smiled weakly as Nobby held up a thumb, indicating that everything was all right at home. Her legs still shaky, she entered the bathroom and washed her face and hands, then rinsed her hair under the tap with some soap, wishing fervently she could climb into a piping-hot bath filled with lashings of bath oil up to her neck. As it was she had to make do with tidying herself up as best she could.

When she came out, Nobby was waiting in the sitting room, a pair of large blue pyjamas wrapped over his arm. Grace took the clean garments gratefully, quickly taking off her soiled clothes while Nobby was himself having a wash.

She picked up her glass of brandy and took a long sip, her mind going round in circles. That could have been either of them lying dead in the street tonight. Up until now she had never fully appreciated just how precarious life was. It was something she had tried not to dwell on. But now, having seen how frail human life was, and how quickly it could be wiped out, it caused her to rethink her own life. Looking towards the bathroom door she admitted to herself for the first time that she was in love with Nobby, *really* in love; a love that bore no resemblance to the feelings she'd had for Stanley. And Nobby felt the same way about her. What if they had been killed tonight in the raid? What if they'd never had the chance to tell each other how they felt? And, more importantly, what if they'd never had the chance to express that love to its fullest extent? A slow, burning rush of excitement rippled through her body. Maybe it was the brandy making her reckless, or maybe she was just being honest with herself about what she wanted. And she wanted Nobby, wanted him in her arms, in his bed, their bodies entwined together.

Grace threw back the last of her brandy and laid back on the armchair, waiting for Nobby to emerge from the bathroom. Tonight had brought home forcibly just how precious life was – and she wasn't going to waste another minute of it.

'You look thoughtful. Not frightened I'm gonna suddenly jump on yer and inflict a fate worse than death, are you?'

Nobby stood in the doorway grinning mischievously while rubbing his wet hair with a towel. Going over to wind up the gramophone, he selected a record and placed it on the turntable. 'Well, yer don't have to worry, Gracie. You can trust me, though it'll stretch me willpower to the limit, and—'

'Oh, I know I can trust you, Nobby.' Grace was gazing up at the tall figure, the love she felt for this man showing in every contour of her face and body. 'It's myself I don't trust. That's why I've always asked Polly along with us. But these past few weeks, I've begun to resent her always being there. I wouldn't admit it to myself at first, but now, after seeing that poor man, I realised there would be no more tomorrows for him. No chance to achieve any goals he might have had, or maybe he'd just been putting off something he'd been meaning to do and never got round to it, telling himself there was always tomorrow. That could have been us lying dead in the street, Nobby, with no chance to be together ever again, no chance of belonging to each other. I want you, Nobby. I want you to take me to bed and love me, even if it is the only time it ever happens; at least I'll have the memory of this night.'

Nobby's eyes were alight with adoration. He hesitated

for a moment, his gaze dropping to the empty brandy glass.

As if reading his mind, Grace said softly, 'No, it's not the drink that's talking. All it's done is given me the courage to tell you how I really feel about you.'

Walking slowly towards her, Nobby bent down and gently picked her up in his arms, while Grace's slender arms wrapped themselves around his neck. Trembling with anticipation, Grace buried her face into Nobby's neck, and when he laid her down lovingly on to the quilted cover of his bed, she felt no fear or guilt. Perhaps tomorrow she might feel some remorse, but tonight belonged to her and Nobby, and she was going to make the most of every treasured moment.

The melodious voice from the gramophone in other room sang softly, *'I'm gonna love you, like nobody's loved you, come rain or come shine'*.

And Nobby did just that.

CHAPTER TWENTY-TWO

Aggie was having a short break from the housework, her huge hands clamped around a mug of steaming Camp coffee, with two digestive biscuits balanced on her knee as an extra treat. With the house to herself she let her mind wander aimlessly, her ever-active brain leaping from one thought to another. Although the war was far from over, there was a new optimism in the air, now that the threat of invasion had been lifted.

Her eyes flickered towards the clock on the kitchen wall, and with an impatient click of her tongue, she quickly downed the last of the coffee before debating whether to give the floor a good wash or start on the pile of stockings waiting to be darned. No! She'd do the floor, the darning could always be done later that evening while she was listening to the wireless. It would give her something to do and take her mind off her worries. As the thought crossed her mind, Aggie shook her head. What worries? she demanded of herself. You ain't got anything ter worry about. All the girls had jobs, so there was no need to worry about money. Polly's friendship with Linda Castle was still going strong, in fact the pair seemed to be joined at the hip

at times. Then there was Vi, still head over heels with that
Yank, Chuck Downing. He had been transferred overseas
some three months ago, but he wrote faithfully every week,
sometimes twice, promising to get back to London as soon
as it was humanly possible. Aggie hardly recognised her
headstrong granddaughter these days. Gone were the sullen silences, the bitchy remarks, and the air of superiority
that had always got up Aggie's nose. The two women hadn't
been so close since Vi's adolescence, and Aggie was glad of
the change.

As Aggie half-filled her bucket to wash the floor, she
thought wryly that, six months ago, she would never have
thought that out of her three granddaughters it would be
Grace who would cause her concern. Yet that's what had
happened. It was obvious that Grace was having an affair
with Nobby – at least it was obvious to her. She didn't know
if Vi or Polly suspected, but if they did, they hadn't said
anything; not to her anyway.

Sighing heavily, Aggie knelt awkwardly on the floor, her
bucket and scrubbing brush close to hand. The only thing
that mattered to her was seeing her granddaughters happy,
and Grace was happier now than she'd been in a very
long while, as were the other two. But Gracie's happiness
couldn't last, not unless Stanley didn't return home . . . !
Aghast at the callousness of her thoughts, Aggie plunged
the scrubbing brush into the soapy water and began to
wash the floor with such ferocity that the knuckles of her
hands turned white. God Almighty! What a thing to think
of. To practically wish for the death of someone, just to
make life easier. 'I didn't mean it. Oh, Lord! I didn't mean
it. I wouldn't wish Stanley no harm, honest I wouldn't.'

Ever since that first and only communication from the
Home Office to inform Grace that Stanley had been taken
prisoner, there had been no other news. The poor sod could
be anywhere for all they knew. And when last year, on 3

September 1943, the Allies had invaded Italy, prompting the Italians to surrender six days later, the officers and guards had simply walked out of the camps, leaving the prisoners to fend for themselves. Many of the men had died waiting for the Allies to arrive, but a good majority of the poor creatures had been rescued and taken to military hospitals. Back in England, thousands of families had waited eagerly for news, hoping some of the rescued would include their husband's, sons or brothers, but no such letter had arrived at the Donnelly household.

Preoccupied as she was with her private thoughts, Aggie didn't hear the front door open and close until a sneering voice said, 'Say one for me while you're down there.'

As always, the sound of Beryl's voice sent Aggie's hackles rising. But before she could make a suitable retort, Grace, who had come into the house behind Beryl, cried in exasperation, 'Nan! How many times do I have to tell you to leave the heavy housework for me and Poll. Now get up from there and into the sitting room and put your feet up.'

Beryl, her well-built body making for the larder, said harshly, 'For Gawd's sake, she ain't gonna drop dead from washing the bleeding floor, is she.' While beneath her breath she added, 'Worse luck.'

Immediately Grace turned on her sister-in-law. 'No she won't. Not while I'm around to prevent it. You'd better be careful, Beryl, because one of these days you'll bite that spiteful tongue of yours, and that alone will poison you. And you can get your sticky hands out of our larder. You're always stuffing your face these days, well not any more. In future you'll either contribute to the housekeeping money or buy your own. I'm sick of you sponging off us, and when Uncle Danny comes home on leave next week, I'll tell him as well.'

Beryl, her face white with temper, slammed the larder

shut, saying harshly, 'You can tell your precious uncle what yer want, lady muck, but I'd save yer breath if I was you, 'cos once I get him upstairs, he'll believe anything I tell him. So if yer know what's good fer yer, keep yer mouth shut and yer nose outta me business.'

Incensed at the hated woman's tone, Grace sprang across the room, and as the two women faced each other in mutual dislike, Aggie, standing by the door, eyed them both wearily. Beryl wasn't in the house much lately, using it like a hotel when it suited her, but when she was at home, there was always an atmosphere, and more often than not, an argument with one of them.

Her voice sounding tired, Aggie said, 'Leave it, Gracie, love, she ain't worth it.'

Aggie appraised the two women, both looking as if they'd like to tear each other apart, and it was as they both turned around, both showing their profiles, that Aggie's heart kicked hard against her ribs, followed by a rising sense of panic. Oh, no! Her eyes were playing tricks on her, surely. She wouldn't be so stupid or careless to get herself caught out. But there before her eyes was the evidence. Gawd Almighty! How hadn't she noticed before?

Her weariness lifting, she strode towards the table, and, grasping the edges, asked in horrified disbelief, 'Yer up the spout, ain't yer? About four months gone by the looks of yer. Yer silly mare, how could yer have been so bleeding careless?'

Two heads turned towards her, then Beryl, her face flushed, blustered, 'I don't know what yer talking about. Yer should get yer eyes seen to. You're going doo-lally in yer old age. Anyway, what if I was – which I ain't,' Beryl's head came up defiantly. 'But just supposing I was pregnant, so what? I'm a married woman, there's no shame in it.'

Staring at the painted face with incredulity, Aggie shook her head slowly. Then, her voice deceptively soft, she said,

'Well, well! All these years I've known Danny, and I never twigged there was something extra special about him. In fact, he's got something so rare, I think I'll write to the newspapers about him.'

Warily now, Beryl looked into the wrinkled face. 'What you on about, yer daft old bat?'

Aggie's lips spread into a chilling smile as she answered, 'Well, it's obvious, ain't it. If that's Danny's child you're carrying, then he must have the longest cock in the world. He'd have ter have, wouldn't he, ter be able to stretch it across the English Channel, halfway across London and up the stairs ter your room.' The smile dropping from her face, Aggie glared into Beryl's eyes with open disgust. 'No wonder yer was so bleeding happy about him getting leave. Oh, I can read yer sort like a book. You'll have him at it morning, noon and night while he's here, then I suppose you'll have ter write and tell him at some point that the baby's arrived early. In fact yer won't even have ter tell him that, will yer, 'cos he ain't gonna know when it was born. Not unless the war ends before you're due, an' I can't see that happening. Then again, you'll have ter have a birth certificate, but I suppose that'll go conveniently missing, won't it?'

Leaning up against the larder, Grace looked on in shocked silence, unable to utter a word. Then Beryl, her confidence returning, looked first to Aggie and then to Grace, and asked scornfully, 'And which one of you is gonna tell him, eh?' Bouncing her head at Aggie, she shouted, 'More ter the point, when was yer thinking of telling him? As soon as he steps through the door? And knowing your dear Danny, what effect d'yer think it'll have on him, eh? Especially as he'll be going straight back into the line of fire after his leave's up.'

Feeling more in charge of the situation now, Beryl drawled spitefully, 'He'll go back under enemy lines, knowing his wife's got herself knocked up by another bloke. How d'yer think he'll cope with that? It's amazing he's stayed alive this long, 'cos while we're being honest, we might as well be blunt as well. And the fact is that Danny's not cut out for soldiering. He hates every minute of every battle he's forced in to. His conscience bothers him every time he's forced to kill, he's told me. Know what else he told me?' The kitchen was eerily quiet except for Beryl's rapid breathing. 'He told me he sometimes hesitates before pulling the trigger because he hates the thought of taking a life. So how long d'yer think he'll last if he goes back knowing he's been made a mug of? His mind will be so jumbled up he won't know what he's doing. He'll be lucky to last a week without catching a bullet. So you think on that, the pair of you, before yer think of blabbing yer mouths off.'

When no answer came, Beryl's head bobbed in satisfaction. She had them in the palm of her hand. They wouldn't say anything to Danny, not now; they wouldn't dare take the chance; they loved the silly old fool too much.

Glaring from one woman to the other she nodded, confident now she had nothing to worry about. Then she made the mistake of testing her luck a bit further.

As she passed Grace, her hard eyes fastening on the young woman's lovely features, she gave a short, derisive laugh and said, 'What a pair of hypocrites you are. You've got the cheek to slag me off when we all know what's going on with you and that Nobby Clark. At least my old man's not banged up in a POW camp with his so-called loved ones sitting at home wishing him dead so he won't upset the apple cart . . .'

The cutting remark struck both women forcibly, for what Beryl had just said was partly true, and it was because of the guilt Grace and Aggie harboured, that they reacted as they did.

Aggie made a move towards the smirking figure, but

it was Grace who, with a howl of rage and before Beryl knew what was happening, swung her hand up and round, catching the side of Beryl's face with such force it almost lifted the woman's feet from the floor. Then, in a near perfect reconstruction of Aggie's actions with Mrs Collins months back, Grace gripped Beryl by the back of the neck and, marching her down the hallway, threw open the front door and sent the detested figure sprawling. Not bothering to see if her sister-in-law was all right, Grace slammed the door so hard that the noise reverberated throughout the house.

Shaking with rage Grace practically ran back into the kitchen, then, just as suddenly as her anger had flared, it evaporated. Placing her arms on the table, she rested her head between them and began to sob wildly, her voice coming out in disjointed words.

'She was r . . . right, Nan. I . . . I have wish . . . wished Stanley wouldn't come home. I . . . I don't wi . . . wish any ha . . . harm to him, hon . . . honest to God, I don't. I just sometimes wi . . . wish, he just wouldn't co . . . come home. But I've never wished h . . . him dead, Nan, n . . . never . . . !'

Aggie's own eyes misted over with unshed tears, and she stroked the back of Grace's head, murmuring softly, 'I know you haven't, love, I know.'

But I have, she added silently to herself. *God forgive me, I have!*

CHAPTER TWENTY-THREE

'Aw, come on, Aggie, it'll do yer the world of good ter get outta the house fer a couple of hours. It can't be much fun stuck in 'ere all day with that miserable cow upstairs. And it's a marvellous film, ain't it, Jeannie?' Rene Castle looked to her friend for support.

Jean Butcher nodded her agreement.

'Rene's right, Aggie. I've seen it twice already, an' I cried me eyes out both times.'

Aggie snorted loudly. 'I thought yer said it'd cheer me up. If it's that bleeding sad, I'd rather stay at home and be miserable, ta very much.'

Rene and Jeannie looked at each other in resignation, their faces glum. Then a spark of optimism flared as Aggie asked gruffly, 'What's it called again?'

The two women leant forward eagerly, and it was Rene who answered.

'*Gone with the Wind*, Aggie. And it's got Clark Gable an' Vivien Leigh in it. Eh, she's a right bitch, ain't she, Jeannie? But yer liked her anyway. But I was a bit disappointed with Leslie Howard. He played a proper wally . . .'

'Yeah, I know,' Jean agreed. 'But that scene when Clark

Gable sweeps Vivien Leigh up in his arms, then carries her up the stairs. Ooh, I came over all hot an' bothered at that bit. And what about the part when—'

'Fer Gawd's sake!' Aggie interrupted loudly. 'It won't be worth me while going if yer tell me any more about it. Why don't yer tell me how it ends an' all while you're at it?'

'Then yer'll come, Aggie?'

Both women held their breaths expectantly, and when Aggie shrugged and said gruffly, 'I don't suppose I've got anything better to do,' Rene and Jeannie shared a delighted grin of triumph. They had been trying for over two years to get Aggie to go to the pictures with them. Mind you, they could understand her reluctance to go after what had happened to Sam and Hetty. As far as they knew, none of the girls had been inside a picture palace since that day either.

Anxious to get Aggie out of the house before she could change her mind, the two friends practically bundled the elderly woman out of the door, keeping up a steady stream of talk as they walked.

'. . . I prefer ter go ter the matinee performance, it means I'm back home in time for the kids getting outta school. Not that they'd care. First thing they do after tea is run off ter play on the bomb-sites, and if I ain't at home when they get in, they're off ter the nearest one. Play there fer hours they would. They think it's all a game, which is just as well. Mind you, if their dad was at home they wouldn't have as much freedom as I give 'em. An' seeing as how Tom's due fer a short leave soon, they'd best make the most of it.'

Looking past Aggie, who was sandwiched between the two women, Jeannie asked Rene, 'How about your Bert, Rene? Any news of when he's due some leave?'

Rene shook her head dolefully.

'Nah, I ain't heard from the bugger in weeks. But then my Bert was never any good at writing letters . . . 'Ere, d'yer remember that time when that incendiary bomb landed over the house at the back of us, an' the handpump at the bottom of the street wasn't working?' Nudging Aggie in the ribs, Rene laughed gleefully. 'Yer remember that, don't yer, Aggie? A crowd of us went running over to see if we could help out, and there it was, a long bleeding silver tube, laying on the bedroom floor of the old couple who lived there, and them running round like blue-arsed flies, not knowing what ter do. And that horrible burning smell coming from it. Lucky our old men were on leave that day, wasn't it, Jeannie? 'Cos what with the handpump being out of order and the old couple in such a state, if it weren't fer our Bert and Tom, the bleeding thing would've gone off, and likely taken the lot of us with it.'

Noting a slight tremble pass through the large frame tucked neatly between her and Jeannie, Rene hurriedly continued her story.

'Then when the white smoke started to pour out of the end bit, me and you legged it, didn't we, Jeannie? 'Cos once that smoke starts coming out, yer know the bleeding thing's gonna explode. But Tom and Bert didn't turn a hair. There was us screaming at them ter run fer it, and waiting fer the bloody thing ter go off, and no sign of either one of them. Then, about five minutes later, when we didn't hear anything, we crept back up the stairs, and their was our old men just buttoning up their trousers. They'd only pissed on it, hadn't they? Gawd! Did we 'ave a laugh that day. You remember, don't yer, Aggie?'

A nudge in the ribs jerked Aggie out of her nervous silence. Throwing back her shoulders she barked in her usual voice, 'Course I do. I remember saying at the time it was a good job the men were on hand to deal with it, 'cos you wouldn't have caught me squatting over a smoking bomb trying ter piss on it.'

The notion of the enormous bottom of Aggie Harper

squatting over the incendiary bomb sent them all off into howls of laughter, with Aggie joining in, her spirits lifting temporarily – until they reached their destination. As they waited in line outside the rebuilt Plaza in Mare Street, neither Rene nor Jeannie could have guessed at the violent flutterings going on in their friend's stomach. And when the three women were finally seated, Aggie experienced a moment of blind panic as the lights went down. She felt as if she was enclosed inside a dark tomb, with memories of Sam and Hetty flashing through her mind, wondering if they'd had any warning before the bomb hit the cinema. Gripping the sides of the plush chairs Aggie tried to breath normally, calling on all her courage not to get up and run. Then the screen lit up and the familiar 'Cock-a doodle-do' of the big cockerel heralding the start of the Pathé News jerked Aggie out of her revevie, and as the news progressed she felt herself relaxing. Suddenly it was as if she had never missed her weekly visit to the pictures.

Then the news finished and when the haunting melody began to play the theme tune of the film, Aggie found herself settling into her seat, eager to watch the much-publicised film, just like old times. Within ten minutes she was deeply engrossed, her fear slowly subsiding as she was drawn into the exploits of Scarlett O'Hara and Rhett Butler. Opening her bag of boiled sweets, she began to stuff the confectionery into her mouth, her mind no longer in Hackney, but in the Deep South of America.

Hearing the three women leave the house, Beryl waddled slowly down the stairs and into the kitchen. Raiding the larder, she made herself a cheese sandwich and cut herself a large slice of the carrot cake that Aggie had baked that morning.

She had barely finished her midday snack when she heard the rattle of the letterbox and, as quickly as her cumbersome body would allow, she shuffled out into the hall and picked up the two letters from the mat, instantly recognising the scrawled writing of Chuck and Donald. Placing Vi's letter on the hall table, Beryl eagerly made her way back to the kitchen, her trembling fingers tearing at the long white envelope.

As she pulled out the letter a photograph fell on to the table. Picking it up Beryl saw a big, white house set inside what looked like acres of open land, and slap in the middle stood Donald, dressed in a brightly patterned shirt, denim trousers and a large cowboy hat perched on his head. Underneath the photo was the date the picture had been taken, July 1937. Beryl's eyes hungrily devoured the house and land surrounding it; then she turned to the letter. Donald wrote about how much he missed her and couldn't wait to see her again, and was longing to bring her over to America to visit his home, adding that he hoped she liked the look of it. He didn't say when he would be returning to England, only that it might not be for another few months. Then at the bottom of the letter he had added a PS: *But don't be surprised to find me on your doorstep one day very soon, if all goes well.*

Beryl read the letter twice, then turned her attention back to the photograph. God! If only she could be there right now, instead of stuck here with those three bitches and the growing lump inside her. Thank goodness Donald had gone back overseas before she had started to show. Maybe, if the baby had been his, he might have accepted responsibility for it, but General Donald Laine was no Danny Donnelly, ready to believe anything he was told without question. She had already been six weeks overdue when she had first met Donald, but that hadn't stopped her sleeping with him on their first night together. She had been just starting to show when he'd been transferred back overseas and that, as she had thought, was that. Oh, he had made the usual promises of keeping in touch, and telling her how he'd fallen for her, but she'd heard it so many times before that she hadn't attached much importance to it. Now, though, it seemed she had really struck gold. The life Donald was offering her made this place look like a hovel, and it was far from that.

Looking at the photo once again, Beryl grimaced as the baby gave her a hard kick in the ribs. Glancing down on the enormous lump, she said softly, 'Get a move on, will yer. 'Cos the sooner you're out the sooner I can get on with me life. But don't worry, I'm sure yer *granny* will take care of yer 'til yer daddy gets back home, 'cos I'm afraid yer mummy ain't gonna be around fer long.'

'I can't believe it, Nan. You actually went to the pictures with Rene and Jeannie. Weren't you scared . . . I mean after what happened to Mum and Dad?'

Polly, Grace and Vi were staring at Aggie in stunned amazement, threaded with admiration at their nan's courage.

As she poured out the tea, Aggie smiled weakly.

'To tell the truth, girls, I was shitting meself, especially when the lights went down and the whole place was plunged into darkness. I was all for getting up and running out, but I didn't want ter show meself up in front of Rene and Jeannie, not after all the trouble they'd taken to get me there. But yer know what?' She bounced her head at all three of them. 'After a while I forgot me fear and settled down ter enjoy the film, an' it was bleeding marvellous. In fact I might even go and see it again while it's still showing,' she added bravely. 'It wasn't only the film I enjoyed either. I'd almost forgotten watching the Pathé News. They've got a piece with Hitler and his Nazi chums doing the Lambeth Walk, yer know, with that trick photography, or whatever they call it. Gawd! Yer should have heard the audience laugh. And then they showed our lads landing at Normandy last

week. Oh! The cheers that went up when that was shown.
Course, it wasn't only our lads, there was plenty of Yanks
there as well. I'll bet by the time this war is over they'll be
knocking out a war film a week, with the Yanks winning it
fer us, of course . . . No offence to Chuck, Vi.' Aggie grinned
at her granddaughter.

'Oh, don't be daft, Nan. He'd probably agree with you if
he was here.'

The atmosphere in the kitchen was warm and cosy, and
each woman in turn felt the harmonious feeling binding
them together. Then Beryl lumbered into the room and the
warm glow suddenly dropped a few degrees.

Flopping heavily on to a chair, Beryl held out a letter to
Vi, saying tiredly, 'This came by the second post. I got one
an' all.'

Vi took the letter, her face lighting up as it always did
when Chuck wrote. She barely had time to open it when an
ominous sound filled the air outside in the street.

'What the bleeding hell's that noise?' demanded Aggie
as she lumbered down the hall and yanked open the front
door.

Everyone in the street was out in force, all eyes looking to
the sky. Then suddenly the noise ceased, only to be followed
moments later by an almighty explosion.

As they ran back inside the house, Grace stuttered, 'I don't
understand, I didn't see any planes.'

'Never mind that, girl,' Aggie barked. 'Get down them
steps ter the cellar.'

Hurriedly they all scrambled down the stairs below, but
they barely had the trapdoor closed when Beryl gave a loud
scream.

'Oh, me Gawd! I think the baby's coming!' she shouted,
before being brought bent double as the first contraction hit.

Helping hands guided Beryl to the settee, while Aggie
shouted out orders left, right and centre.

And while Beryl screamed and struggled to bring a new life into the world, the first V1 rocket had landed on London, killing many, and shattering the newly found confidence of the people of London.

After the first attack, the V1s, or doodlebugs as they soon became known, rained down thick and fast, more terrifying than any other bomb. It was all right as long as you could hear the drone of the engine; it was when the engine cut out that people either ran or threw themselves to the ground, waiting for the explosion. The craters they caused were relatively small compared to the bomb craters of the Blitz, but they were nonetheless deadly, and as the death toll rose steadily, the government began to think about ordering yet another evacuation of mothers and children.

It wasn't only lives that were shattered: homes and businesses that had been rebuilt were now being destroyed again. One such business was the Davidsons' illegal empire. After the war from the air had eased off, the brothers had become confident enough to buy a warehouse and stock it to the hilt, only to watch horrified as one of the dreaded doodlebugs dropped directly on to their Aladdin's cave, wiping out everything they had stockpiled over the years, and leaving them almost back where they had started.

Before the war they had been petty criminals, barely making enough to survive. With the onset of the war, Phil and Pete had avoided the draft for as long as possible but had eventually been conscripted. The first battle they had engaged in had left Phil with a badly damaged eardrum, and Pete, less fortunate than his brother, had been shot in the calf by one of his own platoon, leaving him with a distinctive limp. Neither man had minded his injury, seeing as it had got him discharged from the army. George hadn't even been considered for service – not with his history of mental instability.

Once back together in London, the men had returned to their petty thieving, until Phil realised there was a fortune to be made on the black market. They had started out on a low scale, but had soon realised how easy it was to obtain goods not available to the general public, and had steadily progressed their shady business until they were on a par with the big men running the same racket. The climb up the ladder had been so simple that the Davidsons couldn't believe their luck. What with the blackout and a serious shortage of police manpower, due to the large proportion of able-bodied policemen being sent off to war, at times it was like taking sweets from a baby. A few months back, 14,000 ration books had been stolen from a government office in Hertfordshire, 600,000 supplementary clothing coupons from a London employment exchange, and 100,000 ration books from the Romford food office. None of the culprits had ever been caught, nor any of the stolen items recovered. It was these particular robberies that the Davidsons were discussing as they sat hunched together at a table in a backstreet pub in Bow. They had become used to the good life, and weren't about to see it disappear. What was needed were a few good jobs, like the ones they had just been talking about, and they would be set for life. And Phil had just the jobs in mind.

'Now look, I'm telling yer, I got the information from an old mate who used ter work at the warehouse before he got sacked fer pilfering.' Phil Davidson, his face alight with enthusiasm, was detailing his plan to his brother and cousin. Seeing their doubtful expressions he banged his fist down hard on the table, almost overturning the three glasses of beer atop of it. 'What's the matter with the pair of yer? Lost yer bottle, 'ave yer?'

Pete Davidson, his face turning hard, growled, 'Don't talk cobblers, Phil. I've never lost me bottle in me life, but it's a big job you're talking about. It'll need more than just the three of us, and if you've heard about it, then yer can bet yer life the other gangs will 'ave got wind of it by now.'

Leaning forward eagerly, Phil said in a more moderate tone of voice, 'Nah, they won't. That's the beauty of it. This mate I was telling yer about went back ter the warehouse after they sacked him, looking fer some easy pickings. Anyway, he gets into one of the offices, hoping to find a cashbox lying around, and comes across these invoices fer two lorries expected to arrive at the warehouse next week. Arthur, me mate, knowing he'd stumbled on to a gold mine, copied down all the information. Times, routes and the loads the lorries are carrying. Now Arthur knows the job's too big fer him, right outta his league, so he comes ter me, knowing I'd see him all right. Which I did. Cost me a packet an' all, but it was worth it. At least I thought it was, now I ain't so sure. I thought you'd both jump at the chance of earning some easy money, but yer look like two old ladies frightened someone's hiding under their bed . . . Huh!' He laughed derisively. Finishing off his drink, he pushed back his chair, saying roughly, 'All right, if yer ain't interested, I know plenty of geezers that'd snatch me hand off fer the chance at a job like this . . .'

'Just a minute, Phil.' Pete was glowering at his brother, his eyes narrowing in anger. 'Me and George never said nothing about not being interested. It just seems too easy ter me. I mean, how about this Arthur bloke? Can yer trust him not ter go to one of the other gangs with the same information?'

Feeling more confident now, Phil sat back in his chair.

'Not Arthur, no way. He knows what'd happen ter him if he double-crossed me.'

George Davidson, who had remained quiet throughout the conversation, now spoke.

'So what are these lorries carrying that's worth nearly half a million then – gold bullion?'

Phil glanced at his cousin, his face grimacing in disgust.

'Fer gawd's sake, put that knife away, George. Can't yer clean yer nails like the rest of us without using that thing?'

George shrugged and put the penknife back into his pocket.

'Yer ain't answered me question, Phil. What's in these lorries? And if they're so valuable, they ain't gonna be that easy ter knock over. There'll be more than just the driver fer a start, and maybe a couple of guards an' all. And you're talking about doing two lorries at the same time. Like Pete says,' he jerked his head at his cousin, 'we're gonna need more than just the three of us if we're gonna pull it off. And one other thing.' He pulled a cigarette out of a packet and stuck it into the side of his mouth. 'If there are guards, they might be carrying shooters; did yer think of that?'

'Yeah, I thought of that, smart arse. That's why we'll be carrying shooters an' all – just ter be on the safe side.' At the sudden gleam that lit up George's eyes, Phil growled softly, 'An' yer can get that look off yer face, yer vicious bastard. The guns will only be used as frightners, so don't go thinking you're Al Capone when the time comes, or you'll have me ter deal with, understand?'

Pete, seeing the savage look that sprang into George's pale eyes, intervened quickly.

'All right, so you've got it all planned, except fer one small detail. Like I said earlier, we're gonna need more men, men who'll keep their mouths shut and not lose their nerve on the day. Got anybody in mind?'

Phil signalled to the barman for more drinks, confident now that he had them hooked.

When the drinks were deposited on the table, Phil sat forward and grinned.

'As a matter of fact I have.' He reeled off four names, all

known to the men at the table, who nodded in agreement at Phil's choice of manpower.

'That still makes only seven of us, Phil.' Pete flicked his cigarette into the flowing ashtray. 'I'd feel better if we had another bloke. That way we'd have four men ter each lorry – and yer still haven't told us what the lorries'll be carrying. I mean, we'll have ter know, so we can sort out what kind of transport we'll need to load it on to.'

Well pleased with how the conversation was going, Phil smirked. Then, taking a quick look round the pub, he lowered his vice and said, 'Over a million fags in one lorry, and half a million quid's worth of booze in the other one. There! That satisfy you're curiosity?'

Now all three men were on the edge of their seats, their hearts beating fast at the thought of the enormous wealth that could be theirs if things went according to plan.

Then Pete said quietly, 'We'll still be a man short, Phil, an' . . .'

Phil raised his hand and winked.

'Don't yer worry about that, Pete,' he smirked evilly. 'I've got just the man in mind.'

CHAPTER TWENTY-FOUR

As Aggie came through the front door, her face sullen at not being able to get a decent piece of meat for the Sunday dinner, and having to settle for mutton yet again, she cried out in pain as her shin collided with the large pram stuck in the hallway.

'Damn and blast that lazy, fat cow!' she stormed as her shin began to throb. Standing at the bottom of the stairs she shouted, 'Oy, Beryl, you up there?' Without waiting for an answer she yelled angrily, 'I ain't telling yer again about leaving that pram in the hall. If it ain't out in the garden by teatime, I'm gonna get rid of it meself.' The threat was an idle one, but nevertheless Aggie was sick to death of the cumbersome vehicle being left wherever Beryl chose to park it.

There was still no sound from upstairs, not even the blaring of the gramophone, which was constantly on day and night. Well, if Beryl wasn't home, and the pram was stuck in the hall, then where the bleeding hell was the baby? Raising her eyes upwards, her mouth formed a thin line of anger. Surely she hadn't gone out and left the poor little mite on its own? It wouldn't be the first time she'd done it, despite Aggie's threats to inform the welfare people – as if Beryl would worry about that. In fact it would suit her to have the baby taken away, because in the three months since its birth, Beryl had hardly bothered with it.

Sighing heavily, Aggie made her way up to the attic rooms, and sure enough, there, in the far corner of the sitting room, lay the baby in its second-hand cot, his poor little face red from crying itself into an exhausted sleep. And the smell! Lord, it was enough to knock you over.

Her features set into lines of grim rage, Aggie left the room, returning a few minutes later with a warm bottle of milk and a change of clothing for the baby. She lifted the small child from the cot and deftly changed its soiled nappy, wincing at the sores and bright redness covering the entire lower half of the little body. Gently, Aggie applied a good layer of Fuller's Earth to the infected area, then, leaving the baby's sore lower body exposed, she laid a towel over her lap and placed the teat of the bottle into the baby's mouth. Instantly two tiny hands grabbed at the bottle, and the poor little mite sucked for all his worth as the warm milk coursed its way down to his stomach. So hungry was the child that Aggie didn't even have time to wind him, the milk disappearing almost in one go. Wrapping the towel around the lower half of his body, Aggie lifted the baby to her shoulder and almost instantly a loud burst of wind came rumbling out of the small mouth.

'Well, that was quick, me laddo. I bet you were waiting for that, weren't yer, yer poor little sod. Oh, I'll have something ter say ter that mother of yours when I get hold of her. Mother! Huh! That's a good one . . .' She stopped mid-sentence as the baby looked up at her trustingly and smiled – a sight that melted Aggie's heart, bringing her close to tears.

Cuddling the warm body close, she began to sing a lullaby while stroking the downy hair. She hadn't wanted to become attached to the child, in fact she had gone out of her way to try and ignore it. If it had been her Danny's, that would have been different. Still! It was a good-natured baby, when he was fed and clean, always a smile for everyone, and would lie in his cot happily for hours gurgling to himself.

Aggie had been surprised when Beryl had announced her intention of calling the baby Patrick, before realising that naming the child after Danny's father was simply a ploy on her part, thinking probably that by naming the child after Patrick Donnelly, the thoughtful act might make the rest of the family feel more kindly disposed towards her. Well, it hadn't worked.

Giving the baby's tummy a tickle, and being rewarded by a wide smile, Aggie said, 'I don't know who yer daddy is, little man, but you must take after him fer yer temperament, 'cos yer sure as hell don't get yer good nature from yer mother . . . Oh, oh, speak of the devil.' The smile slipped from Aggie's face as Beryl bounded into the room, only to come to an abrupt halt at the sight that met her eyes.

The accusing stare etched on Aggie's features needed no interpreting, and Beryl, a rare stab of guilt attacking her conscience, stammered, 'I got held up. I'd've been back ages ago, but one of those bleeding doodlebugs landed right in front of the bus. We was lucky not ter be killed, but it made a right mess of the roads. I've had ter practically walk all the way back from Whitechapel.'

Aggie stood up, gathering the towel around the tiny form. 'He's been fed and changed, but I'd leave his nappy off for a few hours if I was you. His poor little arse is red raw from being left in a stinking mess fer Gawd knows how long. In fact, don't bother, I'll take him down with me ter the kitchen; he can lie on the floor and get some air to his skin while I get on with the dinner – that's if you've no objections!'

Whether Beryl had any objections or not was irrelevant. Aggie, holding the baby tight in the crook of her arm, swept past the shame-faced woman, the look of disgust on the elderly woman's lined face saying it all.

Flopping down on the bed, Beryl stared at the ceiling, her eyes bleak. She hadn't had a letter from Donald since before the baby had been born, three months previously. She kept telling herself that what with all that was happening overseas, he probably hadn't the time to write. But the nagging fact was that, at fifty-five, Donald was no longer in active duty. Because of his age and high rank he was stationed at Headquarters behind a desk; yet Chuck, who was in the thick of it, had managed to get two letters to Vi since the Normandy landings. And Beryl was getting desperate. Not out of any fear of Danny twigging the baby wasn't his, because by the time he returned home, there'd be no evidence of any premature baby. She had written and told him the baby had come early, but not to worry as he was coming along nicely. No! It wasn't Danny that was worrying her, but that blasted Nobby Clark. No matter how hard she tried to keep out of his way she was always bumping into him, and always he would look at her in puzzlement, as if trying to place her face. At such times she would make a quick departure before he had time to start asking awkward questions, but she couldn't dodge him for ever.

Beryl closed her eyes and tried to sleep, but she was far too restless. Sighing, she swung her legs over the edge of the bed and made her way downstairs. As much as she hated the old bat, at least Aggie was a bit of company, and with Vi giving her the cold shoulder lately, and the other two barely giving her the time of day, Beryl couldn't afford to be choosy if she wanted someone to talk to.

She entered the kitchen, ready to try and make peace with the old girl, then came to a dead halt. For there, sitting at the table as if he belonged in the house, sat the very man she had been thinking of. For a moment she froze, then with a resigned shrug she came in and sat down by the baby lying on the floor on a thick blanket.

'Hello, it's Beryl, isn't it? We always seem to be passing each other, but we've never been properly introduced. I'm Nobby Clark, but I suppose you already know that, don't you?'

The grey eyes twinkled at her in merriment, but behind the laughter Beryl could sense he was giving her the once over.

Leaning over to pick up the baby, she said off-handedly, 'Well, it's a busy house, ain't it? Anyway, I'm not stopping. I'm gonna take Patrick out fer a walk in the pram. It'd be good for him ter get some fresh air.'

Aggie went to make a remark but abruptly clamped her lips shut. She didn't want any unpleasantness in front of Nobby.

It was as Beryl was at the kitchen door that Nobby, twisting round on his chair, asked casually, 'You know, I'm sure we've met before. Didn't you used to work in a pub down the Old Kent Road?'

Without turning, Beryl said sharply, 'No, I didn't, yer must be thinking of someone else. Now, if yer'll excuse me, I want ter get out before it turns too cold.'

But Nobby wasn't going to be put off so easily. Drumming his fingers on the table he murmured, 'Yeah, I suppose I must be. The woman I'm thinking of had red hair. Lovely it was, right down ter her waist. The blokes used to swarm round her like flies. Lucky for her, her husband ran the place, and kept them in order. Big bloke he was, not the type you'd mess with. Handy with his fists by all accounts. Trouble was, he was a bit too handy with them, especially when he caught his wife flirting with the customers. Last I heard she'd left him. Done a runner with some bloke. I wonder where she is now?'

Her body shaking, Beryl tried to answer nonchalantly,

but when she spoke she was horrified at the tremor in her voice.

'Life's full of mysteries, ain't it? See ya.'

Almost stumbling in her haste to get away from the prying eyes, Beryl dumped the baby in the pram, covered him up and, negotiating the heavy pram down the stone steps, almost ran to the top of the street. Out of sight of the house, she stopped and lit a cigarette, her whole body trembling from head to foot. He knew! The nosy bastard knew. What the hell was she going to do now? Six years it had been since she'd left that pig of a husband, and the bloke she'd run off with had got cold feet and dumped her a month later, fearing the landlord of the pub in the Old Kent Road would come after them. Left on her own, the first thing Beryl did was cut her hair short and dye it blond. Then she had changed her name and found work in different pubs, never staying too long in any one place – until she'd landed the job in the Hare and Hounds three years later. For the first time in years she had felt safe. Then she'd latched on to Danny Donnelly and thought all her troubles were over. She should have known she wouldn't be that lucky. Though maybe that Clark fellow wouldn't say anything! Her head drooped in despair. Of course he would. He was thick with the family, wasn't he? She couldn't see him keeping quiet about her marrying Danny when she was already married. Her body sagged wearily. This was it then. As soon as Aggie found out, she'd be out on her ear, and the baby with her.

Hardly knowing where she was going, Beryl pushed the pram forward, the collar of her coat turned up against the October wind. And as she walked she prayed. 'Please, Donald, please write. You're my only hope now. Please, God, let him write to me soon, or I don't know what I'm gonna do. I'm too tired ter start all over again on me own.' The image of the big white house in America burnt into her brain. If only he would write and send for her. Even with the war on, there must be a way for her to get to America, there must be. Especially with Donald's considerable clout. After all, he was a general, so there must be something he could do to get her over to the States.

In the pram, the baby had fallen asleep, completely unaware of his mother's distress.

Back at the house, Nobby was trying to fend off Aggie's persistent questions without much success.

'Look, Aggie, I only said she reminded me of the woman I was speaking of. It don't mean ter say it is her.'

Bridling angrily, Aggie stormed up and down the kitchen, her face stretched this way and that in agitation.

'Don't give me that old cobblers, Nobby Clark. You know fine well it's her. And it'd explain why she did a runner whenever yer was around. 'Cos an old slapper like her wouldn't ignore a good-looking chap like you. She'd have been all over yer. Nah! She recognised yer, probably fancied yer from when yer used to visit that pub she worked in. Then with yer picture in the papers an' all, well, it must have put the wind up her—'

As a new realisation dawned. Aggie grabbed at the table for support, and in a voice little more than a whisper she said, 'That means she ain't really married ter my Danny. Oh, my Gawd!' Her legs turning to jelly she sank down on a chair. 'I thought it was bad enough her trying to palm some other bloke's bastard off on the poor sod, but this takes the cake.' Then, a determined look creeping across her face, she said in a stronger voice, 'Well, that's it then. She's out on her ear.' Pushing back the chair, she was about to get to her feet when Nobby's hand came out to stop her.

'Listen, Aggie . . . All right, it is her, I never forget a face, and yer was right, she was after me, but I didn't fancy getting me face bashed in by her old man. Mind you, she was a looker, and I can't say I wasn't tempted, but not to that extent. But for all we know her husband might be dead, or she could have divorced him, yer never know.'

'Oh, yeah, then why did she look about ready to pass out when yer started asking her questions? If she had nothing ter hide she'd have come clean.' Shaking her head furiously, Aggie said, 'Nah, she's had our Danny fer a mug, and I ain't gonna let her get away with it. It'd have been different if she'd been faithful ter him while he was away, but she's been round the track more times than a greyhound.'

Slipping a DE Reszke cigarette from a crumpled packet, Nobby lit up, his eyes squinting against the spiral of smoke, wishing he'd kept his mouth shut. But, like Aggie, he didn't like to see any man taken for a ride, especially when that man was away risking his life for his country. Still, he could have kept quiet a bit longer. But the damage was done now. Not that he felt sorry for Sandra, or Beryl as she now called herself. Women like that always found some mug to take care of them. No, it was Danny he was worried about, and the baby of course. Out of all of them, that little innocent was the one most likely to suffer, because he couldn't see a woman like Beryl keeping a baby with no man to support them. She'd probably dump the poor little sod as soon as possible.

The phone rang in the hall, making Aggie jump as it always did. In the kitchen Nobby smiled as he heard her bellowing down the instrument as if talking to someone miles away, then she was calling him.

'It's fer you, lad.'

His forehead creased in puzzlement Nobby went down the hall and took the phone from Aggie, wondering who could be calling him here. As far as he knew he hadn't given this number to any of his friends.

'Hello, Nobby Clark here, who's that?'

A sinister chuckle came down the line.

'What, forgotten me already, Nobby? Tut, tut, and us such good mates an' all.'

A chill went up Nobby's back as he recognised the voice. Gripping the receiver harder he hissed, 'What the bleeding hell you playing at, calling me here? And how'd yer get the number, 'cos I never gave it to yer?'

The voice at the other end of the line sounded amused. 'Give over, Nobby, it wasn't hard ter find. There ain't that many Donnellys in the phone book.'

Nobby, his voice hard, said, 'Don't piss me about, Phil. We made a deal, remember. One job, and our partnership was finished. Well, I kept my part of the deal and—'

The voice cut in sharply, all trace of humour gone. 'Yeah, well, things have changed, mate. I don't know whether yer heard, but our warehouse copped it in the last raid, and we need ter replace what we lost, and quickly. Now, I've got a couple of jobs lined up, both on the same night, so yer could look on it as just one more job fer old time's sake. I wouldn't 'ave bothered yer, mate, I mean we did make a deal, and I'm a man of me word . . . usually, but the thing is we need one more man, and you're the only one I can trust ter keep his mouth shut. So there's the deal . . .'

'Oh, no . . . Oh, no, yer can forget that, Phil. I'm out of all that now. I make enough to keep me comfortable, and that's just the way I want ter keep it . . .'

'NO! You listen ter me, Nobby. Yer'll do as yer told, or else. Don't forget that other job yer did with us. I told yer we needed some insurance on yer before we let yer out of the game, and now we've got it. You're in it up ter yer neck, the same as us. But this'll definitely be the last one. If we pull this off, none of us need ever worry about money again. We'll be set fer life, an' that includes you, Nobby. But if yer gonna try and wriggle outta it, then that insurance I was talking about is gonna get cashed in. Know what I mean, Nobby?'

His breathing coming in rasping tones, Nobby said grimly,

'Go on, then. Go ter the coppers. I'd rather take me chances with them than scum like you any day of the week. And one more thing, in case you've forgotten, Phil, it works both ways. You grass me up, and by God, you and your brother and that nutter of a cousin of yours will be standing right alongside me at the Old Bailey.'

A surprised tone entered the gravelly voice at the other end of the line.

'Coppers! Who said anything about the coppers, Nobby? Nah! I was thinking more about that nice bit of skirt you're so fond of. Gracie, ain't it? Posh piece by all accounts. Not one ter take kindly to villains hijacking lorries and stashing the proceeds. Then again, I may be wrong. Maybe she knows all about your little deals . . . Well! Does she, Nobby?'

Nobby closed his eyes in defeat. Grace wasn't stupid. She knew he dabbled in the black market, but she had no idea to what extent. And if she ever found out about the hijacking a few months ago . . .

Wearily, he said, 'All right, you bastard. One more. But by Christ, if you pull another fast one, I'll take me chances with Grace and tell her meself.'

A hearty laugh came down the phone.

'That's the spirit, me old mate. I'll phone yer at home with more details later in the week. By the way, you got a shooter?'

Nobby's feet nearly left the ground.

'A shooter? Fer fuck's sake, Phil! What yer getting me into? Of course I ain't got a shooter. Who'd yer think I am, Legs Diamond? Now look, I'll have ter think about this, Phil, I—'

'I'll be in touch, Nobby.' Then the line went dead.

His face ashen, Nobby slowly replaced the receiver, then jumped as he turned to face Aggie.

'I think you and me have got some talking ter do, son.

And don't try any of yer boyish charm on me, 'cos for once I ain't in the mood.'

Nodding slowly, Nobby followed Aggie into the sitting room. And after pouring out a glass of brandy for each of them, Nobby began to talk.

CHAPTER TWENTY-FIVE

Two days later, on the Tuesday before the planned robbery, three letters clattered through the letterbox. Beryl, unable to sleep for worry about her future, was the first one up, and at the sound of the post arriving she almost shot out of the kitchen and into the hall.

As she feverishly gathered up the envelopes she almost fainted with relief when she saw Donald's familiar scrawl. There was another envelope identical in design, which was for Vi, and the last was a plain brown official-looking letter addressed to Grace, which Beryl threw back on the mat. Lady Muck could pick up her own mail.

Beryl hurried back to the warm kitchen and ripped open the envelope, her eyes scanning the scrawled writing, her hopes rising with each word. When she had finished the two-page letter, she felt tears spring to her eyes, but they were tears of relief. Quickly now, she raced up the stairs and into Vi's bedroom, and without any preamble she shook the sleeping figure awake.

'Vi! Vi, wake up. Look, a letter from Chuck. And I've got one from Donald an' all. Oh, come on, Vi, wake up.'

Vi, her eyes bleary from lack of sleep, mumbled irritably

before struggling up on to her pillows.

'What the bleeding hell you playing at, Beryl? What time is it?' Glancing at the bedside clock she gave a wail. 'Are you mad, waking me up at this ungodly hour?' she said angrily. 'It's only seven o'clock. I didn't get home until three. You'd better have a bloody good reason for waking me up, Beryl.'

Trembling with excitement, Beryl sat down heavily on the side of the bed and handed Vi's letter to her, all the time talking excitedly.

'Donald wants me to go to France to join him, until they get their orders to return to the States. Look! He's sent visas and all sorts of forms, and he said Chuck was sending the same to you.'

Fully awake now, Vi sat further up in the bed, and as she read Chuck's letter a flutter of apprehension and fear coursed through her body. It was what she had been waiting for, but now it had arrived, she was suddenly afraid. It was one thing to dream and make plans, it was quite another to bring them to fruition.

She reached out for the packet of cigarettes on the bedside table and lit up, also handing one to Beryl absently, her mind whirling. This wasn't the way she had expected it to happen. She had imagined she would go to America when the war was over, which among other things would give her time to bring her nan around to the idea. That was what she was dreading most: telling her nan she was off to the other side of the world.

Lighting up another cigarette from the first one, she said to Beryl, 'Look, go and make us some tea, will you, Beryl? I'm still not properly awake yet.'

Eager to please, Beryl bounded off the bed, her eyes alight with excitement. Pausing at the door she said breathlessly, 'It's happening at last, Vi. We'll soon be outta this dump and living in luxury.'

Vi looked at the open door, her face showing distaste at Beryl's eagerness. Since she had discovered the truth about Beryl's past life, and that she had married Uncle Danny bigamously, Vi had found it harder and harder to remain civil to her so-called sister-in-law, let alone go back to the friendship they had once shared. For a moment she forgot about herself and thought of Danny, and the welcome home he would receive. Not, as he imagined, with a wife and child waiting for him, but the news that he had no wife, and the child he had thought his could have been conceived by any one of a dozen men. That had always puzzled Vi – that Beryl, with all her wordly ways, had got herself caught. Especially all the warnings and advice Beryl had given to her after she'd met Chuck and begun sleeping with him. Then again, everyone was fallible, but never in a million years would she have imagined Beryl getting herself pregnant through sheer carelessness.

The truth was, Danny would be better off without Beryl. Her uncle might be a bit of a wally at times, but he deserved better than Beryl, or whatever her real name was. Trouble was, he wouldn't see it like that, at least not at first. But in time he'd get over it. He'd have to, wouldn't he, poor sod. Shaking her head, she re-read the letter then lay back on her pillows to think. That she loved Chuck, she had no doubt, but to leave London within the next couple of weeks to stay in a foreign country for goodness knows how long before they could safely travel to the States was another issue entirely. Then there was the small matter of breaking the news to the rest of the family.

'Here we are, a nice cuppa tea.' Beryl was back with two steaming mugs of tea. 'I couldn't find any sugar, but the milkman's been, thank Gawd . . . Well! What d'yer think?'

Sipping slowly at her tea, Vi shrugged.

'I don't know, Beryl. It's all a bit sudden, and not like I imagined it would happen.'

Beryl's heart took a nosedive at Vi's lack of enthusiasm. She didn't lack guts, but she didn't relish making that journey by herself.

Swallowing hard, she uttered a false laugh. 'What d'yer mean, it's a bit sudden? You was saying only the other day how yer couldn't wait ter get outta London and be with Chuck. 'Ere, yer ain't changed yer mind, have yer, Vi? I mean, well, Chuck would be heartbroken if yer said yer wasn't gonna go out ter be with him.'

Vi flicked a cursory glance at her so-called sister-in-law. As if Beryl cared about Chuck's feelings, or anyone's else's for that matter. All Beryl cared about was herself. And the truth was that if Vi didn't go as planned, then Beryl would suffer.

Desperate to revive Vi's interest, Beryl held up her letter and continued excitedly, 'Listen, Donald says the top brass have taken over a château on the outskirts of Paris, and there's enough room for both of us to live in comfort until they're ready to ship out. And him and Chuck are top brass, ain't they? So they'll be able ter pull some strings to get us both to America safely. I don't know how they'll wangle it, but that's their problem, ain't it? Then there's the accommodation they've found fer us. I mean it ain't as if they was ordinary GIs offering ter put us up in a crappy old farmhouse fer Gawd knows how long. Oh, come on, Vi, please. Don't let me down. I can't go without yer . . . Well, I could, but I wouldn't fancy it much on me own. And, like Donald says, with all these bleeding doodlebugs landing wherever it takes their fancy, we could easily cop it. It ain't safe in London, Vi. We've been lucky up ter now. We came through the Blitz, and the other raids, but our luck can't last for ever. We've gotta get out while the going's good.' She stared in desperation at the lovely face lying against the pillows, her heart racing, waiting for Vi to say something.

Replacing her mug on the tray, Vi sighed heavily, her mind going round in circles. Beryl was right in one respect. It wasn't safe to be in London right now, and maybe if she waited until the war was over it might be too late. But what about the rest of the family? If all this had happened a couple of years back she wouldn't have hesitated, but things were different now. She had changed. She no longer felt herself to be outside the family circle, but a part of it, and it was a good feeling. She'd grown up a lot during the war. As Grace had pointed out, she was no longer the spoilt, petulant young girl she used to be, with no other thought in her head but having a good time . . . Oh, Lord! She didn't know what to do. She had to have time to think, she had to talk it over with someone. Not Beryl, Oh, no! But Grace would listen. She might not condone what Vi planned to do, but she would listen and give a fair and unbiased opinion. Yes, that's what she'd do. She'd talk to Grace. But first she had to get rid of Beryl.

'Look, this has all come as a bit of a shock, Beryl, and I'm still half-asleep. We'll talk about it more tonight when the others are in bed, all right?'

Heartened by Vi's change of attitude, Beryl rose hastily from the bed, saying, 'Yeah, all right, mate. You have a think about it. And while you're thinking, have a thought about that château. I've heard they're like palaces. We'll live like royalty.'

Her head beginning to thump, Vi said wearily, 'Don't get too excited about the château, Beryl. Now France has been liberated, it'll be returned to its rightful owner, so we could still end up in that crappy house you were talking about.'

Laughing gaily, Beryl replied, 'Nah, yer don't have ter worry about that, Vi. Donald told me all about it in his letter. It belonged to some Jews who got taken off ter one of the concentration camps over a year ago. They must be all dead by now. Hitler didn't hang about using those gas chambers, did he? That's if those stories are true. Anyway, I'll let yer get some rest, and we'll have that little chat later.'

The callousness of Beryl's remark brought the gorge rising in Vi's stomach. Stumbling from the bed she just made it to the toilet before throwing up. Shaken, she climbed wearily back into bed, shuffling down as far as she could under the bedclothes, trying to shut out the faceless family who had once occupied the château that Beryl was in such a rush to inhabit. But try as she might, she kept seeing a dim outline of a man and woman, the parents, maybe grandparents, and children, grandchildren, all taken away and murdered, for no other fault than being born a Jew.

Vi burrowed deeper under the bedclothes and closed her eyes. If she did go to France, and if she had to share a home with Beryl for a time, so be it. But once in America, she would make sure she never set eyes on the woman again.

Later on that afternoon, Aggie made a trip to the police station in Mare Street. At first the desk sergeant imagined her to be one of a dozen women coming in with far-fetched stories of spies and traitors in their midst. But once she mentioned the name Davidson his manner instantly changed. Soon she was being interviewed by an inspector, but try as he would, the only information he could get from the old woman was that the Davidsons planned to carry out a major job in the early hours of Thursday morning, on a stretch of road about a mile from the docks. Furthermore, they would be carrying guns. As for where she had obtained this information, Aggie's lips remained tightly sealed.

Having said her piece, Aggie made to rise from her chair.

'Just a minute, madam.' The sergeant placed himself in front of the stout figure. 'If we could just have your name and address . . .'

The look Aggie gave the unfortunate man would, as he

told his colleagues later, have stripped paint from the walls quicker than turpentine.

'What do you think, sir?' the sergeant asked after the formidable figure had left the office. 'She seemed all there, but you never know these days. And if she is making it up, there'll be an awful lot of manpower wasted.'

The inspector, a veteran of thirty years in the force shook his head.

'No! She knows what she's talking about, all right. Probably someone in her family's been pulled into it, and she wants the Davidsons stopped before her son or grandson gets hurt.'

The inspector rubbed his chin thoughtfully then rose to his feet, saying tersely, 'Come on, Fred. We've got a lot of work to do, and not much time to do it, so let's get moving.'

'France, Vi! Oh, no. I mean, I know how much you want to be with Chuck, but couldn't you wait a while longer? And what about nan? It'll break her heart, you know it will. Not only Nan, but me and Poll as well. We might never see you again.'

Tears welled in Grace's eyes as she stared at her sister across the table in the dimly lit kitchen, and when she saw Vi's eyes beginning to glisten she reached over and grasped her hand tightly.

'I'm sorry, Vi, I'm being selfish. If that's what you really want to do, then I'll help in any way I can. But how on earth are you going to get to France? It's not like you can just get on a boat and sail across, is it?'

In answer Vi pushed Chuck's letter across the table for Grace to read, saying weakly, 'Chuck and Donald have got it all worked out. Beryl and me will catch a train to Dover, and from there we'll board an American convoy ship bound for France. They've organised all the necessary documentation, and as it's all been arranged by two of the top brass, as Beryl calls Chuck and Donald, there shouldn't be any problem.'

But Grace was far from reassured.

'And what about the German bombers, Vi? They're always on the look-out for convoy ships. You could be bombed out of the water before you got halfway across the Channel.'

Vi's lips twisted in a wan smile.

'Oh, I think we'll be safe enough, Grace. All convoy ships have heavy escorts and, as Beryl says, we could just as well be killed by a doodlebug if we stay in London. I'm willing to take my chance on the ship if it means being with Chuck.'

Hiccuping and sniffing, Grace attempted to smile, even though every fibre in her body wanted to scream and beg Vi not to go.

'All right, Vi, it's your decision, and as you seem to have made up your mind, I won't stand in your way.' Forcing a laugh, she added in a quivering voice, 'At least we'll get a cheap holiday once a year, once you're settled in America.'

Vi gripped Grace's hand tightly.

'Thanks, Grace, I appreciate it, really I do. And there's one thing Nan will be pleased about, I'll be taking the ghastly Beryl with me, though I wouldn't like to be here when Uncle Danny gets home.'

Wiping her nose on a clean handkerchief, Grace smiled weakly.

'You're right there, though Nan'll miss little Patrick. She's become quite fond of him, we all have. After all, he didn't ask to be born, did he, poor little devil, and he's such a cheerful little soul. He deserves much better than a mother like Beryl.'

Vi gave an unladylike sniff, her eyes suddenly dropping to the table, unable to meet Grace's glance.

'I was wondering if you'd . . . well, if you'd break the news to Nan, only I . . .'

Immediately Grace pulled her hand away.

'Now hang on, Vi. I said I'd help in any way I could, but that's asking a bit much. Bloody hell! I think I'd rather come face to face with Hitler than tell Nan you're off to the other side of the world . . . Well, it'll seem like it to her.'

'Please, Grace,' Vi pleaded, the tears now running unchecked down her cheeks. 'I know it's a lot to ask, and I know you've your own worries, what with not knowing what's happened to Stanley and then there's you and Nobby . . . Oh, Lord, Grace, don't look at me like that. It's obvious you're in love with the man, and he's mad about you too! But there's no one else I can ask . . . Please . . .'

And Grace, looking into the tear-stained face, the face she was going to miss more than she had ever imagined, shook her head.

'All right, Vi. I don't know how I'm going to break the news, but it'd better be after you've gone. Oh, Vi, I'm going to miss you . . . !'

As of one accord the two women rose and held each other close. And the more they hugged the more they cried, because even with all the talk about having holidays every year, they both knew that after Vi left, they might never see each other again.

'Look, Aggie, I'll have to go. I've gotta be up by five,' Nobby protested as Aggie poured him another good measure of whisky from one of two bottles he had brought with him that evening. Though to be truthful Aggie had been more delighted at the two bars of soap he'd also brought. You couldn't get the stuff for love or money these days, unless you knew the right people, of course.

'Don't be daft, lad. I've never known you not to be able to hold your drink. An' I could do with a bit of company, seeing as how everyone seems ter have decided ter have an early night. Now, get that down yer before yer leave.'

Knowing it was useless to argue, Nobby took the drink.

He'd have to go careful tonight on the way home. The last thing he needed was to be stopped for drunk driving – and asked awkward questions about how he happened to have a full tank of petrol. Then again, it would get him out of tomorrow's escapade.

The thought of the morning brought a nervous quiver to his stomach and he took a large gulp of the amber liquid. All those years he had flown, been shot at and finally brought down, never in all that time had he felt as scared as he did right now. So much for the local hero, he thought scathingly.

All of a sudden he felt faint. Shaking his head he sat up straighter. That was funny, he'd never felt like this before after a drink. Downing the last drop he thought, *It's probably nerves, thinking about tomorrow*. But still, he did feel a bit odd, like he was going to pass out. He shook his head again, trying to clear his vision, and a suspicion dawned on him. The way everyone had suddenly become sleepy and headed off for an early night just after nine o'clock. With tremendous willpower he turned his head to where Aggie was standing by the wireless. The news had just finished, and *Sincerely Yours – Vera Lynn*, the sentimental half-hour linking the men in the forces with their wives back home, was just starting.

'How about another one fer the road, lad?'

Aggie was standing over him, and in a flash he knew.

'Aggie, what'd yer put in me drink? Aggie, yer silly cow, yer bl . . . bloody, si . . . silly . . .'

The glass dropped from his hand and Aggie smiled triumphantly. She'd slipped him enough sleeping pills to keep him out for at least 24 hours, by which time it would all be over and hopefully the Davidsons would be under lock and key. Humming to herself she replaced the sleeping pills in the kitchen cabinet, pills the doctor had prescribed for Polly during her bad period. She'd meant to chuck them, but was glad now that she hadn't, for not only had she slipped them into Nobby's drink, but also into the rest of the family's nightly mug of cocoa. Not as many as she'd given Nobby, of course, just enough to ensure they were out of the way, while she put Nobby out of action. Going back to the sitting room she lifted Nobby's feet up on to the settee and covered him over with a thick blanket, then, impulsively, she leant over and kissed him tenderly on the forehead.

'Sleep well, lad. By the time you wake up, it'll all be over. I've got it all worked out, don't you worry. You was with me on the night of that first hijack, and I'll swear on God and the Holy Bible itself if I have to. I'll look after yer, lad, 'cos let's face it, what would we all do without yer!'

She sank down into the armchair opposite Nobby, humming along to the wireless until the music ended.

Turning out the light Aggie went up to bed, singing softly, 'We'll meet again, don't know where, don't know when, but I know we'll meet again, some sunny day.' And there would be plenty of sunny days now she had made sure her lad was safe.

Before she turned in, she checked on her girls, who were all fast asleep, then she went happily to her own bed, sure in her mind she had done the right thing.

On a dark, lonely stretch of road between Dover and the Kent borderline, seven men sat huddled in their cars, their faces covered with woollen balaclavas, not only to avoid recognition, but also to help keep out the penetrating October cold that was seeping deeper into their bones with each minute that passed.

In the first car sat the Davidsons; behind them, in a black Ford, sat four well-known villains, all of them awaiting the arrival of the two lorries that would make their fortunes. But there was one man missing, and the absence of that man was making the others very uneasy.

'He ain't coming, is he, Phil? The bastard ain't coming. I told yer yer shouldn't 'ave trusted him. What if he's squealed to the coppers? Yer should've got someone else, he—'

'Shut yer gob, Pete, before I shut it for yer,' Phil Davidson growled menacingly. 'I'll deal with Clark, don't you worry about that.'

'And what about yer mate Arthur,' Pete persirted. 'Those lorries should've been 'ere half an hour ago. If we've been had fer mugs I'll . . .'

His words were cut off by the sound of a heavy vehicle approaching. In the darkness, Phil smiled grimly.

'Yeah, Pete. Yer was saying?'

'All right, all right. This ain't the time fer arguments. Now yer know what ter do, George. Yer should do. We've been over it enough times.'

Crouched behind the wheel, George Davidson grinned.

Phil climbed out of the car and clicked his torch twice to the men sitting in the vehicle behind before getting back in. Their hearts pounding with excitement and fear, the men waited. Then, as the masked headlights of the first lorry appeared in sight, Pete Davidson shouted, 'Now, George. Now!'

Immediately, George Davidson started the car, swinging it across the lorry's path. Almost simultaneously, the Ford roared forward to form a complete roadblock.

Within seconds all seven men were out of the cars, the Davidsons moving towards the first lorry, the other four men racing to intercept the second lorry before the drivers realised something was wrong. All seven men were carrying guns, confident that the mere sight of the weapons would stop any heroics on the drivers' part.

But no sooner had the hapless drivers been pulled from their seats than a strong voice, amplified by a loud hailer, called out, 'This is the police. Throw down your weapons, and lie face down on the ground. I repeat, this is the police. We are armed and have you completely surrounded.'

The seven men stood transfixed as the light from dozens of torches flickered on and off all around them as the police moved in.

'Come on, Davidson. Don't try anything stupid. There's no way out. Give yourselves up quietly. It'll go easier on you if you do.' The voice from the loud hailer was speaking again as swarms of uniformed policemen moved in on the stunned men.

Then George, his eyes glittering wildly behind the mask, screamed, 'Yer ain't taking me in, copper!' before opening fire, his gun spewing out bullets indiscriminately. The very second the first bullet was fired, the police marksmen returned fire.

'Fucking hell!' Phil and Pete Davidson spoke almost as one, then dropped to the cold ground, their guns aimed at the uniformed officers.

George Davidson was the first to fall, still screaming his defiance. Pete and Phil Davidson continued shooting, knowing they had no chance of surviving the merciless hail of bullets coming at them from all sides. Pete Davidson died with a single gunshot to his head, while Phil, deciding to make a run for it, was shot twice in the chest. The other four men had already thrown down their guns and were lying stretched out on the ground screaming, 'Don't shoot! Don't shoot!'

Two senior officers moved in, their faces impassive as they stared down at the dead bodies of the Davidson clan.

'Well, at least it's spared the country the expense of a trial,' commented the elder officer. Then, barking out orders to his men, he and his fellow officer returned to the warmth of their car to await the arrival of the ambulances and the press.

In those first few seconds between sleep and awakening,

Nobby licked his dry lips, turned over and promptly fell off the settee on to the floor. Still drowsy from the sleeping pills and whisky, he lay stupefied, his face a comical mixture of surprise and bewilderment. Then he remembered. With a loud oath he peered at his watch, his mouth falling open at the time displayed. Stumbling to his feet, he was about to run from the room when Aggie entered with a tray containing a mug of tea and a plate of spam and chips, the very smell of which made Nobby want to retch.

'Afternoon, lad. I was beginning ter worry yer might have popped yer clogs yer slept that long, but I didn't want ter disturb yer. There yer are, lad, get that down yer. You'll feel a lot better with a hot meal inside of yer. Grace and Polly are both at work, Vi's out shopping, an' that other one has taken herself off somewhere, so we've got the place ter ourselves.'

Nobby slumped back on the settee, his mouth gaping wide. Then, in a voice only a little more than a whisper, he groaned, 'Aggie! Oh, Aggie, yer don't know what you've done. I don't care what happens ter me, but you and the girls . . . I told yer, Aggie. I bloody well told yer . . .'

'Yeah, yer did,' Aggie replied cheerfully, putting the tray down on the coffee table in front of him. 'And I told you I'd think of something ter get yer outta it, an' I did . . . Look!'

Triumphantly she handed him the midday edition of *The Standard*. There, splashed all over the front page was a picture of the Davidsons, with the headline screaming, GANGLAND SHOOTING – THREE KILLED, FIVE POLICE OFFICERS INJURED IN SHOOT-OUT.

Wide awake now, Nobby hungrily devoured the rest of the story, and when he had finished he lay back, a look of total bemusement on his face, then he lifted his eyes to where Aggie was standing over him like a guardian angel and said hoarsely, 'Dead! All of them. Dead! I can't take it in. It was you, wasn't it, Aggie? You tipped the coppers off, didn't yer? Otherwise they'd never have known about—'

'Yeah, it was me,' Aggie interrupted sharply. 'And I ain't apologising fer it neither. 'Cos the way I saw it, it was either them or you, an' that being the case, there was no contest.'

Shaking his head in disbelief, Nobby said, 'You daft old cow. But I'm grateful ter you, Aggie, because I don't think I could've gone through with it, not when the time came. Then it would've been me lying on a slab in the morgue with a bullet in me back. And it wouldn't have been a police bullet that hit me either.'

Without thinking, Nobby began to eat the meal Aggie had prepared for him, talking between mouthfuls.

'I'll still have ter do time fer the first job I did with them, an' I ain't gonna wait 'til the law comes fer me. I'll give meself up an'—'

'What job?' Aggie cut in, her eyes wide with feigned surprise.

After he had shovelled another forkful of food into his mouth, Nobby said wearily, 'Now don't start that lark, Aggie. You know fine well what I'm talking about.'

'And who's gonna tell the coppers about that, eh? The Davidsons are dead, remember! But if one of their mob does try an' put the finger on yer, well then, it'll be their word against ours. As a matter of fact I remember that night well, 'cos we was all out celebrating me birthday, weren't we? Now who's gonna take the word of a known villain against that of a decorated hero and a family of law-abiding citizens?'

The food on the plate suddenly appeared unappetising to Nobby, and he was having to swallow hard to keep down what he had eaten. How on earth could he have eaten at a time like this? He sat quietly, humbled to the very core of his being by the sheer enormity of what this proud woman had already done on his behalf, and what she was further prepared to do if need be.

Aggie, realising Nobby needed time to think, waited silently.

Then Nobby lifted his head and looked at Aggie through red-rimmed eyes and said almost angrily, 'Aggie, I was in it up ter me neck. Oh, I didn't do any of the dirty work, at least only that once, but I made a packet out of the Davidsons. I ain't the decent bloke yer think I am. I'm a crook, Aggie, plain and simple. I want yer to know the truth before yer think about perjuring yourself on my behalf.'

Coming to sit beside him, Aggie put a fat comforting arm around his shoulders and pulled his head into her ample breasts as if he were a child in need of comfort.

'You ain't no crook, Nobby, love. Just a decent fellow trying ter get by as best yer could in hard times. You saved us from going short many a time – and plenty of others as well. All right, so what yer did was illegal, so what? There's worse than you walking the streets. But listen, lad, I want yer to promise that after today you'll have no more to do with the black market. I know it'll be hard on yer, but there's always a bed here for yer, and a plate of food, even if it is only tinned spam or tripe and onions. Yer won't go hungry or be out of a home, not while you've got us.'

Nobby couldn't raise his head to meet Aggie's eyes. He had enough supplies stashed away to see him comfortably off for at least another couple of years. But he'd be careful. There'd be no more selling from underneath the stall to special customers – well, maybe to a few of his regulars. After all, a leopard couldn't change his spots overnight, now could he? And he'd make sure Aggie and the family didn't go short either. Once this ordeal was over, he'd be straight with Aggie and tell her about his secret hoard. He smiled at the thought, then felt a stab of alarm as he felt tears spring to his eyes.

Patting Aggie's hand he attempted to rise, muttering shakily, 'I've gotta go, Aggie. There's things I gotta see to an . . .'

But Aggie pulled him back down, saying soothingly, 'There's no shame in crying, lad. Not even for a hero. So you let it all out, there's no one here to see but me, and I won't be telling anyone. Go on, lad, let it all go. You're safe now. You'll always be safe in this house.'

Nobby swallowed and cleared his throat and tried in vain to stem the rising flood of tears of relief. But it was no good. So, like a child, he laid his head on Aggie's comforting breasts and let all his bottled-up emotions out.

CHAPTER TWENTY-SIX

During the following week, the normally implacable Aggie was in a state of nervous strain, waiting for a knock on the door that would herald the arrival of the police and the subsequent arrest of her dear Nobby. If she hadn't been so preoccupied, she would have noticed the unusual tension among the women of the house, but with other matters on her mind, the preparations Vi and Beryl were frantically making went unnoticed.

The convoy ship Vi and Beryl were due to sail on was set to leave port in two days, and while Beryl couldn't wait to be gone, Vi was still having second thoughts. Not about seeing Chuck again – that she was deeply in love with the man she had no doubt – it was the sneaky way in which she was planning to leave that was racking her with guilt.

The last day at home was spent packing, with Vi's nerves on edge at every sound in the house, fearing her nan would suddenly appear and discover what she was up to. Then it was the last night. Her cases packed, the house silent, Vi looked at the bedside clock. It was one o'clock. In four hours she would be gone, maybe never to return. Her eyes burnt through lack of sleep, but she couldn't rest.

She moved slowly around the room, touching each item of furniture poignantly. Then, quietly, she went downstairs, wandering around the silent house, remembering all the times she had spent in these rooms during her lifetime. Finally coming to rest in the sitting room, she curled up on the settee, her eyes drawn to the old piano at the far side of the room. Making sure the blackout curtains were firmly closed, she switched on a lamp and stared at the piano. How many times had her dad sat there quietly playing some classical tune after a hard day's work or initiated a knees-up after a night out at the club? She remembered, too, how she had never joined in the jollifications, thinking herself too grand for such common behaviour.

Tears of shame stung her eyes at the memory. Then another memory sprang to her mind, bringing a smile to her quivering lips. She had been about seventeen at the time, and they'd been having a bit of a party. As usual, she had stood in a corner, her eyes scornful, boredom oozing out of every pore in her adolescent body. Then Sam had passed the piano over to Hetty and advanced on the scowling teenager skulking in the corner. Vi could remember clearly the devilment in his eyes as he'd approached her. Then she was being twirled and flung this way and that; at one point her father had thrown her over his shoulder, revealing her knickers to the loud amusement of the onlookers. And that was before the jitterbug dance had ever been heard of! Oh, she had been mortified, fleeing to her room in a paroxysam of angry tears at being so humiliated. A short time later, Sam had come into her room and taken her in his arms, saying over and over again how sorry he was for upsetting her. But she had been in too much of a temper to accept his apologies. Before he had left the room he had looked at the weeping form on the bed and said softly, 'Oh, my darling, I wouldn't hurt you for the world, not intentionally. I love you, Vi. Always remember that, even when you're hating me, like now, I love you, and always will.'

Burying her face in her arms, Vi wept silently before whispering, 'And I always loved you, Dad. Even when you showed me up, or took me down a peg or two. I deserved it, I know that now. I was a horrible person back then, but I only did it because I knew I could get away with it. Because I knew that no matter how badly I behaved you and Mum loved me. Thank you, Dad, and you too, Mum, for giving me such a loving childhood, and the security that allowed me to be such a horrible cow.'

Her conscience eased somewhat, she fell into an exhausted sleep.

She was awoken by a rough hand shaking her none too gently by the arm.

'Come on, Vi, wake up. We've gotta leave in half an hour.'

Shrugging off the persistent hand, Vi sat up, angry at being awoken so roughly.

'All right, all right, keep your hair on, I'm coming. I can go to the bathroom first, can't I? That's if you don't mind waiting another few minutes.'

The sarcastic tone was wasted on Beryl, who was in a fever of excitement to be away from the house before anyone woke up – especially that old bag Aggie.

After she had washed her face and hands, Vi took one last look in the bathroom mirror before going quietly into Grace's room.

But Grace was already up and at the door. Placing a finger to her lips, she whispered, 'Have you carried your suitcases downstairs yet?'

Vi gave a tremulous smile. 'Beryl's already done it. It must be the first bit of hard work she's done since she moved in.'

Beryl was standing impatiently by the open door, her foot tapping anxiously, terrified that something might happen to prevent their departure.

Then Grace and Vi were clinging together as if they never wanted to let go of one another.

'You'll explain to Nan, won't you, Grace? And Polly. I'll write as soon as I'm settled, I promise.'

'Fer Gawd's sake, get a move on, Vi,' Beryl said harshly, her eyes flickering down the dimly lit hall, fearful of seeing the awesome sight of Aggie descending the stairs.

They were out on the porch in the dark November morning when Grace suddenly exclaimed, 'Just a minute. What about Patrick? Aren't you taking him with you?'

Expecting just such a question Beryl answered, 'It'll be too dangerous fer him. Besides, he'd be better off with you lot. Like you're always telling me, I'm a rotten mother, so he'll be better off without me.'

Dumbstruck, Grace could only stare at the hard, painted face. She had imagined Beryl capable of many things, but abandoning her child wasn't one of them.

But before she could say any more Aggie's voice floated down the stairs, 'That you down there, Grace. You all right, love?'

The dreaded voice spurred both women on.

Vi gave Grace one last hug, saying tearfully, 'Bye, Gracie, I love you.'

Grace stood on the porch, watching the departing figures for as long as possible, but the darkness of the morning soon swallowed them up. She closed the door and turned to find Aggie facing her, her eyes questioning.

Grace took a deep breath, gently took hold of Aggie's arm and led her towards the kitchen, saying softly, 'We'd better go and make a cup of tea. You're going to need it, Nan.'

*   *   *

'Look, Vi, there's a taxi, quick . . . Oy! Oy! Hold up there!' Beryl screeched.

The black cab, barely visible in the dark, with its head-lights covered, slowed to a halt.

The cab had barely pulled away from the kerb when the deadly drone of the familiar V2 rockets sounded.

'Oh, shit!' The taxi driver, an elderly man, put his foot down, not knowing if he was driving into or away from the doodlebug. Then its engine cut out, and in those few seconds of deadly silence the three occupants of the cab froze. The explosion came almost immediately, followed by another engine close by, then another.

The taxi driver pulled over shouting, 'I'm staying put. There's no telling where those bastards will come down. I'll take me chances here. It's up ter you what yer do.' With that he hunched down on the front of the cab covering his head with his arms.

Thinking quickly, Beryl swiftly followed suit. The man was right, if she tried to run, she could be running straight into its path. She didn't hear the door opening at first, then, peering up from her hunched position she saw Vi running down the street.

'Come back, yer silly bitch. Yer'll get yourself killed.'

But Vi paid no heed. That blast had come from the direction they had just left, and there were at least another two ready to drop their deadly missiles. Gasping for breath she rounded the corner into her street, her legs going weak as she saw her house still standing. Then one of the engines above ceased, and Vi flung herself to the ground, covering her head with her arms. The explosion rocked the ground she was lying on, and when she gingerly opened her eyes she saw that the two houses next to Benji's had been directly hit. Screwing up her eyes against the flying debris and dust she tried to look further down the street, then the other engine cut out. It seemed a long way off, but as Vi got shakily to her feet, she looked up and screamed as the other rocket's load came down, directly over the end house – her home.

'NO! NO!' Her legs barely able to keep her standing, she stumbled on. She was barely a few feet from the house when the next bomb found its mark. The explosion lifted Vi off her feet and flung her high in the air, her body landing with a sickening thud, face down on the debris-covered ground.

Back in the taxi, Beryl waited, her body tense with each explosion. Then, after all was quiet for ten minutes, the cabbie lifted his head and asked, 'D'yer wanna go back to see if yer mate's all right, love?'

Beryl looked at her watch. The train to Portsmouth was due to leave in just under an hour. If she missed that . . . Her lips set in a grim line, she said tersely, 'No! I've a train ter catch. She'll have ter get a later one. Drive on.'

The contemptuous look in the cabbie's eyes wasn't lost on Beryl, but she no longer cared. This was her last chance for a bit of happiness and she wasn't going to blow it for anyone. As the taxi headed off towards the station she had a fleeting stab of guilt about Patrick, wondering if he was all right. Then she hardened her heart. Whether he was or not, there was nothing she could do about it now. Leaning back in the seat she stared fixedly out of the window until they reached the train station.

'They've bleeding well what?' Aggie, her face stretched in disbelief, stared accusingly at Grace, as if she herself had betrayed her. Grace kept her head down, not able to look her nan in the face.

'Hello, you're up early, I heard the front door banging, then you two talking down here. Nothing's wrong, is it? Oh, by the way, Grace, I noticed this letter sticking out from under the hall mat. I don't know how it got there.'

Grateful for the distraction, Grace took the letter, her heart skipping a beat as she recognised the official letterhead.

While her nan ranted on to a sleepy-eyed Polly about what had transpired, Grace read the letter, her hands beginning to tremble as the words sunk into her brain.

'. . . the ungrateful pair of cows. And she's left her baby here. The bloody cheek of it. Well, I ain't gonna look after it, not at my age, I—' She broke off her tirade as she saw the whiteness of Grace's face, and the letter held between her trembling fingers.

'What is it, love? Not more bad news, I hope. I think I've had me fair share of shocks fer one day, and it ain't even light outside yet.'

Through dry lips, slack with relief, Grace murmured, 'No, Nan, not bad news. Stanley's in a military hospital, it doesn't say where. There's not much detail, just enough to let me know he's alive and will be moved to England as soon as it's safe.'

Her voice softer now, Aggie asked tentatively, 'Does it say how badly injured he is?'

Grace shook her head.

'No. Just what I've told you. I expect I'll hear more at a later date.' Reaching out she grabbed Aggie's hand. 'Thank God he's all right, Nan . . . Oh, thank God! I'd never have forgiven myself if . . .'

Aggie squeezed the cold hand, knowing exactly how Grace was feeling. She too was experiencing a great sense of relief at the news. It was as if a giant weight had been lifted from her shoulders, the weight of guilt. For, like Grace, she too at times had thought how much simpler life would be if Stanley didn't make it home, and those secret thoughts had weighed heavily on both women's minds. Now their consciences were clear, for if Stanley had died, neither of them would have known a moment's peace for the rest of their lives.

Polly, who was reading over Grace's shoulder, suddenly threw her arms tightly around Grace's neck.

'Oh, Grace, I'm so relieved he's all right. I was so sure he must be dead by now, but he's alive, and he's coming home. Stanley's coming home.'

Grace turned to look up into the beaming freckled face, but before she could say anything they heard the sound of the V2 rockets overhead.

Quickly now, the women rose to their feet with Grace shouting, 'You get down the cellar, I'll get Patrick. Hurry!'

Racing up the stairs Grace grabbed the sleeping baby from its cot and hurried back downstairs. She had just reached the cellar when the first bomb dropped. Then the second. They never heard the third one.

CHAPTER TWENTY-SEVEN

Lester Road, that once ordinary East End backstreet had been turned into a raging bomb-site. Out of the twenty-eight houses only eleven remained intact. Out in the road, sheets covered the dead, while firefighters fought to contain the blaze that was spreading from one house to another. The street was choked with fire engines, ambulances and dozens of people, some neighbours, some strangers, all fighting desperately to find and rescue any survivors in the piles of dust and rubble that had only hours ago been homes. The early hour of the attack had caught almost everyone unaware. The residents of Lester Street had still been in their beds when the rockets had been launched, and even though some had been awoken by the terrifying noise, most had been too late to get to the shelters in time.

At the site of Paddy's Castle, Nobby Clark, his face black with grime and smoke, tore frantically at the rubble with his bleeding hands, praying like he'd never prayed before, knowing that if the Donnellys were dead, a part of him would die with them. He knew himself to be of strong character, but everyone had their breaking point and this would be his. The death of his beloved parents had almost been the undoing of him, then he had met the Donnellys, and from that first meeting he had felt as if he had found a second family. Not that anyone could ever take the place of his parents, but the warmth and genuine hospitality of the Donnelly family had helped ease his pain. Now it was happening all over again, but this time there would be no kind-hearted, good-natured family to help him through his grief. If he lost the women of this house, especially his darling Grace, then life wouldn't be worth living. The bomb had landed on the top of the house, demolishing the attic rooms, which in turn had collapsed on to the second floor. Every window had been blown out by the blast, but by some stoke of luck the majority of the main building was still intact, even though the inside of the house was a mass of choking rubble.

''Ere, lad, slow down. You'll do more harm than good by going at it like a bull at a gate.' Reg Watson, the local warden pulled at Nobby's arm. 'It's got to be done right, lad. Now come away and let those of us who's trained get on with it.'

Nobby shook his head, almost demented with worry.

'I'll help then. Show me what to do, and I'll help, but I ain't leaving. That's my . . . my family in there.'

Reg took Nobby's arm gently and led him to one side, signalling to the other rescuers to carry on. Slowly and carefully they moved the wreckage brick by brick, then they proceeded to do the same with the timber. Nobby, standing alongside, watched then joined the rescue party, carrying out instructions without question. By his side, Reg Watson tried to give the frantic man some hope.

'They might have made it to the cellar, Nobby. If they did then there's a good chance they're all right. Old Paddy Donnelly built that place well underground. It's the safest place in the house.'

Nobby gasped for breath as he lifted a large piece of timber with care from the wreckage.

'They wouldn't have had time to get there, Reg, not at that time of the morning. They were probably still in bed like those other poor bastards lying in the road.'

Reg glanced sorrowfully over at the pile of covered bodies and wondered why he wasn't crying. Those people lying out there were his friends, people he had grown up with, people he had loved. Like Jeannie Butcher and her bunch of lively kids, and Rene Castle and her children – all dead. God! He couldn't believe it. And what about Bert and Tom away fighting for their country. How in God's name would they react when they heard their entire families had been killed? Poor old Benji had copped it as well; not from the bombing, but from the shock. His heart had given out when he had seen the mass destruction in the street in which he had lived for over thirty years, and the covered bodies lying so pathetically on the ground. Then there was was poor Violet Donnelly, so smashed up he, Reg, had hardly recognised her at first. She had been one of the first to be ferried to the hospital, but whether she was alive or dead, Reg had no idea. But the state her face had been in, Reg doubted if the once-beautiful young woman would thank the doctors for saving her.

Reg glanced at the young man by his side; he would be destroyed if the Donnellys were dead. For a brief moment Reg closed his eyes in utter desolation, then his training took over and he carried on with his job.

Nobby, his eyes reddened by smoke and dust, was passing a long beam to another man along the line. After a few minutes Reg held up his hand for silence, and the men and women lining the street held their breath. But no sound came from the pile of rubble that had once stood so proudly at the top of the street, dominating all the terraced houses adjoining it. Reg nodded, and the men resumed their work, passing pieces of debris and wooden floorboards and window-frames from one to the other. On Reg's orders the men were concentrating on the lower part of the house, praying the Donnellys had made it to the cellar before the bomb had dropped. Because if they had been still asleep then there was no hope for any of them.

One of the men at the top of the line held up his hand for silence, and once again the crowd fell quiet. Then a cheer went up as the frail sound of a baby's cry reached them. With renewed effort the men bent their backs, heedless of their bleeding hands and aching bodies. Reg held up his hand once again, and the crowd responded instantly. After a few agonising moments the sound came again, stronger this time, and with renewed effort the line of men concentrated on the area from which the sound could be heard.

Then three of the men were inside the house and looking down into the large crater that had once been the cellar. The lead man, his blackened face lighting up to reveal white teeth that stood out in startled contrast to the blackness of his face, called out, 'I can see them.'

Someone else shouted, 'Are they alive, mate?'

But here the man couldn't give a reply. That the baby was alive was obvious from its now frantic wailing, but as for the others . . .

Nobby, covered from head to foot in sooty dust and dirt, was almost unrecognisable, as, heedless of the hands that came out to grab him, he stepped carefully over the rubble, coming to a heart-stopping halt as he stared down into the vast hole. A hole that was filled with large, broken beams criss-crossing the opening, and large chunks of the ceiling that had fallen down on the occupants of the cellar.

Then Reg was by his side, saying quietly, 'Steady, Nobby, steady. I've seen worse than this, and got people out alive. Now, just do as I tell you. Don't try shifting or moving anything on your own, or you could make matters worse. OK, mate?'

Nobby nodded dumbly, too dazed to argue.

The professional rescuers resumed their work, and after twenty minutes, one cried out, 'I can see them. Three women and a baby.'

'Can you get to them, Norman?' replied another voice.

'Yeah, but it's gonna be difficult. There's beams everywhere. Some of 'em are holding up what's left of the ceiling. If we move the wrong ones, the whole lot could come crashing down.'

Reg Watson, his face grim, caught the man by the arm.

'Well, that's what you're trained fer, ain't it, Norman? To do the job properly. So let's get on with it.'

The man Norman took no offence at Reg's harsh words. He knew the strain the elderly man was under. The women trapped below were friends of his, and the poor bastard had already lost enough of those today.

It was twenty minutes before the baby was handed up through the hole, alive and well and screaming its head off. The cheer that went up as a woman rushed forward to take the squirming, filthy bundle was deafening. The woman, who was lucky enough to have a home to return to, quickly took little Patrick into the safety of her house, followed by other women, eager to help in any way they could.

Ten minutes later another body was lifted out.

Nobby, standing at the edge of the entrance, was almost afraid to look. It was only when one of the men shouted, 'She's still breathing, get her into the ambulance quick!' that he opened his eyes and put out his arms to take the unconscious figure. Stumbling over the debris, he laid his face against the deathly white cheek of Polly before handing her over to the doctor waiting by the ambulance.

He had barely delivered Polly into the safe hands of the doctor when another shout rent the air. Turning swiftly, Nobby saw Reg and another man carrying Grace carefully over the mound of debris. As if new life had been injected into him, Nobby bounded forward, his eyes wide and questioning.

'It's all right, mate. She's alive an' all, but like her sister she's gonna have ter get to the hospital as quick as possible.'

Too full of emotion to speak, Nobby once again held out his arms and took Grace tenderly from the men's hold.

Burying his face in the dirty hair, he sobbed, 'Oh, Gracie, Gracie. Hold on, darling, you're gonna be all right. You're gonna make it, I promise.'

The chalk-covered face looked lifeless, then the eyelids fluttered and a pair of brown eyes were gazing up at him.

'No . . . Nobby. Is that you, Nobby?'

A sob of relief tore at the back of Nobby's throat as he answered, 'Yeah, it's me, darling. Where else would I be when you needed me?'

Grace's eyes closed again as she whispered, 'Poll . . . and Nan, an . . . and Patrick . . . ?'

'Poll and the baby are fine, darling. They're just getting Aggie out now and . . .'

The doctor and a nurse bustled forward.

'There, give her to us, sir, we'll take it from here.'

Reluctantly Nobby handed over his burden, desperate to go in the ambulance with the two girls, but knowing he couldn't leave until he was sure Aggie was all right. Then he was pushed aside as the woman who had taken Patrick into her care gently handed over the now-silent child to the nurse, who just as gently carried the baby into the ambulance.

Nobby watched helplessly as the ambulance sped off, then he returned to the bomb-site to await news of Aggie. But as he tried to climb the steep pile of rubble his legs suddenly gave way beneath him and he was forced to sit down and rest awhile. His back, left leg and arm were beginning to cause him extreme pain, but not for the world would he admit it. Not while Aggie was still down there in the cellar, and the street littered with dead bodies. He may well be in agony, but at least he was alive.

A woman appeared before him with a hot mug of tea, which he accepted gratefully, gulping down the scalding liquid as if it were water. Two other men came to sit beside him, their faces weary, their bodies slumped in exhaustion. And as Nobby looked at their haggard faces he felt a rising admiration for these men who risked their lives, never stopping until they were sure there were no more bodies left alive in the ruins of the bombed-out houses – and for this heroic work, they were paid the measly sum of three pounds ten shillings a week. The woman appeared with more tea, which was again gratefully accepted.

'How's it going in there?' Nobby jerked his aching neck behind him.

One of the men looked at him warily, then turned to his mate before answering, 'You're a friend of the family, ain't yer, mate?'

Nobby thought he had no more emotion inside of him, but at the sound of the man's voice he flinched, his stomach turning over painfully.

Gulping loudly he said, 'Yeah, I am. Why? What's happened to Aggie . . . I mean the old lady?'

Running a calloused hand over his dirt-streaked face, the man answered sympathetically, 'I don't know, mate, an' that's the truth. She's pinned down under some beams, an' we're frightened to move them in case the whole ceiling falls in. I'm sorry, mate, but it don't look good.'

Nobby slumped back on the hard rubble, his face a picture of despair. Slowly he got to his feet and painfully returned to the house.

'How about trying ter get a rope round one of the beams? We might be able to lift it off. What d'yer think, Reg?'

The old man looked fit to drop any minute, but he stood erect, determined to see the job through.

'Yeah, it's worth a try. I don't see as we've got any choice anyway. We can't leave her down there much longer or she'll croak fer sure.'

Hearing the sombre words, something inside Nobby snapped. He felt his head spinning, then he was falling. He heard voices call out to him, then the darkness came up and swallowed him.

He came to in an ambulance, lying flat on his back on a stretcher. His first reaction was to try and sit up, then a familiar voice said croakily, 'Lie down, lad, and have a rest. By the look of yer, yer need it.'

As Nobby turned his head he looked straight into the vibrant eyes of Aggie Harper. Her face was covered in powder dust, and her hair was almost black with dirt, but the eyes were unmistakable – as was the voice; even choked with smoke there was no mistaking Aggie's voice.

A man in a white coat was bending over her, telling her to lie still and keep quiet and rest. Nobby closed his eyes, waiting for the tart retort the formidable woman would levy at the young doctor. But to his surprise, and profound relief, Aggie merely answered softly, 'All right, Doc, anything yer say. I ain't up ter arguing with yer, not today.' Then her eyes closed and her head lolled to one side as the pain-killing drug the doctor had administered took effect.

'Doctor!' Nobby pulled anxiously at the white coat. 'How is she? The last I heard she was pinned under some beams.'

The doctor took hold of Nobby's wrist and carefully checked his pulse before replying, 'I won't lie to you, sir. She's an elderly woman, and she's had a tremendous shock to the system, as well as lying trapped under a heavy beam for hours. She was pinned under her stomach. We won't know if there's any internal damage until we get her to the hospital. I'm sorry, that's all I can tell you for now. As for you, I think you could do with some rest yourself. I've been told you have a back, leg and arm injury sustained during a plane crash. You must be in some considerable pain. I'll give you something for it to make you comfortable.'

'No, no, I don't want anything, thanks, Doctor. I'm fine, really, I'm fine.'

But the doctor had already injected the morphine. As the drug took hold and Nobby felt the familiar euphoric effect of the drug, he felt a moment of panic, remembering his dependency on the drug after the crash. Then he was floating away, the pain vanishing as if by magic, and within seconds, he too, like Aggie, was out for the count, free from suffering and worry – for the next couple of hours at least.

They had all been very lucky, at least that's what the doctors had told them, but then the doctors hadn't been buried under a pile of rubble in total darkness for over five hours. Grace and Polly had suffered severe bruising and cuts to most of their bodies, and both were still in a deep state of shock, but none of their injuries were life threatening. And by some miracle, the baby had hardly sustained any injuries at all, apart from severe fright. It was Aggie and Violet who were causing the most concern. And as Nobby accepted his third cup of tea from a passing auxiliary nurse, he sipped the scalding liquid, his mind running around in circles.

His relief at discovering Grace and Polly hadn't sustained any serious injuries in the bombing were compounded with his anxiety over Aggie and Vi, who were both still in the operating theatre. Unable to sit still any longer, he made his way towards the ward where Grace and Polly were still sedated. Kissing them both gently on the forehead, he then walked unsteadily back to wait outside the operating theatre, stopping any passing doctor for news of the other two Donnelly women. But the doctors and nurses, although kind and sympathetic, had no time to stop and chat; they had too many patients to see to after the morning's raid.

Pacing the hospital hall, Nobby remembered Aggie in the ambulance. She had seemed all right, but, as that doctor had told him, she had been trapped under a heavy beam for goodness knows how long, and she wasn't a young woman any more. Nobby's face twisted into a grimace. Yeah, well, that doctor didn't know Aggie like he did. She was a tough old bird, and a fighter. If anyone could pull through such an ordeal then that person would be Aggie. He wasn't so sure about Vi though. He hadn't been allowed to see her, as the doctors were already operating on her by the time he'd come round from his morphine-induced state. The effects had long worn off, and Nobby looked for the umpteenth time at his watch, thinking it must have stopped, for the time didn't seem to be moving at all.

Knowing he would go mad if he stayed here much longer, Nobby was about to go upstairs to see if Vi was out of surgery when the green doors of the operating theatre swung open, and there was Aggie, lying on a stretcher, looking pale but peaceful.

Clutching at the nearest doctor's arm, he asked fearfully, 'Is she gonna be all right, Doc? Is she gonna . . . ?' His throat seemed to seize up as he waited for the news, mentally preparing himself for the worse.

The doctor, seeing the anxiety in Nobby's face, took him to one side and, after pulling down his mask, said kindly, 'It's all right, she's not in any danger now. But she was very lucky. She has some internal injuries which we've seen to, but if she had been a slighter-built woman, then her injuries would have been much worse. You could say her, shall we say, fuller figure cushioned the weight of the beam.'

Nobby felt his head spinning, the relief making him feel sick, but he stayed silent as the doctor continued.

'She'll have to stay in the hospital for a few weeks I'm

afraid, maybe longer. It all depends on how fast her body recovers. But when she does get home, she'll have to take it easy, and I mean just that. No heavy lifting, no walking around the shops for hours. Just plenty of rest is what she'll need.' He paused. 'I'm presuming she has family who will take care of her when she gets home.'

Nobby blew out his cheeks, then attempted a lopsided grin.

'Oh, yeah, you've nothing ter worry about on that score, Doc. She'll be waited on hand and foot for as long as it takes, but she ain't gonna like it, not Aggie. She can't bear to be fussed over, and as fer sitting around fer months doing nothing . . . Well, she's gonna drive the family mad. Not that they'll mind. The fact that she's alive and well is all they'll care about. Thanks, Doctor, thanks fer everything.' Now he was pumping the startled but pleased man's hand in gratitude, before following Aggie's stretcher up to the ward. He sat by her bed for an hour, hoping she would wake, but although her eyes flickered a few times, she remained unconscious.

As he had done earlier with Grace and Polly, Nobby leant over and kissed the wrinkled brow before leaving the ward, his heart lighter now he knew they were all going to be all right. He found himself humming beneath his breath – but then he stopped dead in his tracks. Vi! He still didn't know how Vi was. Hurrying back up the stairs, he made a few enquiries and was told Miss Donnelly was out of surgery and in intensive care. The sister would offer no more information until Nobby, lying blantantly, told the starchly uniformed woman that he was her fiancé, then she unbended, her whole attitude softening. She led Nobby into a side room and waited until he was seated. As Nobby looked into the solemn face and saw the pity reflected in the sister's eyes, he felt a moment of panic. He should have known it was too good to last. If he was a betting man, he would have laid a thousand to one against the possibility that an entire family could be struck by a bomb and have them all survive. He listened as the woman spoke, trying hard to register what she was saying. The good news was that Vi, like the rest of the family, wasn't in a life-threatening position. The bad news was that the nature of her accident would leave her face permanently scarred.

Nobby didn't remember leaving the hospital, or thanking the sister for her kindness. The next thing he knew he was in a pub, knocking back pint after pint, as if trying to block out the image of Vi; Vi with the beautiful face that had drawn men like flies around a jam jar, now cursed to spend the rest of her life disfigured. It would be bad enough for any woman to suffer such a fate, but for a woman like Vi, who relied on her looks to get her through life, it would be a devastating blow, and Nobby didn't think she would be able to tolerate or accept her injuries; her character was too shallow. He wouldn't be a bit surprised if she swallowed a bottle of pills at the first opportunity.

Shuddering at the thought, Nobby ordered another beer. He was desperately sorry for Vi's predicament, but at least she was alive, as was the rest of the family. They had all survived. And as soon as they were ready to leave the hospital he would be there waiting for them. And while he was waiting he would find a place for them to live until Paddy's Castle could be rebuilt. That's if it was possible.

He swallowed the last of his beer and debated ordering another; then he decided against it. Instead he headed back to where he belonged, at the hospital with his family.

CHAPTER TWENTY-EIGHT

As Grace prepared to leave the corner shop on a warm April day in 1946 she paused, turned back and gave the man behind the counter a stern look.

'Now don't forget what I said, Uncle Danny – no tick. I mean it now. No matter what sob story you're told, you've got to say no, or better still, tell whoever asks they'll have to come back this afternoon to see me. Because as soon as I'm halfway up the road, they'll be in here like a swarm of bees.'

Danny Donnelly, back home these last four months, smiled sheepishly.

'Aw, Gracie, you know I haven't your strength of character. I don't mean to give tick, but somehow I always end up doing it. I'm sorry, love. Maybe it'd be better if you found someone else to help you out here.'

Grace sighed in loving exasperation. Staring at the red-faced man behind the counter, she wondered how any-one could have fought in such a terrible war and remain unchanged by their experiences. Yet Danny had managed to do just that. From the moment he had landed on their doorstep in his cheap demob suit, he had been the same old

Danny. Shy, unsure of himself, still dependent on others, he had cried in Aggie's arms at the sheer relief of being safely back home. And it had been left to Aggie, still bedridden at the time, to tell the excited man that his wife had never been his wife at all, and that she had run off with an American in 1944 and hadn't been heard of since. Worse still, she had callously left her own baby behind without a second thought.

The old woman had watched helplessly as Danny's face crumpled at the news he was hearing. Then, much to Aggie's amazement, he had squared his shoulders and said in a soft but steady voice, 'It's all right, Aggie. I half expected this to happen, especially seeing as I never received any more letters from her after the baby was born. It would have been daft of me to think a good-looking woman like Beryl would stay in every night listening to the wireless. And with a million Yanks over here chucking their money and nylons around, well, it must have been hard on Beryl not to give in to temptation, because she always did like a good time, did Beryl. But at least she left me my son. It must have been hard on her leaving him behind, but she did it for me, so that at least I'd have my son to come home to. You have to give her credit for that, Aggie.'

And while Aggie had lain in her bed, her mouth flapping open and shut like a fish out of water, Danny had left the room, returning with Patrick in his arms, a nervous Grace and Polly following close behind him. Then Danny, his face alight with pride as he held his child, had turned to his nieces and said kindly, 'Don't worry about me. Your nan's told me all about Beryl, but like I told her, at least she left Patrick behind, and for that act of kindness I'll always be grateful, whatever else she may have done.'

The three women had made frantic eye contact, wondering who should tell the delighted Danny that the child he was holding so proudly in his arms wasn't his. Breaking the news about Beryl had been bad enough, but to tell Danny about the baby . . . !

As usual it was Aggie, always the one to get bad news over with as quickly as possible, who painfully leant across the bed and took hold of Danny's hand, saying, 'Danny, son. There's something else you have to know, an' it ain't gonna be pleasant. But someone's gotta tell yer. It's . . . it's about Patrick . . . he's—'

All three women jumped as Danny, his face no longer genial, rounded on them all in turn, and said in a voice reminiscent of his dead brother, 'I may have lost my wife, but Patrick is my son, and whatever other inadequacies I have, and believe me I know them all, one thing I know I'm capable of is being a good father. So before we all leave this room, I'll say it one more time, and then I never want the subject raised again. Patrick is my child and will be raised as such. Now, does everyone understand?'

Dumbfounded, the women had all looked into the sombre blue eyes, which at this moment bore no resemblance to those of the Danny they knew, and each had nodded in agreement, too stunned to do anything else.

The matter had never been referred to again.

'You look miles away, love. Anything wrong?' Danny asked as his eyes scanned his niece's vacant expression.

Grace, returning to the present, looked at her uncle affectionately. He was wrong to say he had no strength of character. He had shown it that first night he had returned home, almost daring them to say Patrick wasn't his child. And also the night he had first brought Beryl home and announced they were married – he had stood up to Aggie when she had loudly voiced her disapproval. Oh, Danny had character all right; unfortunately it only emerged in times of severe crisis.

'No, nothing's wrong. You just remember what I said. I'll be back about three to give you a break, that'll give me time to get the dinner done and put Patrick down for his afternoon nap. See you later, Uncle Danny.'

Waving goodbye to his son, Danny began to tidy the shelves. Within a minute of Grace leaving, the doorbell tinkled and two women entered the shop, smiling broadly.

'Hello, Danny, lad. On your own, are yer?'

Danny replaced the jars on the shelf and groaned. Out of all his customers these two were the worst for asking for tick.

As he pasted a sickly smile on his lips he asked in a resigned voice, 'And what can I do for you ladies today?'

As Grace opened the front door and lifted the wheels of the pushchair over the doorstep, she could hear laughter coming from what used to be the library and was now Stanley's bedroom. Placing the pushchair in the hall she checked on the sleeping Patrick, hung up her coat, fixed a smile to her face and walked into the converted bedroom.

'Hello, Grace, I didn't hear you come in.' Polly, her face alive with laughter, looked up at her eldest sister.

'Sorry, I'll make a bit more noise next time.' Grace smiled back. Walking over to where Stanley lay propped up by pillows she leant over and kissed his forehead, saying brightly, 'How are you feeling today, Stan? A bit better by the sounds of it.'

Stanley Slater looked up at his fiancée, his eyes losing a little of the sparkle that had been evident when Grace first entered the room.

'Not too bad, thanks, Grace. I'm being well looked after.' Nodding his head at Polly he added cheerfully, 'I've told her she should think about becoming a nurse. She's looked after me better than any of the nurses in the hospital.'

'Oh, you.' Polly laughed as she gently punched Stanley's arm. Stanley looked at the freckled face, the warmth coming back into his eyes, a look that Grace was quick to notice.

As Stanley continued to talk to Polly, Grace's eyes moved over the emaciated body lying in the bed and felt her heart go out to him in pity. The strong, able-bodied Stanley that had gone off to war bore no resemblance to the frail frame of skin and bones that lay in the bed. Even his face had aged, but that wasn't to be wondered at, with what he had been through.

Grace left the room, saying she was going to make the dinner, but once in the kitchen she sat down at the table, making no move to prepare a meal. Instead she laid her arms on the table and rested her head between them. God, she was tired, so very tired. The war had been over for ten months now, and Stanley had been in the house for six of them.

When he had first arrived by ambulance into her care he had been so grateful for every little thing she did for him, even thanking her for something as simple as plumping up his pillow. It had been as if he was afraid that if he proved to be too much trouble he would be carted back to the hospital. He had been in a pitiful state the first time she had visited him at the military hospital in Kent. The dysentery and almost daily torture by the Italian guards in the POW camp had left their toll, and if the Italians hadn't thrown in the towel and gone over to the Allies' side, Stanley would surely have died. Bert Harris, the friend Stanley had joined up with, hadn't been so lucky. He had died a horrible, lingering death brought on by constant ill-abuse.

The prisoners had woken up one day in early September 1943 to find the camp deserted, the guards and officers having left hurriedly before the approaching American and British armies had arrived and seen the indescribable conditions under which the POWs had been living during their confinement.

Stanley, along with his fellow prisoners, had been taken to the nearest Red Cross centre, and from there moved to a military hospital in Italy, where he had remained until the end of the war. During his time in hospital, Stanley had often thought of writing to Grace to let her know he was all right, but he had been so ill, both in body and mind, that the effort always seemed too much. Besides, he had reasoned with himself in his lucid moments, the authorities would surely let her know. After all, she was down as his next of kin, even if they weren't married. But somehow, during the confusion of the war, he had slipped through the net. And when, after over a year in the hospital he hadn't heard from Grace, in his morbid, weakened state, he had presumed she no longer cared what had happened to him. Then he had contracted pneumonia, his life hanging in the balance for weeks. Yet although he pulled through the illness, his body had almost given up on him. That was until June 1945, when they had transferred him and dozens of other patients back to England, and into another hospital in Essex. It was from that day his spirits had begun to lift, although his physical state remained unchanged.

The first time Grace had visited the hospital she had walked right past Stanley's bed, not recognising the almost skeletal frame between the crisp white sheets. He had cried in her arms for hours before falling into a deep, exhausted sleep. The doctors had told Grace he would never make a full recovery, his body had taken too much punishment, and she was also warned to expect unpredictable mood swings – yet another legacy of his time spent in the camp. But the good news, they had informed her, was that he could live for many years if taken proper care of. Grace wouldn't have minded taking care of Stanley, no matter for how long; after all, she had once loved him – her deep sense of loyalty would never have allowed her to turn her back on anyone who had once been a part of her life – plus he had no one else to look after him. But Stanley had changed recently, and not for the better. The mood swings the doctor had warned her about had got worse and, as the months had dragged on, he had become more confident of his permanent residence, and then the sly digs had started.

First it was Patrick who came under investigation, with Stanley making comments about his parentage, until one night, in a fit of petulant rage, he had openly accused Grace of being the child's mother. The next morning he had been full of contrition, but still from time to time she would catch him watching her suspiciously when she came into the room holding the toddler. These cruel taunts had continued at various times until Danny had returned home and claimed Patrick as his son.

Yet the worst incident by far was the night Stanley begged her to get into bed with him. Just for a cuddle, he had promised, laughingly pointing out that he wasn't capable of doing anything else. Trembling, she had pulled back the covers, only to be asked to take off her clothes first. She had taken off her dress, but left her undergarments on, claiming that it was too cold to lie naked on the cool, cotton sheets. She had lain by his side trying with every fibre in her body to relax against him, knowing that she owed him at least this bit of comfort. But when his hands had begun to roam her body she had flinched and pulled away from the skinny, wandering fingers. Horrified by what she had done, she had remained there for an agonising five minutes, with a silent Stanley lying stiffly by her side, afraid to move for fear of setting off his unpredictable temper. It was Patrick who had saved her. His sudden wail for his supper had drifted down the stairs, and with a shaky laugh Grace had said, 'I'd better go. His nibs still likes his bottle of milk before he goes to sleep, and seeing as Uncle Danny's down the pub, it looks like I'll have to see to him.'

Still Stanley hadn't said a word, until she was at the door. Then, his words hitting her like a knife in the back, he had said bitterly, 'Don't let me stop yer. I wouldn't want ter deprive a child of his mother's company.'

The nastiness of his voice stopped Grace in her tracks, but she refused to rise to the bait. But Stanley hadn't finished, his sneering words following her out into the hall.

'Don't think I believe that old cobblers about Patrick being Danny's. We all know it's not true. Even Danny knows, the poor old bastard, he just won't admit it.'

Lifting her head wearily, Grace rose from her chair and began the preparations for dinner. Even now the war was over, the rationing still applied. Though Nobby, bless him, always managed to bring around some treat on his weekly visits. She didn't know what she would have done without him, or Polly for that matter. What with her nan still not able to do half of what she had done before her accident, and having to rest for the best part of the day, and Vi lying upstairs in a darkened room, not allowing any visitors to see her, Grace couldn't have coped without Polly's help. It was hard to believe how much she had come to rely on her youngest sister. In the aftermath of the street being bombed, and the terrible news that all of their friends had been killed, including the vivacious Linda Castle, whom Polly had been so fond of, the entire family had expected Polly to fall apart as she had done at the start of the war. But that young, vulnerable, frightened girl had gone for good, and in her place stood an independent, stoic woman capable of taking anything else life had to throw at her.

And thank God for the change, Grace thought tiredly, for without Polly's help, she didn't know how she would have coped.

Grace raised her eyes upwards as she thought of Vi. Poor Vi, scarred for life when her face had hit the ground at full impact as she was running back to see if her family was safe. If she had gone with Beryl, she would now be safe in America, happily married to Chuck. Instead she seemed doomed to a life as a recluse, for Grace couldn't see Vi ever showing her face out of doors again. If only Chuck had stood by her. He had come over after the war and spent some hours up in Vi's room, laughing and talking, and for days afterwards Vi's spirits had risen. But after that one visit she had never heard from him again. Since then she had gone into a deep depression, which no amount of pills could lift her out of.

Then Grace's thoughts turned to Benji. She had grown to love the gentle man, and had been deeply upset by his death. But with most of her neighbours dead – people she had been genuinely fond of – and the worry of Vi and her grandmother, Grace hadn't had the time to grieve for just one person, except at night when the tears would fall silently as she remembered her friends, hardly able to believe she would never see any of them again.

But by far the greatest shock she received was the notification from Benji's solicitors that he had left her everything he owned. She hadn't been able to take it in at first, but, as the solicitor had pointed out, the elderly man had no other living relatives, and he had been very fond of her and grateful for the extra time she had spent with him to ease his otherwise lonely life. As if that news hadn't astonished her enough, she had been struck almost dumb to find that apart from the shop, which had escaped the bombing, Benji had also left her almost five thousand pounds – every penny he owned. And there wasn't a day went by that she didn't send up a prayer of thanks to the elderly man for his thoughtfulness and generosity. For without the legacy she, and the rest of the family, would have had to remain in the temporary accommodation Nobby had found for them on their release from the hospital. She had used the money to rebuild their shattered home. It had taken time, but as most of the outside walls were still intact, the family had been able to move back into their home within a few months. The restoration had taken up most of the five thousand pounds, but Grace had still had enough left over to buy a goodly assortment of second-hand furniture. None of it was anywhere near as beautiful as the items they had once owned, but nobody complained, being only too grateful to be under their own roof again.

Then she also had the shop, and that had been a godsend as well, since only Polly was able to work, and she was needed at home to look after the family. She didn't look on working at the corner shop from nine in the morning until six at night as work, for she was her own boss – and there was a great deal of difference between working for an employer and working for oneself. And now with Danny working as her assistant, she had more time to herself.

With everything taken into account she was one of the lucky ones, only she didn't feel lucky, she felt trapped and on edge, not knowing from one day to the next what mood Stanley would be in. Then there were the nightmares, when he would wake up screaming and begging for mercy, believing himself to be back in the camp. On these nights, Grace would have to strip the soaking sheets and pyjamas and replace them with dry ones. Usually Polly helped, if she heard Stanley's cries, but sometimes she slept through the agonising sounds, and Grace never had the heart to wake her. Then there was the gruesome task of treating Stanley's infested bed sores, although at least in this task Polly was always on hand to help out.

In an effort to shut out her melancholy thoughts Grace returned her concentration to the dinner. She was in the middle of peeling the potatoes when the doorbell rang. Quickly she wiped her hands on a tea cloth and opened the door, her face lighting up at the sight of Nobby.

'Is it all right to visit, Gracie? I mean, what sort of mood is he in today?'

Smiling, Grace dragged him into the hall.

'Polly's with him at the minute, so he's in a good mood. He saves the bad ones for me.'

A deep frown of concern settled over Nobby's face.

'You can't go on like this, Grace, otherwise it'll be you being carted off to hospital.'

As she pushed him down the hall in front of her, Grace replied, 'Don't worry about me, Nobby. I haven't time to be ill. Look, go on in, I'll come with you. The dinner can wait another few minutes.'

'Well, well, if it ain't me old mate, Nobby. How are you, yer old rascal?' Stanley pushed himself higher up on to his pillows, a thin hand coming out in greeting.

'Oh, there's nothing wrong with me, mate, it's you we've gotta look after. How yer feeling, Stan?'

'Oh, yer know, Nobby, up one minute, down the next. Still, it's good to see yer. 'Ere, sit down. Don't stand there like a stranger.'

Nobby sat on the chair by the bed, keeping the conversation going as only he could. It was as Grace was about to leave the room that Stanley's voice stopped her.

'Hang on, love. Since you're both here, there's something I want ter say.' Turning first to Nobby he said, 'I haven't thanked yer properly fer looking after me girl while I was away, Nobby. Now there's another favour I want ter ask yer.'

Nobby raised his eyebrows questioningly.

'Course I will, if I can, Stan. What is it, mate?'

As Stanley looked over to where Grace was standing at the edge of the bed, a crafty look crossed his face as he asked casually, 'I was wondering if you'd be me best man. The doctor says we can get married here, with a special licence of course, and I can't see any reason fer putting it off any longer, eh, Gracie?'

Grace felt her face blanch with shock. This was the last thing she had expected. Clearing her throat she answered tremulously, 'Well, let's give it another few months, Stanley. When you're feeling better.'

'But that's the point, darlin'. I ain't gonna get any better, and we all know that. So will yer see ter it, Gracie? Danny can give yer away, and you, Nobby,' he swivelled his head around to the stunned man sitting by the bed, 'will yer be me best man?'

Like Grace, Nobby was dumbstruck. Then, with every ounce of willpower, he smiled and said, 'Course I will, mate. But I think Grace is right, you know. Maybe it'd be better if yer—'

'NO!' A mulish expression settled on Stanley's face. 'It's what I want. Unless, of course, yer've changed yer mind about marrying me, Gracie. If so, you've only gotta say. I'll understand.'

Grace twisted the tea cloth between her hands.

'No, of course not, Stan. Look, we'll talk some more after dinner, all right?' Then she fled the room before she broke down completely.

Once back in the kitchen she stood at the cold sink, her head bowed. And when a strong pair of arms came round her she gave a muffled groan and turned and buried her face into Nobby's broad chest.

'He knows, Nobby. I don't know how, but he knows about us, and this is his way of getting his own back. If only there was some chance he'd get better, then I could tell him the truth, but as things stand, I can't. I can't do that to him, Nobby, not after what he's been through. I mean, where would he go? Who'd look after him? Oh, what are we going to do, Nobby? What are we going to do?'

And for once in his life Nobby could find no answer. He had thought life after the war would get easier, especially as he now had nothing to fear from the Davidsons or the law. Then Stanley had come home, and, like Grace, he had hoped that his old school friend would make a full recovery, and be able to stand hearing the truth about him and Grace. But that wasn't going to happen. Not now. Not ever! Gathering the precious body tightly to him, Nobby clung to Grace as if he was never going to let her go. And also like Grace, he knew this may well be their last chance to express their love.

On the last day of June, almost two years to the day since the war had ended, the parish priest attended to the duty that had been asked of him. And when he left the house, a house that had seemed to resemble a funeral gathering rather than a wedding celebration, Grace had become Mrs Stanley Slater.

CHAPTER TWENTY-NINE

'Why don't you come with us, Stan? The fresh air would do you good, and it's a lovely day outside. The doctor said you should get out as often as possible – that's why he got you the wheelchair.'

Grace sat on the side of the bed, her eyes pleading, but Stanley's face remained sullen.

'No thanks. I wouldn't want ter spoil yer afternoon. After all, three's a crowd, ain't it?'

Nobby, who was standing at the end of the bed, felt his stomach muscles tighten. How on earth did Grace stand it day after day? His mind shut down on the nights she had to spend in the same bed with this man he had grown to dislike intensely.

Jutting out his jaw, Nobby said tersely, 'All right, mate, your loss. Me and Grace'll take Patrick over the park by ourselves, seeing as how you don't want to come and Danny's working. See yer later. Come on, Grace.'

As she bent forward to kiss Stan's cheek, Grace flinched when he deliberately turned away his head.

Once outside she breathed in the fresh August air, a welcome change from the bedroom she was forced to share with

Stanley. For no matter how often she and Polly changed his
sheets and pyjamas, and cleaned the room thoroughly, the
room always held a sickly sweet smell. The smell of illness,
and they were powerless to do anything about that.

Nobby and Grace didn't talk much on the way to the
park. It was only when she let Patrick out of his pushchair
to run around on the lush grass that Nobby finally spoke,
and when he did his voice was filled with bitterness.

'You know something, Grace, I could have hit him back
there, the way he spoke ter you. I don't care how ill he is, that
doesn't give him the right to treat you like a piece of shit.'

Grace swallowed hard, not knowing how to answer.
Nobby was right, of course, but what could she do? And
Stanley wasn't always rude and surly. It was the illness,
and the mental anguish he'd gone through that had changed
him. Sometimes he could be so sweet, apologising for his
behaviour, promising it'd never happen again. But it always
did. He couldn't help himself. No one could ever know what
he had been through, or how they would have been affected
in his position. Yet living the life she had been forced into was
taking its toll on her. If the days were bad, the nights were
infinitely worse. Since her wedding night, she had come to
dread going to bed. Often she would stay up as late as
possible, hoping Stanley would be asleep by the time she
went to bed, but he was always awake, waiting for her, and
then the nightly ordeal would begin. Not that anything ever
happened, for Stanley's illness had left him impotent, which
was the cause of his frustration and increasing bitterness.
Night after night, he would try to make love to her, only for
his efforts to end in humiliating failure. The nightly ordeals
were torture for them both. If Grace had still been in love
with Stanley, it might have made things easier, but as it was
she could hardly bear him to touch her. The fumblings that
grew rougher, the kisses rained over her face with his urgent
breathing, breath that was soured by his general ill-health.

Sometimes Stanley stopped trying after a few minutes, too tired to exert himself, but other times, like last night, he had gone at her for over half an hour, his actions becoming more urgent and frustrated as he realised that nothing was happening in the lower half of his body. Finally, in a fit of rage, he had summoned up the last of his dwindling strength and kicked her viciously in the back, knocking her out of the bed. Sobbing, she had stayed in the sitting room for the rest of the night, wondering how much more of this kind of treatment and abuse she could stand.

Then, this morning, when she had brought him in his breakfast, he had been all contrition, blaming his illness and the drugs he was taking. But Grace had heard it all before. He had remained in a good mood for the rest of the morning – until Nobby had turned up and suggested a walk over the park with Patrick. The reason for his change of mood was one of two things: either he was jealous of Nobby's good health and vitality or he had somehow guessed there had been something between Nobby and Grace. And judging by the way he had rushed Grace into marriage, and practically demanded that Nobby be best man, Grace could only assume it was the latter that was eating away at Stanley.

'Are you listening to me, Grace? I don't care how ill he is, I'm not gonna stand by and see you treated like that. It's not right.'

When Grace didn't answer, Nobby pulled her roughly by the arm, then gasped in alarm as Grace cried out in pain.

'What is it, love? I didn't pull you that hard. What's wrong?' Then, a wave of suspicion coming over his face, Nobby's eyes clouded over. 'Has he been hitting you, Grace? 'Cos if he has, by God, ill or not, I'll have him. Not with me fists, though I'd be sorely tempted, but I'd let him know what'd happen if—'

'No, Nobby, stay out of it.' Grace laid a restraining hand on his arm. 'He's my husband, and if there's any problems, then I'll work them out, understand? If you try and interfere it'd only make matters worse.'

Looking into the stony eyes, Grace shivered at the ferocity reflected there. Then, without thinking, she sat back on the park bench, and once more let out a yelp as her bruised back came into contact with the hard wooden slats.

Nobby said nothing. He simply turned her around gently and lifted up the back of her blouse, and when he saw the enormous bruise in the centre of her back, a fierce hatred washed over him.

Gritting his teeth he growled, 'That's it, Grace. That's the last straw. I'll have him for this, the bastard.'

Her eyes following Patrick as he raced around the park, Grace answered calmly, 'Don't be silly, Nobby. There's nothing you can do. But I can. Tonight I'm going to tell him that if he ever raises a hand to me again, I'll move back into my own room, and I'll do it too. No matter what the provocation, I won't be used as a punchbag. Now, I don't want to talk about it any more . . .'

A shadow fell over them, and a vaguely familiar voice said tentatively, 'Gracie! Is that you?'

Grace, shielding her eyes against the sun, looked up towards the voice, her expression showing no recognition at first. Then she let out a whoop of delight.

'Jimmy! Oh, Jimmy. You made it back all right. Oh, Lord, but I've often worried about you. How are you? . . . Oh, I'm forgetting my manners.' Turning to Nobby she exclaimed happily, 'This is Jimmy Potter, he used to work with me up the City, until we were bombed out. The last time I saw him he was thinking of joining up.'

Nobby stretched out his hand in greeting. 'Pleased to meet yer, mate. Any one that can bring a smile to Grace's face is a friend of mine.'

In her excitement Grace forgot the pain in her back and all her other worries, and patted the bench next to her.

'Well, sit down, Jimmy, we won't bite,' she laughed.

Jimmy, grinning from ear to ear at the genuine welcome, sat down, and began to talk about his stint in the army.

'Cor, I was scared ter death at first, Grace. Not at the training centre, that was a laugh. But when I was shipped overseas and head first into me first battle, Gawd, I thought I'd die of fright, never mind a German bullet. Then we was all charging and shouting our heads off, and firing our rifles, and the next thing I knew we was back in the trench. I couldn't believe I was still alive. It got a bit easier after that, but it wasn't the great adventure I thought it'd be. Anyway, it's all over now, thank Gawd, and I'm back in one piece.' He nudged Grace's arm gently, grinning, 'It must be true what they say about only the good dying young, or I'd be six feet under by now.'

Smiling fondly, Grace let her eyes roam over the young man sitting beside her, dressed in an ill-fitting cheap suit and wearing a hat that was far too big for him, and had to stifle the desire to take him in her arms and cuddle him. She might have done just that if a petulant voice hadn't suddenly appeared out of nowhere.

'Thanks fer leaving me and walking off without a word, Jimmy. You might 'ave said yer was going off.'

Jimmy, his face apologetic now, jumped swiftly to his feet, his arm going protectively around the girl's shoulder.

'I'm, sorry, darlin'. I didn't mean ter go off like that, it was just that I saw an old friend, an' I thought I'd wander over and make sure it was her.' His face taking on a proud expression, Jimmy faced Grace and said sheepishly, 'This is me fiancée, Hilda. We're getting married next year. Well, say hello to Grace, love, and her friend.'

The girl's pretty face remained unconvinced, her mouth busily chewing on a piece of gum.

'Yeah, well, yer could 'ave said something. So we going now, or what?'

Grace and Nobby exchanged amused glances. Then Nobby, ever the one to smooth over a difficult moment, jumped to his feet and held out his hand to the startled girl.

'Hello, love. Sorry ter have taken your boyfriend away from you like that, but him and Gracie used ter work together, and they had some catching up to do.' The handsome face combined with the charming, boyish smile quickly dissolved the girl's resentment.

Adopting a more pleasant tone she said, 'Yeah, well, sorry I sounded off like that, I didn't mean ter be rude.'

'Think nothing of it, love. I'm Nobby, by the way, and this is Grace.'

The girl simpered. 'Pleased ter meet yer, I'm sure. Me and Jimmy was just gonna go and listen ter the band play. Would yer like ter come with us?'

Grace watched with amusement at the open admiration in the young girl's eyes. Poor Jimmy, he'd have to watch out if he was serious about marrying the girl. She seemed to be a bit of a flirt. Still! She was young yet; maybe she'd change as she got older. Grace hoped so for Jimmy's sake.

A loud wail brought Grace to her feet, and there, running towards her, his arms outstretched, was Patrick.

'I felled over, Auntie Grace. I hurted me knee,' the youngster informed his worried aunt.

Lifting him on to her lap, Grace examined the slight injury and said breezily, 'It's not too bad, love. But I think we'd better get you home and give it a bit of a wash and put some ointment on it, OK?'

Glad of the excuse to get out of accompanying Jimmy and Hilda to the bandstand, they all shook hands and said their goodbyes, but not before Grace had given Jimmy an affectionate hug.

'I'm so glad we bumped into Jimmy. He was only seventeen when I last saw him, and couldn't wait for his eighteenth birthday so he could join up. I've often wondered if he made it through, and now I know.'

Beside her, Nobby gave a short laugh.

'He may have made it through the war, but by the looks of his intended, he'll have a few more battles to put up with in his lifetime.'

They were nearly home before Nobby tried to bring up the subject of Stanley once more, but Grace quickly forestalled him.

'I nearly forgot. Polly's enrolled in a nursing training college. That is, she's applied and taken a written test. She's just waiting to see if she's been accepted.'

'Poll! Our Polly, a nurse. Good Lord! Whatever put that idea into her head?' Nobby asked in amazement.

'I think she's been debating about it since Stanley came home. She's been so good with him, I mean helping him to wash and shave, and sitting with him whenever she gets the chance. I don't know how I'd have managed without her, honestly I don't. Not with Nan still not fully recovered, and not able to lift anything heavy, and Vi locked away in her room like the princess in the tower. I'd have gone mental if I'd had to see to him all by myself.' They were just entering the house, so Grace lowered her voice slightly. 'She even helps me clean and medicate his bed sores, and that from a girl who used to practically faint at the sight of a bit of blood. So if you want my opinion, I think she'd make a damn fine nurse, because, apart from everything else, Polly has compassion, and plenty of it, and that's essential for a good nurse.'

'Bloody hell, I thought you'd never get home.' Aggie, hobbling slowly towards them, her face alight with excitement, whispered. 'We've got a visitor. You'll never guess who . . . Well, come on then, and see who it is, the pair of you.'

Nobby and Grace, raising their eyebrows at one another, followed Aggie down the hall and into the sitting room. For the second time that afternoon Grace gave a cry of joy, and rushed towards the man sitting awkwardly on the edge of the armchair.

'Chris! How wonderful to see you. Does Vi know you're here? Oh, that'll cheer her up seeing you.'

Chris Green stood up to greet her, his face taking on a doubtful expression.

'I don't know about that, Grace . . . Oh, hello there, Nobby,' he added as the dark-haired man entered the room carrying Patrick, who immediately squirmed down from his arms and ran to his nan to tell her about his injury.

With Aggie preoccupied, Chris turned a sceptical look at the couple.

'To tell the truth, I'm dreading seeing Vi after what your nan's been telling me. According to Aggie, Vi won't see anyone except the family.' Directing an appealing glance at Grace he asked hesitantly, 'Would you come up with me, Grace? Sort of prepare the way, so to speak.'

Grace looked to her nan for support but found Aggie studiously examining the superficial cut on Patrick's knee, and she felt her stomach lurch. Despite her previous words to Chris, Grace knew there was no chance Vi would allow him to see her as she was now. The doctors had done all they could to repair Vi's face, a process that had taken place over many agonising months, but on her last visit to the hospital, driven to the front entrance by cab with her face covered by a black net veil, they had told her as kindly as possible that there was nothing more they could do. In fact Vi's face, although still scarred, was ten times better than when she had first been admitted into hospital, but Vi didn't see it that way, and who could blame her, poor cow?

Her stomach fluttering in nervous agitation, Grace led the way up the stairs, with Chris, apprehensive about seeing Vi after all this time, hanging back. That is, of course, if Vi agreed to see him.

Pausing outside Vi's room, Grace thought, *Lord, what with*

last night, and Nobby's anger when he discovered what Stanley had done, then meeting up with Jimmy, it's been a day and half so far – and it isn't over yet . . .

Grace entered the room. Vi, who was sitting in the armchair by the side of the bed reading a book, smiled when she saw her sister, a smile that soon vanished when she heard the reason for Grace's visit.

'NO! NO! Never! Do you hear me, Grace? How could you do this to me, knowing how I feel about people seeing me in this state? And Chris of all people.' Uttering a mirthless laugh she said bitterly, 'I suppose he's come to gloat over what happened after the way I treated him, and maybe I deserve it. What's that old saying, Grace? "How are the mighty fallen"? Lord! I think that would be an apt description for me, don't you?'

Pity rose in Grace's throat at the anguish in Vi's voice, then both women jumped as a voice from behind them said softly, 'Not as far as I'm concerned, Vi.'

There in the doorway stood Chris, his attractive face solemn as he looked directly at Vi's face before she had the chance to cover her scars with her hands.

'Would you mind leaving us, Grace? Vi and me have a lot of talking to do.'

Instantly Vi let out a wail of panic.

'NO! Grace, please, don't leave.'

But for once Grace ignored her sister's request and shut the door gently behind her, praying that she had done the right thing in allowing Chris into Vi's room. Hesitating, she waited outside the closed door for a few minutes, ready to rush back in if Vi became hysterical, but all she heard was a low sobbing and Chris's gentle, soothing voice.

Feeling a bit better, Grace returned downstairs, wishing she were a fly on the wall so she could listen in on the conversation that was taking place.

*   *   *

For the first ten minutes Vi cried ceaselessly, while Chris sat on the edge of the bed and waited patiently for her to compose herself. He couldn't see her face now, as she had her head bowed, embarrassed and humiliated at having this man she had treated so contemptuously seeing her in her sorry plight.

Then, the strength of character Vi had always possessed came to the fore, and, drying her tears, she lifted her head and said defiantly, 'Well, go on then, have a good look. You must be laughing your head off remembering all the times I gave you the brush off, whereas now you wouldn't have me if I paid you, would you? So now you've seen what you came to see, you can go.'

Chris had remained silent throughout the tirade. Now he smiled fondly and came to kneel by her side. Taking her trembling hands in his, he said tenderly, 'You don't understand, Vi, you never have. I love you, and I always will. I don't care about your face, it's what's inside you that counts.'

'Oh, yes, I'm a model of virtue and compassion,' Vi spat back sarcastically.

Shifting his position slightly to make himself more comfortable, Chris answered softly, 'Tell me, Vi, how was it Beryl got away safely and you got caught in the bombing? Because from what Aggie was telling me, you were both in the taxi heading for the station when the rockets appeared. So how was it you ended up back here in the street?'

Vi's chin wobbled, her throat filling with emotion as she recalled that dreadful day for the hundredth time. Too choked to speak, she tried to lower her head, but Chris gently placed his fingertips under her chin and lifted her face to his.

'The reason you got caught in the raid was because, unlike Beryl, you were worried about the safety of your family and came running back to see if they were all right. Now if that isn't a sign of a person of virtue and compassion, then I don't know what is.'

They were staring into each other's eyes, and what Vi saw reflected in Chris's gaze gave her new hope. Instead of revulsion or pity, all she could see was love shining from Chris's eyes. The sudden revelation that this man truly loved her was nearly Vi's undoing. She wanted to cry and wail, but found she no longer felt the need to wallow in self-pity.

Through misty eyes she whispered hoarsely, 'Oh, Chris. I don't deserve you. Not after the way I treated you. I . . .'

A fingertip came out and covered her lips.

'That's all in the past now, Vi. It's the future we have to look forward to . . . Hang on, don't interrupt,' he said firmly as Vi made to protest. 'In all the time we've known each other we've never really talked, have we, not properly. So now I'll tell you the reason I came to see you. Firstly, to see if there was any hope for me, and secondly, to tell you I might be able to help you. I never told you before, because the subject never came up, that my father is a plastic surgeon. Oh, not the type that treats old biddies who want a few wrinkles removed, but a medical plastic surgeon. He operated on hundreds of men during the first war, men who had been badly burnt or disfigured, and he's still working now, patching up the poor devils who received the same kind of injuries in this war. Anyway, Vi, what I'm trying to say is, would you be willing to see my father? He runs a hospital for burns patients in Essex. I've already spoken to him and he's agreed to see you to see if he can help.'

As Vi listened intently to what Chris was telling her, her hopes began to rise. She had imagined her life would be spent in this room until the day she died, and now there was a chance her face might be restored to its former self.

Chris quickly noticed the rising hope racing through Vi's body, and he held up his hand, saying gently, 'Look, Vi. I'm not offering any guarantees. My father's good, in fact he's the best in his field, but he's not God. There's no use me taking you to see him if you're expecting him to perform some kind of miracle. If you come with me, it has to be on the condition that you go with an open mind, and are prepared to accept it if you're told there's nothing he can do that the other doctors haven't already tried. If anyone can help you, then my father can, but as I've already said, you have to be prepared not to let your expectations run too high, otherwise I won't have done you any favours by giving you false hope.'

He waited for what seemed an eternity, then Vi took his hand and smiled.

'I've nothing to lose, and everything to gain. So, yes, Chris, I'll see your father, and no matter what the outcome, I want you to know I'll be forever grateful to you for giving me some hope, however small. When can we go to the hospital?'

Taken aback by the eagerness in Vi's voice, Chris thought frantically. He supposed he could take her now – after all, his father's hospital was open twenty-four hours a day. Recovering his aplomb, he stood up. Maybe this was the best way. To get Vi to the hospital before she had a chance to change her mind.

'How long will it take you to get packed?'

Vi's eyes lit up with excitement.

'About half an hour. After all, I won't be needing my party frocks, will I?'

Heading for the door Chris looked over his shoulder.

'While you're packing, I'll phone my father to let him know we're on our way. It'll give him a chance to get a room ready for you . . . Oh, don't worry, Vi,' he added kindly at the sudden look of apprehension that sprang to her eyes. 'You won't be put in with the other patients. The family has its own house adjoining the hospital and that's where you'll be staying. Now, get moving. I'll phone my father and then tell the rest of the family what's happening.'

After Chris had gone, Vi stared hard at the closed door. Don't get your hopes up, Chris had warned her. But how could she not? She was realistic to know that no amount of surgery would ever make her beautiful again, but if it could make some improvement, some considerable improvement so that at least she could leave the house without having people stare at her, at least that would be something – wouldn't it?

With new enthusiasm injected into her body, Vi raced across the room and began to pack only the bare essentials she would need. She had no idea how long she would be under Chris's father's care, or if indeed she would be coming back home the next day after being told there was nothing more he could do that the other doctors hadn't already tried. But try as she might to keep her feelings under control, she couldn't stop the raging hope that was surging through her mind.

With a lightness in her step, she snapped her suitcase shut and waited for Chris to return.

'Gawd Almighty, well if that wasn't a turn up fer the book.'

Aggie was sipping her nightly cocoa, the rest of the family gathered around her. Even Stanley, who had allowed himself to be wheeled into the room to be with the others rather than lie in his room alone, determined not to be pushed out of the family conference. Also he was feeling dreadful about the way he had treated Grace last night. What he had done was unforgivable, but God help him, he couldn't seem to control his temper. When the rage swept over him, it was like he was on the outside looking in on a different person.

He was vaguely listening to Aggie rambling on about the

afternoon's events, saying she hoped Vi wasn't expecting too much, or she would return home in a worse condition than when she'd left, and it was as he moved his head distractedly that he caught Nobby's eye. The look reflected there was nothing short of murderous. So he knew what had happened, or guessed, because Stanley couldn't see Grace telling tales to anyone, she wasn't made that way.

Shifting his glance towards his wife, he saw her look up at Nobby, and the way she looked at Nobby was the way she used to look at him before he went off to war. His head fell forward. So he had been right all along about the two of them. All at once Stanley experienced a sense of hopelessness. He had known there was no future for him, and yet he had used moral blackmail to get Grace to marry him. A great weariness came over him, and with it a desire to be rid of this life. He wasn't living, merely existing. A bout of coughing brought his frail body forward, and immediately Grace and Polly were at his side, their faces filled with concern, which only added to his guilt.

Within minutes he was back in his bed, alone with Grace, who was giving him his medicine, saying worriedly, 'You should have stayed in bed, Stan. You know what the doctor said yesterday.'

Yes, he knew what the doctor had said yesterday. Plenty of rest and no physical exertion. Fat chance of the latter, he thought wearily, not after last night's fiasco. What Grace didn't know was that he had managed to get out of bed and listen at the door to what the doctor was telling her. He could still recall the words clearly, as if they had been burnt into his brain.

'He should be in the hospital, Mrs Slater, he's not doing as well as I first hoped. I'm afraid the pneumonia has left his chest very weak, and his heart is in a bad way too. The human body can only take so much, you know. And his mental state doesn't help matters either.'

Then Grace's voice, anxious and afraid.

'But he will pull through, won't he, Doctor? I mean . . . He's not going to die, is he?'

There had been a short pause before the doctor had answered, and Stanley had felt his heart hammering against his ribs, his mouth dry with fear at what the doctor's answer would be.

Then it had come.

In a deep, sorrowful tone the doctor had said kindly, 'I'm sorry, Mrs Slater, but there's nothing anyone can do for your husband now except to make him as comfortable as possible. Maybe take him out in his wheelchair for a change of scenery. He may last another few weeks, or he could go tomorrow. There's just no way of telling. I'm very sorry.'

Stanley had crept back to bed, trembling with fear at what he had overheard. Then last night, in a fit of desperation and frustration, he had made one last attempt at making Grace his wife properly, and as usual he had failed. Then in a fit of fear and temper he had kicked her out of the bed.

'Would you like me to stay with you a while, Stan? I can always catch up on the gossip about Vi's hasty departure later. In fact . . .' she laughed, 'I expect there'll be talk of nothing else over the next few weeks.'

Tiredly Stanley shook his head, thinking that Grace was one in a million. After the way he had treated her last night, and other nights, he had no right to expect any sympathy or nursing from her. Yet here she was, willing to sit with him, not wanting him to be on his own to brood. A deep sense of shame swept over him. She deserved better than him. Furthermore, he owed her more than words could say. She didn't have to take him in and look after him, she didn't have to marry him, but she had, because that was the sort of person she was. Never would she hurt anyone's feelings, even if it meant her own suffered.

'No, I'll be all right, love. To tell the truth, I feel a bit tired. You go back to the family gathering. You can tell me all about it in the morning.'

When Grace had left, Stanley lay for a long time staring into the darkness. His life, as he had known it, was over, and this new one would be too, very soon. Perhaps it was the medication that Grace had just given him, or maybe he was just tired of it all. Whatever the reason, he reflected, the idea of dying no longer frightened him.

The bedside clock showed it to be ten o'clock, and Stan heaved himself up in the bed and looked at the rows of pills arranged neatly on the bedside cabinet. He heard the women calling out their goodnights, and calmly opened first one bottle, then another. Throwing as many pills as he could swallow in one go into his mouth, he managed to empty both bottles and return them to their rightful place before Grace entered the room.

'Oh, I didn't expect you to still be awake, Stan,' Grace said, a note of fear entering her voice.

'I was just dozing off, love,' Stan answered, tears springing to the back of his eyes at the obvious fear Grace was endeavouring to hide. Closing his eyes, he pretended to sleep. He felt Grace gingerly slipping into bed beside him, her slim figure tense as if expecting another assault on her body. After a few minutes had passed he felt her relax, then she whispered, 'Night, love. See you tomorrow,' before her soft breathing told him she had fallen asleep.

His own eyes heavy, Stan turned to look at his wife, his mind travelling back down the years to a time before the war. They had been so much in love, so happy together, and then the war had started and nothing was ever the same again.

He could feel himself drifting off, and fought the effects of the drugs for as long as he could, his mind remembering every happy, carefree moment he had shared with the woman by his side. Now it was all over. And by this last act of his, maybe it would prove to Grace how much he had truly loved her, and how sorry he was for the way he had made her life a misery, when all she had shown him was kindness.

His eyelids were growing heavier, and he knew the end was near. With a last effort, and remembering Grace's final words to him, he whispered into the darkness, 'There isn't going to be any more tomorrows for me, darling, but there will be for you. I loved you, Grace, I still do. That's why I'm setting you free. Goodbye my darlin', and thanks for all the good times we shared.'

Then his eyes closed for the last time.

When Grace awoke in the morning, refreshed after the first good night's sleep she'd had in months, she quietly slipped out of bed and into the kitchen.

'Morning, love. You look bright today. Had a good sleep, did yer?'

Aggie was already at the stove preparing the breakfast, the kettle boiling furiously away on top of the hob.

Grace ran her fingers through her unruly hair, gave a small yawn, then smiled.

'Yes, I did, actually. I can't remember the last time I slept so well.'

When the breakfast was ready, Grace, who had to be at the shop by eight, asked Polly, 'Would you mind taking Stan's breakfast into him, Poll? I'm running a bit late, but I'll pop in to see him before I leave.'

'Yes, of course I will, Grace. I've got to practise my nursing skills, haven't I?' She grinned.

Placing a lightly poached egg on a slice of toast together with a mug of tea, Polly left the room.

It was some fifteen minutes later as Grace was ready to leave that she suddenly wondered what was taking Polly so long. She hoped Stanley wasn't keeping Polly talking, otherwise Poll would be late for work.

As she opened the door to the bedroom, Grace looked towards the bed, her words dying in her throat at the sight that met her eyes. For there was Polly, lying with her head on Stanley's chest, weeping silently, the untouched breakfast tray lying by the side of the bed. Grace's stomach rose in alarm, her heart beginning to race frantically.

Touching Polly's heaving shoulders lightly, she said softly, 'Polly!' And just that one word was all Grace could manage as the awful truth sank in.

Her eyes reddened and swollen with grief, Polly looked up at her sister and sobbed, 'He's gone, Grace. Stanley's gone.' Then her head dropped back on to Stanley's still chest.

Grace stood motionless, watching the poignant scene, a voice inside her shouting it was all wrong. It should be her sobbing over Stanley, and Polly trying to comfort her, instead of the other way around.

As if in a daze, Grace walked slowly back to the kitchen where Aggie was enjoying her second mug of tea. Without any preamble she said dully, 'Stanley's dead, Nan.' Then she sank down on to a chair, staring into space, her mind a blank. She never noticed Aggie leave the room, nor did she remember the doctor arriving. Everything seemed to be happening around her, without actually touching her in any way. It was when Danny appeared and put his arms around her that Grace finally came out of her self-induced trance. Her lips trembling, she buried her face against her uncle's chest and let the tears fall.

Stanley was buried four days later on a sunny August day beside the rose bush Grace and the family had planted in memory of Sam and Hetty. Grace watched silently as the coffin was lowered into the ground, the death of her husband weighing heavily on her conscience. How unfair it was that he should have suffered so much in his short life. Maybe if she had been more affectionate towards him, pretended that she still loved him, then he wouldn't have been driven to take his own life. She would never know the true reason behind Stanley's decision to commit suicide, but some part of her felt she was in some way to blame. No matter what anyone else told her, even the doctor who had reminded her that Stanley would have died soon anyway, it did nothing to alleviate her guilt. She would always think that Stanley's death was somehow partly her fault. And as the small party of mourners walked away from the cemetery, Grace knew the burden of Stanley's suicide would remain heavily on her conscience for the rest of her life.

CHAPTER THIRTY

It had been five months since Stanley's death, and Grace had never felt so lonely in her entire life. There was nobody in the house except herself and Polly. As she thought of her youngest sister, Grace's head gave an involuntary jerk. Since the funeral, Polly had been very short with her. The friendship they had once shared was gone, and for the life of her Grace couldn't understand what she had done to turn Polly against her.

Finding the subject too painful to dwell on, Grace switched her thoughts to Vi, who was still staying at Chris's house in Essex, although she had been home for a few flying visits, each visit showing a marked improvement in her face. And not only in her physiognomy but in herself as well. For with each new operation, painful though they were, Vi's confidence slowly returned. She would have to undergo more surgery until Dr Green, Chris's father, decided there was no more he could do. Grace had listened in fascinated horror as Vi regaled her with tales of skin grafting, and chemical peeling, and also of the marvellous work Dr Green did for his burns patients. By all accounts, Chris's father was a remarkable man indeed, and Vi was deeply appreciative of all he had done for her.

Grace had also noticed a new warmth between Vi and Chris whenever they visited. Grace wasn't sure if the new intimacy was due to Vi's undying gratitude to Chris for turning up at a point in her life when she had been in such a desperate state or whether she was falling in love. Grace fervently hoped it was the latter. If not, then Vi was a fool. She would never find anyone who would love her as Chris did, but like everything in life only time would tell.

Sighing, Grace looked around the empty sitting room, her heart heavy. She had never known a time when the house had been so empty, so quiet. Aggie had gone for a short walk around the shops, promising she wouldn't be too long, Patrick was playing at a friend's house, and Uncle Danny was working in the shop. If she weren't expecting Vi and Chris to arrive at any minute, that's where Grace would have been too. At least in the shop she was never short of company.

She raised her eyes to the ceiling, imagining Polly sitting in the bedroom they had once shared; and was tempted to go up and talk to her. Today would be the last chance Grace would have to mend the breach that had sprung up between them, for Polly was all packed and ready to leave home this afternoon to enter the nursing training college at St Bartholomew's Hospital. She was waiting for Vi and Chris to show up; they had promised to come and drive her to the hospital and see her safely installed in her new quarters. And of course Polly would want to say a final farewell to her nan when she got back from the shops.

As regards Nobby . . . ! The handsome face flashed in front of her eyes making Grace jump. No! She couldn't think about Nobby. That was too painful. She had to put him out of her mind. Trying to keep herself busy, Grace half-heartedly flicked a feather duster around the furniture, her ears listening out for the sound of Chris's motor car.

When Grace could no longer find any more to do, she

took a deep breath and went upstairs. She knocked twice on Polly's bedroom door and, receiving no answer, she pushed open the door.

'You're supposed to wait until you're invited into someone's room, and I don't remember inviting you.'

Grace, gulping loudly, stayed by the door, her gaze taking in every detail of the sister she had once been so close to. Polly's red hair was arranged neatly into a French plait, and as Grace looked closer she suddenly realised that the freckles, which had been the bane of Polly's life, along with the colour of her hair, were fading into pale brown spots, instead of the large dark mass that had once covered her face entirely. Why hadn't she noticed the change before? Grace wondered idly. But then, the two sisters hadn't spent much time in each other's company recently.

Clearing her throat, Grace was about to make some trite comment to break the hostile silence. Instead she found herself blurting out, 'For God's sake, Poll. What have I done wrong? We used to be so close, the best of friends, ever since we were children, now we're like strangers. What's happened to change your feelings towards me? Please, Poll, I have to know, especially now you're leaving.'

When no answer was forthcoming, Grace's voice grew almost in panic.

'Now look, Poll, either you tell me why you've changed your feelings towards me, or I'm not letting you out of the house, at least not without a fight. I mean it, Poll. You must tell me. It's killing me not knowing what I've—'

Polly spun round, her face hard, her eyes as cold as ice.

'Like you killed Stan, Grace?'

The words were spat at her so venomously that Grace staggered back in shock.

'Oh, yes, you can play the surprised innocent, but we both know you drove him to it. Flaunting Nobby under his nose every chance you got. Standing at the foot of the bed when you deigned to talk to him, instead of sitting by his side and comforting him . . . Like I did . . . !'

Polly's voice broke, and as the red-haired head bowed in sorrow, Grace suddenly knew the reason behind Polly's animosity. Polly had been in love with Stan. Oh, dear God! How could she have been so blind? Looking back over the years she could see clearly now that what had started as a crush on her big sister's boyfriend had turned into true love. And she'd never noticed, never had the slightest suspicion.

Now Polly's voice came at her again, high with pain and anger.

'Why did you marry him, Grace? Why? You didn't love him, you didn't even want him in the house. It was me that did most of the nursing for him. You got out of it at every chance you got. Oh, you did your wifely duties, but it was under sufferance, and Stanley knew. He may have been ill, but he wasn't blind or stupid. That's why he killed himself, because he knew it was Nobby you wanted, not him, and I'll never forgive you for that, Grace – never!' Her slim body began to shake, but when Grace sat down beside her, Polly pulled away violently.

'How many times did you tell him you loved him, Grace? I mean since he first came home. How many times did you sit with him and say, "I love you, Stan"? Well, Grace, I'm waiting. How many times? Once, twice – never . . . Oh, get away from me, Grace, just get away.'

But Grace was going nowhere. Sitting as far away from the shaking body as possible Grace began to talk. She didn't expect any answer, but she talked anyway.

'At least we still have something in common, Poll, because I blame myself for what Stanley did too,' she said quietly, staring over at the far wall. 'There's not a day goes by when I don't think of him, and how he must have suffered over the past years, and then the guilt comes over me, almost crushing the very breath from my body. You asked why I married him. Well, you were there when he suggested it, so you know I tried to put him off, but he was so persistent, what else could I do but say yes? Would it have been better if I'd said, "Sorry Stanley, but I don't love you any more, and I've no intention of marrying you"? What effect do you think that would have had on him? And where would he have gone, who would have looked after him—'

Polly, springing round on the bed, her face contorted with anguish, shouted, 'I would! I would have looked after him. I loved him, Grace. Do you hear me? I loved Stanley. I think I always did, but he would never have looked at me while you were around. Yet I could have made him happy, even if it would have been only for a short time.'

'Oh, Poll, why didn't you tell me? If you knew I didn't love him any more, why didn't you say something?' Grace looked with pity into the blotchy face.

Wiping her eyes, Polly's body sagged as if all the fight had gone out of her.

'What would have been the point, Grace? You were always the only one for him, I never stood a chance.' Getting to her feet, she mumbled, 'Well, you're free now, Grace. Free to marry Nobby, because that's what you want to do, isn't it? I'm just surprised you haven't already made plans.'

Now it was Grace's turn to be angry.

'That's not only unfair, it's also utterly uncalled for. I haven't been alone with Nobby since the funeral. I told him then that there was no future for us, that I could never marry him now, not after Stanley had killed himself because he knew about us. I don't know if that was the reason, but I'll never know now, will I? But, yes, there's nothing in the world I'd like better than to marry Nobby, because I love him, Poll, just as you loved Stanley. I didn't mean to fall for him, but it happened, just the way it happened with you and Stanley. Stan may have thought he was doing me a favour by taking his own life, but in a way he took mine with his.'

More composed now, Polly asked, 'What about Nobby? What does he have to say about it?'

Grace looked down at her hands, her fingers pulling and stretching at the lace handkerchief she held.

'He wouldn't accept it at first. If you remember he was round almost every night after the funeral, but I never stayed long in the room with him. I left him with Nan, and she's another one who keeps on at me. To marry Nobby, I mean. I tried to explain how I felt to her, but you know Nan . . .' She lifted her shoulders in a resigned shrug. 'Anyway, if you hadn't been so preoccupied with getting into the training college, you'd have noticed he hasn't been around for some time now. Hopefully he's finally realised I meant what I said and won't pester me any more.'

'And is that what you want, Grace? Not to see Nobby again, not ever?' Polly had now moved over to the window, keeping a wide distance between them.

Outside in the street, a car horn hooted.

Polly walked towards her suitcases, saying, 'You haven't answered my question, Grace.'

Polly's eyes told Grace that she didn't fully believe her about the affair with Nobby being over and done with. And how would Polly react if Grace was to tell her of the abuse, both verbal and physical, she had suffered from Stanley? Grace quickly dismissed the idea of revealing the secrets of her short married life. For one, Polly would never believe Stanley capable of such cruelty, and secondly, if Grace did tell her, then the animosity between them would be stretched even further, maybe beyond repair.

Getting up and walking to the door, Grace replied dully, 'No, it's not what I want, as well you know, Polly. But then we can't always have what we want in this life.' Then, without a backward glance she proceeded down the stairs to open the door to a smiling Vi and Chris.

It had been nearly two months since the couple's last visit and Grace couldn't help but gasp in amazement at the change in Vi. Her face now bore only slight traces of the injuries she had received in the blast. But it was more than that. There was something about Vi that Grace couldn't put her finger on. She seemed almost agitated with excitement.

'Hello, Grace. Is her ladyship ready?'

Behind them a voice called out, 'Yes, her ladyship is ready. We're just waiting for Nan to come back. She's gone for a walk round the shops. Said she was going mad looking at the four walls.'

As if the words had conjured her up, Aggie appeared around the corner, her face wreathed with smiles.

Taking hold of Vi, she scrutinised her granddaughter's face with such intensity that Vi became embarrassed.

'Gawd Almighty!' she exclaimed in wonderment. 'Yer can hardly see the scars any more.' Turning to Chris she laughed, ''Ere, I don't suppose yer old man could do some work on me. I could do with a few years taken off me face.'

Chris grinned at her in merriment.

'Sorry, Aggie. My father doesn't do cosmetic surgery, he doesn't hold with it. He reserves his talents for those who really need them.'

Suddenly Polly looked at her watch and exclaimed, 'Lord! Look at the time. We'd better get a move on. I don't want to be late on my first day. I've heard the Matron's a right old dragon.'

With much laughing and joking, Vi, Chris and Polly piled into the car, and when Aggie asked hopefully, 'I don't suppose there's room for another one in there, is there? I'd like ter see Polly settled in, and the sort of room

she'll be living in,' she was already halfway in the back of
the car beside Polly.

'We'll see you when we bring Nan back home, Grace. Bye
for now. See you in a while.'

Grace stood waving until the car disappeared. It wasn't
until she closed the door that she realised that Polly hadn't
even said goodbye.

A lump rose in her throat, then, with fierce determination
she said to the empty house, 'Well, sod her, then. I'm not
going to cry any more. I'm done with crying. Do you hear
me, Paddy's Castle? You'll hear no more tears from me. I'm
going to get on with my life. I'm going to . . .' Her hand flew
to her mouth as the lump grew bigger. Her eyes flickered
around the empty hall, then with a determined thrust of
her chin, she said, 'Right then, seeing as there's no call on
my time, I think I'll go to the pictures. If I'm going to get on
with my life, then that's as good enough place to start.'

She'd been back only ten minutes when the family returned,
and over a hastily prepared tea Grace told them where
she'd been.

'An' about time too, girl. Yer used ter love the pictures.
What d'yer see?'

Grace smiled as she answered. '*White Christmas.*'

Vi echoed, '*White Christmas*? They're showing that a bit
early, aren't they? We're only at the start of December.
They showed it about this time last year, didn't they, Nan?
I suppose it's to get people in the mood for the festivities.
But since you've brought the subject up, there's something
Chris and I would like to ask you.' She looked at Chris and
took hold of his hand as if for support. 'We'd like you all
to come and stay with us for Christmas. Uncle Danny and
Patrick as well, of course,' she ended on a nervous laugh.

Aggie's face fell.

'Oh, I don't know, love. I've never spent Christmas away

from home. It wouldn't be the same somehow. Christmas is
for families. And what about Polly? It'd be a bit of a trek fer
her to get up ter the middle of Essex from Bart's, that's if she
can get the time off, with her just starting an' all.' She shook
her greying head. 'Nah, sorry, love, but I'd prefer ter stay
by me own fireside at Christmas. But thanks fer the offer,
it was good of yer both.'

Again Vi and Chris exchanged meaningful looks, and when
Chris smiled and nodded, Vi, her face turning pink said
shyly, 'What, not even to celebrate your granddaughter's
engagement party?'

The room fell eerily silent, then they were all talking and
laughing at once.

'Oh, Vi, I'm so pleased for you. You've got a good one
there. Get him up to the altar before he has time to change
his mind.' Even Aggie, caught up in the excitement, forgot
her reservations about spending Christmas away from home
and accepted the invitation happily.

'Bleeding hell! This calls for a drink ter celebrate. Get the
brandy out, Grace.'

'We haven't got any, Nan. Remember, you finished the
last drop a week ago.'

A look of acute disappointment came over Aggie's face.
Since Nobby had stopped coming around, her drink supply
had dried up considerably. What with the rationing still in
force, even though the war had been over for two and a half
years, spirits and many other goods were still hard to come
by, unless you knew the right people.

Grace, seeing the look of disappointment on her nan's face
and afraid that the lack of Aggie's favourite tipple would
lead to Nobby's name being brought into the conversation,
said quickly, 'Look, I'll pop down to the pub and see what
I can get.'

It was with considerable relief that Grace managed to
get hold of a bottle of wine. She'd had to pay over the

odds for it – but so what! This was a celebration. Vi was getting married and they were going to spend Christmas in a posh house in the country. What more could anyone ask for? she thought in silence as they all lifted a glass to Vi and Chris. Yet though her face was smiling, inside Grace felt desolate, and she didn't have to ask herself why.

In a strong, firm voice she raised her glass high and said, 'Cheers. And the best of luck to both of you.'

'Bleeding hell! How much further is it? I'm near frozen,' Aggie complained from the back seat of Chris's Bentley, squashed between Danny and an excited Patrick while Grace sat in comfort at the front.

'Not long, now, Aggie. Just a few more minutes,' Chris reassured the grumbling woman. As good as his word, within three minutes they were driving through the gates of the hospital, and then round to the side to a house of equal proportion. Both buildings were lit up with fairy lights and boasted a huge Christmas tree outside.

Patrick, his face squashed against the window, breathed, 'Cor, look at that, Dad. Isn't it lovely? Like the pictures in my fairytale books.'

Danny, his face as bright and excited as the small boy's, replied, 'You're right, there, Patrick. That's just what it does look like.'

As they emerged from the car, Chris and Danny took down the suitcases from the roofrack, and as they did so, Grace stared at her uncle, marvelling at the sudden changes in character he could display. Only two days ago he had received a letter from Beryl, begging for some money so that she could come back home.

Aggie and Grace had watched with inquisitive eyes as Danny read the letter, all the while trying to disguise their curiosity. They knew the correspondence was from Beryl because of the stamp. Both of them had held their breath, praying that whatever Beryl wanted, Danny wouldn't fall for her old tricks again. Even so, when he crumpled the letter up and threw it into the bin without a word, they had been amazed at his indifference. As soon as he had left to open the shop, the women had eyed the bin with hungry eyes, dying to know what the letter contained. Finally Aggie could contain her curiosity no longer. Picking out the crumpled letter she smoothed it out and began to read, ignoring Grace's half-hearted protest that they shouldn't be reading Danny's mail, which was a laugh, seeing as she was herself peering over Aggie's shoulder at the time. Beryl hadn't gone into any detail as to why she wanted to return, but it hadn't taken a genius to work out that her American general had either thrown her out or died. And when the two women finished reading the rambling letter, they looked at each other and said simultaneously, 'Good for him.'

Stamping her feet against the cold, Grace heard her name being called, and there was Vi, standing in the lighted doorway, wearing a royal blue dress, looking marvellous.

Slipping and sliding on the icy ground, Grace and Chris helped Aggie into the house and straight into a large room with a blazing fire, with two enormous armchairs set either side of the hearth.

'I'm afraid my father's been held up at the hospital,' Chris explained 'but he promised he'd be over as soon as he can get away.'

Aggie, by now snuggled comfortable in one of the armchairs, her coat taken my a maid wearing a black dress with a white pinafore and a starched white frilled hat, looked around her in awe.

'Gawd help us! Yer never said yer was rich, Chris. I mean, I gathered yer weren't short of a few bob, but I never thought yer was this well off.'

Coming to stand beside Chris, Vi slipped her arm through his and grinned mischievously.

'I don't blame him for keeping it quiet, not the way I was when we first met. I'd have probably dragged him up the aisle before he knew what had hit him. Though I'm not complaining, I've always known I could adapt to the life of the rich very easily.'

Watching the couple together, obviously so much in love, Grace felt a pang of jealousy. Then she looked at Vi more closely and remembered all that her sister had been through. Under the bright lights, the evidence of Vi's scarring was still visible, and she had been told that her face now was as good as it was going to get. Yet in spite of that, she looked radiant. The beauty that had always been reflected on the outside was now glowing from the inside too. Vi would never again be as beautiful as she had once been, but she no longer cared. She had found something more important than outward appearances.

Detaching herself from Chris's side, Vi said to Grace and Aggie, 'Would you like to see your rooms?'

Aggie shivered. 'Not me, love. At least not until me old bones are a bit warmer.'

As they climbed the stairs, Vi said, 'Oh, by the way, Polly's coming over tomorrow. Just for the day. Chris is picking her up then driving her back after tea. So at least we'll all be together for Christmas dinner. Then we can have our own private engagement party before Polly has to leave.'

Grace kept her eyes averted as she replied, 'Oh, that's good news. Nan'll be pleased . . . And of course I am too,' she added hastily.

Vi had no idea of the acrimony that now existed between her sisters, and Grace wasn't about to tell her. She didn't want anything to spoil the Christmas festivities, and maybe, after being apart for the last few weeks, and having time to think over what Grace had said, just maybe, Polly would have come round, and they could be friends once more. Oh, she hoped so. There had never been a cross word between them in all their lives, and Polly, although she had changed in many ways, was still possessed of a kind and forgiving nature. That much Grace was sure of.

Laying her small suitcase on the floor, Grace said, 'It's a lovely room, Vi. Will Nan be sharing with me?'

Vi nodded. 'I'm afraid so. It may be a large house, but there's only five bedrooms, and the maid sleeps in one of those.' Leaning against Grace's side she added slyly, 'The smallest one, of course.'

Grace grinned back. 'Oh, but of course. We can't have the servants getting above themselves, can we?'

Giggling like a couple of schoolgirls they re-entered the lounge to find a distinguished man, with white hair and a pair of half-moon glasses perched on the end of his nose, seated opposite Aggie, chatting away as if they'd known each other for years. But then, Aggie had always been able to make conversation easily.

After supper, they all rose and headed back to the lounge. Patrick was already tucked up in his room with his stocking hanging at the foot of his bed. Danny watched as the small boy tried valiantly to keep his eyes open, hoping to catch a glimpse of Father Christmas, but the effort was too much for him after the long exciting day. As soon as he was sure Patrick was fast asleep, Danny laid back on the other single bed, his mind going back to the letter he had received from Beryl.

He had been totally surprised at the indifference the begging letter had aroused in him. The old Danny would have sent her the money she requested immediately, but not now. He would never possess the character of old Paddy Donnelly or Sam, but he was trying, and one thing he was resolute on was that no one would ever take him for a mug again. He'd learnt his lesson, he wouldn't be so easily caught again. Then he thought of the women who came into the shop asking for tick when Grace wasn't around and smiled to himself. All right, so he hadn't changed that much, and probably never would. The only thing he wanted out of life now was his son, and Patrick was his son, in every way that mattered.

Danny had told the boy his mother had died during the war, and the young boy had solemnly accepted the lie without question. Looking at his watch he saw it was nearly ten thirty. He really must get back downstairs, or his hosts would think him very rude. And that was the last thought he had until the early hours of the morning when he awoke with a start and hastily filled Patrick's stocking with the presents he had hidden in the extra suitcase he had brought with him. Relieved beyond measure he had woken up in time, Danny quickly slipped into his pyjamas and immediately fell fast asleep.

'I wonder what's happened to Uncle Danny. He's been upstairs a long time,' Vi queried.

'Yeah, well, he's probably fallen asleep, and that's just where I'm heading for, if nobody minds.'

Jonathan Green stood up as Aggie got to her feet and bade her goodnight, adding that they would have more time to talk the following day. And, if they would care to extend their visit to Boxing Day, they would all be more than welcome.

By eleven, Grace was the only one left in the lounge, the others having retired just ten minutes previously. Although desperately tired, Grace didn't fancy going to bed just yet. It was so peaceful sitting here by the fire, a mug of cocoa held between her hands, alone with her silent thoughts. In fact she could easily curl up in the expansive armchair and go to sleep right now.

When the mantle clock struck eleven thirty, Grace yawned, stretched her arms and rose reluctantly to her feet. She was putting the fire guard around the still glowing fire when a voice behind her nearly made her jump out of her skin with shock.

'Hello, Gracie.'

And there, only a few feet away stood Nobby, his face drawn and pensive.

Clutching at her throat Grace stuttered, 'How long have you been here, I mean in the house?'

Lifting his shoulders in a resigned gesture he answered wearily, 'About half an hour. Vi let me in by the back door.'

Her emotions running riot, Grace shot back, 'Well, she had no right to. I'd never have come if I'd known you'd be here.' Even as the words left her lips Grace knew they were empty. Her whole body was trembling at the sight of him.

Coming further into the room, Nobby nodded to the armchair and asked, 'Mind if I sit down a minute? I won't be staying long.'

Unable to speak, Grace inclined her head, and it wasn't until Nobby was seated that she felt more in control of the situation. That was until she sat down opposite him and saw the desolation and weariness etched into every line of his face. This wasn't the Nobby she knew. The Nobby that was always laughing, always a joke ready on his lips. A sudden appalling thought struck her. Maybe he was ill. Oh, God, no. But he looked so dreadful.

Licking her dry lips she asked worriedly, 'You look terrible, Nobby, are you ill?'

Nobby lifted his head, a wan smile touching the corners of his mouth.

'If you can call not being able to be with the woman I love being ill, then, yes, I'm ill, desperately so.'

Grace could feel her former intentions slipping away as she stared into the face of the man she loved. It was one thing telling herself that she would never be able to marry Nobby after what had happened to Stan when Nobby wasn't around; it was another matter entirely when he was sitting only a few yards away from her. Watching his gaunt face, Grace felt her resolutions and self-induced sacrifice rapidly fading.

Then Nobby looked across at her and said sombrely, 'I'm gonna ask you one more time, and then I'll go an' I promise I'll never bother you again.' Holding her fixed gaze, he said, 'Do you still love me, Grace? If you don't, then say so and you'll be rid of me for good.'

The churning in her stomach was making Grace giddy. Her heart was aching to reach out and take Nobby in her arms, but she couldn't seem to speak, or even move.

Nobby looked on as Grace fought her own private, tortuous battle, his heart thumping so loud he was sure she must hear it. The silence in the room was becoming unbearable, and Nobby, never one to stay where he wasn't wanted, stood up.

'All right, Grace, you've given me your answer. I'm going now, and like I promised, you'll never be bothered by me again.'

Like a man drunk, Nobby headed for the door, and in that moment a cry of anguish sprang from Grace's lips.

'No! Nobby, don't go, please, don't go. I've only been half-alive since we parted. I do love you, I always will, but I made a promise to myself that I'd never see you again, out of respect for Stanley. But I can't do it, Nobby. I can't live without you . . . I love you, Nobby . . . I love you so much . . . !'

The fatigue and despair seemed to leap from Nobby's body, and with one bound he was across the room and holding her in his arms.

'Oh, Gracie, my darling Gracie. I've missed yer so much. Don't let's ever be apart again.'

'We won't be, darling. I couldn't bear to lose you now. I've been so miserable without you.'

Then she was being crushed in his arms, his warm lips

pressing against hers. At the back of her mind Grace thought of Polly's visit tomorrow, and what she would say when she saw Nobby and Grace back together. But she hardened her heart against Polly's feelings; after all, she was a grown woman now, no longer a child to be shielded from life's unpleasantness. And what if Grace stuck to her promise and then, in a few months, Polly arrived home telling them all she had fallen in love with one of the doctors or an intern? It could happen, and probably would one day. What of Grace's noble gesture then? She would be left alone, while everyone around her was happily settled with their own family.

Then Nobby was leading her to the large settee, and as he pulled her down beside him, all thoughts of Polly and everything else vanished from her mind. She had tonight with Nobby, let tomorrow and all the other tomorrows take care of themselves.